CH00868711

FIGURE OF EIGHT

Also by Inga Dunbar

The Chequerboard
Candlemaker Row
Tanners' Close

Figure
of Eight

Inga Dunbar

SIMON & SCHUSTER

LONDON · SYDNEY · NEW YORK · TOKYO · SINGAPORE · TORONTO

First published in Great Britain by Simon & Schuster Ltd, 1994
A Paramount Communications Company

Simon & Schuster Ltd
West Garden Place
Kendal Street
London W2 2AQ

Simon & Schuster of Australia Pty Ltd
Sydney

A CIP catalogue record for this book is
available from the British Library

ISBN 0-671-71877-0

Typeset in 11/13 pt Sabon by
Hewer Text Composition Services, Edinburgh
Printed and bound in Great Britain by
Butler & Tanner Ltd, Frome and London

To
The Marquess of Linlithgow
for the privilege of using his ancestral home,
Hopetoun House, as the springboard
of this book.

*

To
Jack Priest
local historian of Reawick, Shetland Isles
for providing such entertaining information.

*

To
The Tulloch family
for happy memories of
Reawick House.

*

To
The editorial staff of Simon & Schuster,
especially to Lucy Ferguson and Catherine Reed
for all their care and hard work in preparing
this book for publication,
I am greatly indebted.

For my sister, Brucie.

'What matters it how far we go?' his scaly friend replied.
There is another shore, you know, upon the other side.
The further off from England, the nearer is to France.
Then turn not pale, beloved snail, but come and join the dance.
Will you, won't you, will you, won't you, will you join the dance?
Will you, won't you, will you, won't you, *won't* you join the dance?'

Lewis Carroll

1

O N an August night in 1813 the ragged row of fishermens' cottages slumbered peacefully on the Braehead in the East Neuk of Fife, watched over by a pale sickle moon. Suddenly a light flared in the window of the end cottage and shortly afterwards a man ran out to one of the other doors. He knocked as loudly as he dared until the door finally opened and a stout woman appeared.

'She's started,' he said. 'Can ye come quick, Bertha?'

'Did the waters break yet?' she asked with a yawn.

'Ay, they broke half an hour ago, and noo the pains are bad.'

'They'll get worse, Davy Gourlay,' Bertha assured him. 'Weel, weel, there's plenty o' time, but I'll come as soon as I can. Let me get some clothes on, man! Go hame and get a good fire going, for I'll need hot water.'

'I'll do that, but come quick for God's sake,' he pleaded.

Six hours later tears were pouring down his face as he watched the midwife fighting to bring his second child into the world.

Burrowed deep under the blankets, their five-year-old son had cried himself to sleep long ago in the other room. His mother's last two terrible screams woke him up again. He stuck his fingers in his ears and shook with fear.

'Oh . . . *God!*' Davy moaned, and then Bertha held up a bloody, steaming scrap of humanity.

'It's a wee lassie,' she told him, setting about cutting the cord and wiping the baby's eyes, nose and ears as fast as she could while little mewing wails proclaimed that his daughter was living.

'Here,' she said a few minutes later, placing the white-wrapped bundle in his arms, 'I've got to attend to Ruth.'

Davy Gourlay looked down at the tiny red face in the bundle. Even then, minutes after her birth, he could tell that this daughter of his was going to be as determined as her mother. Perhaps even more so, he thought uneasily, as her tiny arms and legs flailed angrily inside the shawl. Her eyes opened and she gave him a hard stare. Then, her mouth opening into an uncompromisingly square shape, the mewing sounds changed to a demanding bawl.

He stood up with the baby in his arms and went through to the other room of the small cottage. With one hand he pulled down the blankets.

'Look, Andra,' he said. 'Here's yer wee sister.'

Andra looked at her scornfully.

'I wis wanting a brother,' he said.

'Well, she's yer sister.'

'Huh! What's her name, anyway?'

'Ay, what's her name?' Bertha asked from the back room, still labouring over the box bed, taking away the afterbirth and finishing her ministrations with the expertise born of long experience.

Ruth Gourlay's face was like white marble, but she dragged open her eyes and managed to speak in a voice hoarse with screaming. 'That's easy,' she croaked. 'She prickled me most of the nine months she wis inside me, and noo she's scratched her way oot o' me, as joggy and jaggy as a thistle! There's only one name for *her*, as near to a thistle as I can think o'! She's to be called Thirza.'

At the age of two Thirza was never still for a minute. Her tongue was never still, either, and she was just embarking on what was to prove a two-year running battle with her mother for supremacy. Worst of all, when she sprouted hair at last, it was bright red.

'Will ye look at it!' Ruth tried to brush the tangled curls while

Thirza raged and stamped her feet. 'There wis never any red hair in *my* family,' she exclaimed, smacking her daughter's hand with the back of the family hairbrush and taking a tighter grip of her.

'There wis never any in mine, either!' Davy protested, feeling guilty – as he was made to feel every day of his life now – for Thirza's very existence.

'Huh!' said Ruth, brushing harder than ever.

By the time Thirza was four years old she had learned to obey her mother and father, but that was only because it was expedient to do so. She had discovered she could get her own way much more often if she appeared to be behaving herself, and if she behaved herself she sometimes got to go out with Andra, her very reluctant hero.

She didn't mind if he got socks and boots to wear while she went barefoot. Boys, men and heroes always wore socks and boots, she told herself. She loved him dearly, even if he took no notice of her, and didn't even own her in front of his friends.

'Can I come wi' ye the day, Andra?' was the daily question she asked her brother, now nine and almost a man in her adoring eyes.

'Nah,' he said, as he nearly always said, and pushed her away, a clear illustration of the way the Gourlay children were being brought up – in the Scottish tradition that men ruled the world. The minister was a man. The doctor was a man. Their father was a man, the breadwinner for the family and the head of the house.

But already Thirza had formed the opinion that it was her mother who was really in charge, and not her quiet, patient father. All *he* did was go fishing, come home, eat his meals and then sit sighing and brooding into the fire.

Ruth Gourlay didn't put out her washing on a Monday, like all the other women in the cottages. She put hers out, sparkling, on Friday mornings, took it in by midday wet or dry, had it steaming on ropes above the fire in the afternoon and ironed it all flat that evening. All day on Saturday the washing aired while she cleaned the house from end to end and cooked the meals for Sunday as well as Saturday. After the evening meal she got the whole Gourlay family, one by one, into the tin bath in front of the dying fire – still full of soapy water saved from the washing.

Thirza went in first, being the smallest and needing only one kettle of hot water to bring it up to lukewarm. Then another kettleful was boiled for Andra. After that, when Thirza and Andra were in the other room in their own beds, they lay and listened while more water was added for their mother's bath. Their father always went outside and paced up and down on the brigstones while this delicate operation was in progress. Finally, when she had struggled into her flannel nightgown, Ruth heated up two kettles of water to top up the bath and called their father in. He went last, for he liked to lie and soak.

Neither Andra nor Thirza ever heard the final tipping out of the water onto the washing green. By Sunday morning the tin bath was hanging from its nail on the kitchen wall again, their parents were dressed, and after their porridge the children were dressed in their Sunday clothes, with their hair brushed and their Sunday shoes polished until they shone. Then the Gourlay family, clean from head to foot, set off for the Kirk, the most important occasion of the week.

At five, Thirza understood that her family was very poor. She took all her mother's thriftiness for granted. Sometimes her father caught very few fish although he worked long and hard at sea, and if he didn't get any fish at all the family were forced to go hungry.

The Gourlays walked to the nearest Kirk of Scotland. Nobody ever told Thirza that it was the Kirk of St Monance. All she knew was when they passed the cave of Sinfillin on the way she and Andra would exchange knowing glances. It was their favourite place to play, and strictly forbidden because the tide might come up and drown them. But, so far, it never had and so they continued.

Sometimes when Andra pushed her away and wouldn't play with her, Thirza would wander off by herself on her skinny little legs past the Kirk and down the climbing, curving streets of St Monance where she explored the busy workaday harbour overlooked by red-pantiled stone houses. She hung over the wall and watched the men building boats and gazed curiously at the bigger ships which were occasionally there, ships she thought of as 'furrin' because the sailors spoke to her in funny voices.

The ones who came regularly got to know the little girl who fearlessly boarded their ships and graciously allowed them to give her presents. Sometimes it was a few bones for her mother to make soup with, sometimes a cabbage or a few carrots, but whatever they were Thirza stowed them away in the white canvas bag she had persuaded her father to make for her from a bit of old sailcloth and took them home to her mother who never failed to scold her for begging. All the same, she carried on, because she knew her mother was secretly pleased no matter how much she scolded her.

Besides, there was another fascination. At first she was terrified of the huge black-bearded captain of what she learned was a Dutch ship. When he spoke it was in a deafening roar, and his booming laugh echoed all around the harbour. Then he noticed Thirza.

Before she knew where she was, one of his sailors was carrying her aboard, kicking and screaming. 'Captain Gerrit van der Haar is asking to see you,' he tried to pacify her. 'He doesn't hurt little girls. He likes them. He wants to give you a present.'

Everything her mother had ever told her about strange men was coming true, and when the sailor put her down on her feet before the captain and he looked down at her from an impossible height she burst into tears. His great hands gently lifted her up and before she could shrink back he had deposited a smacking kiss on each of her cheeks.

'*Ja, ja,*' he boomed, 'you are a little flower, just like my Minna! I have a little girl at home like you, my dear. What is your name?'

'Thirza,' she told him, disarmed. His beard tickled so much that it made her laugh.

'Well, Thirza, little girls like sweets, no? Here are some for *you*.'

'Thank ye, Captain . . . I canna say yer name.'

'Captain Gerrit will do, my dear. Come and see us the next time we are here.'

From that day on Captain Gerrit became Thirza's best friend when he was in port. He always had a box of toys for Minna, and he always allowed Thirza to choose one for herself. Sometimes there were the loveliest wooden dolls with black hair painted on, and pretty pink faces and thin white wooden bodies. There were whistles with tassels dangling from them, but usually she picked one of the balls. They were made of rubber, she liked the smell of them, and she could have any colour she liked.

And then, when she was six years old came the day that was to change her life for ever.

2

THE Gourlays received a letter, the first that Thirza had ever seen. Her father laid the long, flat white packet with a red seal on it face up on the table, and they all looked at it with the utmost respect.

'What's inside it?' Thirza asked.

'It's a message,' Davy Gourlay said.

'A message, Father? Who to? Who from?'

'Haud yer wheesht,' her mother said, and the respectful and almost fearful silence continued.

'Do ye mean it's writing?' Thirza ventured again, only to be ignored.

That was how she deduced that there was writing inside that packet, right enough, just like what was inside the Bible, only none of them could read it.

'Open it,' her mother said.

Thirza understood that this was a crisis, and without raising her eyes from the letter, put up her hand and took a firm grip of her mother's apron.

'Open it, Father,' her mother said again. 'Go on.'

Davy Gourlay took his bowie knife from his pocket and wiped the blade on the seat of his trousers. 'I will,' he said, slitting open the packet and withdrawing a folded piece of paper. He opened it slowly, with great care, and then held it at arm's length with a doubtful expression on his face.

'Is it the right way up?' her mother asked.

Her father turned the paper the other way and looked as doubtful as before. 'It's a puzzle,' he said at last in his quiet, shy way.

'Then take it over to the minister and get a reading,' Ruth snapped.

Thirza didn't understand her mother's tone of voice. She couldn't read it, either, so why should she snap at her father?

'Can I come?' she asked him, but no one paid any attention to her.

Her mother reached into the closet for her father's Sunday hat and, while he was putting it on, Thirza slipped out of the door and hid around the corner of the house. She waited until she saw which way her father was going, and then took the short cut to join him by the shore. There were to be no more knickers for her, her mother had said the last time she'd torn the seat out of them so, holding her skirt above her bare bottom, she slid down the sandy embankment from the Braehead to the path and trotted along behind him.

'So ye're here!' he remarked.

'Ay, Father,' she said avoiding his eye.

There was no more conversation until they reached the manse door which, to their disappointment, was opened by the minister's wife, Mistress Selkirk.

'We've had a letter,' Davy said.

'Weel, the minister's out. So ye can either come back again later or step inside and I'll read it to ye mysel'.'

Thirza watched as disappointment and curiosity fought it out on her father's face. So did Mistress Selkirk. 'I was educated mysel', ye ken,' she said, holding open the door and smiling at them. Curiosity won and they went inside. Mistress Selkirk spread the letter out on the table and Thirza and her father stood behind her and watched her pointing finger. 'It's come from a place called Springfield,' she said, showing them an address on the top right-hand corner, and it says, '*Dear Ruth.*'

'Who's it from?' Father asked.

Mistress Selkirk's finger travelled down to the bottom of the writing. 'From Ellen,' she said.

'Weel then, it's to my wife from her sister. If ye'll read it, I'll pass the message on.'

'*Dear Ruth,*' Mistress Selkirk read slowly, '*This is to tell you*

8

that my man died while we were in Kirkcaldy. Nobody ever liked me there because I did not belong to the place, so I travelled back home again to the old house. It has been my duty to tell you this. Your loving sister, Ellen.'

'I didna ken that wifies could read, Father,' Thirza said on the way back home, more to show him sympathy than anything else. Her mother should not have ordered him about and now Mistress Selkirk had proved herself his superior as well. On the other hand, a man as big as her father should not have allowed it. It never would have happened if he had been able to read for himself.

'Some can,' he answered shortly.

'What did she mean, she wis educated?'

'She went to a school.'

'Will I be going to a school, Father? I wish I could read.'

'There's no school here, lassie. Now wheesht!'

Thirza sincerely believed she lived in a town called Sinfillin. She didn't realise that she lived in a no-man's-land between Pittenweem and St Monance on the Fife coast where there was a big cave called Sinfillin and not much else, besides the cottages and a disused saltworks.

'Where *do* they have a school, then, Father?'

'Pittenweem, mebbe.'

She must get to Pittenweem, then. She would like fine to read. She saw that it made people powerful. It could make girls as good as boys and women equal to men.

A few days later when she was down at the harbour again a brougham arrived on the scene. She had never seen such a vehicle before in her life. Awestricken, she stood and stared as a fine gentleman got out of it and left a lady sitting waiting for him, the driver motionless on the open seat in the front. It was all too interesting for Thirza to bear, and she sidled up until she was standing beside the open door.

The lady smiled down at her. 'Do you belong here, my dear?'

'Nah. Sinfillin.'

The lady looked mystified. 'Does your mother know you're here?' she asked.

But, besides being unwilling to answer this question, Thirza was now running her small fingertips luxuriously over the plush

9

upholstery, and it was giving her a feeling too vague and too adult to put into words. Nevertheless it was positive. Her feeling was that this was the way for Thirza Gourlay to travel through life, as well.

'Can ye read?' she asked, looking up with a serious expression.

'Of course, my dear,' the lady laughed a little uneasily. 'Perhaps some day you may be able to read, too,' she added doubtfully.

'Can yer man read?'

'Oh, yes,' the lady said, 'and he can write and count as well. That's how he earns our living.'

'That's why ye're rich?'

But then the gentleman came back, jumped in beside the lady and looked down at Thirza. 'Has the child been annoying you, my dear?'

'No,' the lady laughed and waved her hand at Thirza as they began to drive off. 'She was only asking if I could read.'

'Oh,' Thirza's sharp ears made out the man's next remark, 'the poor little thing will grow up the same as all the others around here. These people can't afford to have an education.'

Education! There it was again! Now Thirza knew it meant being able to read, perhaps even to write and to count, and it was the key to another world, leading to riches, soft velvet, carriages and ladies and gentlemen. By hook or by crook she must get it.

She achieved her ambition in a roundabout way when she was almost seven. Andra went to a farm near Pittenweem every day for the milk, but he would never take her, and if she tried to go with him he simply lengthened his twelve-year-old stride and shook her off.

One summer evening, she followed him when he went to meet his friends. Skulking along behind them she soon guessed where they were going. It was the only place to go in Sinfillin – to the cave. Laughing and giggling, they went inside. It was too shallow a cave for Thirza to follow them in without being discovered, so she cautiously lay down flat on the grass above it. That way she could hear everything they said, and if she craned her neck she could see them sitting on the stone shelf inside.

'We shouldn't be sitting on this shelf,' a serious smaller boy informed them. 'It's sacred.'

'Gahn!' they yelled at him. 'What do you ken aboot it?'

'I do know. My father told me. An old mannie used to live here. This shelf was his bed. He was a saint.'

'A *saint*!' the boys shouted and laughed and the oldest, Alicky Birnie, pulled a bottle out from under his jacket. Thirza was shocked beyond measure to see it. It was a bottle of beer, and she and Andra had been brought up to believe that no Christian person had anything to do with the drink of the devil.

'He was so a saint! Father said his name was Saint Fillan. That's where this place got its name from.'

Saint Fillan! So that was the real name of her birthplace! Thirza wriggled with delight at this discovery, but nobody else was paying any attention to the boy with such interesting information. With scandalised eyes Thirza saw that they were all jostling each other to get a mouthful of the beer, Andra included.

'Saint Fillan used to drink from this spring,' squealed the knowledgeable boy and, at that, the rest of them rushed up to it, opened up their buttons and with one accord made their water so that the spring rushed down yellow instead of sparkling clear.

Boys, except Andra, were horrible in Thirza's opinion, peering down at the little white worms hanging out of their breeks. Then Alicky Birnie took a hold of his and, before an admiring audience, rubbed at it. To Thirza's distress the white worm turned red. It stood up. Alicky Birnie rubbed harder than ever and shouted, 'AH, AH, AAAH!' when suddenly a stream like milk spouted out of it.

In the awe-filled silence that followed Thirza sensed something that filled her with fear, something to do with boys, when she had never known a minute's fear before. And there was something wrong with Alicky Birnie. Something terrible – and it might be catching. Andra might get it. Thirza got up in alarm and ran all the way home to tell her mother, clinging to Ruth's hands and sobbing bitterly. She cried so much that she fell asleep, and was only vaguely aware of the terrible row that her brother got when he arrived home later.

Next day, everything had changed, especially her mother. Thirza was allowed to wear her Sunday shoes and socks and

11

even her knickers. From that she sensed that the divisions in the family had somehow subtly changed. Her mother took her hand and scowled at Andra. 'From now on, ye'll take her wi' you,' she commanded. 'Yes, now! Ye'll take her wi' you to get the milk. I dinna want to hear o' you wi' that Alicky Birnie again!'

Thirza danced along the path with her brother, beside herself with joy. 'It was the beer,' she told him. 'Ye shouldna drink beer, Andra.'

'Aw, shut up,' Andra scowled. 'I'm going into Pittenweem before I get the milk, and ye'd better say nothing about it this time.'

'I won't,' Thirza promised him fervently. Pittenweem, where the school was! The place of her dreams! It was too good to be true, and so there must be a snag in it. Sure enough, when they got there Andra wanted to be alone.

'Say nothing about it, and I'll let ye walk about yersel'. But ye've got to be back here quickly. I've to get the milk yet, and take ye back home before I go off wi' my father – we canna miss the tide.'

'Go off? Where?'

'To the fishing, of course! God, girls are silly!'

So why was he going down that wee close to meet up with a girl with black hair, then? Shaking her head at the mysteries of men Thirza followed them at a discreet distance. Then her attention was abruptly diverted from Andra's activities when they turned into Low Street, and were passing by a cottage with a thatched roof. If the door hadn't been standing open she might have missed it, but being Thirza with her over-developed curiosity, she had to look inside.

She saw benches set out, children sitting at them with their books and slates and a woman sitting on a high stool near the fire. Thirza marched right in, in a fine state of excitement. 'Is this a school?' she asked the woman.

'It is, and I'm the Dame, Katie Docherty. Miss Docherty to you.'

'Can I come to yer school, Miss?'

'It's a penny a week, mind.'

'I'll ask Father. I'll be here the morn,' Thirza promised.

But there was a lot to be gone through before 'tomorrow' came. Davy was dead set against it. Andra had never gone to school, and Andra was a boy. Girls didn't need to go to school. They were better off at home learning from their mothers how to cook and clean. Besides, it would cost a penny a week.

'So that's it, is it, Davy Gourlay?' Ruth stood with her arms akimbo ranged up alongside her daughter and glaring at the men of the house. 'It's because it would cost a penny a week that oor Thirza canna learn to read and write and get on in the world? Well, dinna fash yersel'! She'll get the money from me. Wait and see!'

3

THE following Monday morning Ruth, with Thirza at her side, stood on the brigstones and watched the little fleet of fishing boats putting out to sea.

'There's my father!' Thirza cried excitedly. 'Mother, can ye see my father? Can ye see him?'

'Ay,' Ruth said.

'And, Mother, there's Andra! He's waving,' Thirza danced down to the end of the washing green waving both her arms and jumping up and down.

'Ay,' Ruth said again.

'Aw . . . They're away round the Point,' Thirza's voice went flat and she stopped waving.

'Come inside and change into yer best clothes,' her mother said. 'We're going a message.'

This was such a novelty to Thirza that she willingly tore off her everyday pinafore and pulled on her Sunday dress, and when the signs indicated that her mother was about to do the same Thirza flew to fetch her shoes and her best shawl. 'Where are we going, Mother?' she asked.

'Never you mind. Just walk.' Ruth looked down at her severely, but Thirza only smiled back up at her with pleasure and wriggled her hand into her mother's. It was a happy, happy day, for Ruth rarely left the house except to go to the Kirk every Sunday and, in the summertime, to go down to the Cowrie Beach where she kilted up her skirts and waded in, teaching her

15

children to swim. On that, she was adamant.

'Everyone living near or *on the sea* should be able to swim,' she kept saying, and from the careful way she never looked at Davy when she said it, and from the way his head went down when she did, Thirza knew that her father couldn't swim. It worried her. What if he fell out of the boat one day? He *should* have learned to swim. It was easy.

Then one day, goaded beyond endurance, her father spoke back. 'Do ye no' ken it's unlucky for sailors to be able to swim, woman?' he asked Ruth. 'It's tempting Providence.'

Thirza tried to follow the argument, but her own conclusion was that her mother was right, and it was no wonder that she kept scanning the Bay every day until the little fishing fleet came home.

But now, excitedly, she tightened her grip on Ruth's hand as they walked along. They were heading for the manse, Thirza saw, but she knew better than to remark on it with her mother in one of her determined moods. Ruth marched right up to the front door and rang the bell while Thirza watched these momentous events and waited in a frenzy of excitement. What could her mother be wanting to see the minister for – and on a Monday morning, too?

Once again it was Mistress Selkirk who answered the door. 'Ye'll be wanting to see himsel'?' she asked.

'No, mistress, if ye've got a minute. It's Thirza here, wanting to go to the school. We havena' the money. I wis wondering, would ye be needing any help wi' yer washing, mebbe?'

'I do my ain,' Mistress Selkirk replied. 'But it's a great thing, the bairn wanting to go to the school. Let's see . . . Weel, if ye go up to the big hoose, Mistress Dundonald might be interested.'

Ruth thanked her and together she and Thirza toiled up the hill. The first glimpse of Dundonald House, half hidden in trees, four storeys high and topped with circular towers, stopped them both in their tracks.

'Oh my,' Thirza breathed. 'It's a castle!'

Ruth walked on warily up the driveway to the front door.

'Ye're no' feared, are ye, Mother?' Thirza whispered, her eyes round with wonder.

'I am not. But we should be at the back door, not the front.' Before Ruth could move or say another word Thirza had pulled on a brass handle at the side of the door and a loud pealing of bells sounded inside the house. 'Ye shouldn't ha'e done that,' she frowned. 'But we'd better wait here now.'

Almost immediately the door opened and the lady of the house herself came out, dressed to go visiting in a blue and gold ensemble. Her blue poke bonnet was trimmed with gold silk. The skirt of her blue velvet coat, buttoned tightly to the waist, flared out to reveal the front panel of her dress which was of ochre-coloured glacé silk.

'Why, it's that sweet child again!' she smiled at Thirza. 'And you are her mother?'

'Yes ma'am, Mistress Gourlay, and this is Thirza.'

Mistress Dundonald laughed gently. 'Thirza? Yes, it suits her. I met her, you know, down at the harbour. Quite delightful. She asked me if I could read.'

'She wants to go to the school and learn to read hersel', but we canna afford to send her. So I wis wondering if you were needing any washing done?'

'Washing?' Mistress Dundonald's gay young laugh rang out. 'Oh, there's always plenty of that here! Come with me and I'll show you the kitchen door — oh! Here's my husband come for me, and we're late already! I must rush — but it's just round there,' she pointed. 'Tell Helen I sent you, and what for,' and with a quick pat on Thirza's head Mistress Dundonald tripped daintily into the waiting brougham.

'Ye didna tell me ye'd seen that lady,' Ruth said as they were walking home with their bundle of washing.

'It was only for a minute, Mother.'

'Well, she remembered ye, anyway,' Ruth looked down at her daughter and sighed with a mixture of pride and dismay. Who could forget her, with her scrawny elbows and knees poking through her dress, her terrible red hair and those eyes as brilliant as the bluest sea?

From then on Ruth Gourlay put out her own washing as usual on Friday mornings, and on Tuesdays the other women in the cottages chattered like magpies amongst themselves at the sight of lace petticoats and snow white shirts ballooning in the breeze on the Gourlay washing lines. Ruth never explained it to anyone.

*　　*　　*

A week after their first outing, she readied her daughter again and went, this time, to Pittenweem with the money in her hand for Katie Docherty.

'She's sharp in every way,' she told the school dame. 'Always has been. Ye'll ha'e yer work cut oot wi' Thirza Gourlay.'

Thirza ran after her mother as she retreated out of the door and clasped Ruth's skirts in her arms. 'I love ye, Mother,' she said.

She had never said such a thing in her life before. Nobody in the Gourlay family ever expressed any emotion.

'Ay,' Ruth disentangled herself. 'Noo, behave yersel', lassie.'

'Come here, Thirza Gourlay,' Miss Docherty commanded when her mother had gone. 'It's the King's English here, and nothing else. You should have said "I love you, Mother".'

'Ay – I mean yes, Miss Docherty.'

'Another thing – everyone must speak distinctly. None of your slovenly speech in this school.'

'Yes, Miss Docherty.'

No matter if twenty-nine other children were crammed onto the benches of Katie Docherty's Dame School, no matter if the floor was earthen, the walls covered with dull religious pictures and two maps, one of Scotland and the other of Europe, Katie herself sat by the fire in a commanding position where she could not only supervise her pupils but also attend to her soup pot. And Thirza was in her glory.

She had to be shown the alphabet only once to know it, and when Katie strung the letters together on the blackboard, 'c-a-t', and 'm-a-t', Thirza could sound them out immediately and then recognise the words, laughing with pleasure. Soon she could read 'The cat sat on the mat'. She was speechless with joy, and simply couldn't believe that most of the other children couldn't read it, too.

Soon Thirza could sound out three, four and five-letter words and was given her first Primer. She ran all the way home to show her mother her 'reading book', dog-eared and dirtied by dozens of pupils before her, but to Thirza a thing of absolute beauty.

'I've to put a cover on it, Mother,' she told Ruth.

'A cover? What sort of cover?'

'She *said* brown paper, but newspaper will do.'

Ruth raked through all the drawers in the press until she unearthed a sheet of newspaper John Thomson the butcher had wrapped a few sausages in, some time in the past when the fishing had been good and there were a few coppers to spare. 'Will this do?' she asked. 'All the other old newspapers have been used long ago in the privy.'

Disregarding the faint stains where the sausage fat must have come through, Thirza folded the paper around the covers of the book with her small nimble fingers the way Katie Docherty had shown the children.

'Now I've to put my name on,' she told her mother. 'How do ye – *you* – write down Thirza Gourlay?'

'I dinna ken,' Ruth said. 'But ye'll soon learn.'

Penmanship was Katie Docherty's forte. It began on slates with slate-pencils that screeched and little wet smelly bits of sponge to wipe off the mistakes. It was a long time before Thirza was judged good enough to progress to a jotter, and was given a pen to dip into an inkwell. It was even longer before she found a way for herself to make her letters slope to the right. This was absolutely mandatory. They were not allowed to slope any other way. For this she had to twist the jotter around sideways and arch her hand, for Thirza was that most awkward thing of all, left-handed.

But she read her third Primer until she could say it backwards and every spare minute she had she practised writing on an old tile she found on the beach along with a round white stone that must have been made of chalk.

Best of all, she loved to count. The patterns that two of everything made, then three of everything right up to ten of everything fascinated her, and she drove her family almost mad, doing her best to talk 'posh' as Andra called it, and counting all day long. She counted the spoons, the forks and the knives. She counted the dishes and the pans, and when she had exhausted everything inside the house she dragged in shells from the Cowrie Beach and counted them, bursting to share her new-found knowledge with her brother.

'Leave her alane!' their mother commanded Andra, who only jeered at Thirza jealously.

Then Katie Docherty showed her how to write down the numbers, and how to add, subtract, multiply and divide them.

Thirza could sign her own name and she could recite the Shorter Catechism almost from beginning to end. She had very unwillingly learned how to sew a hem and darn socks and, with dogged determination and many a tear when she had to rip it back because she'd let some stitches run, she knitted a jumper for her beloved Andra, for now Andra was fourteen and doing a man's job, fishing with their father full-time.

'Now I've got two of them to worry about,' Ruth said.

It was when Thirza was twelve that she came to the sad realisation that her father might be a big, strong man but he was an ignorant one all the same, when one night he took Andra and went off on a rough sea.

'It has to be a full-blown gale to stop *me*,' he boasted.

'Ay, but ye're risking Andra's life as well,' Ruth raged.

Yes, Davy Gourlay was, in his daughter's view, not only irresponsible, but he couldn't even read or write. All this she kept to herself, however. She didn't even want to think it, for Thirza loved her family fiercely and loyally, and would have defended any one of them to the death.

Next morning Davy and Andra brought their boat back empty except for a fry of fish for the family.

'There's a lot o' driftwood around this morning,' Andra observed as they hauled the boat up on the beach.

'There is that.'

'Where has it come from, Father?'

'We'd better take a look.'

His father strode off along the shingle to the Point, where most of the driftwood was washing in and out with the tide, and Andra followed him. 'It's been a boat, broken up,' Davy Gourlay said when they climbed up the rocks to get a better view of it.

'Ay, and there was someone on her.' Andra had spotted a sodden heap further along. 'If that's a man, he'll be deid, Father.'

They clambered down the other side of the rocks and, landing on a strip of sand, approached the heap cautiously to find it was a man, right enough.

'No! He's still living,' Davy said, bending over the body.

'My God, only a boy he is, too! Only a boy like yersel', Andra.'

'What'll we do, then, Father?'

'We canna leave him here,' Davy gazed down at him doubtfully. 'We'd better take him home.'

'Mother won't be pleased to have another mouth to feed.'

Andra kicked the prone body with the toe of his boot and the boy's eyes opened, jet-black and flashing.

'Furrin as well,' Andra added. 'Look at his skin.'

'Ay. He could be an Indian or from somewhere in the East by the look o' him . . . Weel, Indian or no', I canna help what yer mother says.' Davy suddenly made up his mind. 'I've been a God-fearing man all my days and it's not right to leave the laddie here to die. We'd only land up in hell-fire if we did. So you take his shoulders, and I'll take his legs.'

Contrary to Andra's expectations his mother clucked around the castaway 'like a bloody old hen', he told himself. Thirza was even worse, giving up her place in the bed for the stranger and sleeping on the bench in the kitchen, on the other side of the room from her parents' box bed in the recess. She even refused to go to school.

'My mother's needing me,' she said, hanging over the prostrate boy, her arms outstretched along the brass railing at the foot of the bed and swinging her legs in her excitement.

'Get off there, Thirza!' Ruth said, shaking the boy and asking him his name.

'Jordi,' he said faintly, opening his eyes a fraction. 'Jordi Wishart,' he repeated and closed them again, fading away into troubled sleep.

'Mother, if he's sleeping, why are his eyes rolling around like that?' Thirza asked in alarm.

'If ye're no' going to the school there's the windows to wash,' Ruth said sharply. 'They're covered wi' salt again from the sea winds. And leave the boy alane. He's only dreaming.'

4

THIRZA had a good idea already of how many beans made five and how many farthings made a penny when she was introduced to the money table. She took to it like a duck to water. Money, in her opinion, was the most important thing in the world. Katie Docherty had got the blacksmith to make imitation coins out of tin-plate for the school and, at the end of her first day of handling them, Thirza came home with a cut finger.

'And how did ye manage this?' her mother asked her.

'On a ha'penny, Mother. It had a sharp edge.'

'Like a razor, by the look o' it,' Ruth frowned, plunging Thirza's hand into hot water to clean it and then into cold to stop the bleeding.

'The edges should ha'e been filed doon,' Davy observed.

'Katie Docherty's an old maid, as ye very well ken. She's got no man to help her, let alane one wi' a file. I don't suppose there's such a thing as a file in this hoose, either?'

'No,' Davy agreed.

'I had tools in my boat,' said Jordi, who was now well enough to be allowed out of bed. 'Tomorrow I'll go and see if I can find them. You never know, the box might have been washed up.'

'And pigs might fly,' Andra sneered, proud of this brand new saying he had picked up recently, and determined to get the better of this cuckoo in the Gourlay nest not even as old as he was, but taller and infinitely better looking.

In the morning Jordi got up early with the Gourlay men and, parting company with them on the beach, heard Andra saying to his father in a loud voice, 'Ay, it takes a man to go to the fishing, not a stuck-up boy.'

'Wheesht!' Davy said sharply. 'If he's willing, I'm going to take him wi' us on the boat tomorrow. Six hands must be better than four.'

Jordi raked about the rocks and narrow inlets of the shore to no avail, before he came back to where he'd started, reasoning that anything as heavy as a tool box couldn't have been carried very far by the tide. At last he found a sharp wooden corner sticking up out of the sand at the base of a rock. He started to dig swiftly with his hands, and then dug faster still. It was the tool box all right and, seeing it again, he sat down on the rocks unable to stop his memories.

If only he could forget! He thought he *had* forgotten but the memories came flooding back now with a vengeance.

Jordi recalled his childhood in the large mansion in the Grange district of Edinburgh, India House. Madeleine, his mother, was always there, and hovering always in the background was Bess, plump and cheerful. She was in charge of the housekeeping and the maidservants, and her husband Robbie looked after the horses and the carriages and supervised the men who did the outside work.

Jordi's early life wouldn't have been the same without Robbie, who never failed to spare a little time to play with him every day, just as a grandfather would have done. Robbie was the one who got a little pond built for him to sail his toy boats, for boats were Jordi's passion from the beginning. Robbie even made his boats for him.

His father, George Wishart, had come home from the East India Company on furlough every two years or so. The first clear memory Jordi had of him was that of a large fair-haired man leading what seemed, to his infant eyes, a huge horse.

'This pony is for you, Jordi,' George Wishart said. 'You must be a little soldier and learn to ride him. I want you to grow up and become a soldier, just like me.'

He could remember the fear and horror he felt when his father lifted him onto the back of that horse. He could remember screaming in terror, screaming and screaming . . .

Mercifully, George Wishart's Indian servant came into the picture next, gently lifting him off the horse with his strong brown hands. His name was Viaz Mohammed, a kind man who smiled at him and calmed him down. Jordi looked into his beautiful, liquid black eyes, quite different from his father's cold ice-blue ones, and loved and trusted Viaz from that moment on. Viaz didn't expect him to be a little soldier when he was only four years old. He spent many patient hours helping him to conquer his fear of the animal, and when Viaz had to go back to India again with his father, he handed over the reins to old Robbie, who taught Jordi to ride.

George Wishart was pleased that his son could ride the next time he and Viaz came home. Jordi didn't think he liked his father very much, although he loved the stories that he and Viaz recounted for him. Sometimes he didn't understand them. He didn't think his mother did, either. He often thought that she looked bored, especially when she whisked him away to his nursery.

'I like *some* of the stories, Mother,' he told her.

'Which ones? Do you mean the one about how Father saved Viaz in the battle with the French soldiers?'

Shivering a little, Jordi could well visualise his father standing over a Frenchman who was about to slit Viaz's throat. Instead, George Wishart had run his sword clean through the French soldier. He didn't think that would have given his father a second thought. The truth was, he was frightened of his father . . .

'I'm glad he saved Viaz, Mother.'

'Oh, so am I,' Madeleine smiled softly. 'So am I.'

'But,' he closed his eyes, 'sometimes, if I close my eyes like this, I can see Viaz leading Father into the Marigold Palace. That's the story I like best. I can see them killing all the snakes, hitting them with their burning torches! And then, Mother, the worst snake of all! The one Viaz shot so that it splattered all over the wall!'

'Ah, yes,' Madeleine shuddered. 'The cobra.'

'It was guarding the treasure chest, Father said. And he thought there was a baby cobra hanging from the lock, but Viaz showed him it was only the key. Do you believe that story, Mother?'

'Sometimes I do. But we've never seen any treasure, have we? Seeing is believing, Jordi. Don't believe everything you hear.'

When Father and Viaz were away and they were left alone again in India House, Madeleine would tell him stories of her own, but her stories were very different.

'You see, Jordi, I was one of a very poor family in Paris and had been sent to live with the nuns. They taught me to sew and helped me to become an expert at embroidery. Then, when I was still only fifteen, a great Scottish lady called Lady Hope happened to see my work displayed at an embroidery exhibition held by the nuns, and was so taken with it that she wanted me to go back to Scotland with her so that I could embroider her linen.'

'And did you, Mother?'

'My parents were overjoyed. It was a godsend to them. Lady Hope was very good to me and never treated me as a mere sewing woman in her house, more like a young distant relative of her own, one who could sew beautiful pictures.'

'And you were happy?'

'Very happy with my Lady. And there were so many interesting people at Hopetoun House.'

'Hopetoun House? Where is that?'

'A few miles outside Edinburgh to the north, right on the mouth of the River Forth. It should have been called Hopetoun Palace, Jordi, for people say that it rivals the Palace of Versailles. It is certainly the most beautiful house in all Scotland.'

'Was it there that you met Father?'

'Yes. He came with his brother, David Wishart, who was an excellent horseman. Lord Hope engaged your Uncle David that same day, I remember . . .'

Jordi could tell by the expression on his mother's face that she didn't like Uncle David very much. He wondered why, but he knew her so well that he believed she didn't know quite why, either, otherwise she would have told him. He made up his mind to try and find out but, in the meantime, he went back to her story.

'You fell in love with Father?'

'Oh no, dear,' Madeleine smiled a little bitterly. 'But when he asked permission to marry me, my Lady was very happy about it.'

'And were *you* very happy, Mother?'

'I suppose I just wanted to please everyone,' Madeleine sighed.

After that Jordi couldn't help noticing that it was always Viaz who sat down beside Mother and spoke to her gently about her embroidery. He also noticed that when he did, his black eyes glowed into hers and she flushed like a rose. Sometimes his brown hand would touch her soft white one and then their eyes would come to rest on him.

Then his mother would hold out her arms to him, and when he got up from his toys and ran into them she would hold him so fiercely that he could feel the heat and strange passion running like invisible threads between her and him and so to Viaz, binding all three together.

Of course, he didn't understand it. Not then.

'Look at his eyes, Viaz,' she murmured once, 'so black and so deep. Whenever I look into them I feel I am drowning in you. It makes all the waiting between your furloughs worthwhile.'

How could you drown in somebody's eyes? Jordi wondered if he should ask Robbie who, up to now, had only explained that you could drown in the pond if you weren't careful, rather than interrupt this interesting conversation. They spoke so much about the past. When his father was there his mother and Viaz didn't get a chance to talk much; his father did all the talking.

But when George Wishart wasn't there, his mother wanted Viaz to tell her over and over again how it all began, so that by now even Jordi knew it had been at his parents' wedding. Viaz had come from Madras with George for the first time for that occasion, and when he had looked at Madeleine, and she at him, something had happened.

'It was at your wedding to Wishart-Sahib,' he said. 'So many strange and unexpected things happened that night ... It was also the first time for years that Wishart-Sahib met his brother again.'

'Yes. David Wishart.'

'He said something derogatory to your new husband. They might have come to blows, but I stood behind Wishart-Sahib, and his brother didn't like the look of me.'

'No,' Madeleine smiled, 'David Wishart wouldn't like the look of you. I can understand that many men would think twice before they crossed you. You can look so fierce when you want to, Viaz, with your eyes flashing murder as they did that night, and your hand on the dagger at your waist.'

'But you weren't frightened of me, Madeleine?'

'I suppose it was the danger that I sensed in you that thrilled me from the start . . .'

Viaz bent down and whispered something in her ear so that Madeleine flushed and trembled and looked across at Jordi. 'Later,' she whispered. 'Later, Viaz.'

A few days later the name of his uncle, David Wishart, came up again and Jordi pricked up his ears. Surreptitiously he moved his toy soldiers nearer to where his father and Viaz were sitting, their long legs stretched out before them, laughing and chatting and drinking a tot of whisky out of crystal glasses.

'So, Wishart-Sahib, you have never seen your brother since you were married? Never run into him any time we have been in Scotland?'

'No, and I don't care if I never see him again, either.'

'You had a quarrel?'

'Oh, my friend, that was a long time ago!'

'Over a woman, perhaps?'

'A woman?' George laughed and glanced down at Jordi, who kept his head bent. 'Women are not to his taste, Viaz. You understand?'

'Ah . . .' Viaz nodded his head. He obviously understood. Jordi only wished *he* did.

'Yes, he even tried *me* on once, you know, his own brother! It was a great mistake. I punched him on the nose, and that was more or less the last time we were ever in each other's company.'

All that Jordi gleaned from that exchange was that his father didn't like his brother David.

The next conversation he overheard was between Madeleine and Viaz, and that was one he brooded over for years.

'I don't know for sure, Viaz, but all these years I've had the feeling that something happened, or something was said, between you and George the night of our wedding. Tell me, what was it?'

'Nothing that night. In fact, nothing that month. But later, before we went back to Madras . . .'

'Yes? What are you trying to tell me, Viaz?'

'Something I have never told you before. Something, perhaps, that I shouldn't tell you now, either.'

'And you would leave me in suspense, wondering for the next two years? Oh, Viaz! It isn't like you to be so cruel!'

'Well then, I will tell you. Your feeling has been quite right, Madeleine. Wishart-Sahib did take me aside the night of your wedding, to tell me that everything he possessed belonged to me as well as to him.'

'What did he mean?'

'He was repaying the compliment of one of our customs. India is another world, Madeleine, a different world altogether from Scotland. You see, I had said exactly the same thing to him in my own home before we left Madras. I meant I would even offer him my wife, Ameera.'

'Then you do not love Ameera?'

'I am very fond of Ameera. It was no disrespect to her. She was brought up with our customs, you see.'

'I'm so glad you've explained it all to me. I feel much happier now. What is between you and me doesn't feel so wrong any more.'

Jordi's mind jumped forward several years to when the news came from the East india Company that his father was missing in action, presumed dead. Neither he nor his mother shed a tear for him, but not long afterwards she began to pine.

'What is it, Mother?' he asked her. 'What's wrong?'

'There's nothing wrong, dear,' Madeleine hastily dabbed at her eyes and turned back to the canvas stretched on her embroidery frame. 'You mustn't worry. Your father left us with plenty of money. We'll be all right.'

'I'm not worrying about that,' Jordi told her, as he thought of the image of his own face, seen so often reflected back at him from his mirror. It was the image of a ten-year-old boy with a golden oval face with a thin, slightly hooked nose over a firm mouth, and black eyes under heavy eyebrows. The whole face was crowned with shining blue-black hair.

'I'm not worrying about money, Mother,' he added, 'but I

am worrying, the same as you are, about my real father. What happened to Viaz?'

It was the first time that the truth of the relationship had come out in the open between them, and Madeleine burst into tears. 'Oh, Jordi!' she wept, rocking him back and forth in her arms so that something hard and cold under the bodice of her dress hurt him.

'What have you got around your neck?' he asked.

'Oh, this?' Madeleine took out a heavy gold necklace. 'George gave it to me just as they were leaving. It was at the last minute, and the expression on his face was very strange when he said it would be safer with me than with him. Could he have had a presentiment of his death? Anyway, he seemed worried about the necklace, and said he must remember to tell Viaz what he had done with it. I have been hoping to ask Viaz about it, but there has been no word from him yet . . .'

Jordi's memories then took on a nightmarish tinge, from when the fine fat purse of money George Wishart had left them ran out. His tutors were dismissed and some of the servants.

'Don't worry,' Madeleine told him again. 'I've always hated these eastern ornaments, anyway. I shall sell them. They are worth a lot of money.'

So the jewels and ornaments disappeared one by one, then the silks and draperies by the yard and, when the pieces of ornately carved furniture went at last, the rooms they had occupied were closed up and became disused.

He must have been nearly twelve when Madeleine said, 'I know you're going to be very disappointed, Jordi, but I've had to let Bess and Robbie go. Now we're on our own. We're poor.'

'There's still the house, Mother.'

'Yes. Before she left, Bess gave me the name of a man who buys houses and then allows the previous owners to lease them.'

'Who is he?'

'His name is Marmaduke Elliot, and he's coming to see me today.'

Marmaduke Elliot was a huge man, brutish-faced and ginger-haired, and Jordi hated him on sight. But Madeleine took him into the only sitting room left furnished in India House and shut the door on her son. An hour later they both came out smiling.

'Say goodbye to Mr Elliot, Jordi,' his mother said, but he remained tight-lipped.

'That was very rude,' she lashed him later with her tongue.

'I don't care. He's horrible. Oh Mother, you didn't sell him this house?'

'Of course I did, for a thousand pounds.'

'A thousand pounds! But you know it's worth more than *ten* thousand pounds! He's swindled you.'

'A thousand pounds will last us a long time, Jordi. We'll just have to be very careful with the money and try and save as much as we can in between paying Mr Elliot every month for the lease.'

'Paying him for the lease? When he's stolen the house from us already? You haven't signed any papers, have you?'

'Yes, I signed. Don't you see, Jordi? It was the only way to get some cash. We have to live,' Madeleine protested in tears.

'If I had been twenty-two instead of twelve this would never have happened,' Jordi stalked away after the first quarrel he had ever had with his beloved mother. Sure enough, within a year the payments to the smiling, gloating Mr Elliot were becoming more and more difficult, until finally Madeleine found herself unable to meet them at all.

'What are we going to do now, Mother?'

'I'll talk to him. Do stop worrying, Jordi.'

That afternoon Madeleine showed Mr Elliot into the best room again and shut the door. Jordi sat down on the floor outside and listened.

'You're behind again this month?' Mr Elliot said. 'It can't go on, Mrs Wishart.'

'If you would allow us a little time, sir, I feel sure . . .' her words trailed off in a sob.

'I've been allowing you time already,' he said flatly. 'No, it can't go on.'

'Do you mean you're evicting us?' Madeleine's voice rose hysterically.

'Now, now . . . Madeleine, isn't it?' Jordi heard a creak from the easy chair beside the fire, heavy steps across the room to the door, and then the key was turned in the lock. There was another creak over where his mother must be sitting on the chaise-longue, and where he was now joining her. 'You must call me Marmaduke. There, there . . . Give me your hand, my dear. There is another way to pay, you know.'

'What other way? Tell me, and I'll do it.'

'You will?'

'Yes, yes,' Jordi heard the desperation in her voice. 'Anything.'

'Well then, it's called "in kind", if you're sure about it.'

'Oh . . .' Madeleine's voice seemed to be cut off, and after that Jordi heard a strange thud, thud, thud coming from the direction of the chaise-longue. It went on for a long time. It went on for so long that he became frightened for his mother. He tried the door desperately, and then he knocked on it. What was Mr Elliot doing to make that queer noise? What was happening to his mother?

Jordi rushed out of the house and ran round to the window of the best room, in time to see Mr Elliot getting up from straddling his mother and buttoning up his breeches.

'You'll still have to pay next month, you know, one way or the other,' he said, and the next minute he was out of the door before Jordi could recover from the shock. Feeling came back into his legs only when he heard Mr Elliot riding away on his horse. Rushing back he found his mother with her face ashen except for the red weals across her mouth where Marmaduke Elliot must have pressed his hand to stop her from screaming.

For the next three weeks they were both silent. There was nothing to say. Nothing could alter the fact that they had been cheated out of money. Far worse than that in Jordi's view, was what Mr Elliot had done to his mother. Sooner or later he would see Marmaduke Elliot again, and then he would kill him.

The days dragged on while he became more and more determined, until the morning came when Madeleine was standing at his bedside. 'Wake up, Jordi,' she said. 'We're leaving.'

The implacable resolve on his mother's normally gentle face alerted him immediately. 'Where to?' he asked, pulling on his clothes.

'For a long walk. It's eight miles, so put on your stout shoes.

I've taken the last of the bread and the milk in the house. We can eat and drink on the way.'

Jordi fell silent. He didn't like the black clothes she was wearing. In fact, he couldn't remember her ever wearing black before. The gold of her necklace and her golden wedding ring burned like fire against the sombre colour. Suddenly everything felt strange to him, and somehow frightening. It seemed in keeping that he had never seen his mother in such a strange mood before, either. As they walked along, side by side, she talked – not mentioning Marmaduke Elliot once, but speaking as usual about her past, often quite tearfully.

'I think it is only right that you should know the whole story now, before . . . Well, *now*, dear.'

'Yes, Mother?' Jordi asked gently.

'Oh, Jordi, I tried so hard to please everyone,' Madeleine sighed, 'and let that be a lesson to you. Try to please everyone and you please no one. See you look out for yourself first, Jordi, in this life.'

'Well, you'll be here to see that I do,' he laughed. But something in her expression worried him, and he went back to her story. 'Tell me why my father went to India.'

'I was still a young girl at the time. I remember a very important gentleman arriving at Hopetoun House, called Henry Dundas, Viscount Melville.'

'Henry Dundas? Everyone knows about Henry Dundas, Mother. My tutor used to tell me he was called 'Henry the Ninth' because he more or less ruled Scotland until he was impeached.'

'There was something about Navy Funds,' Madeleine agreed vaguely. 'He was too casual with them, people said.'

'Too casual? Don't you know what he did, Mother? He invested them and pocketed the profits, while the ordinary seamen were getting no wages,' Jordi said indignantly.

'This was long before all *that*, dear. Henry Dundas arrived, bringing two young men with him in his carriage. They were George and David Wishart. He introduced David to the Earl, hoping he would take him into his household, which Lord Hope agreed to. But your father,' Madeleine sighed, 'had no such ambition.'

They always referred to George Wishart as his father, Jordi

thought, although they both knew better. Still, he had been accepted as his son, and given his name.

'Instead,' she went on, 'it had been decided that George would join the East India Company at Fort David near Madras. I'm afraid he was rather wild as a boy, and that's what they used to do with wild young gentlemen – send them as far away as possible. In his case it was to India.'

'In what way was he wild?'

'You don't need to know these things, dear.'

'You said I should know it all, and now.'

'Yes, well . . .' Madeleine dried her eyes momentarily and rushed on. 'Your father liked money, Jordi, and when he had it he spent it. On other women, on gambling and on anything that took his fancy, as you saw by that awful India House. I never liked it. It was built in such a rush that I never believed that the foundations could possibly be sound. It will fall down one day, mark my words. We are best out of it.'

'Yes, Mother. But where did Father get so much money? He was only a junior officer in the East India Company, wasn't he?'

'He wouldn't have told me even if I'd asked him. It was Viaz, his batman, who used to tell me everything. And then, during an engagement with some French soldiers, George saved Viaz's life, as you know. After that he never left your father's side. He always came home with him on furlough.'

'That was when you fell in love with him, Mother?'

'Oh, Jordi,' Madeleine wept, 'Viaz was the only man I ever loved! And when you were born we were both so happy . . . He was delighted to watch you growing up, furlough after furlough.'

'Viaz was already married, Mother?'

'Don't look so disapproving, Jordi! Yes, he was married with a home near Madras. We both knew our happiness would be brief, and then it was crowned by your arrival.

'I think George always thought of you as his son. He insisted you should be called by his name, although I never liked George for a name. So when I sewed your christening robe I embroidered "JORDI" on the hem. Being French, you see, I didn't know any better when Lady Hope told me that, in Scotland, Geordie was the pet name for George.'

'What does it matter how it's spelt?' Jordi asked impatiently. 'Tell me some more about Viaz.'

At that a light came into Madeleine's face and a smile to her lips for the first time during that long walk, and he saw that Viaz was all she wanted to talk about. 'I came across him one day with some gold and such delicate little tools, Jordi,' she told him, 'and I asked him what he was doing.

'"Copying this key," he told me. "George wants a duplicate made in case his own gets lost."

'"And you can do that?"

'Viaz laughed. "My father was a goldsmith, and his father before him. Some day I'll go back to it, Madeleine."

'"It looks more like a serpent than a key."

'"It's a cobra, all coiled up. See, the mouth and the fangs make the mechanism to turn the lock."

'"What lock?"

'"The lock of a large trunk in Alistair Fisher's strongroom. But Wishart-Sahib will tell you all about that."'

'Well, Jordi,' Madeleine sighed, 'your father never did tell me. I don't even know who Alistair Fisher is, or where his strongroom may be. George simply gave me the original key without a word of explanation except that it must never be lost, and I had to wear it round my neck day and night on a gold chain until he came back.'

'So Viaz has another just like it?'

'He had,' Madeleine began to weep softly. 'Before he died.'

'Oh, Mother, he might not be dead! I don't believe it! How do you know he is dead? Wouldn't we know? Wouldn't we be bound to feel it?'

As soon as he could manoeuvre it after his return to Camp David, George Wishart set off with Viaz for another secret visit to the Marigold Palace in the desert beyond the swamp. The night was filled with the beating wings of fruit bats and fireflies danced in front of their eyes like stars. George thought the heat and the smells were going to suffocate him. He became increasingly uneasy.

He sensed excitement in the air and all around in the dense shadows. Yet he felt none of it within himself except for the thrill of finding more treasure – only a sort of dread to be visiting the deserted, ruined palace half-buried in the sand again. Perhaps it was because Viaz was so dead set against it.

'Why do you think we shouldn't go, Viaz?'

'I never said we shouldn't go back to the Marigold Palace, Wishart-Sahib. Only, not tonight. For weeks the camp has been surrounded by the fanatics. They come under cover of darkness.'

'Not even the fanatics would brave the snakes in the Marigold Palace,' George laughed.

'It is not sensible to risk all these dangers when there may be no more treasure anyway. And even if there were, do you not remember all the trouble we had smuggling it into the camp and then guarding it until we could get it shipped with us to Scotland?'

'You are too cautious, Viaz. Let's go! There is nothing out there but sand and snakes and jewels!'

But Wishart-Sahib was wrong. Silent black shapes rose out of the sand and ambushed them by the ruins of the Palace, leaving them for dead. It was hours before Viaz came back to consciousness and saw Wishart-Sahib lying near him.

Somehow he managed to drag his master's body into the shelter of a sand dune and, failing to find any sign of life, he then discovered that Wishart-Sahib must have been robbed as well. The cobra key he always wore on a chain around his neck was gone.

The key would be of no more value to a thief than the gold it was made of. Fortunately, Viaz thought immediately, he had left his own copy at home with Ameera, so all was not lost – not only for his own family, but also for Madeleine and Jordi.

It was days before he managed to crawl back to his own house and another week before he could speak to the terrified Ameera holding tightly to their growing daughter's hand, as if frightened she would run away and leave her, too.

'We can't stay here,' he told her.

'But you cannot walk, Viaz, not with that wound.'

'Get word to your father up in the hills, to send carts here for us and Jorjeela.'

Ameera looked incredulous. Perhaps he was still raving. 'You would leave . . . ?' she nodded down at the earthen floor.

'It's not time yet to dig it up. It will take more than a month for the carts to get here. By that time I shall be recovered.'

Or dead. Ameera wept to herself, while Viaz went over and over the ambush in his mind, worrying most of all about what could have happened to Wishart-Sahib's cobra key. Two things crossed his mind. The first was that it had been a long time since he had actually seen the necklace around Wishart-Sahib's neck. The second was that he might have left it with Madeleine, but that thought he swiftly dismissed. His master would have told him something so important as that.

Now Madeleine would be a widow and Jordi would be brought up without the protection of a father. How, Viaz worried, was she going to manage? Of course, if Wishart-Sahib really had left his key in India House, she would have access to the fortune in the trunk in Alistair Fisher's strongroom . . .

But supposing he hadn't? Viaz took to brooding. There was only one solution. His own key would have to go back to Edinburgh, to that lawyer's office. He had Jordi to think of, a son he would never tell his gentle Ameera about. No, after he had recovered and got his own life in order he would go back to Edinburgh himself. He swore it.

In the meantime he would have to content himself with the memory of the large sum of money Wishart-Sahib had taken home and left with Madeleine. Although it wouldn't last for ever, it might last until he himself got back to India House.

Four weeks later Viaz was still very weak but he breathed a sigh of relief when Ameera managed to get the heavy tin box up from under the floor.

'Now,' he said, 'wrap it up in some rugs and tie it with ropes ready for moving. Nobody must ever see it or know about it. We could be killed for just a fraction of what is inside. It is our passport to a better life.'

'And you can really leave Madras behind you – the place where you were born? And the Company, and the excitement of the fighting?'

'That all died with Wishart-Sahib, Ameera. Thanks be to Allah that I left you and him alone together for a month before that happened. We would not have this beautiful daughter now, for it seems that you and I cannot make a child together. Truly, he gave us the gift of life. For his sake, and for the sake of all he left us,' Viaz hugged Jorjeela, 'it is time to look to the future. It will be a long, weary journey, first to Calcutta and, beyond that, north to Darjeeling. But, once there, we shall be safe on the trade route to the East, and I can be a goldsmith again.'

Ameera turned her face away to hide her tears. She was glad that Viaz was going back with her to her own people. They would see to his funeral pyre.

Madeleine and Jordi walked on, but they had to stop frequently so that Madeleine could rest. As time passed, Jordi became more and more uneasy at the way she was talking to him, as if she wanted to tell him everything about her life – as if she would never see him again. Finally they sat down as the sun was setting in a flare of glorious red, extending orange fingers across the sky. Soon dusk would fall.

'I want you to have this necklace,' Madeleine said with a shiver, taking the key from around her neck and putting it around Jordi's. 'Remember, you must never lose it. It was your father's last wish. Come, let's go. Hopetoun House isn't far away now.'

'That's where we're going?'

'You mustn't feel it strange. You were born there, Jordi, although there is a new Earl now, and his Countess. Before he came back to Hopetoun to be the fourth Earl, he was General Sir John Hope, a very famous soldier. If you see him you must call him Lord Hope and tell him you have come to ask him for work. Although he won't know you, he'll recognise the name when you tell him your uncle is David Wishart. Your uncle works for the new earl, too.'

'When I tell him? But you're coming too, Mother?'

'I want you to do this on your own, Jordi. You have been the man of the family for a long time now, and I'm afraid the time has come for you to find a job. You can't do that with your mother trailing behind you.'

'But we have never been parted before, Mother . . . Where are you going? When will I see you again?'

'Don't worry, Jordi,' Madeleine's voice sounded firm and resolute for the first time that day. 'I'll see you later, when you are settled,' she said, opening a little side door beside the huge iron gates. They stood for a moment looking at Hopetoun House, black and graceful, silhouetted against the darkening sky. Jordi could see that there was a very long path up to it, through gardens shadowed by the surrounding trees.

'Now go, Jordi,' his mother smiled and kissed him. 'I won't be very far away.'

When he looked back she had slipped away. Like a ghost, she had disappeared, and he was alone.

The tears blinding Madeleine's eyes didn't stop her. Melting into the black shadows she was a shadow herself gliding along the Sea Walk. She knew every step of the way. Nothing had changed since she used to live at Hopetoun House.

Only she had changed – from the happy girl she had been when she first came here, to the heart-broken woman she was tonight, her whole being consumed with grief, humiliation and despair. Once she had had it all, home, money, husband, lover and child. Now it was all gone. Mixed with the black bitterness in her soul, there was now a red core of anger burning deep inside her, driving her on, threatening to erupt.

The moon came out, but Madeleine didn't need its light to find her way through the trees to the glinting, dancing silver streak ahead. She stood for a moment on the river bank, then walked across the little strip of sand straight into the waters of the Forth.

For a few brief seconds her black cloak bellied out above her, and then it sank too, with scarcely a ripple as the river flowed on.

5

JORDI walked on alone down the long eerie path towards the lighted windows of Hopetoun House. The nearer he got the larger it loomed, and he remembered his mother's words. It was not a house at all. It was a palace, with its huge main structure four or five storeys high flanked by curving wings which were flanked in turn by two more wings connected by curved and pillared verandahs, each topped by a tower. It was a different shape from Holyrood, the only other palace he'd ever seen, but twice as big and much more beautiful.

He was struck by its perfect symmetry. It resembled a fan spread out in a great semi-circle. Within the semi-circle there was a courtyard in front of the house, and at the end of the courtyard there was an imposing set of wide steps up to the front door.

He started to climb them, feeling only the size of a fly, and then he was confronting a massive door and ringing the bell. But obviously no visitors were expected at Hopetoun House that night, for there was no reply at first. Jordi kept on ringing and ringing until at last the door was opened. 'Lord Hope?' he asked.

The servant looked down at him incredulously. 'Does he expect you?'

'No, sir. My mother sent me. My name is Jordi Wishart and my uncle, David Wishart, is here. My mother said Lord Hope would know, and perhaps find me some work.'

'Wait in here while I ask,' the servant said.

Left alone in total silence, Jordi sat on the edge of one of the leather chairs and looked at the white marble chimneypiece. In the centre of it was an Apollo head, and on either side were white marble busts of famous men. Above them were white marble roundels on the golden wall, and even the floor of this magnificent entrance hall was made of marble.

Through the open door to the inner hall he could see a longcase clock at the foot of a graceful staircase, its pine walls carved with flowers and fruit, and portraits set in each panel. Far away he could hear voices, then a door closing and, after what seemed a long time, the old servant was pulling him to his feet and taking him outside again.

It was not a pleasant experience when he was introduced to his uncle, David Wishart, in the stable courtyard. Burly, and clearly irritated by such an interruption to whatever he had been doing, he just stood there, tapping a whip on his riding boots. 'Who did you say he was?' he snapped.

'It seems he is your nephew, Jordi Wishart. The Earl's orders are that you will take charge of him until he has the time to look into it.'

'Leave him, then,' David said imperiously. 'I'll soon deal with him.'

Jordi noted the sour, tight-lipped way that the old servant glowered at David, from which he gathered that he neither liked nor respected his uncle.

'So you are George's son, are you?' asked David, when they were alone. He spoke in a high-pitched voice and there was speculation in his eyes as he stepped all around him, looking him up and down.

'Yes, sir. He died in India, and since then my mother has found it very hard to support us. She has sent me to work here, if Lord Hope will have me.'

'Well, you bear no resemblance to your father, nor to that French slut he married.'

Jordi didn't reply to that, just as his uncle hadn't responded to the news of his brother's death. He realised immediately that he would find no kindness from this man.

'I suppose I shall have to find a place for you to stay, but not tonight. Tonight I am too busy.'

David was pacing up and down the stalls in an agitated manner. Suddenly he stopped as if he had made up his mind about something, and unbolted one of the doors.

'There's plenty of hay in here,' he said. 'You can bed down beside Sinbad for the night. It might be different tomorrow – that is, if his lordship allows you to stay, which I doubt.'

At this sting Jordi found his tongue again and gave back as good as he got. 'Surely he will, sir, since you are my uncle.'

'Get in there, cheeky little bugger!' David cuffed him on his ear so hard that he propelled Jordi into the stall, where a huge black stallion whinnied.

Jordi heard three bolts being slammed in from the outside, and he was left alone with a very angry animal pawing the ground. In the dim lights of the stable he saw the whites of the horse's eyes. In another minute the beast would rear and trample him with his hooves.

He could not allow his terror to show. That much he remembered from Viaz's teaching long ago. Summoning up all his courage he put a hand on the horse's neck. 'Sh! Sh, Sinbad,' he said over and over again and went on stroking the quivering horse and hissing into his ear. It seemed hours before the animal settled bit by bit. Jordi just kept stroking him and whispering until Sinbad gave a great snort and finally quietened. Eventually Jordi lay down in a corner, and they both fell asleep.

'Jesus!' a voice woke him next morning, and he looked up into the round eyes of a boy much the same age as himself peering in over the door of the stall. Sinbad was becoming restless again. It was clear he didn't like this next intrusion. 'Quick!' the boy said, snapping back the bolts. 'Come on out! How did you ever get in there, anyway?' he asked when he had locked the horse in again. 'Sinbad is the most dangerous horse here. He's a killer!'

'My uncle put me in there for the night.'

'Your uncle? Who's he?'

'David Wishart.'

'Ah . . . Well, my name's Joe Tennant. What's yours?'

'Jordi Wishart. My uncle said he was too busy to find me a place when I arrived last night.'

'Come along with me then. I'll show you the ropes here.'

*   *   *

43

For the next three weeks Jordi tried to settle down into his new life, but it was hard. The other stable-lads were split into two groups, those who wouldn't meet his eyes at all and seemed frightened, and those who looked at him knowingly but shunned him all the same. Only Joe was friendly enough, but even he didn't seem at all surprised by David Wishart's cruelty on the night of Jordi's arrival. He just accepted it.

Jordi hated his uncle. He couldn't stay on at Hopetoun. Then he had second thoughts. How else would his mother find him again except by sending a message through David? No, he must just stay here and wait for her. And since she had vowed never to go back to India House . . . Where had she gone? Jordi worried continually, but all he could do now was wait until she got in touch with him, or else he would lose track of her for ever.

In the meantime, he only set eyes on his uncle again from a distance.

With Joe's help, Jordi got to know all the different parts of the stables, where the blacksmiths and the farriers worked, the tack room, how the machines for mixing the feed worked and where the areas for exercising the horses were. He discovered that if he were allowed to stay on at Hopetoun he would be only one of a whole army of servants. Now and then he saw the factor of the estate going about his business, and the grooms, henwives, gardeners, and dairymaids. Then there were those in the house itself whom he never saw, from the steward, the butler, the housekeeper, the house chaplain and the chef down to the footmen, the housemaids, the under-footmen, the laundry-maids, the sewing women and the scullions.

But the best place was down beside the river where he discovered the boat house on one of his solitary expeditions. And in it, at long last, two friends. John Bryson and Bertie Simpson, men in their fifties, who talked to him. He told them about his mother and father and, to his delight, they remembered Madeleine well. They, along with all the other servants, had been at her wedding in Hopetoun House when she was married to his father.

After that Jordi was happier, but back in the stables he sensed that there was something very wrong in this all-male society. He couldn't put his finger on it, and therefore he couldn't understand it. He only knew that the atmosphere was secretive and subdued. The one bright spot was when Lord Hope, every inch a soldier, came to visit the stables, speaking a few words to all the men and boys.

'Jordi Wishart, isn't it?' He shook his hand and Jordi looked up into a thin ascetic face and very blue eyes well used to weighing up men, situations and battle horizons.

'Yes, my lord.'

'I am almost as new here as you are,' Lord Hope said. 'Like you, I am still finding my feet. If you have any problems, let me be the first to know,' the Earl added and passed on to the next hand.

Jordi smiled with relief. Then he was to be allowed to stay on.

He plunged in to his new way of life with vigour. He progressed to a bunk in the long quarters which housed nineteen other men. Their days began very early in the morning when the horses were ridden out for gallops, and Jordi and the other stable-lads had the job of mucking-out and getting in fresh hay, oats and water before the horses and grooms came back. One morning, finding themselves alone together, Joe spoke a few more words to him.

'They don't trust you here, because you're David Wishart's nephew,' he told him while they were trundling out with their steaming barrow-loads.

'Why? What's that got to do with it?'

'I hope you never find out. I hope to God I don't, either. So far I've escaped,' was all Joe would say, leaving Jordi more mystified than ever.

In December, a blast of excitement shot through the stables. The date for the servants' ball had been set for the fifteenth. On that afternoon the horses were brushed, fed and watered early and there were more buckets of hot water for the men to wash in when they removed their riding boots and breeches and dressed up in their own clothes.

Samuel Grant, the Master of the Horse, strode down the length of the quarters with David Wishart beside him, slapping his whip on his boots. At once silence fell. Jordi could feel the thrill of terror from one end of the long room to the other before the two men stopped at his bunk.

45

'You needn't bother to change,' his uncle told him. 'You're going nowhere tonight. You're to stay here.'

Joe, in the next bunk, was trembling and actually whimpering when they went out. 'Oh, for Christ's sake,' he kept saying. 'For Christ's sake . . .'

'What's the matter, Joe?'

'Run away, for God's sake! Do it now!'

Jordi shook his head, feeling very disappointed, for he had been looking forward to seeing the inside of the great house after the tiny peep he'd had the night he arrived. 'I can't go. I've got to stay here, Joe. There is a reason. The only thing my uncle can possibly want with me is to give me a message from my mother.'

'Oh, Jesus Christ,' Joe said despairingly, and left him to it.

One by one the others departed hurriedly, and eventually Jordi was left all alone. It was unnaturally quiet and depressing. The battle against his disappointment at having to miss the ball made him so tired that he stretched himself out on his bunk. In a few minutes he was fast asleep.

But then, to life as well as out of his sleep, he was very rudely awakened.

At first Jordi was only dimly aware of men's voices wakening him out of his sleep. Then he opened his eyes and saw his uncle's face above him. It was red, his eyes were bright with an evil excitement and his pink tongue kept wetting his thick lips.

Now he knew what Joe had meant. He was in for a beating. But why? Why had his uncle taken such a dislike to him?

'You can go first. I'll watch,' he said to the man beside him and Jordi saw that it was Samuel Grant.

'Bloody right, I'll go first,' Grant threw Jordi onto his stomach and pulled him down to the end of the bunk so that he was sprawled with his feet on the floor. 'I'm the master here!'

It was bad enough to be getting a beating at all for something he'd never done, Jordi thought, but to pull off his breeches to do it was monstrous. He shut his eyes and waited for the whip. Instead, something big and hard was being forced into his back passage in a nightmare of pain. It was pumping in and out. Screaming, Jordi knew that his skin and his flesh were being ripped apart.

It went on and on while Jordi vomited, then fainted, and then came back in a red-hot mist to find that the invasion was still going on. When it stopped he was in such excruciating pain that he vomited again, and then he heard his uncle's high-pitched voice.

'Now it's my turn!' His falsetto was almost at screaming point in his panting excitement. 'His father would have nothing to do with me. Disown me, did he? Well, now I'll get my own back at last! Let me get at that little bugger of his!'

Jordi lost all consciousness in the brutal and savage attack. How long it went on, he didn't know. How long he lay bleeding and half-dead afterwards, he had no idea and, struggling to get to his feet, he fell over backwards and cracked his head. All he knew, much later when he was coming to, was that Joe had been right. He should have gone long ago. Now he must get out, at once.

He willed himself to move. Somehow – faint, sick, bleeding and torn – he crawled outside. That was a feat in itself, but the shock of the icy air overcame him. Finally he came to himself again and, utterly determined, crawled on, inch by inch and foot by foot over the frozen lawns.

Lord Hope took one last look out of his bedroom window, high up in Hopetoun House. The Round Pond wasn't dancing and sparkling as it usually did. It must be frozen solid to gleam so dully. He shivered, cold now after the heat and laughter of the ball. It had been a great success, the servants clearly enjoying the dancing when he had left with his wife, Lady Louisa.

He was just turning towards his warm and inviting bed when something moving caught his eye. 'Good God!' he exclaimed, and looked again. 'Louisa, come and look at this!'

'It's an animal,' she said, standing beside him.

'It must be wounded, then. See how slowly it's crawling along? I'll take Adam and go and see.' The Earl rang for his most trusted footman and pulled on his dressing-robe.

'Good Lord, Adam,' Lord Hope said when they reached Jordi, 'it's the Wishart boy from the stables! Help me to carry him inside.'

'Very good, my lord. He's bleeding, you know.'

'What? Where? Oh, my God! The doctor will have to be fetched! In the meantime, who can we trust to keep his mouth shut? You'll need someone to help you.'

'James, my lord,' Adam named another senior footman. 'I'll put the boy in the small room next to mine. No one will ever look in there.'

Jordi woke up to find a doctor attending to him. He was in a narrow, spartan room, and Lord Hope was there, as well as Adam, hovering in the background.

'Well, my lord,' the doctor said, 'as far as I can tell there are no serious internal injuries. He has been lucky – if you can call it that.'

'Who did this to you?' Lord Hope demanded sternly.

But Jordi only shook his head, lay flat on his stomach and refused to speak. The agonising physical pain was not quite so bad, now that the doctor seemed to be finished, but the humiliation made him speechless with shame.

'Very well,' Lord Hope said grimly. 'I have my own ways of finding out,' and he marched out of the room.

Left alone except for Adam, Jordi didn't feel he had been a victim. Far from it. He felt murderous. He swore that one day he would kill his uncle. And he had not forgotten the burning outrage of his mother's abuse by Marmaduke Elliot. That man would be number two on his list. But, in the meantime, he could only lie there helpless, with tears of frustration oozing from his eyes.

A few days later, when he was up and hobbling about the little room, though still too badly torn to sit down, Lord Hope came to see him again.

'Samuel Grant and David Wishart have been dismissed from my service,' he said. 'Do you wish me to press criminal charges? They should be locked up.'

'No, my lord,' Jordi smiled wanly. 'That would be locking the stable door after the horses have bolted, I'm afraid. The damage has been done.'

'Damage has certainly been done,' Lord Hope said angrily. 'I found out that they had been terrorising the young stable-lads for a long time. A prison sentence would stop those two from any further attempts to rape other young boys, though. Much more of it and we might have had a nest of abused and perverted stable-lads at Hopetoun House.'

'I knew they were very frightened, my lord, but no one would say why.'

'Samuel Grant and David Wishart must be punished, one way or the other, and another way is to have them shipped out of the country on separate vessels. You have made up your mind, then? You will not press charges?'

Jordi shook his head. 'No, my lord. Let them go. All I want now is just to forget it.'

'Well, you will never manage that in the stables – just going back there will be a constant reminder every day.'

'My lord,' Jordi winced with pain, 'I was thrust upon you in the first place. I appreciate your kindness, but it would be better if I left you now, anyway, and went to find my mother. It has been six months since I last saw her.'

'Perhaps later, but not yet. Even when you are fully recovered you will be more scarred than you can understand now. So where on the estate would you like to work in the meantime?'

'Oh, down at the river with the boat-builders, my lord!'

And so he was put into the care of John Bryson and Bertie Simpson, already his friends, who had been told what had happened. Neither ever mentioned it to Jordi during the time he stayed with them.

He would have been content, as he matured to the age of sixteen, if it hadn't been for the dread he felt every morning for another day ahead, with no word from his mother.

'It's not like her,' he said over and over again to John and Bertie. 'She said she would come back. She's never broken a promise to me before.'

'Never you mind, lad,' John said. 'She'll turn up yet. Wait and see,' and to take Jordi's mind off it he began teaching him how to make a small boat of his own, one he could eventually sail.

In the meantime, John and Bertie took him up and down the Firth in their boat and taught him to row. It all helped, but every now and then the sounds of the maids' soft voices, a woman's laugh or the swishing of her skirts cut Jordi to the heart.

Then, one summer evening while they were all three on another rowing exercise further up the Firth, John and Bertie shipped their oars. The sweat was dripping off them all. Jordi saw that they had stopped at another boat house. 'We'll stop here and visit Sam Bryson,' John said. 'He's a cousin of mine, and it's his turn to pour out some ale, for a change.'

Jordi longed to sit outside in the fresh air and drink his, but the men clearly preferred to sit inside, where shortly the air was blue with the reek from their pipes. Jordi thought it would be ill-mannered not to stay with them, and before long he was glad he had done so, for Sam Bryson was full of stories about the Firth of Forth, and once embarked upon one of them, Sam was hard to interrupt.

After about an hour John got a word in edgeways. 'We'll have to go soon,' he reminded his cousin, 'so if ye're going to tell us the one about the beautiful lady, ye'll have to hurry up.'

'Ah yes, a sad day, that was!' Sam said. 'The new Earl had scarcely come to live in Hopetoun when it happened.'

The new Earl had scarcely come to live at Hopetoun! Jordi looked around the little shed, gone suddenly ice-cold now. He had arrived at Hopetoun himself, just weeks after the Earl — with his mother . . . He didn't want to hear another word from Sam Bryson, and yet he felt compelled to listen.

'One of Lord Hope's first duties was to see that the lady was given a Christian burial,' Sam went on, unaware of the panic and rising horror in Jordi's breast. 'I found her myself, under a bank. Beautiful, she was, and all dressed in black.'

Oh, God – all dressed in black . . .

They were all silent now, Sam himself looking very uncomfortable. 'I never told anyone else this before,' he added. 'I took her wedding ring off her finger before they put her in her coffin.'

'What?' John cried, aghast.

'Well, there was no sense in burying a fine gold ring now, was there?'

'It doesnae seem right to me, either,' Bertie looked just as disapproving as John. 'What did ye want wi' the poor lady's ring, anyway, Sam Bryson? Did ye sell it?'

Now it was Sam's turn to be offended, as well as becoming agitated as he tried to defend himself. 'Certainly not! It wasnae mine to sell, even if I had wanted to! No, I just thought it was a shame, that's all, so I put it in a box and I've kept it ever since. It's here,' he added, reaching up to a shelf. 'Take a look at it!'

On that warm evening, inside the hot, smoky shed, fingers of ice were crawling down Jordi's spine. He was shuddering, and his face was paper-white when John and Bertie pored over the engraving inside the ring.

'G.W. – M.C.' John said. 'I wonder what that stood for?'

'George Wishart and Madeleine Chamberlain! That was my mother's wedding ring,' Jordi whispered, before blackness swirled around him, and he knew no more.

Weeks later, when the sharp edge of his grief was over, and all the tears and the agonising, Jordi came back to the world once more. He turned to his boat again and carried on building it with the help of his two anxious friends. At last, when it was almost finished, John and Bertie saw a gleam in his eyes – eyes that had been dulled with pain for so long.

'Look!' he said to the two old men. 'My dearest ambition!'

'Soon!' he said to himself with mounting excitement as, with the two older men to guide him, he practised sailing up and down the Forth. Now he was a full-grown man and only a stone's throw away from carrying out all his plans.

The Earl came down to the boat house to watch his progress.

'Do I have your permission to sail away in her, my lord?' Jordi asked.

'Where are you proposing to go?'

'I was going to put in at Leith, hoping to find my mother in Edinburgh,' Jordi said sadly. 'Now, I'll just go for a sail along the Firth.'

'How long will you be?'

'Weeks, perhaps even months. If I find a place that takes my fancy, I might even stay there for a while, my lord.'

'In other words, you're off on an adventure, Jordi! Ah, to be sixteen again, with the whole world before you! Of course you may go, with my blessing. I have always believed in a boy's spirit of adventure. It can make him a man. Just remember, you will always be welcome back here.'

'Thank you, my lord,' Jordi shook his hand. A few days later he waved goodbye to John and Bertie.

'Remember all we told ye about that sail!' John shouted.

Then Jordi was on his way with all the bravado, the despair and the impetuosity of his sixteen years taking over. He could go anywhere in the world in his boat. He was the master of his own destiny, at last.

Forgetting all about Marmaduke Elliot in his excitement, he gave Leith hardly a glance as he journeyed down the Firth of Forth. He unfurled his one little sail, then reefed it in again according to the prevailing winds as John and Bertie had instructed, totally unprepared for the sudden squall that hit him broadside when the Firth widened into the North Sea.

It had dashed his frail craft against the rocks in Fife, and that was how he had come to be here today, living in the Gourlays' cottage, and gazing down at his tool box now, the sight of which had brought back his past so vividly. John Bryson had made it for him, and he and Bertie had found some old tools to put in it.

With his hands, he finished digging away the sand embedding it and pulled it up. Then, bit by bit, he dragged it to the Braehead, thinking that it had never been part of any of his plans to be living here with a dour, silent fisherman, his managing wife, his jeering bully of a son and his little red wasp of a daughter.

Well, he would put up with Andra's jibes for just so long. Already he had had enough of bullies to last him a lifetime. And he would only stay here fishing with the Gourlay men for as long as it took him to sharpen up his sailing abilities, which were sadly deficient as he now knew. Then he would go forth on his adventures again, this time the adventure of his life.

6

RUTH was as pleased as Jordi was to find that his tools had come to no harm, and they spent an hour drying them off one by one. Afterwards she gave him directions for the school in Pittenweem, and he set off with his file.

His appearance caused a sensation in Katie Docherty's Dame School. 'Who's this?' she asked Thirza.

'My new brother,' she said, preening herself. 'His name's Jordi. My father and Andra found him on the beach.'

'Then he cannot be your brother. He doesn't belong to your father and mother, like Andra.'

'He does now,' Thirza tossed her red mane, 'and besides, he's going to the fishing with them tomorrow – aren't you, Jordi?'

Jordi only smiled and explained why he was there to Miss Docherty before he retired quietly to a corner with the coins and his file, and after ten minutes even Thirza forgot he was there.

Jordi thought about going out in the *Bluebell* tomorrow. Nothing would suit him better than to go to sea again. His accident hadn't put him off in the least. There was just the little matter of another boat if he was ever to get away from here, and boats cost money.

There would never be another one handed to him for nothing like the *Lady Hope*, so as soon as he was finished filing down the coins he would run back to the beach and rescue what driftwood he could still find. The only thing to do in the meantime was to stay and try and earn some

53

money with the Gourlays by helping them with the fishing.

On the morning of the fourteenth of August, 1825, in the half light before dawn, Ruth and Thirza saw a strange phenomenon on the sea while they were watching for the fishing boats to return. The bay was covered with what appeared, at first glance, to be a great white sheet. They stood for a moment amazed, then ran to get their shawls and, with all the other women from the Braehead, ran to the foreshore to witness a miracle.

The bay was solid with herring.

They were drifting in with the tide, gulls and gannets screaming above them, followed by the fishermen who had shot their nets and hauled them back in again with moderate catches long before dawn. Now they reefed their sails, unstepped their masts, stowed the lot away and took to the oars, the Gourlays and Jordi included.

'Get to the shore side o' them, boys!' Davy yelled from the stern, and Jordi and Andra pulled as hard as they could, although it felt like rowing through porridge.

They pulled in their oars when they could penetrate the mass of fish no longer. Andra stood up on the bow, spearing them in with a boat-hook while his father and Jordi began to scoop up the herrings with anything they could lay their hands on – shovels, basins or buckets. When everything was full they simply scooped up the herrings in armfuls or stabbed them with their knives till *the Bluebell* – like all the other boats – was lying dangerously low in the water.

Panting with his exertions Jordi stopped for breath and looked around at the bow. Andra was nowhere to be seen. 'Where's Andra?' he shouted to Davy.

Red-faced with excitement Davy merely shook his head. Here were riches galore! The fish were almost jumping into his boat, and Jordi saw that the enormity of the possible loss of his son totally escaped him.

There was only one thing to be done, and he did it with his knife still in his hand. Taking in a lungful of air he slipped over the bow himself, down through the solid mass of herrings on the surface and saw Andra just below them, with his foot caught in one of the lines. Jordi imagined he must have struggled to free himself, but now he was still, just floating along under the hull, his hair streaming like seaweed.

With his lungs almost bursting Jordi swam down and cut Andra free, then propelled him through the fish back up to the surface. 'Give me a hand!' he shouted. 'I think he's drowned!'

At last Davy Gourlay paid attention. His eyes lost that glazed look of ecstasy and snapped back to reality. 'My God,' he kept saying. 'My God. What happened to Andra?'

Together he and Jordi hauled him in, flung him face down on top of the herrings and began to press the water out of his lungs, taking it in turns until there was a spasm in Andra's body and salt water spewed out of his mouth. Minutes later he was coughing and retching.

'My God,' Davy Gourlay kept repeating, until he saw that his son was going to live. Then he changed his tune. 'Ye aye were an impudent little bastard,' he said, 'but if I ever hear you bad-mouthing Jordi Wishart again you can look out, me lad! D'ye understand he saved yer life, bloody fool that ye are?'

Jordi continued to rub Andra's back until he was able to breathe easily and then to talk.

'Ay,' Andra said, shivering and crying, 'ye saved my life, Jordi. I'll be yer friend for life, see if I don't.'

'Well then,' Jordi answered, 'it's been a lucky day all round.'

It was indeed a happy day. The people on the shore recognised first one and then another of their own folk on the small boats and never even saw the herrings. All they could see were boats filled with money, full larders, new clothes and security.

Thirza was in a positive frenzy. 'There's my father,' she cried. 'Mother, see my father's boat! See the *Bluebell*, Mother?'

'Ay,' Ruth said. She saw her husband, and Jordi. But where was Andra? Why was he not shovelling in the herrings as well? She had one eye on the empty barrels being trundled in from the curer's, filled, and trundled back full, and the other fixed on the *Bluebell* until she could stand it no longer. It felt as though she and Thirza had been watching for hours, and still Andra was nowhere to be seen. The emptying of the boats of herrings into the barrels would go on all morning and she could wait no longer for news of her son.

'We'll have to go home, Thirza,' she said. 'I want ye to run down with a piece for the menfolk. They're never going to get home for their dinner today. Come on!'

'But it's nowhere near dinner-time yet, Mother,' Thirza objected as Ruth dragged her home almost at a run.

'I don't care!' Ruth said, slapping together slices of bread thickly spread with dripping. 'Take these to them right now! And take a pail of milk as well. Now, Thirza,' she warned her strictly, 'ye've to be back here in ten minutes! D'ye hear me?'

'Yes, Mother,' Thirza darted off.

Ruth waited in an agony of suspense until she saw her daughter running back again. 'Did ye see Andra?' she asked.

'Yes, of course I saw him.'

'Well then, what did he look like?'

'Andra? A bit like a sheep, sitting in the bottom of the boat,' Thirza informed her mother innocently.

Ruth glared down into the clear eyes of her daughter. Trust Thirza to hit the nail on the head. It was the truth. Davy was hot-headed and as weak as water. Andra was turning out to be just like him.

'Go inside and sand doon the table,' Ruth snapped, heading out of the door with a bucket of water and the hard broom. 'Menfolk should always come home to a clean table after a hard day's work. And mind ye put yer back into it, Thirza Gourlay!'

'Yes, Mother,' Thirza droned dutifully. What had she done to put her mother in such a bad mood, she wondered? She would far rather have stayed to watch the boats, but now she sprinkled the fine silver sand onto the table and reflected that she had always tried her best to please. She got the scrubbing brush and rolled up her sleeves with tears threatening to fill her eyes. She could hear her mother brushing away at the brigstones with sharp, short strokes. Why was her mother mad with her?

Outside, Ruth vented her spleen on the stone path up to the door, her heart swollen with frustration and the aftermath of the morning's stress. She brushed and brushed, stabbing angrily at the path until she came abreast of the window. There inside was Thirza, her bare bony arms wielding the scrubbing brush unmercifully.

Oh, Thirza! Her beloved daughter! The sight of her, so schooled, so disciplined, so intent on pleasing her after all the hard years! Ruth's tears ran down her cheeks at last, for in that moment she saw the budding woman who in the end would be worth twenty of her menfolk both rolled together. She knew for certain that Thirza would never fail her.

The men didn't come home until the evening, carrying pails of herrings. After her initial relief at seeing Andra all in one piece, Ruth sent them off to change their clothes and wash. Then she gutted a dozen of the herrings, rolled them in oatmeal and put them in the frying pan while Thirza scrubbed the tatties until they were clean enough to boil.

During their meal, Ruth found out that her only son had been snatched from the jaws of death by her lodger. 'Ay,' her husband was unable to resist adding, 'a fat lot of good it did him in the end, learning to swim.'

'Now, Thirza,' she said, ignoring this and gazing at the brimming buckets instead, 'the men are going to their beds, and we've got all this lot to gut and lay down in brine before we can get to ours.'

Ruth was planning to put all the money they got from the herring glut into an old tea-caddy and hide it up in the loft for a rainy day.

From that day onwards Andra did everything he could to make it up to Jordi who was now more than just a hero to Thirza, he was a god.

When Andra was seventeen and Jordi was almost seventeen and fully absorbed into the Gourlay family, Thirza's school days came to an end. Every Tuesday and Friday Katie Docherty had been sending her on shopping errands, as the most trustworthy pupil she had. At first it had only been on Fridays, but now Katie had given in to temptation and so it was twice a week that she sent Thirza to Matthew Jolly's bakeshop for a cream bun.

'I don't drink wine or spirits,' she told Thirza privately, 'and I don't swear. I hope you won't, either, as you go through life.'

'No, Miss Docherty.'

'But everyone has a weakness of some sort, Thirza. My one and only weakness has been cream buns, and it's one that I cannot conquer.'

So Thirza stepped into the glorious smells of the bakeshop twice a week almost fainting with the hunger they induced.

Mr Jolly was a thin, balding little man in a white apron. He always looked worried, but Mrs Jolly deserved her name. She put the cream bun, its shiny brown lid dusted with icing sugar and its inside filled to bursting with piped cream, into a paper bag and handed it to Thirza to take back to Katie Docherty one Friday morning.

'Thirza,' Katie said, taking a mournful bite out of it so that the cream squelched out of its sides, 'Next Friday will be your last day at my school. Who I can trust to run my errands after you,' she added darkly, 'I'm sure I don't know. But anyway,' she took another great bite, '*your* days here are numbered now. I can teach you no more. At twelve years old you know more about figures than I do.'

On Tuesday, when Thirza went to the bakeshop to get Katie's bun, she saw that Mr Jolly was more woebegone than ever when he sojourned briefly into the front shop, and even Mrs Jolly was agitated.

'He canna get the money and the figures to add up,' Mrs Jolly's jaws clamped together. 'There's no living wi' him,' she added, thrusting the cream bun into a paper bag and whirling the ends of it round and round angrily until it was sealed with two little twists standing up in the corners. 'It's driving him from sleep, and me too.'

'Well, I'll say goodbye, Mrs Jolly. Miss Docherty will be coming herself from now on. She says I've to leave the school on Friday.'

'Oh dear, Thirza! What'll you do then?'

'Nothing, I suppose. Just help my mother.'

On Friday at twelve o'clock Katie wrapped her shawl about her shoulders. 'I'll go to the bakeshop myself today, Thirza,' she said. 'You can clean off the blackboard instead, for the last time.'

'So Thirza Gourlay's leaving now,' Mrs Jolly said when Katie got there. 'She doesn't want to go, I could tell.'

'I don't want her to go, either,' Katie said when Mr Jolly made one of his dashes into the front shop, as he always did when he heard a strange voice. 'She has been the best pupil I ever had, by far – especially at counting and notation. There's nothing that girl doesn't know about a pound note, and you should just see her jotters! Not a slip anywhere in her figures!'

'If only she could add up mine,' Mr Jolly said.

'Why don't you try her, then?' his wife snapped. 'Anything for peace.'

'You'll never get a better,' said Katie as she moved to the door.

At four o'clock on Friday afternoon Thirza gathered together all her belongings, a pencil-stub, a battered old tin box containing her cowrie shells and the small Bible the Rev and Mrs Selkirk had given her. Its pages were very, very thin and the printing on them almost microscopic, but it was a book, and as such Thirza set great store by it. Besides, it was the only one she possessed. Sighing deeply, she packed her things into her white canvas bag thinking it wasn't much to show for over five years of education.

'Now then, Thirza,' Katie said briskly, 'you might as well take your old jotters as well. You never know who might want to have a look at them. Mr and Mrs Jolly, for two.'

'Mr and Mrs Jolly, Miss Docherty?'

'They want you to go and see them on your way home.'

By five o'clock Thirza had taken a horrified glance at Mr Jolly's idea of book-keeping and had been offered a job.

'Seven in the morning till noon,' Mr Jolly said. 'That would give my wife more time at home. A shilling for you and a free loaf every week for yer family. What do you say to that, Thirza Gourlay?'

'Yes, sir. But I'll have to ask my mother.'

'And ye'd better be wearing a clean white pinny, dearie, if ye're coming on Monday morning,' Mrs Jolly told her.

'It still leaves the problem of balancing the books for now.' Mr Jolly looked more doleful than ever. 'Unless,' he said, turning in desperation to his wife, 'you might manage them, my dear, wi' all this spare time ye'll be having?'

'*Me*, Matthew Jolly? G'wa, man!'

'Do you have a clean ledger, sir?' Thirza asked.

'I thought I might have to start another one, right enough. So yes, it's here.' Mr Jolly disappeared into the back and came back fetching one.

'Perhaps, if I took them both home?' Thirza asked. 'I'll try and sort them out, Mr Jolly, if you'll trust me.'

'Oh, I don't know about that,' he said stubbornly.

'If there's to be any peace or pleasure under our roof, Matthew Jolly, ye'll let her have them!' Mrs Jolly brought all her weight to bear. 'Dinna be a bigger fool than ye are already, for God's sake!'

Silence reigned over the Gourlay household all that Friday evening while Thirza wrestled with the figures and Ruth dared the menfolk to open their mouths.

'Have ye got it sorted?' she asked her daughter at bedtime.

'No, I have not,' Thirza scowled, 'unless all the mistakes mean that Mr Jolly's been cheated left, right and centre by the grain merchants. That would explain everything, because at the moment the figures certainly don't add up.'

All day on Saturday Ruth excused her the housework so that she could concentrate on cutting out the best parts of a torn sheet to make into two pinafores. Then she sewed the hems and stitched on tapes, one to go around her neck and one on each side to tie behind her in a bow, and on Sunday in the Kirk the whole family prayed that Thirza would succeed in her first venture into the world of business.

On Monday morning she arrived at the Jolly's bakeshop shining clean, at seven o'clock on the dot, clad in her snow-white pinafore and with her hair scraped back and bound with a scrap left over from the sheet, clutching the books under one arm and her white canvas bag in her other hand.

'What a mess!' she accused her employer as soon as she set eyes on him, presenting him with the old ledger. Then she showed him the new one, written up with her small precise figures. 'Have a look at that! You'll soon see now where the mistakes were, Mr Jolly. I'd better go in to the front shop and start.'

'It looks as though I've been consistently cheated by Cummings, the grain merchant,' he said when they managed to get a cup of tea and a minute to themselves just before twelve. 'No wonder the money never added up!'

'It looks like that, sir,' Thirza agreed, 'but you won't know for certain for another week or two.'

'Ye'll look at the books wi' me next weekend, Thirza? Ye'll help me?'

'Well,' Thirza scowled. 'It was a lot of work, Mr Jolly. Unpaid.'

'If ye'll just look at the books, I'll let the Gourlay family have all their loaves free, not just one.'

'I'll ask my mother,' Thirza squinted up at him, relishing the bargaining.

'Well, if I throw in four cream buns as well on a Saturday night, d'ye think she'll agree?'

'Five. There's five of us now, Mr Jolly, with Jordi as well.'

'Ye drive a hard bargain for a wee lassie, Thirza Gourlay. All right. Five it is.'

'Done! But I'll still have to ask my mother.'

During the following six months Thirza made herself indispensable at the bakeshop, working from seven in the morning until seven at night, and then an extra hour on Saturdays when she and Mr Jolly went over the books and the money, and for that she eventually got two shillings a week, as many loaves as the Gourlays wanted, five cream buns and anything else she fancied from what was left over at the weekend.

She was thirteen years old, a lady of business, and insufferably proud of herself. The men deplored it. Her mother eyed her thoughtfully. 'Pride comes before a fall, Thirza Gourlay,' she frowned. 'Ye'd better watch out, my lady!'

7

In the East Neuk of Fife it had been the best fishing season within living memory. It continued well right up to Christmas, but not well enough for two of the fishermen at St Fillan.

'Och, man,' Davy said to his friend Wattie Jamieson, 'I can never get the picture o' that herring-glut oot o' my mind.'

'I ken,' Wattie sighed. 'All that money in one day, and yet nothing like it for all the rest o' the year put together.'

'Ruth's gey thrifty.' Davy tried another approach. 'She aye puts something by in that old tea-caddy o' hers.'

'Oh, ay?' Wattie suddenly perked up. 'We've saved a bit, too. Never spent any o' the money from yon glut.'

Davy gazed out longingly to the east when they breasted the Braehead. 'I just aye get this feeling, Wattie . . . If only we could get oot into the North Sea!'

'Not in these small boats, we won't.'

'I saw a right one for sale in St Monance last week. A fine, smart vessel she was, rigged as a cutter.'

'What size?'

'Twenty feet, mebbe more. About ten tons as far as I could see.'

'And the price, Davy?'

'I never asked. I could never buy her mysel' anyway.'

'We might be able to, both together.'

'I don't know.' Davy looked doubtful, but inside he was seething with excitement. He'd got Wattie Jamieson interested,

63

anyway. 'We'd need to ha'e a look at her and find oot the price, I suppose.'

'If that was right we'd ha'e to tell the womenfolk next.'

'Ay,' Davy sighed as Wattie went into his own cottage and he carried on alone to the end of the Braehead wondering what would be the best way to approach Ruth, and when. He gave it a lot of thought over the next twenty-four hours and the following night in their box bed he didn't turn over as usual and fall asleep. 'Ruth,' he said.

'Wheesht! Thirza's sleeping on the other side o' the room!'

'I wis thinking,' he whispered, 'shouldn't ye be giving up the Dundonalds' washing, noo that we're all working, even Thirza?'

'Give up the Dundonalds' washing?' Ruth's face was stony when she blew out the candle. 'Never! Besides, Mrs Dundonald keeps paying me more and more as time goes on.'

'How much? How much is there up in that tea-caddy by this time?'

'Never you mind, Davy Gourlay! Up in the tea-caddy it stays!' Ruth turned her back on him and pretended to fall asleep.

But she wasn't sleeping. Once Davy's snores began she listened under them for Thirza's breathing, hoping it might be regular tonight. But no, there they were again, the restless little whimpers, as if she were in pain.

After more discussions with Wattie, a trip to the boat-building yard, and yet more discussions, Davy finally came right out with it at the supper table on Sunday night. 'Wattie Jamieson will put up fifty pounds if I put up the same,' he announced. 'Then we can buy a bigger boat between us.'

If he'd dropped a bombshell it couldn't have had more effect. Even Thirza was silenced at the very idea of the Gourlay family finding fifty pounds.

'It makes sense,' her father continued. 'With us three and him, that makes four of us to sail her, and we could go further out and bring in far bigger catches.'

'It's unlucky to speak about business or strike a bargain on a Sunday.' Ruth nipped such foolishness smartly in the bud then and there, and refused to discuss it all through the week that followed.

So did Wattie's wife, Davy found out, when the Gourlay men and Jordi went to meet him on Friday night. 'I dinna ken *how* to persuade her,' he told them.

'The colour of money might,' Jordi said. 'It persuades most people.'

'That's right,' Wattie smiled. 'If she saw your money first, Davy, that might do the trick.'

'Ay . . . well, it all depends on Ruth.'

Left alone in the cottage with her daughter, Ruth had more to worry her than just money. Thirza's face had gone ashen and she was gripping the table so hard that her knuckles were shining white. 'What's wrong wi' ye, lassie?' she asked.

'A terrible pain down here,' Thirza rubbed her stomach with both hands. 'Oh! Here it comes again!'

'Go to the privy, Thirza.'

'But I've been. I don't need to go again.'

'Go! And take your shawl with you,' Ruth said.

Obediently for once, Thirza flung her shawl around her shoulders and stepped out into the darkness. She knew every step of the way, daylight or dark, to the Gourlay privy which, in her opinion, was far better than anyone else's on the Braehead. For one thing, it was built of stone, whereas all the others were only little wooden shacks down at the end of their washing greens. Thirza thought that they must spoil the Braehead folks' view of the sea something wicked. Fancy looking out of your window straight into a privy!

To get to the Gourlays' you had to go past the shed which was attached to the house, and then you were at the privy which was built on to the shed at the very end of the row of cottages.

It was very discreet. Thirza had thought so all her life, but tonight she wasn't thinking along those lines. Tonight was different. There were black shadows everywhere and she could hear noises, like sharp intakes of breath. She dismissed these almost at once, realising they were coming from her own body as she tried to combat the urgent, terrible pain in her stomach. It attacked her again, just as she lifted the latch to open the door.

Inside the dry toilet, lit as always by a tiny cruisie lamp which her mother lit at dusk every night and blew out before she went to her own bed, Thirza sat down on the wooden bench with the hole in the middle. At one side of her there was a pail containing fragrant peat powder, its little shovel ready on the top. On the other was the hook on the wall from which dangled the little squares of paper her mother provided, but none of them were squares of newspapers tonight.

There was nothing to take her mind off this terrible feeling she had. She stood up again at last and rearranged her skirts, surprised that they were wet. In fact she was wet right through to her knickers, yet when she looked at it the wooden bench was quite dry. Then she saw to her horror that her petticoat was reddened with blood. With a shiver of fear she ran for the door of the cottage.

As she banged the cottage door shut Thirza's searing pain came back again and she looked up into her mother's face. 'Oh, Mother,' she said in tears, 'I'm bleeding.'

'I thought as much,' Ruth said calmly. 'It's sair, but it'll pass. Just remember that all women have to put up wi' this every month, even Mrs Dundonald.'

'But I'm *bleeding!*' Thirza repeated, for quite clearly her mother hadn't understood. This might even mean a trip to the dreaded doctor. 'I have no intention of bleeding again next month, whatever Mrs Dundonald does. What has she got to do with it, anyway?'

'Oh, Thirza, it doesn't mean ye're ill. It only means ye're a woman now,' Ruth said, going to fetch one of the pads she'd had ready for a few months. 'You just have to put on a bandage,' she explained, showing her how to wear it.

But that only made things worse. 'I don't want it!' Thirza stamped her foot. 'I don't want to be a woman!'

'Ye're a lassie, and lassies turn into women whether ye like it or no'. Otherwise ye'd be gey queer. Ye wouldna be right,' Ruth sighed, preparing herself for a long night of argument. She should have known better than to think Thirza would just accept things. She always had to have an explanation. 'Ye'd better sit doon, Thirza, and listen to me.' She started off in the time-honoured way with the birds and the bees, but she was smartly interrupted.

'I know all *that*,' Thirza said loftily. 'I told you when I saw that ewe giving birth to twin lambs.'

Her mother was silent for a minute, for now here came the

difficult bit. 'Yes,' she said. 'But did you ever wonder how the lambs got into the ewe in the first place?'

Thirza was forced to admit that she had never considered it. Her mind had been on higher things.

'The ram put them there, lassie,' Ruth said, and went on to draw the comparison between sheep and human beings. 'Men are just the same,' she added. 'Ye've lived wi' Andra all yer life. Ye've seen him wi' no clothes on. The same thing will happen to him as it did to Alicky Birnie that day in the cave.'

'Is that what you meant when you asked Cathy Emslie if he'd bairned her that time?'

'That's exactly what I meant.'

'Not Andra,' Thirza said stoutly. 'Nor Jordi, either. They're different. They wouldn't do that.'

'Oh, wouldn't they? They're men, aren't they?'

'But they're different, Mother,' Thirza protested. As for her father, another man ... or another ram ... Thirza did not allow herself even to *think* of anything so vile.

But Ruth persisted. 'Ye've got to know about it, Thirza, for yer own protection now that you've changed into a woman. Women have babies. I've told ye what men do to women. That's how babies are made.'

'Well, *I'm* never going to have any, Mother, don't worry,' Thirza burst into tears.

Ruth wasn't worried in the least. She felt she had done her duty, though it gave her no satisfaction whatsoever to see her beautiful, talented child no longer the pouting, bored little lady posing about the cottage, but only a frightened child after all, a little girl needing her mother now. 'Ay, Thirza,' she said sadly. 'Ye've got a lot to learn. God help ye, lassie.'

Ruth spoke her mind the following night. It was Saturday night and they were just finishing off the cream buns. 'Very well,' she said. 'The fifty pounds are here for the cutter, but only on one condition.'

'And what's that?' Andra demanded, for he was as excited as his father at the prospect of it all. So was Jordi.

'Thirza's thirteen now. She's not a wee lassie any longer. She needs somewhere o' her own to sleep.'

'And where's that?' Davy Gourlay frowned.

'The loft.'

'The *loft?*' They all gazed at her.

'We'll need a staircase built up to it. Then it must be floored and lined, and she must have a proper bed.'

There was a thunderstruck silence in the Gourlay cottage while the men gazed next at Thirza. She *looked* the same. She was still a little red wasp in Jordi's estimation. Andra glowered at her. She'd never been anything else but a nuisance from start to finish – and now, this!

'And we'll all go to the Kirk the morn,' Ruth continued, 'and think about it. No new bedroom, no new boat.'

'It's going to take a lot o' wood,' Davy's eyes met his wife's.

'It is,' she agreed, 'and wood costs money.'

'There's the wood I saved from my boat,' Jordi ventured sadly, because he'd been hoping to use it himself one day to build another.

'Never you mind, Jordi,' Ruth said. 'My brother has the saw-mill at Pittenweem. By the time I've finished wi' him, all you men will ha'e to do is carry the wood home.'

She was as good as her word, and with each of them sawing with his saw, planing with his plane and hammering in his nails with his hammer, Jordi saw Ruth's decree taking shape within a week. Better still, Thirza was no longer behaving like an uppity young lady. Something had certainly changed her. She seemed to be clinging to her mother all of a sudden, and she seemed to have softened, ever so slightly.

However, except for her initial dependence on her mother, Thirza had not softened at all. Up in her loft-room she became, if anything, more rebellious than ever. It was all because she had been passing by the window one day and saw and then heard her mother and father in the kitchen.

'We've just managed it out of our own money, Davy,' she was saying. 'I didna touch a penny o' the bairns' money, nor Jordi's either. We couldna expect any of them to put up a penny o' their wages. They'll soon be thinking o' marrying. They'll need all their pennies then.'

'Oh, Ruth!' Davy flung his arms around her in an almost forgotten embrace. 'Ye're the best wife a man ever had!'

'I love ye,' she told him. 'I've tried to do my best for us all.'

'And I love you, Ruth Gourlay,' Davy swung her around with a laugh.

Thirza's blood ran cold. Her mother and father with their arms around each other – kissing each other, with their eyes shining! She staggered back against the stone wall of the cottage, and something rose up from the depths of her being and burst inside her. So it was all true! Her own father was just the same as every other man.

But there was something else, far worse. Her parents would marry her off to some man or another if she stayed at home much longer, and that she vowed would never happen.

All the same, when she cooled down after the trauma of her first period, she realised that she was indeed different. She felt humiliated. None of her accomplishments meant anything now, caught in the trap of her own flesh, a weak woman every single month of the year for the best part of her life. Many a night she went up to the loft and cried herself to sleep at the unfairness of it all.

Her father and Andra and Jordi shouldn't have discussed the maiden voyage of the newly painted *Golden Acres* where she could overhear them, she thought, a little surprised that it was going to take place towards the end of January, when everyone knew the North Sea was at its most treacherous. But it was her opportunity to redeem herself in her own estimation and to show the world she was as good as any man, any day.

They were all experienced sailors, weren't they? They were *men* after all, she told herself bitterly. They were supposed to know what they were doing.

Thirza came to the decision of her lifetime.

8

FORTUNATELY, the men had built the loft-room and the little stair up to it securely. They must have hammered in hundreds of nails to hold the planks of wood so taut – not one of them creaked when Thirza stole downstairs in the middle of the night.

At the bottom she paused and listened. Everyone was sleeping.

Ruth had baked bannocks before she went to bed. They were on the table wrapped up in a white cloth, and under the table four pint cans of milk stood in buckets of cold water.

Thirza put one of the cans of milk and four bannocks into her faithful white canvas bag and, taking a deep breath, she opened the door, closing it behind her again as quietly as she could.

Now her adventure was starting, and here outside in the cold, crisp January night the skies were starry and, in a strange way, curiously lit. Far away to the north there were flares of colour, but only for a moment before they danced down to the ground and then disappeared. As she ran towards the *Golden Acres* she couldn't help looking back to admire them again, but they had gone.

The first thing she noticed when she boarded the new cutter for the first time was the mainsail, double reefed. She had expected that there would be a wheelhouse but, lifting a hatch on the deck, she discovered there was only a forecastle space for the anchor chain and a few stores, besides a hold for cargo, empty except for a spare sail and some ropes.

This was where she would have to hide. She lay down on the floor and covered herself with the sail, waiting and listening for the men to come, praying that they wouldn't discover her until it was too late to turn back. When they came at last it was Wattie's voice she heard first.

'I dinna ken, Davy,' he was saying. 'I wis oot bye half an hour ago and I saw the Northern Lights. That's aye the signal for bad weather.'

'Hoots, man, it's only a bit o' a breeze from the south,' her father laughed. 'That won't stop us.'

Thirza lay still under the sail, hardly daring to breathe when they weighed anchor. She heard it groaning upwards, the chinking and clanging of its chains rattling to rest in the forecastle, and then her father's voice again.

'Keep her well out, Andra,' he shouted, 'away from the rocks.'

So Andra must be at the wheel. In another minute both head sails were set. She heard the the men tying the ropes and felt the vessel heeling over on her port side and moving fast.

All went well for the next hour. Thirza tried to relax and beat back the seasickness she had made no allowance for, determined not to give in to it. It was only another sign of weakness, anyway.

But soon, seasickness became the last thing on her mind. She felt, rather than saw, that they were now sailing around Fife Ness and into the North Sea. The sea itself told her in the huge surges of a colossal swell from the very depths of caves and caverns miles below, and she judged the time had arrived to come out of hiding.

She went and sat near the foot of the companionway leading down to the hold. Through the open hatchway she could now see her father, Wattie, Andra and Jordi in their oilskins and heavy leather seaboots up above and she could distinctly hear their voices when a heavy sea struck the *Golden Acres* and she gave a great roll.

'Jesus Christ! The main sheet's broken!' Wattie Jamieson screamed.

'The main boom! It's swung off to the port rigging,' Davy shouted. 'Come on, Wattie, rescue the sail first!'

Thirza tried to climb the steps to see what was happening but fell back to the floor of the hold as the cutter lurched and was knocked out. Davy and Wattie got the boom almost into the sailing mark when the sail slipped again. In that same instant another massive wave made the *Golden Acres* roll again heavily and the boom swung off for the second time.

It pulled the two men, both still holding the sail, and threw them overboard on the port side. Down below Thirza rallied and heard Andra's voice. 'Get away the small boat!' he was yelling. 'My father canna swim. Jordi, take the helm!'

The *Golden Acres* was rolling about so much, and there was so much noise that Thirza thought they had struck a reef. This time she succeeded in climbing the steps up to the deck far enough to get her head out and saw to her amazement that they were nowhere near the coast but in the middle of an angry, molten sea, that her father and Wattie Jamieson had disappeared and Jordi was holding the small boat steady for Andra.

'Don't go, Andra,' he was saying. 'It's hopeless. Look at the speed we're doing! You'll never find them now.'

'I've got to try,' Andra said. His face was white and glistening with spray. 'I've got to find my father,' and Thirza saw him rowing away as fast as he could.

It was only then that she realised that her father and Wattie Jamieson were overboard and she came right out on deck screaming.

'My God, Thirza!' Jordi gasped. 'You bloody little fool! What are *you* doing here?'

'Where's my father?' she screamed. 'And now, Andra! Can you see him?' she pointed. 'He's gone, too!'

The rudder was shifting with every lurch, the boom was swinging to and fro, the thunder of the loosened mainsail was flapping in the wind, blocks were flying about and spray and waves were dashing onto the deck as every second the storm was mounting.

Then Thirza screamed again and clutched Jordi's arm. 'Oh, my God! Look! Look!'

Perhaps only fifty yards away, and at least twenty feet high, a huge wave was rushing towards them, curving inwards to come down on top of them, green, vicious, foaming dangerously and building as it came.

'Get down below!' he pushed her back down into the hold, jumped down behind her, closed the hatch and managed to beat the terrible wave before it thundered along the deck.

It would have killed them. And three men were dead already, Jordi thought in those few moments, expecting each one to be his last.

This little cutter could not survive seas like these, Thirza thought, expecting the same fate. And soon it would be dark. 'If you go back up there you'll be swept away,' she said, clinging to him in terror, 'and then I'll be all alone. Don't leave me, Jordi.'

'I couldn't get up there now, anyway.' Another tremendous wave hit them again and they were thrown from one end of the hold to the other. 'Here, Thirza, hold on to this rope.' Jordi put a rope dangling from the roof into her hand and grasped another himself. 'Hold on tight, and then we won't be flung about. We can sit still.'

Thirza had time to think, sitting there in the cold wet darkness all through that terrible night. 'Jordi,' she sobbed, 'do you think my father and Andra could have survived?'

He knew they could never have survived, but he didn't want to dash any hopes she might have.

He was taking a long time to answer, Thirza thought. Too long. 'No, you don't need to answer,' she sobbed, her heart plummeting to her boots. For hours she cried and cried, and Jordi didn't try to stop her. He knew that in the end she would exhaust herself, and then she might even sleep a little.

But Thirza didn't sleep when her tears diminished. It was time to think about the living. What would happen to her mother now? Ruth would believe she had lost her whole family, and there was no way that Thirza could tell her any differently, certainly not while they were heading through the North Sea, going to God alone knew where. She sat miserably beside Jordi in the darkness, as together they clung to their ropes.

Daylight on Tuesday morning brought little cheer. Jordi managed to lift the hatch a few inches but, even as he did so, hail and snow and gusts of spray threatened to tear it out of his hands and fill the hold. 'We'll have to wait until it eases a bit,' he said. 'Then I might manage to crawl along to the forecastle. We left milk and bannocks in there.'

'I've got a pint of milk and four bannocks here,' Thirza pulled out her white canvas bag from under the spare sail. 'I couldn't eat anything.'

'We must eat a little to keep our strength up. But we daren't eat them all at once. I don't know how long they might have to last. I can't get up to steer the *Golden Acres*. She's drifting.'

'We'll make them last, then!' she snapped. 'We'll make them last four days if we have to. Surely the storm will be over by then!'

There was a lot of her mother in her, Jordi thought in those dreadful hours while Tuesday passed and they hung on to the ropes. By nightfall their hands were blistered and peeling. Jordi got out his knife and made a loop for each of them out of one of the spare ropes.

'Rest one elbow at a time in that,' he told her. 'And you're soaking wet in that thin dress and shawl! Here,' he dragged the sail up around her, 'keep that over you, Thirza.'

On Wednesday morning, at Jordi's insistence, they ate and drank a mouthful again. The weather was still as wild as ever. Wednesday night closed dark and cheerless and cold, the sea was running high and, although they didn't say it to each other, they had resigned themselves by then to meeting death itself. They both prayed silently.

Thirza woke up from a fitful doze on Thursday morning to find Jordi with the hatch up, looking out. The *Golden Acres* wasn't rolling about so much. She thought she saw a glint of the sun, and she didn't have to hold on to the rope. Feeling a little more cheerful, she took the last bannock out of her bag and broke it in two.

'I saw land away to the left,' Jordi told her as they finished off the milk.

'What land?'

He shook his head. 'It might have been the north of Scotland, but with the wind veering first this way and then that I lost my bearings long ago.'

'Can you get to the compass?'

'It's smashed, but I think we've been zig-zagging northwards. So it may have been the Orkney Islands I saw.'

'Are there any people on the islands?'

'Perhaps. Anyway, for all I know it could have been Norway.'

'*Norway?*'

'And there are definitely people living in Norway, Thirza,' he tried to comfort her. 'They're called Norwegians.'

'I *know* there are Norwegians – and French, and Germans, and Dutch!' she snapped, and burst into tears again.

He didn't understand her, that was the trouble. Thirza knew she shouldn't be snapping at the only person she was close to now in the whole world. Her terrified thoughts wandered away to those who were left, now that she had accepted the deaths of her father and Andra. There were only Jordi and her mother, if she ever saw her again, and the Jollys who had been so kind as to give her a job – the Jollys whom she'd also let down by running away. She thought of Captain Gerrit van der Haar. Oh, if only he could appear in his brig and save them now!

Early on Friday morning the wind sprang up again and lashed the sea into a boiling cauldron of foam. Jordi took one brief look and closed the hatch again while the next storm raged and they were back to their ropes and their misery once more, cold, wet and exhausted. Ill with hunger, they were just drifting this way and that willy-nilly on the cruel sea at the mercy of the remorseless winds.

Not long after what they thought was midnight on Friday night came the first sign that either deliverance or destruction was at hand. The *Golden Acres* began to strike hard on submerged rocks, finding first one and then another bed to grind and hover on with every rise and fall of the sea, her timbers creaking and groaning now all the time.

The noise of the mast swinging and threatening to give way was terrifying, and what Jordi saw was more terrifying still when he looked out at dawn on Saturday morning. The cutter was bumping and reeling drunkenly off one rock and on to the next and heading straight for a narrow gully, little more than a slit in some cliffs. Its sides towered up steeply ahead. She would wedge in there and be crushed to pieces. There was only one thing to do, and that was to jump.

'Quick, Thirza,' he said desperately, 'we've got to get up on deck,' and he pushed her up the steps in front of him.

'Now hold on to me,' he shouted as they struck. 'Hold on! Hold on!'

There had been no time to lash her to him with a rope. They were thrown clear into the icy sea, still clinging together. There was a rush of green water above their heads. Another wave tossed them onto a hard bed and they were hurled apart.

All Jordi knew was that the sky was above him, shingle was below him, and his last glimpse of Thirza was a broken heap lying a few yards away.

9

A SUDDEN violent pain in his side brought Jordi back to consciousness. He opened his eyes in time to see the black pointed toe of a boot delivering a second vicious kick to his ribs and somehow managed to roll over and so avoid a third.

His blazing eyes travelled up from the boots to the dress and then to the red puffy face of a gentleman who was now poking at him with a silver-topped cane, and Jordi realised by the smell of him that the man was drunk.

He continued to poke and to peer at him out of half-closed, unfocused eyes until, from somewhere, Jordi summoned up the strength to snatch the cane from him and beat him off with it. The man shambled away, giggling, and in his rage Jordi snapped the cane in two and hurled it after him.

'You bastard!' he yelled. 'There's your walking stick! You'll need it to prop you up.'

The man actually bent down and picked up one half of it, staring at it stupidly for some time before he dropped it again and staggered on, his footsteps leaving an erratic zigzag of prints on the shingly sand.

But now another man was approaching from the opposite direction, and in the forlorn hope of protecting Thirza, if she was still living, Jordi dragged himself over to her and prepared to do battle.

'Bairns, bairns!'

They were the only words Jordi could distinguish amongst a

torrent of others, but he realised they were spoken in genuine concern by this old man, dressed very differently from the other in his long sheepskin boots, tough trousers, woollen jumper under a heavy jacket and a flat round cap. When he saw the footprints in the sand he raised his voice and shook his fist at the figure receding along the sands. 'Nicholson! Alec Nicholson!' he yelled, as he gestured angrily towards him.

Then he turned back to the two on the beach, touching Jordi gently on the shoulder as he spoke, gazing anxiously into his face before he looked down at Thirza's, snow-white and framed by what looked more like strands of seaweed than hair.

'Bairns, bairns,' he said again sadly, pointed to where he had come from, and then ran off in that direction as fast as his old legs could carry him.

In the meantime, Jordi cradled Thirza in his arms and tried to keep her warm in the bitter cold. She was breathing, at least, but her eyes didn't open and no colour had returned to her cheeks when the old man came back, this time with three others.

They took over. Between them they carried Jordi and Thirza up from the shingly beach, over jagged rocks and through bogs to firm ground where nothing appeared to be growing but a half-hearted salty stubble of grass. That was all Jordi had time to notice before they were at a dwelling house, its once white-washed stones now sad and peeling, and then they were inside.

'Bairns, bairns,' a woman's voice echoed the old man's before a merciful blackness descended on him.

He was in a bed of some sort, he realised, but not one of a kind he had ever lain in before. In India House, in the Stables of Hopetoun House, and certainly in the Gourlays' cottage, the mattresses had all been like hard thin biscuits stuffed either with flock or with straw.

Now he found himself floundering in a nest of feathers. His back was resting on something quite firm, but the feather mattress puffed up high on either side of him, and on top of him were more feathers in a quilt which, he saw, was tucked in with woollen blanket upon woollen blanket, pinning him down.

He had never felt so hot in his life, and was just struggling to get out of this cocoon when the old woman appeared at his side with a tray. She put it down on a table, pushed him back into the bed, puffed up the pillows and dragged him up to sit.

'Gruel,' she said, and after he'd eaten the thick oatmeal mixture with the salt she'd left, she came back with another plate. On it were sizzling little meatballs he'd never seen before and a scrambled egg. 'Sassermeat,' she said, and left him again. He would have called them sausagemeat at home, but homemade and spicy like this they were far more delicious. In another minute the woman was back, this time with a tin mug of tea. 'Noo, sleep again,' she said as she pushed him back down into the feathers.

'But Thirza?' he asked.

'Thirza? That's her name, dan, da peerie lass?'

'Thirza. Is she alive or dead?'

'Na, na, boy. Your sister's living and life-thinking.'

He sighed with relief. Thirza was doing her best to recover somewhere else in this house, and she had had the wit to call herself his sister. That told him something else. She was terrified of being parted from him. Jordi sank back into the featherbed as if he had been drugged, and slept the clock around. His last thoughts were of Thirza, and they were very protective. He would be her brother from now on.

He judged it was midday when he finally escaped from the featherbed and donned his clothes, which had been washed and ironed and now hung over a chair. Then he went to find out where the voices he could hear were coming from. The old woman was there, and as soon as she saw him she sat him down in a hard chair by the fireside and fetched him tea, hardly pausing in her conversation with a girl a few years older than Thirza.

Jordi just sat there and listened to them. It *was* a form of Scots that they were speaking, but in a strange accent as hard and angular as the rocks guarding this place from any intrusion, with a word here and there he had never heard before . . . This place – where was it?

'Where are we?' he asked when he could get a word in edgeways. 'Where is this?'

They stared at him. Then the girl laughed. She had a merry, laughing face and dark, dancing eyes. 'Do you not know where you are?' she asked. 'You're in the Shetland Isles. This place is called Reawick.'

The Shetland Isles! He did a rapid calculation. That was five hundred miles north of St Fillan and four hundred miles west of Norway. 'Then we're a long way from home,' he said.

'But we thought you had come from one of the other isles, blown here by the gale!'

'We were blown all right. We drifted here all the way from the Firth of Forth. We were out fishing when the storm blew up. Unfortunately Thirza chose that day to stow away.'

'Did anyone else survive?' the old woman asked in horror.

'No. Three men went overboard,' Jordi said carefully. 'Our father and our brother, along with another man. Thirza is very upset. I'm afraid she is suffering from shock as well as from the dreadful experience. Can I see her now?'

'She's been asking for her brother, and crying a lot. I'll take you to her in a peerie minute. By the way, my name is Christina Cheyne, but everyone calls me Teenie. My man's name is Thomas Cheyne, and this is our daughter, Merren,' the woman said in almost perfect English. 'We thought you were Shetlanders and understood us. Noo dan, Merren, du's awa?' she turned and asked her daughter, back in the broad dialect.

A smile came over Merren's delicate features, and she wrapped a shawl around her soft brown hair and small thin body as she spoke to Jordi. 'My mother asked me if I was going,' she explained. 'I have to. I've got to get back to work. Don't worry, you'll soon be able to understand everything we say in the Shetland.'

Jordi smiled back doubtfully as she opened the door to leave, and before it closed a young man came in.

'Magnus, our son,' Mrs Cheyne introduced him.

'I know you,' Jordi smiled. 'You were one of the men who carried us here. We are very grateful to you all.'

'In Shetland everyone helps everyone else,' Mrs Cheyne said, leading him to Thirza's bedside.

'And thank you, Mrs Cheyne, for all *you've* done for us,' Jordi pressed her hand gently.

'Na, na,' she protested as she left. 'And anyway, it's Teenie.'

'Are you feeling better?' he asked Thirza when they were alone.

'I wasn't until I saw you,' she said, clinging to his hand. 'I kept asking to see my brother.'

'Yes. That's going to be our story from now on. My name is Jordi Wishart and yours will be Thirza Wishart as long as we're here. Then, hopefully, we won't be parted.'

'As long as we're here,' Thirza repeated sadly. 'How long might *that* be? We'll never get back home again, never!'

'We'll find a way,' Jordi promised.

But at present he couldn't envisage one.

In a few days Jordi felt suffocated in the Cheynes' house. Its walls were four feet thick and the tiny, deeply recessed windows looked out on a blur of green and brown where nothing seemed to move except an occasional sheep. The peat fire made it very warm and sometimes, depending on the direction of the wind, very smoky. He had to get out and breathe some fresh air.

'Can I come with you today?' he asked Magnus, surprised when the young man hesitated.

'You can, with pleasure,' he answered at last. 'But it will have to be kept a dead secret. So far it's only us, and two Cheyne cousins who know you are here. They hate the Laird as much as we do. If he finds out – or rather, his sister Tamar, now – she'll have you away to the fishing.'

'I'm afraid somebody else knows, too. His name is Alex Nicholson.'

'Alex Nicholson! That idiot!' Magnus snorted. 'His life passes by in a dwam. He doesn't know the difference between reality and his drunken dreams. Nobody ever pays any attention to him.'

'Well, I don't mind going to the fishing, Magnus, if the worst comes to the worst.'

'Neither do I, but not on a sixareen out in the far haaf in weather like this. And not, in the end, to hand over the fish to the Laird just for the privilege of living in his district,' Magnus said bitterly.

'What's a sixareen, and the far haaf?'

'An open boat with six oars, and the far haaf is all round the coasts of Shetland. You've found out already that they're far from hospitable. I've only escaped from it lately myself, because my father is old now and a man has to be fit to work on the croft – once again, only to hand over most of the produce as well.'

'Well, I'll come and help you anyway. I'm not frightened of Alex Nicholson, or the Laird.'

'No, not the present Laird. He's only eleven years old. His two sisters run the estate in the meantime, and they're as bad – if not worse – than the old Laird ever was. Thirza is in as much danger from them as you are.'

'What could happen to her?'

'She could be taken into Reawick House itself, God save her, the same as Merren. Come, let me show you.' Magnus took his arm and led him to a hill near the brigstones. A beautiful bay crowned on either side with cliffs came into view. 'We call that Reawick Voe,' he said, looking out beyond the bay to the long inlet of sea, 'and there to the right of us on the top of the hill is Reawick House. Thank God you were wrecked on those cliffs to the left of us instead.'

'But what's their name?' Jordi asked.

'Umphray,' Magnus sighed, 'and that's a name you must promise me you'll never utter in our house. John Umphray died not long ago. His grandfather stole the Haa – as we call Reawick House – and the Reawick estate from my grandfather. The Cheynes should be living in the Haa now, not the Umphrays. The feud began when the Cheyne family ran short of money, mortgaged the estate to the Umphrays and were never able to fully pay back the loan. Almost, but not quite.'

Jordi smiled bitterly. He knew all about that situation at first hand.

'So you see, the Umphrays are twice as hard on us as they are on everyone else. Tamar, the elder daughter, has gone all to hell with religion, and besides that she's engaged to Alex Nicholson, that drunken pig! That should be enough to tell you she's mad. She would dearly like to get her hands on our house, too, it being the second largest in the district, but my father still holds the deeds to that. What I am trying to tell you is that both my mother and father get very angry at any mention of any of this.'

'But why do they allow Merren to work for them, then?'

Magnus sighed. 'It's very difficult to explain to anyone who comes from the south, Jordi, but in Shetland we still live in a sort of feudal system. The Laird is the landlord, and in return for the land they rent, the people have to pay him many times over in many different ways. They have to buy their meal from his shops. He sets the price for rent, food, fish, everything. The result is that the tenants are always in debt to the landlord. He can take their animals in payment, he can take every fish they catch and he can take their children for servants.'

'I'd better not let anyone see me, then,' Jordi shuddered.

'No. Jink in behind a peat-stack if you ever see any of the Umphrays coming,' Magnus said seriously. 'But all the same I would be glad of your help to do the outside work. My father mustn't be seen doing any, or else they'll say he's fit and I'll be sent to the fishing again. But that suits him nowadays. He's busy studying the seal, instead. That's where he was going when he found you.'

Standing there beside Magnus on the hill in the bitter chill Jordi suddenly realised what was missing. There wasn't a tree in sight, just long fingers of this hard land running down to the sea in every direction.

'Yes,' Magnus seemed to read his thoughts, 'we're even north of the tree-belt here. It's too cold for you to work outside in those clothes of yours. We'll go inside and find you proper clothes to wear for this climate, something for your feet first,' and soon Jordi found himself standing up in the same shapeless boots as the other men, sheepskin worn with the wool inside, and laced with twine to keep them firmly on his feet and legs. 'That's the rivlins,' Magnus said. 'Now for the rest.'

10

'I CAN'T stay here in this bed any longer, Teenie,' Thirza said when the shock of the disastrous voyage began to wear off a little. 'I've got to get up.'

'You look a peerie bit better,' Teenie agreed, looking at her closely, 'but you canna run aroon the place stark naked. You've no clothes. When I took your own off you they were in rags and tatters.'

'Oh,' Thirza wailed, her small recovery dashed. 'What am I going to do now?'

'Hush, lass. There's no fear o' you. We'll soon get you rigged,' Teenie smiled kindly and went to the door for a bundle she'd left there. 'My dresses are too big for you, and Merren's too small, but I've been aroon the folk and collected some things that might fit you. They're all washed and clean,' she added reassuringly, laying them out on the bed. 'Would you like to try them on?'

'Oh, Teenie – you've been *very* kind to me,' Thirza wiped away the last of her tears, got out of bed and stepped into the first dress. 'This blue one? How does it look?'

'That aye *was* a bonnie dress. It was Christine Fraser's best before she grew oot o' it. Now try on her black skirt . . . Yes, that fits as weel. And the blouses?'

'They all fit, Teenie! I've never had so many clothes in all my life!'

'And how long has that been, lass? How old are you?'

'Thirteen and a half. Fourteen in August.'

'My, my, you're a big lass for thirteen. Merren's sixteen. You're a lot bigger than her, poor peerie lass dat she is,' Teenie said mournfully with tears in her eyes.

'Why? What's wrong with her? Where is she?' Thirza asked in alarm.

'At Reawick House,' Teenie said and, taking a deep breath, went on to tell her the story of the feud between the Cheynes and the Umphrays and the bitter hatred of the tenants towards the Umphray lairds. 'Now I've told you, Thirza,' she said at the end of what had clearly been an ordeal to relate. 'Merren is more or less a slave in that wicked house. The name of Umphray is never mentioned in this one. We won't speak of this again.'

Thirza followed her downstairs and for the next few days watched all that went on in the Cheynes' household, helping where and when she could.

With her mother's troubled eyes on her Merren went out every morning with a shawl tied around her, a light straw basket slung across her shoulders and her knitting in her hands. She knitted as she walked, as if there wasn't a minute to lose, and arrived home in time for the evening meal, still knitting.

Teenie's knitting was never far from her hands, either, and she wore a strange belt around her waist.

'What's that, Teenie?' Thirza asked curiously, for the belt had a pad on it, and in the pad there must have been twenty holes.

'It's a knitting belt, lass. We stick the working needle in it, and that leaves our hands free to hold up the garment at the same time.' Teenie demonstrated, the wool flying through her fingers. Thirza had never seen anyone knitting so fast in her life.

Magnus and Jordi went out to work from morning to night on the croft and came home at the same time as Merren. Teenie cooked and baked, fed the hens, cleaned the house, carried in peat from the stack outside the door, washed and ironed and worked non-stop all day.

'Where are you going now?' Thirza asked when she donned her shawl once more.

'Oot to milk the kye.'

'Let me come with you, Teenie,' Thirza begged.

'Na, na, lass! You canna be seen ootside the door, or else

they'll have you at Reawick House! And they'll soon see you, wi' that bright hair o' yours!'

'Not go out? Is that why you never gave me any outside clothes? Teenie, please give me a scarf – anything to cover my head. I am *not* going to sit by idle another minute and watch you doing all this work! I'm coming with you,'

'And can you milk?'

'I've never been near a cow to know how to. But I'll soon learn,' Thirza said resolutely. 'From now on, everything you do I'm going to do as well! You'll teach me, won't you, Teenie? I want to help you as long as Jordi and I are here.'

'That could be for the rest o' your life, joy,' Teenie said sadly. 'You're in Shetland now. Most o' us women have never been off the Isles, and never will.'

'Why?'

'Shetland is a long way from Scotland, Thirza. It costs a lot o' money to go there.'

Ah! So here it was again – even in Shetland . . . *Money*. It always came down to money, Thirza thought bitterly.

'That's why we knit all the time,' Teenie went on. 'It's the only way the women can earn any money. We sell everything we knit.' Then her mood lightened. 'Come on then, Thirza, if you're determined! Let's see how you get on with Buttercup and Bluebell – but mind, try not to be seen.'

'I'm not frightened of cows, Teenie,' Thirza lied stoutly, absolutely terrified.

But in her heart she was much more terrified of the Umphrays. Somehow she would get money and go back and find her mother. She didn't want to be a prisoner on the Shetland Isles which, she now realised, she was. Worse even than that was to be a prisoner in Reawick House.

In February the real snow of the winter came to make the outside work even harder, when Magnus and Jordi had to see to the cows and go amongst the sheep on the hill every day to repair a fence or a dyke along the cliff-tops to keep the sheep from falling over the edge into the sea.

When the first snow came, it went away again grudgingly, leaving some behind the dykes. 'It's waiting there for more,' Magnus said gloomily, and sure enough it kept up this pattern, settling for a couple of days at a time and then almost melting away until the afternoon of the twenty-third.

The sky became a hideous mixture of dark grey, navy-blue and saffron, and out of it fell flakes almost the size of saucers. 'This is it now,' Magnus said. 'It's coming a proper moorie-cavie. We'd better head for home.'

Even as he spoke, the wind whipped the flakes horizontally, powdering the air so thickly that they could no longer see each other walking side by side. It sifted into every nook and cranny, blanketing the sheep, levelling byres and barns and almost suffocating the two men in just a few minutes.

Great drifts of it began to cover the cottages, and the world became a soft white plain bulging here and there where the cottages were, while the icy-fingered sea lay silent.

'Thanks be to The Lord you're home,' Teenie said when they fell in the door.

'But what about Merren?' Thomas Cheyne looked at his wife with a worried expression. 'She'll be stuck in the Haa tonight. The boys and I should go and fetch her.'

'That you will not, Thomas Cheyne! You could all three lose your lives between here and the Haa in a blin' drift like this – and then, where would we all be? Na, na. Merren will be all right.'

But to Thirza her eyes looked frightened when she said it, and she quickly turned away and bent over the peat fire. 'Thirza,' she said, 'we'll put on our shawls and pull them right up over our noses when we go out to milk the kye.' With that, she plucked a fiery peat out of the fire with a pair of tongs and handed it to Thirza and, taking another for herself, explained, 'these braands will light the way.'

By the end of March the land was bare again, the bitter wind from the north died down, the gulls were fussing amongst each other a good way from the ebb and Thirza saw two otters playing in the water just below the house.

'This is the time they all have their weddings,' Teenie smiled her gentle smile.

Thirza helped her to get all the beds changed and the sheets and covers washed and hung out to flap wildly on the lines. It was just the same as it had been at St Fillan, with the tin bath

full of soapsuds out upon the brigstones, only here
was done in the clear water of the burn which ra
the sea.

'Now we'll make brunnies in the pan and boil duck eggs for
the tea,' Teenie said, taking a cup of wholemeal flour, a pinch
of salt, two spoons of baking powder and milk. 'Na, na, lass!'
she added when she saw Thirza copying her. 'You must stir with
the right hand. You must turn the spoon with the sun and the
way of the seasons!'

'I'll try,' Thirza said. 'But it's not easy when you're left-
handed.'

'Poor lamb,' Teenie shook her head and sighed sympathetically. 'Well, well, it's fine that the ducks have started to lay
again. And I think the Leghorn is going to clock, so we'll mebbe
have peerie chickens for Easter.'

'Easter, Teenie? Then we will have been here three months!'

'And have you enjoyed your stay here with us so far, lass?'

'Oh, Teenie!' Thirza put an arm around her plump shoulders,
'nobody could have been kinder to us than the Cheyne family!
But I am so worried about my mother. She will think she has
lost all her family. I've *got* to get home!'

'Reawick is out on a limb, dearie, with poor roads – where
there are roads at all. Lerwick, our capital, is twenty-eight miles
away. I've only been there once in a cart, and it was a horrible
journey. Another thing – the weather here changes so fast. The
best way to travel is by sea.'

'How can we do that? We see ships passing, but they are so
far out to sea, beyond the Voe.'

'Unless the skippers know these waters that's the best place
to sail. It's a brittle coastline. You know that, Thirza! You've
been on the rocks! Na, na! Just wait. You'll get back home
one day.'

But would they, Thirza worried? She was so desperate now
that she even considered going out and about openly, and after
speaking to Jordi she knew he felt the same about leaving.

'We'll get away on a ship,' he told her, 'we must watch for
an opportunity.'

But in the meantime, the pace of life quickened with the spring.
The spring planting, or the *voar* as the Cheynes called it, began.

A green haze appeared over the island and clumps of daffodils poked up through the ground.

Jordi and Magnus helped most of their lambs into the world and Teenie killed off all her old hens and, plucking the feathers, she cleaned them, dried them and stored them in a big sack ready for her latest pillow or quilt.

Then it was off to the peat-banks for the men.

They flayed off the top layer of grass and heather first. Then Magnus handed Jordi a spade with a long narrow blade. 'Here's a tushkar for you,' he said. 'Watch me. You have to dig down through the moor until your blade is full, then lift out the sod in one piece and lay it up on the bank.'

It was hard work. After the first peat came up there was a second underneath it to cut. Magnus, quick and skilled at it, showed Jordi how to lay the peats on the bank in neat rows so that they got the maximum sun and wind. Then Teenie, cautious as ever, allowed Thirza to go with her to the peat-bank – it was so far up in the hills that they never saw another living soul. The two women raised the peats up on their ends into little stacks of four or five so that they could dry and harden, and become lighter and easier to lift.

'How long does it all take?' Jordi asked Magnus.

'It depends on the weather. If it's a good summer the peats are cured by late July, and then we can take them home.'

'July?' Jordi frowned. 'We came here in January. That was six months ago. Thirza and I should be thinking of a way to get back home, Magnus, and the only way I can think of is by sea.'

'Yes, you'll get your chance, don't fret.'

But Jordi did fret, and so did Thirza when, after the terrible winter, it turned out to be a wonderful summer. Every morning started the same way, with mist, but the sun soon burned it all away when it burst through. The Shetland ponies who sheltered all night beside the house would gallop off to the hills, their hooves destroying all the spiders' webs laden with jewels of dew. Now Thirza saw Reawick at its best, and its best was breathtakingly beautiful.

No matter where she was, she could see the sea. It lay so still that the sun sent its sparks to glitter and shimmer on it, while down by the rocks it was a wealth of blues and greens fringed by wide ribbed sand on which the incoming tide left layers of seaweed, etching a pattern of its own in brown and gold right round the bay.

Daisies carpeted the fields, the seapinks vied with the white campions on the clifftops, and the scent of flowers wafted everywhere on the soft clear air. It was time for the family to 'roo the sheep', Teenie said, which Thirza discovered meant to hand-pluck the soft fine wool from them, and then dip them and send them off into the hills to fend for themselves for the rest of the summer.

It was hot in the sun. The men stripped to the waist, and Thirza looked at Jordi's golden body curiously. Now she came to think about it, she had never seen it in all the time he'd been at St Fillan. She had certainly never seen that charm around his neck, either.

Magnus looked at Jordi enviously. 'I go red,' he said. 'It's not until the end of the summer that I turn brown for a few weeks.' Then he, too, noticed the necklace. 'What's that you're wearing around your neck?'

'Oh, this?' Jordi smiled sadly. 'My mother gave it to me. She made me promise never to take it off.'

'It's gold, isn't it?' Magnus looked at the chain with the cobra key dangling from it. 'It looks foreign to me. I've never seen anything like it.'

'It came from India, I think,' Jordi said casually.

It was too casual for Thirza. She knew him better. Andra always used to mutter about 'the Indian boy'. And his skin *was* brown, there was no denying it. There was a mystery surrounding Jordi. He had been washed up out of the Firth of Forth, and she knew very little more about him.

Then and there she made up her mind that one day she would find out *all* about him. After all, he was more or less her brother.

The Cheyne family worked on quietly with the sheep while the sun blazed down, and Thirza never suspected that Jordi was wondering what had happened to his natural father . . .

Was Viaz really dead, as Madeleine had believed?

Viaz looked out of the windows of the large white house he was living in now. He had prospered in Darjeeling. His business of dealing in gold and precious metals had made him a very rich man.

His wife Ameera tried to keep the house very cool for his sake. The extreme heat made him sick nowadays, for he had suffered ill-health ever since that last terrible expedition to the Marigold Palace with Wishart-Sahib. The servants threw water on the baking paving stones in the courtyards around the house, where it sizzled for a few minutes before they brought more.

The heat had never affected Jorjeela, even though she could pass for white. Viaz smiled bitterly as he thought about her – the child for whom he had chosen a name as close as he could get to 'George'. Getting up from his resting-chair, he went to find her. Because of his money, and the beautiful clothes, as well as the education he had been able to lavish on his daughter, she was now accepted in the Anglo-Indian community. Every day she was showered with invitations. Viaz studied each one closely and allowed her to accept only a chosen few.

The gardens around the white house were large and sprawling. It took a small army of gardeners to keep it so beautifully. Viaz found Jorjeela in the rose-bower as he had expected. It was her favourite place.

'Come and sit down beside me, Father,' she smiled. 'It's lovely and cool in here, with the fountain tinkling.'

'Where are you going this evening?' he asked her.

She was almost eighteen now, and sooner or later she would leave him, Viaz thought sadly. He couldn't expect anything else. In fact, it was a wonder he'd been able to keep her this long. Young suitors clamoured for the privilege of her company every day, for Jorjeela was exquisite. But, so far, she'd never shown the slightest interest in any of the young men.

To his surprise, she coloured slightly now. 'If you would permit it, Father, I should very much like to accept this invitation,' she said, handing it over for him to see.

'Mr Paul Justin?' Viaz was even more surprised. 'He's quite old, Jorjeela. He must be forty, almost as old as I am.'

'It's only to dine with him! It's not a proposal of marriage, Father,' she laughed. 'I like him. He's the only man I've liked so far. I find him very kind, and I like his conversation.'

'He's a gentleman, it's true.'

'And in the Diplomatic Service, Father?' Jorjeela teased him.

'Very well, then. You may go. But the usual rules apply.'

If only she'd had a brother to look after her! Viaz hated every minute she was out of his sight in case he lost her, the same way he had lost his natural child, Jordi, years ago.

Taking home the main bulk of the peats, a whole year's firing, was the next job Magnus and Jordi tackled and, true to form, Thirza tagged along, despite their efforts to discourage her. They took their ponies with straw panniers slung on either side to transport the peats, and first picked out all the 'blue' peats, almost black like coal. They were the hardest, the ones which gave out most heat. Then they took home the mossy peats, which burned more slowly. These were the kind Teenie rested on the fire all night long so that there was always a spark in the morning. The mossy peats were stacked around the blue peats in a neat herring-bone pattern and then the whole stack was covered with sods of earth weighted down with stones.

Teenie's evening work from then on was with the plucked wool. First she teazed it out until it was ready for carding, brushing the wool over one card with another until it was smooth and ready to lift off the pins, soft as thistledown and ready for spinning. It was when she was at the stage of spinning the wool that she would tell Merren and Thirza some of the old stories. Stories of the press gang thrilled them: how, out of the misty voes, ships would emerge; how sailors would appear in unsuspecting homes to force young men onto the waiting ships, carrying them off to distant seas and wars – often never to return.

Sometimes Teenie invited a few trusted neighbours to these spinning evenings, and they would tell the girls old stories about the trows, the fairy folk who lived in hillside burrows. It was only when one old woman with second sight read their palms and then their teacups that the magical charm of the long evenings was coloured with foreboding.

'Now I'll let you see your future for yourselves,' she said, dripping a few drops of the white of an egg into a glass of clear water for each of them. As they watched, something strange happened to Thirza's fortune. The clear water in the glass became clouded and three drops of egg-white fell to the bottom of the glass. The old woman drew in her breath and looked a little worried.

'I canna read your future from this, lass,' she said, bringing a pack of cards out from her pocket. 'I'll have to try the cards.'

Thirza could feel it wasn't fun any more, now. The other women were all quiet. They looked apprehensive when the old woman shuffled the pack, spread out the cards and looked at Thirza. 'Pick seven,' she said.

Without a word the fortune-teller glanced at her seven cards, shook her head and put them back into the pack, shuffling it again.

'I'll choose seven for you myself this time,' she said, but once again shook her head at the cards she had drawn. 'It's no use, lass,' she told Thirza. 'As you saw, I tried to change things for the better for you, but I canna change the future. Your fortune's turned up three times, now, first with the egg-white, then with the cards you drew and even in the cards I drew for you. But dinna worry, lass,' the old woman added gently, laying her hand over Thirza's. 'It's not death I see – I can tell you that you'll be married more than once, but you'll never wear a wedding ring.'

'What did she mean?' Thirza asked Teenie after the old woman left.

'Pay no attention,' Teenie said. 'It was only a game.'

Only a game? Thirza hoped it was, but the old woman's words stayed with her.

11

Jordi and Magnus took a rest from their labours one quiet evening in July. They were sitting on the hillside gazing out to sea when all Jordi's old longings came back. 'Do you ever go off in a small boat, Magnus?' he asked.

'How did you know what I was thinking myself? And what sort of question is that to ask a Shetland man? Our cousins and friends have been bringing us fish all this time, because the windows of the Haa look right over the bay and the voe.'

'You mean the Umphrays might see us, now that it's never dark?'

Magnus laughed. 'Well, it *is* called the land of the Midnight Sun, you know! But the Summer Dim has its advantages all the same. Unless they're going off to the fishing most folk go to bed at their usual time. I think that, tonight, the Cheynes could risk going off to the eela, as we call it here. We'll bait the lines and tell the lasses to be ready for half past ten.'

As the sun dipped at half past ten, the sky changed to every delicate shade of opal: lemons and yellows, the pale blues streaked with green, and pinks shading into lavender. Judging it to be late enough to be safe, Magnus and Jordi set off with Merren and Thirza in one of the Cheynes' small boats.

The girls dangled their lines over the stern while the men rowed slowly down the Voe. Thirza, paying little attention to her fishing line, thought that she had never seen anything so lovely as that coloured sky over the surrounding, brooding hills with their atmosphere of certainty and endurance. They would be there for ever, summer and winter, day and night – long after she was dead. Suddenly, although she had not been inside a Kirk for more than six months, Thirza knew that God was *her* rock, but she had had to come to the Old Rock itself, as the natives called Shetland, to find it out for certain.

Just then there was a tug on her line, followed by another and yet another, and already Merren was squealing with laughter and hauling her own fish in over the boat. Thirza copied her and it was not too long before they had filled a bucket.

'That's enough,' Magnus finally said. 'It's well after midnight now and the sun's rising again.' So they rowed back silently under the magic island spell.

When they got back they found Teenie waiting with flour ready and the frying pan heating over a hot fire. Within minutes she had the small silver fish gutted, floured and sizzling on the pan. 'I know all about you young ones,' she said. 'Aye hungry! Look, Thirza! Watch these peerie sillocks! When they're cooked their tails turn up.'

Laughing, half dreaming, and with the sea air still about them, the four young folk bantered with each other while the lamplight hissed and their happiness filled the Cheynes' house.

Jordi, glancing up, caught sight of Thirza, watching the sillocks in the pan with Teenie. He suddenly realised that, almost overnight it seemed, she was different. Gone were her awkward angularities and the flame coloured red of her hair. He saw that she was truly a young woman now, just as Ruth had warned them. Her delicate breasts swelled under her dress, her hair had softened to a glorious auburn and her cheeks – flushed with the night air and then the heat of the fire – were as pink as a rose.

She was beautiful, he thought almost in alarm. And then, when her blue eyes glanced over at him and she smiled, it was as though they had pierced him like two arrows. He was in love with her, he realised – and he was supposed to be her brother!

Only Merren saw it all, and something died in her dark and gentle eyes that night.

In August the beautiful summer was merging into autumn. All

the men were out, Merren was working for Tamar Umphray up at the Haa and even Teenie helped with the hay.

Thirza potted herring in vinegar, taking her covered dish to cool on the brigstones in time to watch Teenie's return from her day's labours with her kishie on her back – knitting, as usual, as she walked.

By now Thirza knew that the jerseys and the gloves and the hats and socks would all be exported to Holland by the Laird's factor. In the grinding poverty of the Shetland crofters, every loop that Teenie cast on her wires meant another fraction of a penny for the Cheyne family.

After a certain amount of argument, Thirza got her way and she took in the hay side by side with Teenie. The two of them took the sacks of corn that the men had winnowed to the mill, where it was ground into flour. And then it was time to dig up the blue tatties peculiar to the district which, when boiled, released their ink and came to the table white and fluffy.

It was when the autumn was well advanced that they all noticed a terrible change in Merren. The soft colour had gone from her cheeks, her eyes looked into the distance and she hardly spoke or ate when she came home.

Teenie made her favourite supper, in an agony of worry over her one ewe lamb. 'Come, jewel,' she coaxed, selecting the finest slices of wind-dried mutton for her, 'here's some vivda. Have a little with a floury tattie. I made it especially for you.'

'I *canna*, Mother!' Merren rose up from the table and dashed outside, sobbing.

'Leave her, Thomas!' Teenie commanded her husband when he made to follow her. 'There's something worrying the lass to distraction. Leave her to me. I'll find out what it is.'

But Teenie didn't find out, at least not then.

Jordi tried to appear merely brotherly towards Thirza, which deceived nobody except Thirza herself, and the Cheyne family went about their business as usual. Until the night of the Thirty-first of October, Hallowe'en. That evening, they told each other stories of witches and witchcraft, and waited to see if the guizers were out, knocking at all the doors.

There were six of them when Thomas went to open the door.

The tallest and burliest of the six, dressed in long straw skirts with pointed straw hats pulled down over their faces, pushed the other five in to do their act. One carried a melodian, another a fiddle, while a third carried a bag for any gifts they might receive.

It was supposed to be funny. But something was wrong. The guizers were very half-hearted when their leader pushed them into the Cheynes' house and, in the middle of their act, they fell silent. The big burly one lifted up his head-dress. It didn't reveal one of the boys of the district as everyone expected, but a woman.

'Osla Umphray!' Teenie screamed.

'Get out of my house!' Thomas Cheyne said in a deadly voice.

'It might be your house, but the ground it stands on belongs to us, the same as you all belong to us,' Osla Umphray said unpleasantly while her eyes searched the room and came to rest on Thirza. 'Yes!' she added triumphantly, 'That's her! I've found her at last! That's the one I want, the one with the red hair.'

'Well, you can't have her,' Thomas was emphatic. 'She's my niece. She's been here on holiday, and she's going back home to Burra Isle tomorrow.'

'Then I'm just in time tonight, isn't that so?' the fat woman smiled. 'Besides, she's been here – to my certain knowledge – for months. I saw her myself out on the Voe at the eela.'

'And we all know why *you* were looking out of your window at midnight,' Teenie put in. 'There were no men crawling up the hill to your bed, then?'

Osla Umphray ignored that. 'You have no relatives in Burra Isle, Thomas Cheyne, and this girl is not going there or anywhere else tomorrow. She's coming to Reawick House. I don't see why Tamar should have Merren Cheyne for a maidservant, while I have none. So you'd better send her with Merren in the morning. What's her name, anyway?'

'Thirza Wishart, and I don't want to work for you,' Thirza blazed. 'I'm not coming!'

'*Oh, you'll come*,' Osla Umphray assured her and, with this threat, strode out.

Teenie burst into tears, but Thirza felt almost relieved as she went to comfort her. Now the fight was out in the open. That's where she preferred it to be, and she wasn't afraid.

The other five guizers lifted up their masks. 'We had no choice, Thomas,' one of them said with a despairing gesture as they turned to go. 'She's had us round every house in the district looking for Thirza, since no one would tell her anything.'

'Don't worry,' Thomas Cheyne patted Thirza's back. 'We'll not let that woman take you.'

'You know fine we can't stop her,' Teenie sobbed. 'Why else would we let our Merren go, either? If that woman is thwarted, just think of all the damage she could do! The Umphreys could put up the price of everything we're forced to buy from them and bleed us to death financially. Then they would take this house and we would be destitute. They've got one of our children already – and now, Thirza, a guest in our home . . .' Teenie was inconsolable.

'Jordi isn't really your brother, is he?' Merren asked as they walked to the Haa the next morning. 'We've all known that for a long time. You don't look alike, for one thing. He's so dark, where you are fair.'

'I regard him as my brother,' Thirza said slowly. To tell the truth, whenever she dwelled on the subject of Jordi, she thought of him more as a friend and a confidant. Whenever they were alone together their conversation was always about how and when they could get back to St Fillan again.

'Well, he doesn't think of you as a sister. He's in love with you, Thirza. I thought I was in love with him myself, not long ago. But I saw it was hopeless. Besides, you'll both be going back to Scotland, won't you?'

'We've got to, Merren. It's almost a year since we came. I can't believe it.' Thirza walked on, for a while thinking how fast the time had gone. Almost a year in Shetland had just raced by, with work for every season amongst these kind people. Suddenly she had a great surge of feeling for them, especially the friend at her side. 'Oh, Merren, I've got to tell you the whole story! It doesn't matter now anyway, does it? The cat's out of the bag.'

There was silence for a few steps after Thirza had related their adventures.

'If it wasn't for my mother I could easily stay here for ever,' she went on, 'but Jordi has a reason for wanting to get back home, as well. There's some man in Edinburgh he's determined to see. Is it Jordi who's making you so unhappy, Merren?'

'No, no,' she sighed. 'You'll see what's wrong when we get to that accursed Haa. I just can't tell my folk, it would worry them more than ever.'

'How many Umphrays are there?'

'Three. Tamar, Osla and the fiend, Laurence Umphray.'

'Is he a fiend?'

'Yes, he's a fiend straight from hell. He makes the lives of all the maids purgatory, although he's only just turned twelve.'

'How?'

'You'll see, Thirza. But here we are now – round here to the back door. Just mind you keep well out of his way. Don't let your eyes light on him. Don't give him a chance to speak to you, even,' Merren muttered as they entered the kitchen and stood upon the flagged floor.

Thirza's first impression of the house was that although someone had lit the fire and the chimney was smoking, the whole place was cold. Worse still, it stank. 'Ugh ...' she whispered to Merren. 'Who lit the fire?'

'Two maids live in,' Merren whispered back. 'God help them.'

'Now, Thirza,' she went on in a normal voice, 'I'll show you where Miss Osla's room is, and then you can start.'

'Hm!' said a tall, very thin woman coming down the stairs as they went up. 'You've arrived, have you?

'Yes, Miss Tamar. This is Thirza Wishart. I'm just taking her to Miss Osla now.'

'I want some washing done, so don't be long. By the way, have you seen Mr Nicholson this morning?'

'No,' Merren shook her head. 'He's probably still in bed.'

'Find out!' Tamar snapped.

Merren, followed closely by Thirza, went upstairs and knocked at one of the doors. When she opened it the stench was awful – stale peat-reek mixed with stale tobacco smoke and, above all, the smell of sour whisky. Mr Nicholson lay sprawled on top of his bed, fully dressed and snoring loudly.

'Get up, Mr Nicholson,' Merren shook him.

Thirza was horrified – what might he do when he opened his

eyes? 'Get behind me, Merren,' she said under her breath. 'I'll soon deal with him,' and went to fetch the jug of water on the washstand.

'You can't,' Merren gasped when Thirza proceeded to pour it over him, and none too gently.

'Oh, can't I? Well, I've done it!' she answered as Alex Nicholson awoke, spluttering and choking. 'And as you can see he hasn't the faintest idea what's happened to him. Right! That's done. What next?' Thirza propelled Merren out of the room.

'Oh Thirza, now for the Bad Woman of Reawick. Now for Miss Osla.'

'What do you mean, "the Bad Woman of Reawick"?'

'Because she's far worse than a whore. At least a whore rents out her body to men for money. It's how she earns her living. This one does it because she's mad for men, mad for sex. It's all she ever thinks about. She's an animal.'

She learned something new in Shetland every day, Thirza thought. Thoroughly intrigued by this information, she followed Merren into Osla's room. Its atmosphere was much the same as Alex Nicholson's, except for the tobacco and whisky.

Osla was awake and, dismissed, Merren withdrew, leaving Thirza alone with her new mistress. By her side lay someone else, and Thirza didn't need anyone to tell her who he was.

A few days later, she came face to face with the creature again. He was large for a twelve-year-old. His thick mop of hair was a dusty black, his eyes were small like a pig's and his mouth was slack. He reminded Thirza of Alicky Birnie and, just as she had been aware of the masculine danger in Alicky when she was a little girl, now she had no doubt that, twelve years old or not, the Laird of Reawick could be much more dangerous still.

'Let me pass!' she said when he barred her way in the narrow passage to the back door.

Laurence Umphray leered and came closer, smelling of manure. Thirza had been out at the washing line, gathering clothes into a small tin bath, and she didn't pause to argue. She lifted up the bath and rammed it down on his head with all her might. Screaming and bubbling with tears, he snatched his hands from Thirza, clapped them over his head and ran into the kitchen.

'What's happened to my brother?' Tamar Umphray demanded.

'He got a clout on the head from me,' Thirza said grimly, 'and he'll get plenty more if he ever lays a hand on me again.'

One of the live-in maids was standing nearby. She burst into tears.

'Now what's the matter with *her*?' Tamar asked irritably.

'I should think it's obvious,' Thirza said, while Merren looked on nervously. 'The girl is pregnant, or hadn't you noticed? She only had to *look* at your brother to be upset.'

'Don't you *dare*!' Tamar fetched Thirza a smack on the face that sent her reeling. 'How dare you speak like that in this house? Some man out of the byre must have done it.'

'It was him!' the maid cried, pointing at Laurence Umphray and, in her rage, Tamar lifted her hand again.

'No, you don't!' Thirza grabbed the woman's wrist and stopped her. 'And if you hit me again you'll get more than you bargained for!'

Tamar Umphray stood speechless. Quite clearly no one had ever stood up to her before.

'He did it,' the maid repeated, sobbing. 'He never leaves any of us alone.'

'Well, well,' a voice slurred in the doorway, 'so it's a shrew I'm to be marrying, is it? What sort of family am I letting myself in for?'

'Come out of this kitchen,' Tamar hastily pushed Alex Nicholson out of it while Osla, drawn to the kitchen by all the noise and the screaming, led her brother away.

'So now you know, Thirza,' Merren said wearily. 'This is what it's like in Reawick House. They're all unbalanced, one way or the other. It comes from in-breeding, Father says. The Shetland gentry are few and far between, and they persist in marrying within that small circle.'

As Thirza was dusting the staircase that afternoon, she overheard the two sisters having a furious row.

'Now there's *another* maid will have to be sent home,' Tamar said, her voice raised in fury. 'And we'll have to pay another family to keep their mouths shut.'

'We can do what we like,' Osla shouted.

'No, we cannot. Who will marry Laurence if this gets out, after all the other girls he's put in the family way? You know he's the last of the Umphrays. If he's like this now, what will he be like by the time he's sixteen?'

'There's nothing wrong with Laurence,' Osla's sulky voice assured her sister.

'Dirty bitch!' Tamar hissed. 'You take him into your bed, don't you? It's you who's corrupted him! I've said it before and I'll say it again, for the last time. Either all the servants go and we must do all the work ourselves, or *he* goes! One or the other!'

'And where would you send him?'

'Oh, I've thought it all out! To the North House on the island. Without a boat.'

'To be a prisoner, you mean? No, you will not, Tamar Umphray! You'll leave Laurence to me. I'll look after him,' Osla waddled up the stairs and slammed her bedroom door.

When it grew dark that night Thirza's mistress was still in a very ugly mood. 'Light the lamps,' she snapped at her, 'and put one in the window.'

'You'll set the curtains on fire,' Thirza warned.

'Fool! Why would I draw the curtains? Fetch me my red scarf, and send Laurence to me.'

But fortunately she didn't have to go looking for Laurence. He sidled into Osla's bedroom, leaving the door ajar.

'Pay no attention to Tamar,' she heard Osla saying. 'We'll have some fun tonight. With any luck, when the sailors out on the Voe see this red light some might come and visit me, and you can hide in the cupboard and watch.'

So that was one meaning of a red light, was it? That explained why Teenie pursed up her lips in outrage whenever it appeared in a window up at the Haa, although of course she never spoke about it.

On Sunday mornings the whole Cheyne household could go to the Kirk now quite openly. And then, as usual, Merren read her mother's favourite verses aloud to her from the Bible in the afternoons, while Jordi and Magnus scanned the newspapers shipped up from Scotland. They were passed from hand to hand around the district and some of them were as much as two months old, Jordi noticed.

'Is there no way we can rescue the girls from the clutches of the Umphrays?' he asked Magnus.

'Of course, dozens of ways. But then the Umphrays would only take revenge on our parents. They could bankrupt them in weeks. Merren knows that, but she also knows, along with all the rest of us, that the politicians are working now on the Great Reform Bill. If it is passed, it will give tenants many more rights, and landlords a lot less.'

'But it might be years before that happens!'

'Oh, I wouldn't say that, Jordi. There's still, even after all these years, huge resentment against Henry Dundas and his kind, for example, from every seaman in Scotland. The system will change, you'll see. One day every man will have a vote.'

'You've taught me a lot, Magnus,' Jordi sighed. 'In fact, Shetland's taught me a lot. And I'm ashamed to say I didn't even know where it was, exactly, before we came here.'

'No? Well, there's many a famous man that has discovered us before *you*, you know,' Magnus laughed, fending off the cushion Jordi flung at him. 'Sir Walter Scott managed to find us in 1814, and went back home and wrote a book about it. Here it is.' He fished around among the books on the shelf. '*The Pirate*. Read it, and give me peace.'

Ships were always coming and going in the Voe. In bad weather they sometimes sheltered in Reawick Bay. One day, in perfectly fine weather, a ship sailed in and dropped anchor, to the intense excitement of everyone in the district. Its square rigging looked very familiar to Thirza.

'It's the Dutchman,' Merren told her. 'He comes here every year. Just shortly you'll see the factor and his men loading up the peerie boats and rowing out to sell our knitting.'

They watched as piles of knitted goods, especially stockings, were ferried over. When the last bale was thrown up onto the deck, the factor himself went aboard.

'Now the goods are all counted and money exchanged,' Merren explained. 'Then, in a day or two, the factor will go around the houses with what we are due.'

But Thirza's thoughts were running along very different lines. Once again she berated herself for possessing too vivid an imagination. She should not allow her heart to leap at the mere sight of a Dutch vessel, and she certainly should not jump to the conclusion that it may be Captain Gerrit who was her skipper. That was too fantastic an idea, and already she had learned that life never worked out that way.

Two days later she was as shocked as Jordi when the factor came to the door to pay the women of the house for their knitting. Thirza thought of Teenie most of all — all the work she'd done from the stage of the fleece — the cleaning, the carding, the blending and the spinning of the wool before she even began to knit it so expertly.

It was a mere pittance.

She herself and Merren got even less.

'Now you see, Jordi,' Magnus said calmly, 'why we don't cause any trouble. My mother gets little enough as it is. She would get nothing at all if we did.'

One evening when Thirza and Merren came home, they met Thomas Cheyne coming out of the 'end hoose', as he called the shed built beside the house in which all the ropes, spare oars, bags of hay and sides of dried salted mutton were stored, along with barrels of salted herring.

'What have you been doing, Father?' Merren asked him.

'I took in the last of the mutton oot o' here and hung it up beside the dried fish in the rafters over the fire. I also moved the hay nearer to the door for when the snow comes. We can expect gales and bad weather from now on.'

As he had predicted, it was soon very much colder, and Teenie got out some red flannel and cut out a petticoat for Thirza.

'While you're sewing that I'll knit you a spencer to go under your blouses,' she said. Before the evening was out, she handed Thirza a short openwork vest with half sleeves.

The next day she was glad of the warmth of her red flannel petticoat and her spencer under her dress when she and Merren wrapped themselves in their thickest shawls and set off for the Haa. The mornings were frosty now. It was still, quiet weather, but there was an uneasy feeling in the air, almost a vibration.

A few nights later Thomas Cheyne got up from his chair and opened the door. He let in a sound like the fanning and flapping of huge wings. 'Come and see them!' he said. 'The Pretty Dancers are here, and it's a wild dance they're dancing tonight.'

Vast sweeping veils of colour swished far up into the sky and shimmered down again snapping, whirring and gathering strength to dance back up to the heavens in ever-changing colours.

'The Northern Lights. The aurora borealis,' Magnus said.

'The *aurora borealis*!' Teenie sniffed. 'They've been the Pretty Dancers all *my* days!'

The family stood and watched the whole performance. They couldn't tear their eyes away from the fantasy and the energy of it. Only Thirza couldn't speak. They were beautiful all right. Beautiful, but dangerous. Once before she'd caught a glimpse of them, and they had heralded terrible trouble and an appalling storm.

The weather broke the next day, when the girls were working in the Haa. And so did the trouble. Merren had not looked well since she'd got up that morning. Now her face turned as white as snow.

'You're not frightened, are you?' Thirza asked in concern.

'Not of the storm,' Merren clasped her thin arms around her stomach.

'Have you got a pain?'

'If only I had a pain, Thirza,' she answered bitterly as the tall house on the hill began to be battered by great gusts of wind.

In the wind were large icy balls of hail. They hurled themselves down the chimneys, covered themselves with soot on the way and scattered, black and hissing, over the hearthstones.

'Oh God!' Merren groaned. 'More work! We'll never get home tonight.'

Then she vomited on to the kitchen floor. Her white face turned almost green. Thirza gazed at her friend, quite frozen in alarm for a minute, before she rushed to help her.

'Merren! You're ill. Go home this minute and get to your bed. Teenie will help you.'

Merren lifted up her delicate face drenched in sweat. 'How can I go home?' she asked sadly. 'Don't you think my mother will know at once what's wrong? I can't do this to her.'

'You haven't been well for months,' Thirza said slowly. 'You're not . . . ? You're not— '

'Yes. I'm pregnant,' Merren sobbed. 'That fiend of hell caught me at last, and raped me that night I couldn't get home. There wasn't a bed for me. I had to sleep here on the kitchen floor and when he shambled in I couldn't get away from him. He's so big and heavy, Thirza. There was nothing I could do.'

Thirza's heart lurched, then sank to her boots, devastated, as she tried to take in the terrible news. No wonder she had been looking so ill – and now she was sick with worry. 'Go home, Merren,' she said again. 'I'll clean this up, and I'll do the hearths before I follow you. You should have told Teenie long ago. She'll help you, you know that. Your mother would have to know sooner or later, anyway.'

'No! She's *never* going to know,' Merren said fiercely, picking up her wool and her knitting needles while Thirza wrapped her shawl around her.

Bitterly shocked and upset, Thirza watched her go. The ground was whitening with sleet and snow as every minute passed, but at least it was of no depth. It shouldn't hinder her friend.

She took her bucket and her cloths and whisked around the hearths as fast as she could go. Then she put on her own shawl and ran after Merren. By now the ground was very white and Thirza's feet were beginning to sink down in the snow, when a relunctant moon came out to light her way.

She came upon the wire first, a knitting needle – the sort all Shetland women used. But when she bent to pick it up she saw that it didn't gleam silver. It didn't shine at all. It was a strange, dark colour and all around it the snow was stained the same dark red.

She found Merren next, huddled under a bank at the side of the road and all around her the snow was turning red. Moaning and crying Thirza raced to the Cheynes' house.

'Come quick!' she screamed. 'Come quick! It's Merren – she's fallen in the snow!'

12

T HE day they buried Merren Cheyne was one of the saddest days in Thirza's life. Men came, hushed, from far and wide, regardless of the gale that was blowing up again, to pay their last respects at her graveside in the late afternoon under gloomy, threatening skies.

Influenced by Magnus, Jordi's opinion was very cynical. All these men wouldn't have known Merren Cheyne, even if they knew her father and mother. People didn't move much out of their districts. No, it was a silent protest directed at Reawick House, at all who lived in it – and every other oppressor in the Islands. It made the Umphrays, conspicuous by their absence, appear even more obscene.

Thirza stayed at home with Teenie and watched the crowd that had gathered at the graveyard on the hillside. Merren would look down over her beloved Reawick Voe for ever now, she thought, and could find no words to comfort Teenie.

As the wind gathered strength, more and more ships scurried in. There had never been so many ships in Reawick Bay before. It was as if they, too, were gathering in sympathy – in defiance even, to swell the ranks and show their contempt for all the Umphrays of this world.

Darkness was beginning to fall when, to Thirza's utter dis-belief – to her *outrage* – a red light appeared in Osla Umphray's window. Teenie saw it too. Without a word she got up from her chair by the window, put on her shawl and left the house.

Thirza ran after her and tried to stop her. 'Come home, Teenie,' she begged. 'The menfolk will be coming back soon.'

Teenie thrust her aside and went on her way, her eyes fixed on Reawick House. Thirza followed her all the way there, and was behind her when Teenie began to shout.

'All you in the Haa of Reawick, listen to me!'

More lights were held up at the windows. Dim faces peered out.

'This house is a place of evil, and everyone in it is evil. For what you have done to my daughter, the Umphray family will have to pay. For every family to live here in the future the price will be the same.

'A life for a life. No son of Reawick House will live to inherit it. That is my vaam. That is the curse I lay upon you this day.'

Thomas and Magnus Cheyne, along with Jordi and many other men, saw and heard her on their way down from the graveyard. The icy chill of Teenie's words sent shudders down everyone's back.

'Oh, my God,' one man muttered. 'Teenie Cheyne has laid on a vaam.'

Coming from a God-fearing woman like her, no one doubted that it would come true.

Laid on in the white heat of passionate grief, the curse didn't take long to materialise. The wind howled and sobbed all evening, and then, from one of the upper windows of Reawick House, a flame shot out.

'It's that stupid Osla and her red scarf!' Thirza cried. 'It's caught fire!'

But when she ran back to the Haa with Jordi and Magnus and all the young folk of the place, Thirza saw that the flames weren't coming from Osla's window at all. The red light was intact, and behind it she plainly saw both Osla's face and Laurence's, still giggling together, still waiting for sailors. Tamar was out upon the grass in front of the Haa, demanding to know what this invasion was about.

'Mr Nicholson's window!' Thirza pointed up to it.

'Alex! Alex!' Tamar Umphray screamed and dashed back inside dragging Thirza with her in a grip of iron. When they got to his bedroom door there was smoke coming out of it. Tamar pushed it open, allowing the flames to wave back towards them in their greed for air. 'Help me to get him,' Tamar shouted, rushing over to the chair where Alex Nicholson was out cold, a bottle still in his hand. Burning peats from the huge fire he had built for himself – halfway up the chimney – were raining out on to the carpet.

They watched the trail of flames reach the window. The wind picked them up gleefully and soon Tamar and Alex Nicholson were enveloped in a wall of fire. Thirza was rooted to the spot. She couldn't move.

'Let them go!' Jordi's voice was in her ear.

'Let them all go.' Magnus appeared at her other side, and she was swiftly carried down the stairs and out of the house.

The chain of people passing buckets of water from the sea up to the Haa must have been of the same opinion. Thirza saw that there was no sense of urgency about them. The buckets took a long time to reach the blazing house and, even when they got there, they were only half full.

Now that it had played its part, the wind suddenly died down. The sailors on the ships crowded up on deck to watch the fiery spectacle. Soon they would sail away again.

Thirza went up to Jordi and whispered in his ear. 'It's now, or never.'

'Magnus,' Jordi said sadly, 'Thirza and I can burden your family no longer, especially now. Would you do us one last favour?'

'Anything. You know that.'

'Row us out to one of those ships.'

'You're going then? We'll all miss you both, especially at this sad time. Thirza . . .'

'It's your mother you're thinking of, I know, Magnus. It will be another shock for her. I must see her and say goodbye. While you're making ready, I'll run back to the house.'

But when Thirza got to the Cheynes' house it was in darkness. No sound came from the room where Thomas and Teenie were lying. Thirza couldn't bring herself to knock on their door and invade their privacy and grief. She was miserable as she gathered her few possessions together with Jordi's. But she couldn't wait. After a whole year of kindness and hospitality from them, she couldn't wait long enough to thank them.

She was crying when she ran back down the hill. 'Your parents are in their room, and the whole place is in darkness,' she told Magnus. 'I didn't have the heart to disturb them, and perhaps upset them further with our goodbyes. Please, thank them for us, and explain what happened.'

Magnus rowed them out to the Dutchman and, when they came up alongside, she shouted up, 'Captain Gerrit?'

'There's no Captain Gerrit here,' one of the sailors shouted back. 'He didn't come this trip. His daughter's been very ill.'

'Minna?'

A man shouldered his way to the deck railings. 'Minna? You know Minna?'

'I've known Captain Gerrit for years,' Thirza yelled desperately. 'Ever since I was six years old.'

'Any friend of Gerrit van der Haar's is a friend of mine,' the current captain said. In minutes, a rope-ladder was lowered to Magnus's boat.

Two days later, in the gloom of the late afternoon, Captain Jan put in for a few minutes at Aberdeen to let them off, and Jordi and Thirza found themselves dazed, almost speechless at this sudden turn of events. They began the long walk up the quay. The only other sign of activity was coming from another ship, in almost complete darkness. Thirza thought what a sinister vessel it looked.

As they walked on silently they gazed at the busy streets of Aberdeen up ahead where there were moving lights and the noise and bustle of a large city.

'What now?' Thirza asked.

'First of all, to see your mother. I'll leave you at St Fillan and go on to Edinburgh.'

'Then you'd better have this,' she handed him a small pouch. 'I remembered to take your purse and my own with our wages in them.'

Jordi couldn't help smiling, even at this critical moment, when God alone knew how they would ever get to Fife, let alone where they might lay their heads that night in a completely strange town. Where money was concerned Thirza was always so practical . . .

'So what should we do first?' she asked, deep in thought.

Thank God Jordi had quite a lot of money in his purse, money he had made from fishing in St Fillan and small sums Thomas and Magnus Cheyne had insisted on paying him from time to time. Her own purse was very thin, in spite of all the hated stockings she had knitted. Wages had been unheard of in Reawick House, of course.

She sighed, coming out of her reverie, and wondered why Jordi wasn't answering her.

She looked up, but Jordi was no longer at her side. He had gone, disappeared into thin air. But where? What would she do without him? Panic engulfed her as she ran up and down in the deserted darkness calling his name.

Finally, she realised he had gone for good.

13

THIRZA sat on the harbour wall in Aberdeen while anger burned away her panic. What did Jordi *mean* by leaving her like that? She had been kind enough to adopt him as her own brother, had she not? He had no business leaving her stranded in a strange city – and at night too, she thought indignantly. The more she thought about it the more she burned with temper, as the night became jet black around her.

There wasn't a sound except for the lapping of waves and the rushing of pebbles with the tide, and in the eerie silence she remembered uneasily the black ship slinking out of the harbour like a ghost. Shuddering, she began to contemplate her most pressing problem. She couldn't stay here all night, sitting on a wall with horrible things that she thought might be rats scuttling about her feet.

Then fear of a different kind chilled her to her very heart as the dim shape of a huge bulky man bore down upon her with a lantern in one hand and a large cudgel in the other. She cowered back.

'Oh, ay?' he said. 'And what are ye doin' here, may I ask? A lassie alane, doon at the harbour? Is it the sailors ye're after?'

His appearing out of the pitch blackness was terrifying enough. His heavy cudgel was even more so. But what winded Thirza more than any of that was the implication of his words. She rose to her feet and faced him.

'No, indeed, sir!' she gasped, spluttering with rage. 'Not

long ago a Dutchman landed us here, my brother and me. Then he disappeared – and anyway, who are you to have the impertinence to accost me in such a fashion? Who are *you*, more like?'

By the light of his lantern Gilbert Stuart saw before him a young girl, perhaps no older than fifteen, with a mass of red hair and a temper to match, to judge by the way she was spitting back at him like a wildcat. 'Noo then, lassie,' he said more gently, 'ye needna' be feared. I'm Gilbert Stuart o' the Night Watch, ye ken. Number Seventeen.' He turned around to let her see his number painted in large white letters on the back of his top-coat. 'It's oor job to stop crime and help folk in distress.'

His words calmed her a little. Besides, his round, moon face under his Tam o' Shanter bonnet was kind enough, although still stern. 'Well, I'm in distress,' she told him. 'My brother would have got us a place to stay the night. We were supposed to be going on to Fife in the morning.'

'By sea?'

'No,' Thirza shook her head violently. 'I've had enough of the sea. I suppose I'll have to find a stagecoach going that way.'

'You will, and in the meantime you need a place to sleep tonight.'

'A proper place,' Thirza snapped. 'A place with no sailors.'

'Ah weel, lassie,' he apologised, and tucked his cudgel under his arm, 'usually the women wandering aboot doon here are no better than they should be. I wasna' to ken who ye were.'

'Thirza Gourlay.'

'A guid Fife name, right enough. I'll tak' ye to John Anderson's New Inn in Castle Street. The coach leaves from there at six in the morning. What's wrang wi' ye, lassie? Are ye cold? Ye're shivering!'

In fact, shuddering with shock and fear, Thirza didn't even feel the icy blast from the North Sea as she walked beside Mr Stuart up to the town. Along the way, he described his job to her, and how much he enjoyed every minute of it. Although she knew she was probably very lucky to have such an escort, Thirza listened in utter misery.

'We report anything wrong to the Town Council,' he told her. 'I work at night only. At seven o'clock in the morning I hand over to one of the Day Patrol. They have different uniforms

– blue suits, tippets of oil-cloth and hats with glazed covers. Patent leather, ye ken.'

'But what could have happened to my brother?' she interrupted him.

'He didna' fall into the sea, did he?'

'No. Besides, he's a strong swimmer.'

'What drew my attention to the harbour in the first place,' Gilbert Stuart said, 'was a darkened ship sliding oot to sea. I dinna ken if ye saw her?'

'I did see her.'

'No lights!' he snorted. 'Up to no good. Mark my words.'

'What do you mean? Do you mean the Press Gang? But I thought there was no Press Gang when there's no war to press the men into,' Thirza cried.

'Och, some skipper must ha'e seen him walking along the pier and taken a fancy to him. A fine upstanding young man, is he?'

'Yes, he is.' A horrible suspicion began to take shape in her mind.

'The captain's sent some of his crew to capture him and take him aboard, then. Shang-hai'd him. Yer brother'll be on the high seas by this time, nae doot . . . Miss Gourlay! Are ye all right, lassie? Here, tak' my arm. We're coming to the New Inn noo. Ha'e you the money to stay here the night?'

At the mere mention of money Thirza steadied up. 'How much will it cost?'

'Well, there's the sign. Seven and six, bed and breakfast. I've a wee lassie like you at hame. I'll gi'e ye the money if ye hinna got it,' Gilbert Stuart said with concern, looking at her face, pale in the street lights.

'I'll manage,' Thirza said proudly.

'The trouble is, I forgot they're having some sort o' a masonic do in here the night. It's gey noisy. Just go in, walk right up to the bar counter. Mr Anderson'll be there. Tell him ye want a room.'

'Thank you, Mr Stuart.'

'I'll be back at six tomorrow morning to see ye get awa' on the stage a' right. Noo, dinna worry!'

Managing to smile a farewell to him, Thirza opened the door of the inn. Noise met her like a wall. Smoke from a hundred pipes and cigars billowed out like steam and, when she took a step inside, it seemed to her that she was in a sea of men – men sitting at tables, men standing in groups, men laughing and shouting, and every one of them with a glass in his hand. She pushed her way to the counter at the far end.

'Mr Anderson, please,' she asked.

At the sound of a female voice the smiles died on the faces of the men nearest to her. They moved as far away from her as they could.

'Mr Anderson, please,' she repeated, loudly this time. Very reluctantly, a man behind the bar stepped along to face her.

'Go away,' he hissed. 'I dinna encourage your kind in here.'

Gasping at the affront, Thirza struggled for breath. This was the second time in one night she had been taken for a whore. An inquisitive silence fell around her. The men waited to hear what she would say to that, and it spurred her on into battle.

'Your sign says Bed and Breakfast,' she said coldly. 'I want a room tonight and breakfast in the morning in time for the six o'clock Stage.'

'I ha'e rooms,' he admitted majestically. She couldn't tell from his cross-eyes whether he was looking at her or his sniggering customers. 'But the thing is, could ye pay for one?'

'Yes,' she said, flashing her open purse in front of him for just a second.

'I'd need the money in advance.'

'Well, you're not getting it in advance,' Thirza assured him before an audience that was hushed now. 'As far as I know, it's an illegal practice to ask for it. It's also against the law to advertise this place as a rooming-house, and then deny me a room ... unless they're all filled up, of course?' she added sweetly.

'Mr Mitchell, you're a lawyer,' John Anderson appealed to a tall, silver-haired man standing quietly by. 'Will ye just listen to her? A barrack-room lawyer if ever I heard one! She thinks she knows it all.'

'Facts and figures, Mr Anderson. I'm afraid she's got you this time,' Mr Mitchell smiled at Thirza. 'The little lady is perfectly right.'

'Hm!' John Anderson said ungraciously. 'Why would you want to travel in November – nobody travels then.'

'Force of circumstances,' Thirza said grandly, 'and they're none of your business.'

The men laughed and applauded her. 'Man, John, let her ha'e a room,' one very drunk man shouted, while his companion guffawed. 'She's a sport, that one!'

'Follow me,' John Anderson reluctantly preceded her up the stairs. 'I see ye've nae luggage?' he added in a loud voice, loud enough to be heard at the other end of the bar.

'I left in a hurry,' Thirza acknowledged in just as loud a voice.

'That's right, lassie,' one of the drunk men roared after them. 'Dinna worry, we'll be up to see ye in a wee minutey!'

With a very bad grace John Anderson showed her into Room number one. 'In here,' he said, lighting a tallow candle.

'No sir. This will not do, I'm afraid,' Thirza said, looking around. 'There's no key in the door.'

'Who's going to disturb ye?' he grumbled, leading the way to number five.

By now Thirza was feeling very tired and, to her horror, in danger of bursting into tears. Aberdeen was a chilly city, and it had given her a frosty reception. 'Thank you,' she said, accepting the key to the door. 'I'll be down for my breakfast at a quarter past five. Goodnight, sir.'

'Hm!' he said, stomping off. When he got back downstairs some of the men looked at him with raised eyebrows. 'I had to put her in number five,' he announced. 'She's a proper little firebrand, that one.'

'That's the kind I like,' the drunk man said, while his companion giggled in agreement.

Upstairs, Thirza turned the key in the lock and looked around the sparse little room. She didn't think it was any too clean. Next she inspected the bed. The sheets were clean enough, but as soon as her hand touched the iciness of them she knew she couldn't lie down between them. The bed was wet with damp and disuse.

Leaving the candle burning, she wrapped her shawl tightly around herself, clothes and all, and lay down on top of the bed, trying to compose herself for sleep – but her thoughts were very agitated. Seven and six would make a big hole in her money, and how much would the coach cost? And where, oh where was Jordi?

Downstairs, the revelry went on. It was a grand night out for some people in Aberdeen, Thirza thought. She soon learned not to move her legs to one side or the other, but to lie perfectly still. In that way she was lying in a clamminess that was almost warm from the heat of her own body. If she moved a muscle in any direction she would freeze to death.

What her mother would have said about it, she shuddered to think, but even to think of Ruth was comforting. With any luck she should be back home with her in another forty-eight hours. She was just dropping off into an exhausted and uncomfortable doze when she heard scuffles at the door.

What was that? Was it mice? There was a tentative knock, then giggles, and she was gripped by pure terror. It was only a flimsy door and she could hear that there were two men outside it. In the dim light she saw that the handle was turning.

'Bloody thing's locked,' a voice said. Someone put his shoulder to the door before he fell down, and there were more giggles.

'Get up, ye bloody auld feel,' another voice said. 'Awa' tae fuck, man! Ye canna stand up, let alane gi'e her a ride!'

After a few more scuffles and giggles there was the sound of drunken footsteps trailing away, and silence fell. But Thirza stayed awake and alert for hours after that, in spite of having had very little sleep the night before, and the rigours of the day. As soon as the city of Aberdeen came to life again in the morning she got up stiffly from the bed, and at exactly a quarter past five she stalked downstairs, ready to do battle with the landlord.

Of course, nobody was there to greet her. Thirza did not expect it. She marched up to the counter and punched the bell, then seated herself at one of the tables still spread with its dirty, beer-stained tablecloth of last night, and waited. Muddy-eyed and yawning, Mr Anderson appeared at last, rubbing his hands together as he approached her. Evidently, he was prepared to play Mine Host today.

'I hope ye slept?' he enquired unctuously, as if to confirm it.

'That I did not! How could I?' Thirza's voice was like ice, and her back was as straight as a ramrod.

At that, his eyes flew open fully. He resembled some animal scenting danger. 'I'll get yer breakfast,' he said, scuttling away.

It was a very different Mr Anderson who returned five

minutes later with a tray. He was certainly wide awake now, as he prepared to lift a piping hot plate on to the table in front of her.

Thirza raised a hand to stop him. 'You are surely not proposing to serve me on *this* tablecloth?' she asked coldly.

'Of course not, Miss.' He whisked it off smartly and came back with another, clean and white and crisp, which he flapped down with a flourish. 'Noo, here's yer bacon and eggs.'

'No, sir, it is not. This bacon is only half cooked and the egg is sitting in a pool of fat. Take it away, please.'

Mr Anderson was about to argue, Thirza could tell. She kept her face set hard. It persuaded him to try again, and shortly afterwards he returned – this time with a plate of crisp bacon and a lightly poached egg. 'And here's a rowie and some butter,' he smiled confidently. 'I'll go back for yer tea.'

'What's a rowie?' she asked, eyeing the greasy slab of bread on her plate suspiciously.

'It's famous for being the best morning roll in the world. It's sometimes called an Aberdeen buttery.'

'I can't eat your Aberdeen buttery, Mr Anderson,' Thirza pushed it away when he came back with a teapot. 'I'm not trying to be awkward – '

'No?' he asked sarcastically.

'No, sir. But that buttery is too greasy, and whichever baker you got it from must have put a half a pound of salt in it. I don't know where you kept your butter-pats overnight either, but this is rancid. Please fetch me an ordinary Scottish bap, some fresh butter, and see that the tea is much weaker,' she said, lifting the lid of the teapot, not surprised to see that the brew was almost black.

'A' this is going to cost ye money, ye ken.' Mr Anderson took his stand, his temper rising – rising nicely to her bait, thought Thirza as she smiled inwardly. 'I'll ha'e to charge ye an extra breakfast.'

'Charge me for even *one*, or for that bed last night – if you dare, sir,' she challenged him calmly. 'That first breakfast you tried to fob me off with this morning was disgusting. The bed was soaking wet. And the dreadful battle I had with you last night in front of a hundred strange men for a room with a lock and key was disgraceful.'

'Jesus Christ! The impidence!'

'Contain your language if you please, sir. You are in the presence of a lady.'

'Are ye sitting there saying ye're no' going to pay?'

'*Pay?* Pay you for allowing drunk men to try and molest me through the night? It is only by the grace of God and my own common-sense – no thanks at all to you – that I am not a disgraced woman today. *Pay*, did you say? Mr Gilbert Stuart of the Night Watch will be here shortly. We'll see what he has to say about the goings-on in this inn last night.'

'Gibbie Stuart?' Mr Anderson asked, his face paling.

'Certainly! Number Seventeen! He recommended you and your New Inn, and he's coming to see me off on the Stage. Now I suppose I shall have to postpone my journey. He will almost certainly wish to take me with him when he reports this to the Town Council . . . I daresay,' Thirza reserved her final blow for the end of her speech, 'you will be put out of business. Oh, here he is now!'

'Oh, God! Please say nothing about it, Miss!'

But before she had a chance to speak again, Mr Stuart was at her side. 'Good morning, lassie,' he said. 'Noo, come awa'. The Aberdeen and Perth Telegraph is ready and waiting. Ye're the only passenger.'

'How much is it?' she asked anxiously.

'How far will ye be going?'

'To the crossroads for Kirkcaldy.'

'Wait here, and I'll go and ask the driver.' Mr Stuart disappeared out of the door again.

'I'll charge ye nothing for last night and pay yer fare today, whatever it costs,' Mr Anderson whispered, his crossed eyes begging her. 'Only say nothing, please say nothing about last night.'

'Twenty-four shillings sitting outside,' Mr Stuart came back to report. 'Thirty-six shillings inside, including bed and breakfast in Perth.'

Mr Anderson took the Night Watchman aside. 'Put her inside,' Thirza overheard him muttering as he took the money out of the till. It was only then that she noticed his withered left arm, which he had managed to disguise up to now. Suddenly, she was stricken with remorse. She should not have been so hard on the man. 'Just get her awa' in good order, for Christ's sake, Gibbie!'

'Ye havena seen much o' Aberdeen,' Mr Stuart said, handing her up into the coach.

'No, indeed. It was not a happy introduction to your home town.'

'I suppose I contributed to that last night, lassie,' he said ruefully, 'and I gather ye didna ha'e a very good night in the New Inn?'

Thirza ignored that last question. 'You have been very kind, Mr Stuart. You tried your best.'

'Aberdeen's a fine toon really,' he smiled at her. 'Full o' fine folk when ye get to ken them. They mebbe seem hard at first, a bit like the granite the place is built o'. When ye get aroon' the bay, just look back! Ye'll see a silver city by the sea – and dinna forget, ye've got a friend in it, any time in the future.'

'Goodbye, Mr Stuart,' Thirza waved at him. 'And thank you!'

She still felt vaguely guilty when she sat back in the slowly moving coach. Everyone knew that Aberdonians were famous for breeding moths in their purses. Because they didn't like to spend money, she should have had an affinity with them – but the fact that she had beaten one of them at their own game gave her no pleasure at all.

After a rapid calculation she discovered she had saved two pounds, three shillings and six pence purely by her wits. Then she remembered what everyone said about Fifers with a sigh. F-L-Y spells Fife. She couldn't have left a very good impression behind her, either. Everyone must have thought she was a sharp, cunning, little red-haired vixen.

Sighing again, she looked back at Aberdeen just as they rounded the bay. The wintry sun struck the cold, grey granite buildings she had been in last night and turned them to a glittering silver. It was a magnificent city.

Perhaps she should not have judged it so harshly or so swiftly.

14

A T eight o'clock that night, after a wearying journey punc-
tuated by numerous stops on the rough roads, the Stage
arrived at the George Inn in Perth. The George was a warm
and welcoming hostelry, and with great relief Thirza climbed
into a comfortable bed at last. She was asleep before her head
even touched the pillow.

The next morning at seven o'clock, she boarded a different
coach, the Union and Waverley Stage, or the 'Edinburgh Fly' as
people called it. The long journey dragged on until the coach
came to the crossroads for Kirkcaldy and stopped.

The driver got down and opened the door. 'Yer stop, Miss,'
he said, helping her down. 'Go along that road for ten miles,'
he pointed, 'and ye'll get to Kirkcaldy.'

It was well through the afternoon of another wintry day as
Thirza hurried along the road, deserted except for an occasional
horse and rider. When she heard the rumble of carriage wheels
behind her, she stopped on the grass verge to look at it hopefully.
But the carriage swept past her in disdain. The driver, with his
head sunk in the collar of his greatcoat didn't even glance at
her, and she hurried on again. St Fillan was a good twenty miles
beyond Kirkcaldy, and she hadn't a minute to waste if she was
to get there before midnight.

The next time, she kept on going when she heard the plodding
of a horse's hooves and the creaking of a wagon. It wouldn't be
anyone who knew her here anyway. But, as it drew alongside,

she glanced across at it and her heart leapt up as she saw its driver. 'Is it you, Ben Clark?' she shouted, running towards it.

The old man took his pipe out of his mouth, spat on the road and examined her closely. 'Aren't ye the wee Gourlay lassie?' he asked, amazed. 'But we thought ye were lost at sea!'

'It's me, Ben, Thirza Gourlay. Are you on your way home?'

'All the way to St Monance. Hop on, and I'll gi'e ye a lift.'

It was almost bedtime when Thirza ran along the shore path from St Monance and then up along the Braehead of St Fillan, but most of the cottages were still lit up. The Gourlay cottage was one of them, she saw with a wildly beating heart.

'Mother! Mother!' she shouted, banging wildly on the door.

She could hear consternation in the kitchen on the other side of the door and, from the backroom came the wail of a baby, startled from its sleep. Then the door opened. A strange young man stared at her, as did a young woman behind him.

'Ay?' he asked.

'Where's my mother?' Thirza gasped. 'What are you doing in our house?'

The young woman departed hurriedly as the baby's wails turned to angry howls and came back holding him in a shawl. 'Who is yer mother, lassie?' she asked.

'Mistress Gourlay. Ruth Gourlay.'

The young man's brow cleared. 'Oh! She sold us this cottage six months ago,' he said, 'and then she went away.'

'Where, sir? Do you know where?'

'No. We never got to know her. She just left the place.'

'Some o' the neighbours might ken,' his wife suggested.

Shocked beyond words, Thirza could only stare back at the small family. Behind them she could see the old kitchen press, but it looked different now. There were different dishes on it. And there was a picture on the wall which had never been there before. They were telling her the truth. It wasn't her home any more.

'Of course,' she said, pulling herself together somehow. 'I'll go and ask the neighbours. Is Bertha still here?'

'Bertha Gilmour? Ay, she's still here. She brought oor wee Eric into the world,' the young mother said, gazing at her infant proudly. 'Ay, she's still here, and her son – I dinna ken his name.'

'Jimmy,' Thirza said. 'I'm sorry to have disturbed you, and your baby. He's a bonnie wee boy.'

The young couple smiled at her and then at each other as the man shut the door. Standing there in the darkness again on the brigstones in front of the door of her old home, Thirza felt lost and lonely and completely desolate. Most of all she felt abandoned by her mother.

What had happened to Ruth?

'Any bairn I bring into the world I think o' as my ain,' Bertha was comforting Thirza half-an-hour later over a supper of bannocks and milk. 'Ye'll stay here as long as ye like. Ye can lie in the box bed wi' me in here. Jimmy sleeps in the other room.'

'I'd be so grateful for a bed tonight, Bertha, but I must find Mother. Where did she go?'

'Well, dearie, she up and sold yer house as ye ken, lock stock and barrel to those young ones. The wife was expecting a bairn and the room in the loft that Ruth got made for you fairly took their fancy. They gave her a good price. Jimmy took her across to Newhaven wi' just a wee bundle.'

'Ay, she was travelling light,' Jimmy agreed.

'But where was she going?'

'Well,' Jimmy smiled his slow smile. His speech was even slower in coming – it made Thirza feel like screaming. 'She said she would take the coach up to Edinburgh.'

'Edinburgh? But we don't know anyone in Edinburgh! She must have been going on somewhere else. Did she tell you where next, Jimmy?'

'Let me see.' Jimmy scratched his head. 'Ay! She did!' he said at last, while Thirza waited in an agony of impatience. 'She said she'd get the Fly for Carlisle.'

'*Carlisle?*' Thirza reeled back in her chair. 'Carlisle, Jimmy?' She had no recollection of any connection with Carlisle, either.

'Ay, well, Thirza . . . She wasn't going all the way, though.'

'No? How far, then? Can you remember?'

'Is there a place called Springfield? I think that's what she called it.'

'Springfield! Of course! To her sister Ellen!' Thirza smiled tiredly. At last she had a clue. 'Well then, that's where I must go tomorrow.'

'Oh no!' Bertha said. 'Ye'll go nowhere tomorrow except yer bed, Thirza Gourlay! Ye're exhausted.'

'Besides, I canna tak' ye over to Newhaven the morn,' Jimmy assured her. 'I will, the day after.'

Thirza was forced to give in. She spent the next day being waited on hand and foot while she rested and told Bertha her whole story. In the evening while they sat around the fire, Jimmy joined them and told Thirza what he had arranged.

'Ye'll ha'e to be ready to go by five o'clock in the morning,' he said. 'I'll tak' ye over to Newhaven on the flood tide, and that'll gi'e ye time to catch the coach going up to Edinburgh. All ye ha'e to do is follow the fisher-lassies. They'll be taking their herring up to the toon.'

Jimmy Gilmour tied up his fishing boat in the semicircle of Newhaven's little harbour and Thirza jumped out. A few boats were already tied up alongside, and further out gulls swooped and screeched raucously as they escorted more fishing boats in with their catches.

Thirza and Jimmy walked up to Main Street, its cobblestones glistening with the dampness of early morning dew mixed with salt from the sea-breezes of the Firth of Forth. They watched as thirty or forty fisherwomen welcomed the men and threw the herring into their creels.

'The first of the coaches will be coming for the women soon,' Jimmy said. 'I'll get one o' the lasses to tak' ye under her wing,' and in a minute he was back with a blonde girl at his side. 'This is Marie.'

Thirza couldn't make up her mind if Jimmy's face was red with pleasure, or embarrassment. She thought it might be a mixture of both, and wondered if she was in the company of the future Mrs Jimmy Gilmour. 'Those are very colourful clothes you're all wearing,' she said admiringly. In fact, they were very picturesque – white lace-trimmed petticoats peeping out under red and white striped outer petticoats and, on top, they wore overdresses looped up round the hips with a string in the hems. 'Are you one of the girls who go around singing "Caller herrin" so that the ladies come out and buy your fish?'

'I am,' Marie laughed, 'and ye'd better stick close to me in the rush if ye want a seat in the Fly to Edinburgh. Here it comes now.'

Girls, women, creels and herring were packed in together until the coach was as tight as a drum as it set off to go the few miles to the Royal Mile. When Thirza got out and waved goodbye to Marie she was covered with fish scales, but well furnished with directions of how to get to the White Horse Inn for the Carlisle Stage.

And she was just in time.

'Four hundred miles,' Thirza counted in her head, hours later. That was the distance from Shetland to Springfield in her quest to find her mother, and this last hundred of them were turning out to be by far the worst. They added up to two days of grinding on in this coach, of never-ending stops and starts, of getting out and getting back in again, while all the time the stench of the herring on her clothes became riper by the minute, wafting under the noses of the other passengers with every move she made.

'Ugh! You shouldn't be in here with civilised people,' one very prim lady told her, waving her handkerchief under her nose in a vain attempt to dismiss the smell. 'You should be riding outside.'

'Yes, indeed,' her parson husband agreed. 'My wife has very delicate sensibilities, you know.'

'I paid the same as you did,' Thirza glared at them, 'and this *is* a public conveyance. It's pot-luck. If we could choose our companions *none* of us would be here.'

That silenced them effectively, but all the same, she felt humiliated, very uncomfortable and – of all the passengers in the coach – she was the one most frustrated at each delay. The dusk of the second bitterly cold afternoon was beginning to fall when, at last, the driver slowed the coach and turned up the sweeping drive to a large and beautiful old mansion, all lit up and welcoming. He stopped in front of gracefully curving steps up to the front door.

'The Gretna Green stage,' he announced. 'This is Gretna Hall. All change.'

'Is this anywhere near Springfield?' Thirza asked him.

'Just up that road,' he nodded his head towards it and, utterly thankful, she got out and ran back down the drive again to the road.

There was a church opposite, with a signpost that said 'Gretna Old Church'. There must have been a funeral in the churchyard that afternoon, for some black-shawled women were walking away from it and streaming up the road towards Springfield in front of her.

She quickened her steps to catch up with them. Perhaps someone would know Ruth or where her sister was living. In the gathering darkness, a gust of wind hurling icy raindrops blew some of the womens' shawls off their heads. Ruth Gourlay was one of them. She half turned into the wind to put it back on again, and saw Thirza. Her stare was terrible. It was as though she saw a ghost.

'Mother! Mother!' Thirza cried, running up to her. 'It's all right! It's all right! It's really me!'

'Oh, my God,' Ruth moaned, swaying for a second before she began to sag.

The other women held her up. 'Who are ye, lass?' one of them asked. 'Mrs Gourlay's had a bad enough day already, without any more shocks. She's just buried her sister.'

'I'm her daughter.' Thirza couldn't stop the tears that poured down her face. 'She hasn't seen me for over a year. I couldn't get word to her that I survived a shipwreck. She must have thought I drowned along with my father and brother. Of course it must be a terrible shock . . .'

'Let's get them home,' another woman said, 'before we all catch our death of cold.'

By now the wind had risen with a vengeance and, between the pouring rain and the tears that wouldn't stop pouring out of her eyes, Thirza could scarcely see where they were going. She was only dimly aware of it when they entered a house in which a fire burned low in a sparkling black grate. Then someone lit a lamp and drew the curtains – and she was alone with her mother at last. They flung their arms around each other and sobbed.

It was Ruth who was first to recover. She broke away, lifting her head and sniffing. 'What's that terrible smell?' she asked. 'Thirza Gourlay, ye're stinking! How did ye manage to get into such a mess?'

'It was the herring.'

'Well, I ken one thing,' Ruth said sternly, putting the kettle on to boil and taking a tin bath off a peg on the wall, 'ye're going into no bed o' *mine* in that state!'

Thirza was half laughing and half crying when she answered. 'Oh, Mother, it's good to be home!'

15

THEIR first day together was spent quietly while Thirza faithfully reported every single incident since they'd parted the previous January – every detail of the storm that night, the disaster, their sojourn in Shetland, and how she had managed to get to Springfield.

She sat on the floor between Ruth's knees for, all the time she was relating her story, her mother was brushing out the tangled web of her newly washed hair and then going through it strand by strand with a fine tooth comb.

'It *seems* to be all right,' she pronounced at the end of her inspection.

The second day, she told Thirza about Springfield, a story which lasted all of five minutes. There were two rows of cottages facing each other, an inn set in the middle of them, called The Queen's Head, a very old farm nearby called Plump and the Kirk down the hill in Gretna Green. And of course, there was Gretna Hall on the rise of the hill, overlooking three busy highways, one from the East, one from the South and one from the West.

'Being just over the border into Scotland makes it an ideal stopping place for runaway couples from England,' Ruth finished. 'They get married in Gretna Hall.'

It hadn't taken her long to acquaint her daughter with the geography of the place. The personalities would take longer to get to know, Thirza felt sure. Most of all, she would like to know the people in Gretna Hall. The house intrigued her.

In the meantime, there was the great ugly loom, occupying a whole wall in the living room of this small cottage, to be investigated. 'What's that for?' she asked.

'When yer Aunt Ellen's man died in Kirkcaldy, so did his wages,' Ruth told her. 'She had to find some work to do herself. But, as ye ken, she never liked Kirkcaldy. Then she heard about these cottages they'd built here in Springfield, and decided to come back to where we were both brought up.'

'How did you come to meet my father, when you were living here?'

'He was fishing around the Solway in his young days.' Ruth's eyes grew misty. 'He was a good-looking lad with a smile that charmed me altogether. Ay, he was a wonderful man.'

Thirza gazed at her in amazement. Had she forgotten that this was her daughter she was speaking to now? She remembered all the little stratagems Ruth used to employ to build her father up in the role of head of the house, and all the trouble she'd taken to disguise from outsiders that he was a weakling. But perhaps, having got used to speaking about him to her sister Ellen, she'd forgotten that Thirza knew better.

'I fell in love with his smile and his beautiful teeth,' Ruth went on dreamily. *Love?* Thirza had never heard her voice the word before, and a tiny seed was sown in her mind that day. Her mother had changed in the past year. She had definitely changed. 'That reminds me, Thirza. I made this for you last night,' she said, presenting her with a soft bleached twig with one end of it teased out into strands like a little brush. 'And here's a dish of salt. Ye've got his smile and his teeth, lassie. Ye've got to preserve them. Did ye ever brush them all the time ye were away?'

'They don't have twigs in Shetland, Mother. There's no trees for them to grow on. And you still haven't told me about this loom.'

'Well, these are weavers' cottages that yer Aunt Ellen heard about. She was lucky enough to rent one, and to learn to weave.'

'Yes. But weave what?'

'Linen. The owner brings us large sacks of flax, and we have to weave it into linen. It's hard, back-breaking work, but that's not what killed yer auntie. When I thought I'd lost my entire family and came to live with her, she was ill already. I looked after her, but she never got better.'

'Then I suppose I'll have to learn to do this weaving.'

'I was thinking ye'd start today, Thirza.'

'What's this you've been doing?' Thirza was examining some linen squares.

'I got an order from Gretna Hall, for six dozen serviettes.'

Thirza counted the squares. 'Well, that makes four dozen you've still to make.'

'Yes. And, after that, to finish by hand.'

'Come on, then, Mother. Show me.'

Painstakingly, Ruth did the drawn-thread work inside the hems of all the serviettes when they were finished. Then she washed them and ironed them and laid them in tissue paper ready to be delivered to the Hall.

'Would ye take them to Mr Linton?' she asked Thirza. 'Tell him who ye are. He'll gi'e ye the money.'

Thirza leapt at the chance. 'Tell me about him first, then.'

'Well, it seems John Linton leased Gretna Hall from the Earl of Hopetoun. He's a very good landlord and his wife is a very good housekeeper. They have several grown-up bairns, but I think they're all away now. I've never seen any o' them, anyway. Now, when you get there, go round to the back door, Thirza.'

A young man with laughing eyes in a roguish face met her when she arrived with her parcel. 'Mr Linton, please?' she asked.

'Yes, I'm Mr Linton but, sadly, I don't suppose I'm the Mr Linton you're looking for.'

'I've come with serviettes from my mother,' she was saying primly when a middle-aged woman wearing a wraparound pinafore and a dust-cap came bustling out. She frowned at young Mr Linton.

'Are you not away yet, Joe Dan?' she said. 'I want those fish and I want them before midday. Be off with you!'

'Hold your horses, Mother,' he grinned. 'Here's a young lady with serviettes. A very pretty young lady, too.'

'Don't pay any attention to him,' Mrs Linton turned to Thirza, shaking her head as Joe Dan walked off jauntily. 'You're—?'

'Thirza. Mrs Gourlay's daughter, ma'am.'

'Well, I'm pleased to meet you, Thirza, and pleased to get the serviettes. We have so many weddings here, you see, besides providing meals for our other guests. Come inside and I'll fetch my husband.'

There must be a feast of some sort today, Thirza thought, when she found herself in a large, well-appointed kitchen. A woman, obviously the cook, was rolling out pastry on a table standing in the middle of a flagged floor. Blue and white china ashets, jugs, cups and plates of every size stood upon the dresser behind the cook. Facing Thirza was a deeply recessed fireplace where a good red fire blazed, flanked by ovens.

On the sideboard a ham lay cooling beside a dish of oranges and apples. A rich plum cake covered with almonds stood on a rack. There were plates of freshly baked scones, others of tiny fairy cakes and, under a sprinkling of sugar, chopped-up apples awaited their pastry lids.

'So ye've come to see the Bishop?' the plump woman smiled. 'Thinking o' getting married, are ye?'

'Not me. Who's the Bishop?'

'That's what the village folk call Mr Linton. He marries the runaways, ye ken – but only the gentry. He doesn't allow any riff-raff in here. *They* can go and get married by some o' the other priests.'

'Why – how many ministers are there?'

'Oh, lassie,' the woman laughed, 'none o' them are ministers! Not even Mr Linton. Ye see, in Scotland any single man and woman can stand before two witnesses and declare their marriage vows, and then they're married. They don't need a minister o' the Kirk.'

'Yes, I know. But is it different in England?'

'Oh, mercy me, yes. That's why we get all these English folk running over the border to Gretna. There are so many "priests" because people don't feel properly married without someone to read the words over them. But since only the rich come here to Gretna Hall we call Mr Linton the Bishop.' A man's footsteps sounded along the passage. 'This is him now,' said the cook.

'Miss Thirza Gourlay, is it?' Mr Linton held out his hand. 'Come with your mother's serviettes?'

'Yes, sir.'

'I hope Mrs Bryson's been looking after you?'

'Yes, sir, she has.'

'I don't see you with a cup of tea and a fairy cake, all the same,' he smiled, opening the parcel.

'Oh no, sir, thank you! It's not long since breakfast.'

While he was examining her mother's work Thirza took stock of him. He was large, pleasant and very affable. No doubt this was who Joe Dan had inherited his good looks and silver tongue from. Mr Linton was also very well-dressed, even at that time of the morning. He was every inch a country gentleman. No wonder they called him the 'Bishop'.

Another rush of footsteps heralded Mrs Linton. 'Thirza,' she panted, 'ask your mother if she could make me four more tablecloths. I've only got eight, and with some in the wash, I really need a dozen to be on the safe side for all the functions we cater for here.'

'Plenty of women are good weavers,' Mr Linton said, 'but your mother's the best finisher in the district, you see. Now, let me give you the money for those serviettes.'

'As soon as she can with the tablecloths, dear,' Mrs Linton scurried off, and Thirza ran back home, greatly enlivened by her visit to the Hall.

Christmas came and went. The New Year of 1829 came and went, with its painful memories of the previous January, and the loss of Davy and Andra. All that winter Thirza and her mother were hard at work. While Ruth hemmed and finished tablecloths, sheets and pillowcases for the Lintons, Thirza worked the loom.

She hated it with all her heart.

On the other hand, she liked running back and forth to Gretna Hall with the linen, especially if she happened to run into Joe Dan. He was so very entertaining.

She became very friendly with Mary Bryson, the cook, as well. 'Are you and the Lintons the only three running this inn?' she asked her one rainy afternoon.

Outside it was a grey day in late February, and Mrs Bryson had made her sit down at the kitchen table with a 'fly' cup and a slice of one of her crusty loaves spread thick with butter. Inside the kitchen it was cosy and – for once – peaceful, with the house cat curled up in its basket at Mrs Bryson's feet.

'I never see any maids,' Thirza went on. 'Mrs Linton seems

to be running about from morning to night. Surely she should have more help?'

'There's nobody to be got, lassie. The women around here are either farmers' wives or weavers. I'm a widow mysel', wi' no bairns, so I'm glad o' the company up here. It's always lively ... Why are ye asking?'

'I was only wondering,' Thirza said. 'I don't like housework any more than the weaving, but I've been a maidservant before. I could be again, if the money was right.'

'Just you leave it to me, Thirza,' Mrs Bryson said.

The following week she became a general servant at Gretna Hall and, in the weeks that followed, she saw Joe Dan Linton more and more, although he didn't actually live there. He only visited.

'Ye want to watch him,' Mrs Bryson warned her. 'He's the black sheep o' the family. They don't even let him live here.'

'Where does he live, then?'

'On the beach, as far as I ken,' Mrs Bryson sniffed.

'He can't just live on the beach,' Thirza laughed.

'Well, in a hovel o' some kind down at the Solway. The Lintons can do nothing wi' him. They gave up long ago. So he just goes his own way.'

More and more, Joe Dan sounded like a man after Thirza's own heart. She thought he must be four or five years older than she was, about the same age as Andra, her brother, had he lived. Indeed, he must be the same age as Jordi.

Jordi.

Jordi, her other brother. Well, not really her brother, but her dearest friend.

In all these months since they'd been parted, when so much had happened, Thirza had thought of him only fleetingly from day to day. Now she suddenly missed him so much there was a pain in her heart like a wave surging up and bursting all over her.

16

U P to that very moment Jordi's feet had not touched dry land since he was snatched from Thirza's side on the quay in Aberdeen.

Bitterly, he lived and relived it over and over again. One minute he was walking along minding his own business and the next minute – from out of nowhere – two strong hands threw a tight gag over his mouth, and other hands swept him off his feet and bundled him away. His own hands and arms were firmly pinioned and two more men pressed their whole weight upon his thrashing legs.

The speed of the silent manoeuvre had taken him completely by surprise and, to this day, he couldn't believe that he had neither seen nor heard a thing until it was too late. Oh, they were experts at it! Many times since then he had seen them repeating it, even in broad daylight. Their quarry never stood a chance.

He was carried on board ship, thrown down below and immediately shackled hand and foot. Finally, he was left to consider his situation. Jordi thought it through and it didn't take him long to do it.

He had been captured. Escape would be his main aim from now on. But how? Ashore, he might have had some opportunity. Afloat, it seemed impossible, especially shackled like this. Whatever happened, the first thing to do was to get out of the chains. They were just long enough to allow him to drag them to the porthole and gaze longingly at one quay after another in the different ports where the ship dropped anchor fleetingly.

He didn't think being loosed would be achieved by ranting and raving at the men who brought him hard biscuits and water from time to time. His best bet would be to appear compliant and bide his time.

He realised he was on the sinister black barque which had been riding at anchor briefly on that dark night in Aberdeen, and that the purpose of the blacked-out ship's brief visit was to recruit manpower. Anyone would have suited them – he had simply been in the wrong place at the wrong time, like all the other men he'd seen whisked off quays at other ports. Why were they not down here with him? Well, someone must come to him soon and release him. He was no use to anyone tied up down here.

The sound of heavier footsteps than usual descending the companionway told him that his calculations might be correct. The next minute he was looking a long way up into two ugly, deep-set eyes, narrow and slanting, in a ruddy white-whiskered face.

'So, boy, they tell me you're a quiet one,' the huge man said, using no particular dialect, although his accent was Scottish. 'That's what I like to hear – except the quiet ones are usually the most dangerous. The other men we picked up have all settled in.'

Jordi stared back at him. He judged he hadn't heard enough yet to answer one way or the other, so he didn't open his mouth.

'I'm the skipper. Captain Jack Hawkins. You've heard of me?'

Jordi shook his head. And yet . . . It was familiar. He thought he had heard Magnus mention it once.

'I took a fancy to you the minute I saw you,' the Captain said and, to Jordi's horror, he slid down into a sitting position beside him. All he could think of were the terrors of the stables of Hopetoun House, and he edged away. 'No, no, lad,' Captain Hawkins laughed. 'I don't mean *that* kind of fancy! There's none of that on board *this* ship! I look for strong, useful men to bring aboard the *Prince* – men,' he winked hideously, 'who want to make a bit of money. We're all friends here.'

Still, Jordi couldn't trust himself to respond, and he didn't trust this man in the slightest.

'Now, tell me your name.'

'Jordi Wishart.'

'Scottish, thank God.' Captain Hawkins sighed with relief. *'Wha's like us?'* he quoted. *'Damned few and they're a' deid!'* In spite of himself Jordi couldn't help smiling wanly. 'You've been to sea before?'

'No,' he lied carefully. Already he had made up his mind to tell this man nothing more than his name. In fact, he would tell nobody on board this ship anything at all, since one careless word about his background might some day lead to his recapture. By now, he was implacably determined to escape, but he had an uneasy feeling, looking into this man's cunning little eyes, that he could read every thought passing through Jordi's mind.

'Well, well, you'll soon find your sea-legs with us. I don't want you chained up down here any more than you do. I want you working up above. You're strong, I can see that. But could you be faithful to your Captain? Can I trust you? And will you be useful? Can I trust you to try?'

'I'll try,' Jordi said shortly.

'Good!' Captain Hawkins beamed at him. 'Then tomorrow morning you can start by swabbing the decks. We'll soon have you up on the rigging!' With what was meant to be a cheering pat on the back, vigorous enough to send Jordi three feet to the left, his captor stood up to go.

Once released and up on deck, Jordi found that the ship was in a very beautiful long inlet bordered by high cliffs. Narrow inlets such as this were called voes in Shetland, but this was a voe magnified a hundred times.

By dint of listening to everything the other men said, he found out that this was a Norwegian fjord, but he couldn't find out the reason why they were skulking from point to point up and down its shores. Everyone else seemed to know. They took it for granted.

Jordi had to admire the Captain's seamanship. He could steer the large ship between rocks so that it slipped like an eel through the neck of a bottle. It seemed that he was fearless as well as very capable and, to a man, his crew had the greatest respect for him.

They obeyed his every command, as he roared from the quarterdeck scrubbed as white as a man-of-war. Wondering if this was what it was like in the Royal Navy, Jordi soon learned to do the same – for, from his elevated position at the stern, Captain Hawkins insisted on a spotless ship and an alert and disciplined crew. His eyes were everywhere.

It was while he was swabbing the decks one day that Jordi lifted up one corner of a tarpaulin covering something big. He dropped it hastily again. It was covering a short, large-calibre ship's gun. As he swabbed further along the deck he came to another tarpaulin, and another, hiding the carronades. In fact, they were positioned at intervals both on the port and starboard sides. The *Prince* was armed, and that meant only one thing. Captain Hawkins intended to do battle.

The weather was calm, and down on the water between the high rocks it became positively warm. The crew took off their shirts and worked stripped to the waist.

'Can you paint?' the Captain asked Jordi.

'Yes, I can paint.'

'The bow needs a bit of touching up. We might as well get it done while we're waiting.' Waiting for what, Jordi wondered? 'Go over the side with McKim here. He's got all the gear.'

McKim threw two rope-ladders over the side with a plank of wood secured between them. Then he gave Jordi a paint-pot, took another for himself and they climbed down with their brushes between their teeth.

'Black paint?' Jordi asked casually, his heart beating fast. Was this going to be his chance? He could easily dive off the rope ladder into the sea. He could easily swim to the rocks.

'Dinna even think aboot it,' McKim told him, an ugly knife suddenly in his hand. 'That's the reason why I'm here wi' ye, in case ye think o' jumping ship. This knife'll be in your back afore ye hit the water.'

All that day they painted the bow, moving the rope-ladder foot by foot as they worked, until they reached the prow where the name *Prince* was printed in white letters.

'Dinna you dare put a spot o' black on that name,' McKim said.

'Somebody's already painted right over another name in front of it.' Jordi peered at the obscured letters. 'The real name is *Black Prince*.'

'Now ye ken,' McKim grinned evilly.

And now Jordi remembered. Jack Hawkins, the Scottish pirate, with his *Black Prince*. They said half his crew were lost in every bloody encounter. Now he knew why he'd been snatched. He was to be cannon-fodder.

The crow's nest wasn't high enough to see over the tops of the tall and densely wooded mountains. At intervals the long-boat was sent out to the mouth of the fjord to spy out what shipping was coming. When, two days later, it streaked back to the *Prince*, the long wait was over.

A dainty brig, well down in the water, was sailing leisurely into the fjord, and now Hawkins' men worked feverishly amidships to cast loose the gun-carriage so that the Long Toms were free to swivel fore and aft.

Jordi watched as two of them were uncovered on the forecastle and two more of the long cannons looked over the taffrail in the stern. Other men moved the carronades forward into their positions before they primed them. Then, with a groan and a rattle, the anchor chain came up.

Captain Hawkins waited until the brig was almost alongside his hiding place among the rocks. There was just time enough to make out her name, *Fleur de Lys*, when Jordi's horrified eyes saw the Skull and Crossbones being run. Then, with all guns blazing, the pirate made straight for the unsuspecting vessel.

He had the advantage of surprise – his usual devious, dirty tactics, Jordi thought bitterly. The French brig responded, but it was too late. The fjord was lit up orange and brilliant white with every explosion, and now it was difficult to see what was happening in the smoke-filled air.

A shot from the *Black Prince* whistled through the rigging of the French ship, followed by another that brought down one of her main masts. Then there was a blast which almost burst Jordi's eardrums and in the tremendous flash that followed he saw a tearing, jagged hole in the *Fleur de Lys*, saw her heel, the rest of her masts topple and then there was silence from her guns.

On the *Black Prince* confusion was roared down by Captain Hawkins bellowing out staccato orders. He and most of his crew threw ropes across to pull the French ship alongside and, before they boarded her, he put McKim in charge of the rest of the men, to fight the fires that had broken out on his own decks. McKim, with his hand on the hilt of the knife at his waist, never left Jordi's side.

The French cargo was discharged at top speed and transferred to the holds of the pirate ship. The ropes were loosed from the *Fleur de Lys*, and Captain Hawkins, piling on the sails, headed straight down the fjord to the open sea. One last blast from one of his Long Toms finished the French brig. She went down with a loud, hideous gurgle – so swiftly that she had disappeared before the *Black Prince* reached the North Sea.

That night, as they sped south the crew members who were still left alive celebrated with their Captain. He broke out two casks of French brandy and left them to it before, as had been his custom every night now, he came to speak to Jordi.

'Can I fill up your glass again, lad?'

'No, thank you, sir.' Jordi had only drunk the first glass to try and stop the dreadful sick feeling in his stomach. All those French sailors dead, their wives now widows and their children fatherless! Then there was something even worse than that, a sight he would never forget, of the dead and dying bodies of his shipmates shuffled over the side to feed the fishes. 'I don't really drink.'

'Well, you're different,' Captain Hawkins said. 'I knew it from the first. And what did you think of our little encounter?'

Jordi looked at the man, the murdering monster, as he stood there with his chest swollen with pride and a happy grin on his face. Now, if ever, was the time for diplomacy. 'I thought you handled your ship with an expertise few could match, sir,' he said. 'It is to be admired.'

To his amazement the big man's eyes filled with sentimental tears. 'Those are the exact words my old father used, Jordi,' he gasped. 'I knew you were the lad for me! I never married. I never had time. But if I ever had, I could have wished for nothing better than a son like you.'

146

Now, what had he done, Jordi wondered? This was the last thing he wanted. Now Captain Hawkins would never let him go.

'You know, lad,' he went on, 'my dearest wish is to see my old mother and father again . . . Just one more time, before they die. Just one more time! I'm a family man at heart, you know.'

No, Jordi decided, his ears weren't deceiving him, and the tears rolling from Captain Hawkins' eyes were real. The man could be drunker than he looked, or perhaps he'd found a chink in the pirate's armour; his parents were bound to live on dry land somewhere.

'Well, why don't you go and see them, then?' he asked.

'Because I'm a wanted man. Rich, but wanted. I can never go ashore with any peace of mind. It's the price I've had to pay for the life I chose – but, oh Jordi, it's a terrible price, to be a wanderer on the high seas for ever!'

To Jordi's consternation Hawkins gave way to his grief. 'Well,' he said, putting a comforting hand on the huge, heaving shoulders, 'We'll just have to make a plan, then, won't we?'

'A plan?' The pirate mopped his eyes and gazed at Jordi.

'Yes. We'll think of a way you can go and see your parents, however long it takes.'

But, Jordi made up his mind, there would be no plan of campaign unless it included some way he could escape from Captain Hawkins' clutches.

147

17

'Is this ye, hame already, Thirza?' Ruth had been concentrating so hard at the loom that she looked up now with a dazed expression.

'What do you mean, "already", Mother? It's six o'clock! I always get home at six, you know that. The last time I saw you was at seven this morning when I set off to go to the Hall.'

'Oh . . . Ay.'

'That was eleven hours ago. You haven't been sitting at that loom ever since, have you?'

'I seem to ha'e lost all track o' the time today. The thread broke on the shuttle. It took hours to fix it so that the knot was on the selvage. What aboot yer dinner?'

'Mother!' Thirza laughed. You know I get my dinner at the Hall. And my tea. And fly cups – all day long!' The fire was out. The lamps had never been trimmed and there was no sign of food anywhere to be seen. 'But *you've* had no dinner, sitting at that loom all day long.'

'I tell ye. I dinna ken where this day's gone,' Ruth said, stretching herself on her stool and arching her back.

'And now you've got a sore back,' Ruth scolded. 'Go and lie down on the couch and I'll get the fire going for a cup of tea.'

'Well, at least I've got all that done,' Ruth pointed to the yards of linen lying in folds where it had dropped behind the loom.

'Is it finished, now? No, I see it isn't. Well, after this cup of tea I'll finish it, and tomorrow you'll have a rest.'

149

'Ye canna work all day and then come hame and take on my work too, lassie,' Ruth protested tiredly, lying down on the couch.

'Oh, no?' Thirza boasted, swiftly clearing out the fire, laying a new one and lighting it. 'I'll be fresh to the weaving after what I've been doing today. We had two lots of runaways.'

While she boiled the kettle, speared bread on the toasting fork and, once that was nicely brown, scrambled eggs, Thirza regaled her mother with her stories of the day.

'The first couple arrived at one o'clock. When Mr Linton married them the bridegroom gave Mary Bryson and me a half a crown each for being the witnesses.'

'He must be rich.' Ruth ate her supper, looking a little better already.

'He is,' Thirza assured her, rushing around with the lamps. 'I saw him giving Mr Linton ten pounds.'

'Ten pounds?'

'He parted with ten pounds for his marriage fee and looked very happy to do it. The bride looked happy, too. Before they travelled on, all they had time to eat was a plate of what they fancied from Mary's cold buffet. Of course, it was washed down with champagne . . .'

'Some are born lucky,' Ruth sighed. 'What about the other couple?'

'They're staying the night in the Bridal Chamber. Mr Linton is taking care of *them*. They pay a lot more, you see.'

'It's all money, money, money, Thirza. Money rules our lives.'

After that day, Thirza got up an hour earlier every morning and worked on the loom to give her mother a good start before she went out to work herself. Nothing more was said, but although she never again came home to a cold house, she began to keep a close eye on Ruth.

Her mother had worked hard all her life and scorned anyone who didn't do the same. But she had never seemed so tired, before. Thirza didn't believe that there was anything physically wrong with her mother. It was more a weariness of the spirit.

'Now then, Thirza,' Mr Linton took her aside some weeks later, 'there's something I want to show you. Follow me,' he said, leading her upstairs and along a passage usually forbidden to everyone except Mrs Linton. 'This is the Bridal Chamber,' he ushered her in and closed the door behind her.

'Oh, it's so beautiful!' Thirza exclaimed.

She had never seen a four-poster bed before in her life. This one had a frill under the canopy and curtains under that, a buttoned headboard and a deep quilt, all made out of a soft cream silk, patterned with pale pink roses. The curtains on the bed and the curtains on the window were tied back with thick silk cords, from which dangled fat pink tassels.

There were pictures on the walls in between candles waiting in their sconces to be lit, and in one corner there was a screen, decorated with pictures of birds and flowers. But it was the panes in the small window which drew her eye. 'What's that?' she asked Mr Linton. 'Somebody's written something on the window-panes.'

'They scratch their names on them with their diamond rings. Now, Thirza, as you can imagine, this is the most important room in a romantic house like this. It takes Mrs Linton a very long time to clean it and leave it looking like this each day, so from now on I want you to do it for her.'

'Yes, sir.'

'But that's not the only reason for bringing you up here,' he went on. 'There's another private room along the passage a bit. Come, and I'll show you.' He took her into another room, very sparsely furnished. 'Sometimes this is a very busy little room, Thirza. It has a secret compartment.' He went over and slid back one of the wooden panels and behind it she could see a small cell.

'We've had to use that hidden chamber many, many times,' Mr Linton told her, sliding the panel back into position again. 'You see, couples wouldn't elope in the first place if they had their parents' permission to wed. I have been actually conducting the ceremony when the holy words were interrupted by furious knocks on the front door and loud demands for immediate entry by irate fathers. Some of them even had guns!'

'Ah! So you hide the bridal couple in there?'

'I was wondering if you could help me? Sometimes I have been hard put to it, to get the young people hidden and fend off their parents at the same time. As long as you are on duty, would you take them to the secret chamber?'

'Oh, yes!' Thirza, who hadn't yet developed a romantic bone in her body, was thrilled by the adventure of all this. 'I'll keep it clean as well,' she volunteered.

Ruth and Thirza had both worked very hard and made themselves comfortable in the weaver's cottage in Springfield, even if they had scarcely been out of it except to go to Gretna Hall and to the Kirk at the foot of the hill on Sundays. But now it was well through March, the days were stretching, and they were both feeling dreadfully cooped-up.

Thirza went to clean the Bridal Chamber as soon as the latest newly-weds vacated it. As usual, the quilt was lying on the floor and the bed was rumpled. What on earth did they *do* when they got into bed, she wondered, to make such a mess? She changed the sheets and the pillowcases, made up the bed again and dusted the room. Then she went along to the room with the secret chamber, shut the door and cleaned it, too.

But all the time she was itching to go behind the panel and have a good look at the secret room where she had already hidden three couples so far for a few hours. She stood for a minute and listened, but no one was moving about up here except herself. Greatly daring, she slid back the panel.

She was in a cell, right enough. It was very small. Its main feature was the window which seemed big in a room as small as this. It commanded a good view of the approach to the inn. She saw that anyone could escape out of it as well, for it opened out on to a staircase.

Where did that lead to? First she carefully closed the panel behind her, then opened the window and stepped out. The steps led down into somewhere dark. Thirza followed them and found herself in the stable. It was wonderful! She could imagine the adventure, leaping on the back of a horse and riding away with a lover . . .

'Ah, ha! Now I've got you!' said a man's voice, strong arms enfolded her and, for a very brief moment, she played the part, turning around in his arms and allowing his lips to press upon hers. He held her closer still, until Thirza came to herself and sprang away.

'Joe Dan Linton! What are you doing here?'

'You mean, what are *you* doing here? There's only one way you could have got here. Does the Bishop know?'

'You shouldn't talk about your father like that, Joe Dan,' Thirza said severely as they walked out into the soft spring air, 'and yes, he knows. Oh, isn't it exciting? And romantic?'

'I know somewhere far more exciting and romantic than this. It's my place, down at the Solway. Why don't you come and visit me some day?'

'I might – some day,' Thirza laughed and ran inside the Hall again, smiling, her cheeks very pink. She went by way of the kitchen, where Mrs Bryson was up to her elbows in her mixing bowl. 'What are you making, Mary?' she asked.

'Getting the puddings ready for the party tonight. They're having a dance as well. Mrs Linton is seeing to the ballroom right now, and she said if I saw ye to tell ye to go and help her to lay the tables in the dining room.'

'I'll go now. I'm finished upstairs, anyway.'

'You didna get *that* blush upstairs, Thirza Gourlay! Not unless that Joe Dan was up there wi' ye!'

'Mary!' Thirza protested with a laugh. 'No, I met him outside.'

'Ye'd better mind what I told ye about that one, lassie.'

In the dining room Mrs Linton was busy counting out fifty of everything. 'He said forty-eight, but we'll have fifty ready, just to be sure,' she told Thirza.

'Who said, Mrs Linton?'

'Mr Elliot, dear. Mr Duke Elliot, poor chap.'

'What's the matter with him?'

'He was a happily married man until last year when he took his wife and children to Carlisle. They all caught a dreadful fever there and died – all except him. He lives in Allison's Bank all alone, now. Do you know it?'

'I don't know any other houses except this one and our little cottage, Mrs Linton,' Thirza said, counting out fifty cups and saucers, and laying them on one of the sideboards. 'Where is it?'

'Over the main road, straight down Lovers' Lane and you're there. It's the big house down by the sea. He says he has so much hospitality to return that this is the best way to do it. Thirza, do you think you could come back for an extra hour or two this evening, and give us a hand? Mr Linton will see that you're well paid for it.'

'Of course I will.'

'Then I think you should run home now and tell your mother.'

'She might come too, if I ask her. She never gets out.'

'That would be better still, Thirza. Tell her I would be very thankful for her help in here. There's still the stagecoach to attend to as well, you know.' Mrs Linton was beginning to get flustered.

There were ten carriages crowding the drive that night when Thirza and Ruth arrived at Gretna Hall and donned their white pinafores. Mr Linton was receiving the guests and showing them to the tables in the dining room. It all looked beautiful, Thirza thought, standing with her back to the wall and admiring the posies of snowdrops and primroses she had managed to find for the little vases on all the tables. Ruth stood at the wall opposite. The party was about to begin.

Last of all a tall, fair and very handsome gentleman arrived. Everyone clapped when they saw him. He smiled and sat down at the top table where another gentleman and two ladies were waiting for him.

'Duke Elliot,' Mr Linton whispered to Thirza. 'He's going to say a few words to his guests, and then you and Ruth can start serving the soup.'

Thirza sincerely hoped her mother would come out of her trance by that time. She was gazing at Mr Elliot as if stunned.

Mr Linton, acting as Master of Ceremonies, rang his silver bell. When the guests had stopped chattering, he announced that their host wished to say a few words of welcome. Duke Elliot stood up, dressed immaculately in narrow-fitting grey trousers, a well-cut grey striped coat and a white shirt with a frothy lace jabot. He thanked them charmingly, even boyishly, for accepting his invitation to come to Gretna Hall that night.

Something didn't seem to ring quite true, thought Thirza. All the guests were dressed with as much style as their host, all were obviously affluent and, in her eyes, quite old. Forty, at least, older even than her mother. True, Mr Elliot didn't look that age, but there was a solidity, a slight thickening of his frame, that told her he was no spring chicken. So what was he trying to achieve?

'It was an inspiration to ask you to come here,' he assured them. 'The menu at Allison's Bank cannot compare with Gretna Hall's.'

There was some sympathetic laughter at that, and a few ladies murmured, 'Ahhh . . . Poor soul . . .'

'Neither can my wine-cellar, I'm afraid,' he went on with a grin that was as attractively crooked as it was brilliantly white – and there it was again, that little-boy-lost appeal which, for some reason, grated on Thirza's nerves. He was definitely touting for sympathy. She wondered if this party was the sprat to catch a mackerel. Were these people a lot richer than he was, perhaps? Was that why he wanted them on his side?

'So, landlord,' he turned to Mr Linton, his voice rising, 'keep it flowing! All I ask, ladies and gentlemen, is that you eat, drink and be merry!' Then he paused. He lowered his voice dramatically. 'God knows, life is short enough . . .'

There was the tiniest pause, and then he recovered. He was smiling at them again. 'It's friends like you who chase all the black clouds away. Please enjoy tonight! Can I count on you?'

'Yes, yes, yes!' they shouted, and clapped as he sat down. And then, since he had very effectively broken any ice that there had been by his sheer charm, the chattering rose to a controlled roar.

To Thirza's disgust, Mr Linton assigned Ruth to serve the top tables near Mr Elliot, and waved her to the other end of the dining room. The soup came and went, and then the dainty plaits of white fish in a piquant creamy sauce, with bottles of white wine emptying at an alarming rate. Mr Linton moved about, re-filling glasses, clearly delighted that Mr Elliot's guests were taking him at his word.

As Thirza was carrying through the gravy boats for the roast beef and Yorkshire puddings, she overheard a snippet of conversation at one of her tables. '. . . a well-known fact that he was tired of her and her parcel of brats, anyway,' declared an acid-faced lady. 'George!' she snapped. 'Keep your feet to yourself!'

'How's it going?' Mary Bryson asked anxiously, mopping her brow in the heat, when Thirza got back to the kitchen.

'Well, they're on to red wine now. Are there any more roast potatoes?'

'Three more tins in the oven.' Mary wrapped her hands in a thick cloth and opened the oven door. Clouds of fatty steam billowed out as she set the tins down on the table. 'And I've had the dishes warming.'

'Mary,' Thirza said as they speared the sizzling golden brown potatoes onto the serving dishes, 'tell me! What do you know about Mr Elliot?'

'Not much, dearie, except nobody knows where he gets his money from. It certainly isn't from any work that he does. He just rides around on that horse of his.'

'And what about his wife?'

'Oh,' Mary said, fanning herself, 'everyone knew they didn't get on. They fought like cat and dog, and she always came off the worse o' it. It must ha'e been a merciful relief to him when she died, her and her spoiled brats wi' her!'

Thirza sped around offering more roast potatoes until she reached the top table, and Mr Elliot's party.

'No, thank you,' they all declined.

'I've had more than an elegant sufficiency,' one of the ladies smiled. 'Tell the cook it was divine, truly divine.'

Ruth stepped forward to clear away their meat plates and Thirza retreated, far from happy at the way Mr Elliot was smiling at her mother, and including her in their conversation.

The guests lingered over their coffee until they heard strains of music coming from the ballroom. Thirza, Ruth and Mary Bryson washed and dried the dishes in the kitchen, working efficiently until the last coffee cup was safely put away, and then they, too, fell under the spell of the music.

'Och, we could go to the door and just peep in,' Mary said. 'We could keep out of sight, I'm sure.'

But they hadn't been there five minutes before Thirza saw Mr Elliot advancing across the ballroom floor towards them. He wouldn't be interested in Mary – and her nearly sixty years old. And he wouldn't be interested in a fifteen-year-old maid either, Thirza thought. No, it was Ruth he had in his sights.

'Come away, Mother,' Thirza tugged at her sleeve. 'We can't go in there,' she said urgently. 'We aren't guests. We're only the servants. It's time to go home.'

18

OVER the following week relations were a little strained between mother and daughter. Thirza was bursting to air her opinion of Mr Elliot but, the trouble was, Ruth didn't give her the opportunity. She was in one of her frosty moods, the moods the whole Gourlay family had dreaded in St Fillans. Nerves were stretched.

They both became more and more edgy until the following Sunday, Thirza's day off. It was a fine spring morning, and a great relief to get out of the house and go to the Kirk. Afterwards they came out into glorious sunshine.

'Oh, don't let's go home yet, Mother,' Thirza pleaded. 'Let's go for a walk instead. I've been here all this time and never seen the sea. Have you?'

'How could I? I've had my nose to the grindstone since ever I came,' Ruth snapped, 'and Sunday or no Sunday there's plenty to do when I get back home today.'

No, Ruth had never had much fun, Thirza reflected, quite startled to find out that she was rebelling – now, at her age.

'Is it far?' Ruth asked impatiently.

'Not according to Mrs Linton. She told me the way. Come on, Mother! You'd like to see the sea again, wouldn't you?'

'I would that, lassie,' Ruth sighed, and suddenly the little rift between them disappeared.

Thirza took her mother's arm as they walked on downhill,

159

then up and over a little rise to arrive at the main road from England to Scotland.

'We've to cross over and go down Lovers' Lane. I suppose this is it.' Thirza led the way down a twisting path where the hawthorns almost met over their heads and on either side the verges were lush with brilliantly green grass dotted with vivid forget-me-nots and huge yellow celandines.

'Be careful, Thirza. There must be plenty of water somewhere near for flowers to grow like that.'

'There is. There's a very deep ditch under the grass at this side, and another at the other side,' Thirza looked to see. 'You can hear the water tinkling.'

'Anyone could drown in them, then, and never be seen again!' Ruth warned, her voice sharp with irritation.

Thirza tried to diagnose it. Was it because she was frightened she would lose the one remaining member of her family in another drowning? No, Thirza suspected there was something else, and it was a secret.

They walked on to the end of the lane and there, just as Mrs Linton had said, stood a large house alone, almost at the edge of the sea. A river, which they found out later was called the Sark, ran behind it into the estuary of the Solway.

This must be Allison's Bank. No smoke came from its chimneys. The windows were blank and uninviting and the door was firmly closed. It was a secretive house in Thirza's eyes, and she hurried her mother past it. With any luck Ruth wouldn't know it belonged to Mr Elliot.

The road broadened in a sharp right hand bend and then turned in a sharp left hand bend, and now the sweep of a little bay curved before them. The rippled sand was silver, the sea was very blue and there wasn't a rock to be seen except right round at the other end, where there was another house. It stood on a tiny peninsula, circled by the sea.

'Well,' Ruth looked at it, 'it's not like St Fillan, but oh! It's glorious to be at the sea again, to feel the breezes and smell the salt!' Nobody else was there, but then it was one o'clock by that time, when most people would be eating their Sunday dinner and, in a totally uncharacteristic fit of abandon Ruth sat down and took off her shoes and stockings. 'Let's just dip our toes in,' she smiled.

Like two children, Thirza and her mother laughed and splashed each other all the way around the bay until they arrived below the house which they saw now was a farmhouse. They stopped giggling long enough to put their shoes and stockings back on again.

'That's a big farm,' Ruth said.

'What do you think of that strange little cottage stuck on the side of it, Mother?' Thirza peered all round it. 'Look! Oh, look, Mother! It's built on top of a cave!'

'Built on top of a cave?' Ruth echoed, when two things happened at once. Joe Dan Linton stepped out of the strange little cottage, and a woman came out of the farmhouse, carrying covered dishes and a milk-pail.

Joe Dan went to take the dishes from her. 'What have I done today, Mrs Bell,' he laughed. 'Have I been a bad boy, to be banished from your table?'

'Don't pay any attention to him,' Mrs Bell smiled at Thirza and Ruth, repeating his own mother's words. 'He usually gets fed in the house, but when I saw you coming, I guessed you must be friends of his and took some food out for you. You can have a picnic on a lovely day like this, up here on the grass.'

'You're a good woman,' Joe Dan hugged her, to her obvious delight. 'She's like a mother to me,' he told Thirza and Ruth.

'Get away with you, Joe Dan Linton! You've got a very good mother of your own! You should behave yourself and help her up at the Hall. But that's the trouble,' she smiled and sighed as she went away. 'He likes it better down here.'

Thirza introduced the black sheep of the Linton family to her mother before she began to tease him. 'So you've got a second mother, have you, Joe Dan? What's she given you for our picnic? I'm dying of hunger!'

'Thirza Gourlay!' Ruth laughed and tried to frown at the same time.

She was looking very pretty, Thirza thought, with her shiny brown hair blown down with the soft sea-breezes, and a flush in her cheeks at last.

'Oh, you needn't bother, Mrs Gourlay,' Joe Dan assured her, uncovering a plate of cold roast beef. 'I know Thirza of old.'

Laughing, Thirza took the cloth off a dish of hot potatoes.

'*Hot* tatties?' Ruth asked.

'And on a Sunday, too,' Joe Dan smiled at her. 'But we're all scandalous down here on the Solway shore . . . Isn't that so, Duke?' he shouted over his shoulder and, to Thirza's absolute horror, Mr Elliot came out of Joe Dan's cottage where he must have been all the time. 'Isn't that right? We all live in sin here. We even boil tatties on a Sunday. Have a couple, man, and a slice of Mrs Bell's beef.'

Mr Elliot sat down on the grass beside them and accepted a share. 'If this is called living in sin, I'm all for it,' he said, looking straight into Ruth's eyes.

The bantering went on. Everything the two men said seemed to have a double meaning and the longer it went on, and the more masculine and crude the humour, the more disgusted Thirza became. She realised that Mr Elliot, the stronger character of the two, was the instigator of it, egging on Joe Dan.

Her disapproval showed on her face, changing swiftly to anger when it became obvious that women were the butt of their jokes. It was insulting to the lady that Thirza considered her mother to be. She glared at Mr Elliot and frowned heavily at her mother.

Mr Elliot grinned back, revelling in her discomfiture and Ruth, oblivious to the undercurrents, ignored her daughter. She just went on smiling in that soft, silly way into Mr Elliot's eyes.

The sea kept washing in with a sigh and then whispering out again. The sun kept on shining, and a shiver of fear ran straight down Thirza's spine.

19

I<small>T</small> was the speed of the next development that took her completely by surprise. She came home from Gretna Hall a few days after the picnic to find Mr Elliot sitting on the couch in their living room.

'Thirza,' Ruth said. 'Mr Elliot has come to offer me a position. He's asking me to be his housekeeper.'

'Allison's Bank has been an empty, lonely house for over a year now,' he sighed, 'and I'm not very good at looking after myself.'

There he was! At it again! He was looking for sympathy. Thirza suddenly discovered the two pet hates she had in this world – men with sandy hair and men with cold green eyes – and this one had both.

'Of course,' she addressed her mother and ignored Mr Elliot, 'you've refused.'

'I'll see,' Ruth said, flushing. 'I'll think aboot it, Mr Elliot.'

'Don't be too long thinking, then,' he stood up and held out his hand to shake Ruth's. In Thirza's opinion they were shaking hands for far too long. It was as if they both had glue on their palms. 'Goodbye, Mrs Gourlay. Please put me out of my misery soon.'

'*Mother!*' Thirza said as soon as the door was shut.

'I ken it's sudden-like,' Ruth sat down suddenly herself, 'but I *hate* that loom, Thirza! Ye dinna ken how much I hate it. Weaving, weaving, weaving, morning, noon and night! Is

163

that all there's ever going to be for me? When do I ever get oot?'

'Will you get out any oftener as that man's housekeeper?' Thirza asked sternly. 'And besides, if you give up the loom, you give up the cottage. It *is* a weaver's cottage, after all. We'll be homeless.'

'Mr Elliot expects me to live in, Thirza.'

'Live in? You mean live alone in that house, with that man? Oh, Mother . . .' She looked at Ruth with disapproval written all over her face.

'He says you can come, too.'

'That must have been easy for him to say. He knows fine well that I would never go. He had that well-thought out, believe me,' Thirza said bitterly, her dislike of the man flaring into full-blown hatred. 'Worse still, you seem very anxious to go yourself, that's all I can say!'

'Yes!' Ruth snapped, her patience running out and her temper rising swiftly. 'I am! It's been my life, looking after a house, and a man. At least it was until I lost yer father. And all *I* can say, Thirza Gourlay, is that I hope ye never lose yer man, if ye ever get one. Ye'll ken then, what it's like trying to live alane!'

'You've got *me*,' Thirza said, wrapping her shawl about her shoulders again, 'but that doesn't count, does it?'

'Where are ye going?'

'To see Mr Linton. He's the agent for these cottages, isn't he?'

Thirza flung out, the night air fanning her burning cheeks. So *that* was it! Now she knew the secret of her mother's unhappiness. She was missing her man, and she simply wanted another, whichever way she could get one. All the pieces had slotted into place, the changes she'd observed in Ruth, her moods, her lightning tempers, her weariness. She just wanted a man to look after.

But some other bit of the mystery still remained – why? Her father and Andra had been nothing to Ruth but two loads of worry. Yet here she was again, determined to take on what Thirza could see would be the biggest worry of them all. *Mr Elliot.* And Mr Elliot wanted a fast answer, so the sooner she could speak to Mr Linton, the better. For her own sake as well as Ruth's.

Mr Linton might have been surprised to see his maidservant back so soon, and quite distraught too, but he remained as urbane as ever. Thirza believed now, after watching the polished and affable way he dealt with so many nervous runaway couples and their furious parents, that there was no human or emotional crisis that he couldn't smooth over.

'Sit down, my dear,' they were in the kitchen, empty now that Mary Bryson had finished her work and gone home, 'and tell me, what can I do for you?'

'It's my mother. She's going to be Mr Elliot's housekeeper. Does that mean we must give up the cottage?'

Mr Linton looked at her gravely. 'That depends on you, Thirza.'

'How?'

'There's a minimum quantity of linen you would have to weave yourself to hold on to the tenancy. But there's no need to worry, my dear. If your mother goes to work at Allison's Bank there's always a room here somewhere in Gretna Hall for you.'

'That's very kind of you, Mr Linton. But you see, I would want to hold on to the cottage if I could, to keep a home open for my mother. I'll do my best at the weaving, to see to it.'

'Well, Thirza, I'll try my best, too. Because you also work here in the Hall for me, I'll try and get you a special concession – but remember, I'm only a very small cog in the wheel of the linen industry, if you can even call me that. I'm only the local agent.'

'I thought you had all the power,' Thirza sighed.

'Only in Springfield,' Mr Linton smiled. 'There is a network of men responsible all the way up to the top, to the Earl of Hopetoun. He's the owner.'

The Earl of Hopetoun.

Jordi used to tell her about the Earl, and his life at Hopetoun House. Oh, how she was missing Jordi! He would never have put her in the position her own mother was putting her in now. He would have been protecting her instead, as a true brother would. A pang of longing to see him again blazed through her – so fierce and so passionate that it was enough to make her legs feel weak all the way home.

*　　*　　*

165

It was a very sad day for Thirza when her mother packed her bag to leave. Ruth took a last look around the cottage, but it was a look which did not deceive her daughter in the least. There was too much of a sparkle in her eyes.

Thirza carried her bag down Lovers' Lane. All the April showers had made the bluebells burst into bloom. They were so beautiful she longed to simply lie down amongst them, close to their fresh, delicate scent and forget that any of this was happening. Her feet faltered when they reached the end of the Lane and Allison's Bank came into view.

'This is it, then, Mother,' she said. 'I see he's got the door open for you. I'll leave you here.'

'Ye're not coming in wi' me?'

'No.'

'Ye'll come and see me?' Without waiting for an answer, Ruth took her bag, smiled and almost ran down the path and into Allison's Bank. The door slammed shut behind her. Turning to go back up to Springfield, Thirza saw the bluebells in Lovers' Lane as just a blue haze through her tears. 'We're all sinners here, down at the Solway.' Joe Dan's words rang in her ears for some unaccountable reason.

As soon as she reached the cottage again she sat down on the stool in front of the loom, Sunday or no Sunday. Her fingers busied themselves, and the shuttle flew furiously; and by bedtime she had woven the minimum requirement of linen Mr Linton had stipulated.

This would be her lot from now on, working every day as a servant at Gretna Hall and weaving every spare minute to keep a roof over her head and her mother's, when she returned. Thirza had no doubt that she would come back.

Well, she would do it, she vowed defiantly. Duke Elliot may have got the better of her mother, but *he would never get the better of her*. With her mind determined on that, she awoke quite refreshed and ready for work on Monday morning.

She gave Ruth exactly one month to settle in to her new life. For three Sundays now her mother had not put in an appearance at the Kirk. On the fourth Sunday Thirza walked past Gretna Old Church and went straight down to the Solway. She met nobody, from which she gathered that her mother wasn't going to attend the service today, either. Summoning up all her courage, she arrived at the door of Allison's Bank, and knocked.

Nobody answered. She knocked and knocked. It was now eleven o'clock and they must be up, but the door remained stubbornly closed. It was something Thirza had never expected and, wondering what to do next, she wandered around the bay to Sarkfoot Farm without conscious decision.

Joe Dan must be out. His door was open and, knocking on it and getting no answer there, either, she peeped inside. What she saw filled her with dismay. Such few possessions that he had were overturned and tumbled into the middle of the mud floor. Empty bottles, and even kegs, were everywhere, on a ramshackle mantelpiece, scattered about the miserable room which was all the cottage comprised. Over all this squalor lay layers of dust and dirt and an atmosphere of hopelessness.

It was not what she would have expected of the cheerful, jaunty Joe Dan Linton, and she stood for a moment on the grass verge outside his door before she made up her mind to go around to the farmhouse and speak to Mrs Bell.

Mrs Bell, her short frame quivering with fat, was bustling about her kitchen all on her own. 'Mr Bell and the girls are out,' she said. 'Would you take a cup of tea and a cake?'

'I really came down here to see my mother,' Thirza explained, 'but I can't get an answer from Allison's Bank.'

Mrs Bell stared at her. 'Your mother's gone to Allison's Bank? What for?'

'To be Mr Elliot's housekeeper.'

'Oh, dear!' said Mrs Bell, frowning and tucking in to one of her own queen cakes thoughtfully.

'You don't like him either?'

'I do not. I don't like the influence he has over poor Joe Dan, for one thing. Sometimes they're as thick as thieves, those two, and goodness knows Joe is bad enough on his own.'

'How's that, Mrs Bell?'

'Has nobody told you, dearie? Joe Dan drinks. He's a hard drinker at the best of times, but when he goes on one of his sprees he's a danger to himself and everyone else around him.'

But it wasn't about Joe Dan that Thirza wanted to speak. Mrs Bell would know a lot about Mr Elliot. She was his nearest neighbour. Their houses stood opposite each other, at either end of the bay.

'Have you known Mr Elliot long, Mrs Bell?'

'Oh, dearie me, yes! He came here first with his wife when she was just a bride, and a bonnie wee thing she was! She lost her looks, though, when the babies came,' the farmer's wife bit into another queen cake even more reflectively.

'How many babies?'

'Four, all boys — and here we are with no boys! Just four girls! Ach, the world is poorly parted! But they're all grown up now,' she digressed. 'Mr Bell says our four girls are as good as two strong men, anyway. They help him with all the work on the farm . . . But, to get back to the Elliots. The youngest was only two when they went to Carlisle and got the fever. At least, Duke Elliot *said* he took them to Carlisle, although we never saw them going, and that was unusual! Between the six of us, the Bell family see most things that go on down here.'

Feeling ill, Thirza wished she'd never asked. To cover her alarm, she went back to the subject of Joe Dan. 'I couldn't get an answer from Joe Dan, either, Mrs Bell. The door was open and I looked inside to find him, but he wasn't there. All I saw was the mess.'

'Oh, dear,' said Mrs Bell again, looking anxious. 'We'd better go and have a look for him. Anything could have happened.' They laid down their teacups and when they got outside they heard a man's moans and groans. 'That's him!' she said. 'He's down in the cave. It's too steep for me to climb down into. Will you have a look, Thirza?'

He was sitting with his head in his hands in a rowing boat.

'What's wrong?' she asked. 'What are you doing in here?'

'Oh, Christ . . . It's you, Thirza. I'm a bit the worse for wear . . . As you can see,' he added pathetically, squinting up at her. Just for a moment, he reminded her of Mr Elliot. Now she saw what Mrs Bell meant.

Her sharp eyes looked around the cave and saw that it took a bend to the right. Cautiously, she made her way along the narrow pathway until she came to the bend. Around it the cave opened up into a cavern. It was all shelved, and on each shelf were stacked kegs of liquor, bales in sacking and boxes and bags of every description. She beat a hasty retreat and came back to gaze down at Joe Dan again.

'My God . . .' she said. 'You're a smuggler! I thought those days were gone for ever!'

She wondered if the Bells were aware of it. They must be. Mrs Bell had just told her that they knew about most things down here on the Solway.

'There will always be smugglers.' Joe Dan laughed and came to life. 'There's plenty of us still around here, anyway,' he said, climbing out of his rowing boat and joining her on the narrow ledge, 'and not too far from here, either.'

The leer with which he said it scared Thirza. She was very glad he was behind her and not in front, to block her way back out of the cave. To make sure he didn't think of grabbing her from behind, she shouted up to Mrs Bell.

'He's all right. He's coming up.'

Mrs Bell's anxious, kindly face appeared above them. 'I've been in and tidied up your house as best I could,' she scolded. 'Now you'd better come inside the farmhouse with me and get yourself tidied up before Mr Bell sees you. You'll be getting thrown out of that cottage if you don't mind!'

'Before you go, Joe Dan,' Thirza said, 'I came down to see my mother, but there was no reply from Allison's Bank. Have you seen her lately?'

'Och, Duke Elliot will be coming out of the drink about now,' he said. 'He was with me last night.'

Doing what? Was he a smuggler, too? Were they all in it? And her mother, was she now unwittingly in the middle of it all? Greatly alarmed, Thirza saw that she should tread carefully until she knew more. In the meantime, she had better say nothing.

'He and Ruth will be otherwise occupied, I should think,' Joe Dan added with a snigger.

'I don't know what you mean.'

'You'll find out.'

'Oh, I'll find out, all right,' Thirza said, thinking that it was now imperative that her quarrel with her mother must be patched up at the first opportunity.

'You would do better to mind your own business and live your own life now, Thirza. Your mother is with Duke Elliot for life,' Joe Dan viciously kicked a bottle Mrs Bell had missed outside his door.

It splintered into shards, into dangerous pieces of glass. Thirza gazed at them, glittering now in the sunshine after the rain. The bottle had shattered, like her life, into splinters.

20

SUNDAY after Sunday Thirza tried unsuccessfully to see her mother, and she always went on to the farmhouse, in case the Bells had any news of her.

'I've never even seen her, dearie,' Mrs Bell said, with no appearance of concern. 'But if anything was wrong we'd be the first to know. Sit down and stop worrying. Ye're just in time for a cup of tea and a scone.'

Over the weeks Thirza got to know the Bell family quite well. All Mrs Bell's interests lay in her home, her family and the farm. The girls lived for the outdoors and, as for Mr Bell, Thirza became convinced that he knew nothing about the smuggling. Joe Dan wouldn't be in his cottage, if he did. Mr Bell was absolutely honest, and Thirza – frightened for her mother's sake – did not speak about it.

Then, one Sunday in June when she had gone, as usual, to Allison's Bank, the door opened and out came Ruth. Thirza could hardly believe how much she'd changed. She looked ten years younger. Her eyes had lost that sad look, her skin glowed and she was the picture of radiant happiness.

'Come in and visit me, lassie,' she said. 'Duke isn't here. He's gone to Edinburgh to see his father. He won't be back for two or three days.'

It was too much for Thirza's curiosity. She followed her mother into the kitchen, discovering that the door that faced onto the road must be the back door. As they explored the house together, she found that this was true, and the rooms downstairs must once have been quite impressive, although they were shabby now. It reminded her of one of the questions she wanted to ask.

'How does Mr Elliot make his money, Mother?'

'Och, he doesn't tell his housekeeper things like that! All I ken is that he goes to Carlisle three times a week, I suppose on business, and to see his father once a month. He aye seems to have plenty o' money when he comes back from Edinburgh.'

'Is he rich?'

'I dinna rightly ken, Thirza,' Ruth said, her face clouding over for a minute. 'Now, do ye want to see the upstairs?'

'I might as well, since I'm here.'

'It was all gey dirty when I came first,' Ruth said, obviously proud of her housekeeping. 'Ye could hardly see oot o' the windows. This one looks right over the Solway,' she stopped at the top of the stairs to gaze out at the view.

It gave Thirza the opportunity to glance, quickly, through the door which was a little ajar, at the one room her mother had neglected to show her upstairs. There was only one bed in it, the Scottish version of a double bed, the three quarter marriage bed.

No, she thought, her mother wasn't only Mr Elliot's housekeeper . . .

Ruth had noticed nothing. 'We'll go back down and have a fly cup,' she said. 'Ye'll stay to yer dinner, after that?'

'It's fine to see you again, Mother,' Thirza said. 'Yes, I'll stay.' She might find out more, she thought, and roamed about downstairs while Ruth made the tea. 'Have you ever thought there's a queer smell in this house?'

'Och, it's coming from his wine cellar.'

'How can wine make a smell like that?'

'You dinna understand, Thirza. It's the sea ye're smelling. He says it comes in and floods the cellar at high tide.'

'Have you ever been down to have a look?'

'He keeps the door locked. He says it's dangerous.'

'Well, the tide's right out just now. Will you come for a paddle with me after we have this tea? We could go around the outside of this house and find out where the sea comes in.'

'Ay, Thirza,' her mother sighed, 'ye never change. Aye wanting to find oot things. But I'll come wi' ye. A paddle would be just the thing in this heat,' and before noon they had found the grill the sea washed through. It was covered with drying, stinking seaweed.

'What did I tell ye?' Ruth said.

The rest of June and all of July passed before Thirza saw her mother again. It was almost as if Duke Elliot kept her a prisoner in Allison's Bank. Although nothing was said, Thirza understood that her mother didn't want to speak to her or anyone else unless he was away. When she saw Ruth this time she wasn't almost dancing on air like before. This time Thirza thought she was limpimg.

'What's wrong with your leg?' she asked her.

'Nothing. I'm getting fatter, that's all, and my leg's feeling it,' Ruth flushed and looked away, but not before Thirza saw tears in her eyes and a strange little smile on her lips.

'Mother, tell me! What's the matter?'

But Ruth shook her head and refused to discuss it. Of all the moods Thirza had seen her in, this was the strangest.

By the time August arrived, her limp was much more pronounced.

'It's nothing,' Ruth repeated. 'I've had this trouble before. The last time was sixteen years ago, and it went away then. It'll go away again this time, too.'

'And what are those red marks on both sides of your neck?' Thirza persisted.

'Och, that! That was the neck of a blouse getting too tight for me. I've thrown it away since then.'

Thirza didn't believe her. The red marks looked like fingerprints, like weals made by fingers. 'Have you been to the doctor?' she asked.

'No, of course not. There's nothing wrong with me,' Ruth assured her. 'Now, come into the house. There's something I want to give ye for yer birthday, and I may not see you again before that.' She unwrapped a parcel lying on the kitchen table. Inside it was a petticoat with a deep hem.

'Oh, thank you, Mother! It's just what I need,' Thirza tried it up against herself, 'and it's got a lovely rustle.'

'Ay, it's a very special petticoat, that one, Thirza,' Her mother told her. 'Don't let anything happen to it. The rustle's coming from weights in the hem.'

'It doesn't feel heavy. What kind of weights?'

'Paper ones. Banknotes. There's a hundred pounds of the money I got for the cottage in Saint Fillan. Then there's fifty pounds that belongs to Jordi, his money for the fishing, and twenty pounds is what I saved for you out of your wages from the Jollys.'

'But that's all the money you've got in the world!' Thirza exclaimed.

'I've kept a wee bit for mysel', dinna worry. It's just that ye were in Shetland on yer fifteenth birthday. The money is for that and yer sixteenth coming up. I want ye to have it *now*. I want it oot o' this house. Now, Thirza, dinna argue wi' me . . .'

'I'm not. But what about washing it when it gets dirty?'

'Just wash it. The banknotes are washed already, and ironed. Then I rolled them loosely and sewed them inside the hem.'

'I didn't know you could wash banknotes, Mother?'

'Well, ye can. They get very dirty and smelly passing through hands. I couldn't put them inside yer petticoat in that state!' Ruth looked shocked at the very idea.

On the way back home with her parcel Thirza thought of everything her mother had said with a glow in her heart. Ruth had missed her when she was marooned in Shetland, then. She was the best mother in the world. But why had she wanted the money out of that house, now – today? And how did she get those marks on her neck? And sixteen years ago, when she last had a sore leg, wouldn't she have been pregnant at the time?

Thirza hesitated on the way up to Springfield, in two minds as to whether she should turn back or not. But in the end she decided her mother wouldn't like any more fuss than she'd made already.

She was much too disturbed to do any weaving that night, nor could she concentrate on subsequent evenings. Finally, at the end of August she could bear the suspense no longer. She would have to go and make sure that her mother was all right. Anxiously, in a rising wind, Thirza made her way down to Allison's Bank and hammered at the door. Of course she got no answer. This time Thirza was furiously angry.

The normally placid waters of the Solway were becoming

angry, too, with the wind throwing them up over the sands in great brown billows. It howled and tore at her shawl, but *somebody* must know something of her mother, she thought desperately, and ran round the bay to the farmhouse.

It was all lit up when she got there.

'Oh, my God, Thirza!' Mrs Bell gasped when she saw her. 'It's been a terrible day! Joe Dan and Duke Elliot were drinking hard the whole day next door, and now they've been swearing at each other and fighting and shouting fit to wake the dead!'

'What about?'

'I've long suspected it,' Mr Bell said grimly, struggling into his coat. 'Duke Elliot has been riding to Carlisle and the English ports. I suspect he is in a smuggling ring. No wonder he always has plenty to drink! He has entirely corrupted poor Joe Dan. As far as we could make out, the quarrel was about money.'

'It's always about money,' Thirza said wearily.

'Duke Elliot staggered back to Allison's Bank,' Mr Bell added. 'We saw him go. And there's not a sound from Joe Dan now.'

'We'll have to find out if he's all right,' Mrs Bell said. 'I promised his mother.'

Half an hour later, Mr Bell laid down his night lantern with a thud on the kitchen table and sank into a chair. 'It's a proper storm,' he said. 'I could hardly keep my feet, but I've searched high and low, and Joe Dan is nowhere to be seen. He's gone.'

'I hope my mother's all right,' Thirza said. 'Have you seen anything of her? She was limping badly the last time I saw her.'

The Bell family stared at her dumbly for long uncomfortable seconds.

'Limping, was she?' Mrs Bell glanced at her husband.

'And she had red marks on her neck.'

'I wish you'd told us sooner,' Mr Bell said gravely.

'Well, I've got to go and try knocking on the door again. Perhaps she'll open it this time.'

'You're going nowhere!' Mr Bell stood up, his tall figure blocking her way.

His wife grasped Thirza's arm. 'Listen to it, lassie! You wouldn't get ten yards in that. By tomorrow the wind will have dropped, and then I'll come with you. You'll stay here the night.'

'You can never trust the sands down here, even without a storm to shift them. They're constantly moving, you know, Thirza,' Mr Bell said, when Thirza continued to look determined about leaving. 'Unless you know them they can swallow you up. So tomorrow I'll be coming with you as well, to see you safely across. If that bugger Elliot won't allow your mother to answer you, I'll soon flush him out.'

In the morning he led them across the bay, pointing out the damp, bubbling danger spots in the sands until they reached Allison's Bank. There was no smoke coming out of the chimneys. The house looked dead. Then the door opened and, to their horror, they saw Ruth trying to crawl out on her hands and knees.

'MOTHER!' Thirza screamed.

Mr Bell lifted her up gently, took her inside and laid her down on a couch. 'Stay with her,' he said grimly. 'Don't move her any more. I'll ride as fast as I can for the doctor.'

'Where's Duke Elliot?' Thirza asked.

'If he's in this house, I'll find him.' Mrs Bell went to search.

Ruth was struggling to breathe. Terrified, Thirza watched the pink froth bubbling from her mother's mouth. Ruth opened her eyes, put up her hand to Thirza's cheek and tried to smile.

'He's not here,' Mrs Bell came back to report as Ruth's laboured breathing changed to a rattle.

Instinctively, Thirza put an arm under her shoulders and lifted up her head a little. For a minute it seemed to work, and then her head lolled to one side and the terrible noises stopped.

Ruth was dead in her arms.

Mr Bell and Dr Graham slithered off their horses and rushed into Allison's Bank. The doctor took one look at Ruth and asked Mr and Mrs Bell to go into another room.

'You're her daughter?' he asked Thirza, and she nodded dumbly. 'I want you to stay while I examine her. Help me to take off her clothes.' They saw that every part of her body except her hands and face was discoloured with bruises, both old and new. 'Good God!' he muttered and shook his head. 'The savage brute . . .'

Fifteen minutes later they had made Ruth decent again, and were waiting until the undertakers should arrive. Dr Graham put an arm around Thirza's shaking shoulders.

'I can see she was beaten to death,' she wept, 'but what made the pink froth come out of her mouth? Why couldn't she get her breath at the end?'

'Because he must have punched her ribs clean through her lungs,' he answered. 'It's the worst case of abuse I've ever seen. By the way . . .'

'Yes, sir?'

'Your mother was four or five months pregnant. But that is for your ears only. Nobody else needs to know.'

'I dreaded as much, Dr Graham,' Thirza sobbed.

After the funeral, Mr and Mrs Bell – with the Linton's approval – insisted that she stay at Sarkfoot Farm for at least a week. In a daze of shock, Thirza could do nothing else. She got up in the mornings, and went to bed at night, but in between it was all a blur. She spoke to Mr and Mrs Bell and their four daughters quite rationally, but afterwards she couldn't recall a single word of any conversation they had.

She re-lived the past, from her earliest memories of Ruth right up to her death. She remembered how Ruth had never failed her, how she had always stood by her daughter, until her own personal dilemma – her need for a man, as Thirza now understood – had overtaken her and brought her to this sorry end.

There were always pictures in front of her eyes, of Ruth out at the washing lines at St Fillan, Ruth spitting on the flat-iron to test its heat, Ruth peering out of the window, waiting and watching for her men to come home from the sea. The visions and the memories were endless.

Mourning Ruth, Thirza wept. And gradually, during those lost, sad days in Sarkfoot, a volcano was erupting within her. It spewed over and hardened into a deadly resolve. One day, God willing, she would see Duke Elliot again.

Then she would kill him.

21

FINALLY calm, and rational once more, Thirza thanked the Bell family for all their kindness to her and to her mother. 'And now, I must go back to Springfield,' she said.

'You'll come down on Sundays and share our dinner?' Mrs Bell made her promise.

'Your days in the weavers' cottage are over, Thirza,' Mr Linton insisted when she arrived at Gretna Hall. 'There's no need now to struggle to hold on to it, is there?'

'No, sir.'

'I'll put a bed and some furniture in the room with the secret compartment. Would you like that?'

'Yes, thank you, Mr Linton,' Thirza smiled bleakly and went about her chores. Somehow, although she wasn't quite able to work out why, she felt she was being manipulated.

The storm on the night before Ruth's death was a mere breeze in comparison with the equinoctial gale that hit the Solway Firth in September, when the bore rushed up the Firth like fifty galloping horses, overpowering everything in its path. It began on Wednesday, and it only abated on Saturday, allowing Thirza to pick her way on Sunday through the debris thrown high amongst the tussocks of grass above the sands.

'Are you all right?' she asked Mrs Bell, when she finally reached the farm.

'Mercy me, lass! We've seen all this before! I'm roasting pork, and I've made the apple sauce. Now sit down there,' she pushed Thirza into a chair at the fireside, 'and let's hear all the news.'

'Not much, Mrs Bell. Just the usual weddings. Mr and Mrs Linton haven't had a visit from Joe Dan for over a month. They wanted me to ask you if you've seen him recently?'

'No . . .' Mrs Bell was starting to make the gravy when Beenie, the youngest Bell daughter rushed in.

'Come quick, come quick,' she said breathlessly. 'The sands have shifted! We've found something!'

'Oh, my God,' Mrs Bell gasped when they got to the end of the tiny pier. Her husband was laying out the bodies of a woman and four children on the beach. 'God Almighty! It's Mrs Elliot and the bairns!'

Suddenly Thirza saw the whole picture. She hadn't been wrong about the smell coming from the wine cellar in Allison's Bank. Duke Elliot's wife and children must have been mouldering, half-preserved, in the sand beneath the house. The mountainous waves had obviously pushed open the grill she and Ruth had found, and flushed them out.

Mrs Bell clutched Thirza's arm. Her fat pink cheeks were now utterly blanched. 'There's someone else. Look at that arm sticking up out of that sandbank!'

'Do you think it's Duke Elliot himself, Mother?' Beenie Bell asked. 'Has he gone down as well?'

Nobody answered her. Mr Bell went with his daughters for strong ropes. Then all five lassoed the arm, lay down flat on their stomachs and began to pull.

'Why are they lying down to do it?' Thirza asked.

'Because, standing up, they would be sucked down themselves. Oh, God, look! It *is* a man!'

The Bells got the man off the sandbank and up onto the grass. Mr Bell wiped his face. 'It's not Duke Elliot. It's Joe Dan,' he said, 'and he didn't fall overboard drunk, either. First he was strangled with that wire wrapped around his neck. Then he must have been pushed out to sea by somebody else.'

'And we can all guess who *that* was,' Thirza said.

'Here are six people, all murdered by that bastard,' Mr Bell stood up. 'Well, lasses, cover them up while I go and report it.'

*   *   *

Joe Dan Linton may have been banished from his home while he was living, but now, in death, he was received back with cries of despair and grief. The uproar didn't cease while urgent arrangements were made to divert the stagecoach, and redirect the runaway lovers to one of the lesser marriage 'priests' who had set up in the Blacksmith's Shop. The whole district was combed, to no avail, for Duke Elliot, and Gretna Hall was closed to the public.

Inside, the rest of the Linton family was gathering from far and wide. Mary Bryson cooked for them, and Thirza ran and fetched and carried for them. Finally, on the night before the funeral, which was timed for three o'clock the following afternoon, she retired to her room with the secret compartment, quite exhausted.

She pulled back the panel, stepped inside the cell and walked over to the window. What on earth was she doing here, she asked herself? What had happened to all her ambitions? Was this her fate, to be a servant for ever?

In the moonlight, the first frosts were sparkling the shrubs all along the driveway, directing her eyes to the crossroads. There were three of them, one to the north and back to Fife, one to the south over the Solway and into Cumberland – or east from there into the black and haunted hills of Northumberland in England. And there was the one to the west. She didn't much care which one she would take. She was as free as a bird now to go anywhere she liked, along any road.

The road! The open road! It was calling to her.

Lunch at half past twelve the next day was a miserable affair. One by one, and two by two, the Linton relatives left the table and went to prepare themselves in soul and in dress for the sad occasion.

That was when Thirza put on the petticoat her mother had given her, packed her few possessions into an old carpet-bag and ran down to the crossroads, still undecided. They weren't just three roads, she thought.

Once again she was at a crossroads in her life.

Last night's frost had long since melted away on that golden afternoon in early October when, purely on a whim and as the fancy took her, Thirza chose the road to the west – and a very pretty road it turned out to be too, quiet and peaceful.

She walked past a white cottage with green painted windows on her left, but there was no one about. The gentle incline of the road ahead was also deserted, and then, also on her left, she passed a graveyard. Behind its gates she saw a man working. He didn't look up, and she didn't stop, because she knew already that he must be digging the grave for Joe Dan's funeral in a few hours' time.

She hurried on, and didn't feel that she'd really left Gretna behind her until she passed another small croft house and turned the corner. Soon she came to a wooden sign-post. 'River Kirtle', it said, and there before her was a narrow stream of the clearest water she had ever seen. With all the time in the world now, she climbed down to admire it.

Water weeds rooted under its stones shivered back and forth and tiny fishes darted in between the weeds. She could have kilted up her skirts and just waded across the clear shallow water of the Kirtle, but there was a bull on the opposite bank eyeing her with too much interest for her liking. So, instead, she took off her shoes and stockings, dabbled her feet in the cool water and looked about her.

She was free, and it was a wonderful feeling, one she could scarcely comprehend after her recent traumas. It was difficult to believe that now she was beholden to no one. She could just go wherever she liked, and on this quiet road there was no one to stop her. At the moment her main preoccupation was nothing more than to let her feet dry in the sunshine. She lay back, wriggling her toes in the cream and lilac clover, her only company a few drowsy bees, and revelled in it.

But, of course, this couldn't go on for ever. Thirza had been brought up by Ruth for long enough to know that there must be some purpose in life, and she had been put on this earth to work towards it. Eventually she put her stockings and shoes back on again, crossed the river by the bridge and walked into a tiny hamlet signposted Rigg. Rigg took only five minutes to travel through, the next slightly larger village of Eastriggs took only ten, and shortly afterwards she was in a third, called Dornoch.

By now, thanks to her dalliance on the banks of the Kirtle, it was getting late. The sun was beginning its descent, wreathed in wisps of trailing mist. The very old church of Dornoch looked black against the sky, and from the tall trees round it rooks swooped and cawed at her angrily for disturbing their rest.

Thirza shivered and walked on until she saw written on a white milestone in the fading light that she had travelled eight miles from Gretna, and she was now descending a hill into the town of Annan. Annan seemed to be comprised of one long street of buildings, some tall, some small, and all built out of pink sandstone.

She walked along the wide street until it narrowed to a bridge over the River Annan. By now it was almost dark, but people were converging all around her. They were heading down a path to the river. Loud music was drawing them there, and Thirza followed, worries about her next meal and where to sleep that night rapidly disappearing.

It was a fair, on one of the grassy banks bordering the river. Long sticks with torches on their ends lit up a circle of stalls, and right in the centre – magic of magic – there was a groaning, brilliantly painted roundabout of imitation horses, heaving up and down. It was from here that the blare of music was coming. After he had pushed it hard enough to get up a good speed, a young man jumped up on it from time to time, walking in amongst the children who were having a ride and screaming with excitement, and then he would jump off again to chivvy the onlookers into trying the horses themselves, or to talk to a young, pregnant woman.

Thirza thought he was quite good-looking in a rough, unkempt sort of way. His matt hair was dark and tousled, his face was long and hard and his eyes were wide-set and expressionless, even when he spoke to the young woman. All this she saw while she sat enthralled on the grassy bank above the scene. Never in her life had she seen such colour and gaiety before. She watched until the moon sailed pale lemon into the cold skies above and the last child was whisked off the painted horses and away to bed.

Immediately, the young man set to work to dismantle the roundabout. The horses came off and lay grotesquely on the grass, their legs still galloping, but motionless and stiff. Next, the wooden flooring was piled into heaps and, with a lot of banging of hammers the rest of it was soon dismantled. She watched while the young man, and an older one with him, threw the bits and pieces of momentary magic into a long, flat float and then sheeted them with tarpaulins.

Four stalls were folded down and packed into another wagon, and then all the jollity was gone. All that was left was a shadowy circle of wagons, caravans and horses under the starry, frosty sky ... and a wonderful smell of bacon frying.

Thirza stood up stiffly from where she'd been sitting on her carpet-bag, pulled her shawl more closely around her shoulders and became conscious that she was ravenous with hunger. She couldn't remember her last proper meal. The smell of the singeing bacon was driving her mad, when she saw the young man of the roundabout climbing up the riverbank towards her. There was nobody else around. He was coming to speak to her and, suddenly frightened, she turned away, grasping the carpet-bag more firmly in her hand.

'Me mother wuz askin',' he said when he came within hailing distance. 'She wuz wonderin' why don't you come an' have a bite to eat along o' us?'

He was a beautifully built young man, there was no doubt of that. He would also have been strikingly handsome if it hadn't been for a mouthful of blackened teeth, and he spoke with an English accent.

'Your mother?' Thirza asked, contemplating a ring of fires now burning brightly down below.

'She'm sittin' in the door of the biggest vardo,' he said, pointing to the caravan in the middle, the glittering one Thirza had been admiring all evening. It had a rounded top and its body was a veritable riot of carving, mostly of grapes and vines picked out in vividly contrasting colours. The hubs of its wheels were made of gleaming, shining brass. 'She'm taken a fancy to you, sittin' yere and sittin' yere. She used to have red hair herself.'

'What does she want?'

'She'm wonderin' iffen you be hungry? And wot's your name?'

It was like a sign, Thirza thought.

'Thirza Gourlay,' she said, 'and yes, I'm very hungry.'

'Follow me then, gal.'

They clambered down the bank together and walked across the wide grassy verge to the encampment. 'Yere she'm be,' he said when they arrived at the largest caravan. 'Thirza Gourlay.'

'How you gittin' on?' his mother asked. 'Come and sit by me. It'll be warmer than where you'm been sitting all evening. I don't 'spect that great gomeril had the sense to tell you our names?'

Thirza sat down and shook her head.

'No,' his mother snorted, but she looked at him with pride all the same. 'That's why I never gits peace to die. He'm not fit to take over the Sharkeys yet. That be our name. Belle Sharkey an' Michael Sharkey. Now, why don't you have some bacon and a sausage?'

The food was well-cooked, if flavoured with the smoke of the fire, but to Thirza it was the best bacon and sausages she had ever tasted. While she ate, and her hostess chattered, she examined her companion.

Belle Sharkey was wearing an overcoat several sizes too big for her. There was a rope around her neck, and Thirza could see that two large tins were suspended from each end of the rope and covered by the folds of the coat. A brightly patterned silk scarf was pulled low over her forehead, and her dangling earrings, glittering in the light of the fire, were hoops of silver from which fell bunches of pierced silver threepenny pieces. The coins tinkled, swinging this way and that whenever she turned her head.

They were Sharkeys from the south of England originally, she explained, although Carlisle was the farthest south they travelled nowadays. They went in a circle from there and through the south of Scotland to Galloway and back. 'That tea'll be about ready, now,' she added, grasping a walking stick and hobbling down the steps of her caravan to the fire, where a large pot hung from a thick crooked stick plunged into the earth beside it. She ladled some of the brown, bubbling liquid into two mugs and came back with them. 'Try that,' she said.

It wasn't tea as Thirza had ever known it. The tea-leaves must have been boiling in the pot for a long time, along with milk and a large amount of sugar, but she drank it gratefully all the same.

'Thank you, Mrs Sharkey,' she said. 'It's very kind of you. I haven't eaten all day until now, you see.'

'Why's that, gal?' Belle's dark eyes peered into her face.

185

'I didn't stop anywhere long enough, I suppose – I was so anxious to get somewhere else.'

'An' where might that be?'

'I don't know yet,' Thirza laughed.

'Ah! So you be on the road, then, the same as we? You want to be careful, lady!' Belle warned her. 'You shouldn't be on the road alone, a young gal like you! Where's you sleepin' tonight?'

'I'll find somewhere, Mrs Sharkey.'

'And stop callin' me Mrs Sharkey. It takes me all me time to know who that is. Call me Belle, like everyone else,' Belle said, and darted another question. 'Does your mother know you'm run away?'

'My mother died not long ago, Belle,' Thirza said.

'Wot? Ah, that's sad that is, and you just a dee-little gal like I wuz myself once. You can sleep in the vardo along o' me iffen you like. I reckons it be better than sleepin' rough. Now, ain't that a fair offer?'

'What else can I say except thank you, Belle?'

'Well, now that we'm finished eatin', the rest o' them'll come and sit by me fire for an hour or two. They allus do, and sometimes we tells the old stories or have a sing-song. Put your bag on that bunk there,' she pointed inside the caravan, 'and come back and meet them.'

The inside of Belle's vardo was a revelation to Thirza. She had seen the travelling folk passing by and had admired their caravans, but she had never been inside one before. Everything was encased in glass cupboards, the panes of glass cut, decorated and sparkling, exposing Belle's obvious weakness for fine china. Three full tea sets were crammed in beside gaudy pink tumblers and right in the middle, facing anyone who came in, was the centrepiece reflected in a mirror, a silver teapot – dented, but silver nevertheless.

The interior wood of the caravan was highly varnished, the covers and curtains were crisp and clean, and in the middle of a small table covered with a lace cloth stood a vase of paper flowers.

Thirza was very impressed.

'You have a lovely home, Belle,' she said, and nothing she might have said could have pleased Belle Sharkey more. She introduced the other travellers as they came to sit around her fire, men called Samson and Snaky and Vesta, women called Mary-Anne and Lily and Sasha, and others with even stranger names. The only one Thirza picked out that night was Sasha, the pregnant young woman, with her long, wild hair. Close up, Sasha's features were coarse, but her apricot skin and large flashing eyes were beautiful and, in them, Thirza read the only message to mar her day. Sasha didn't like her.

However, by now she was too tired to care. She listened to their stories, and their songs with their strange words, while half-asleep. Finally, she saw Michael Sharkey stamping out the embers of his mother's fire and then she got undressed to lie down in her bunk. Her eyes stayed open long enough to see Belle taking off her overcoat and the rope underneath it from around her shoulders.

Before she took off any more clothes Belle went across to the door of the vardo and locked it and, behind her back, Thirza peeped curiously across at the tins. They were full of money. So Belle must look after all the tribe's money, she concluded. The last thing she saw before she knew no more, was Belle locking the tins in a cupboard beside her bunk.

'Oh my blessed Jesus,' the gypsy woman woke her in the morning, 'you musta been tired! Here, drink this tea, gal. By the look of those covers you'm never moved all night! But now it's nine o'clock, and we'm to be out o' here by ten. They keep movin' us on.'

'Where are you moving on to?' Thirza asked.

'West to Dumfries. It be the last Fair of the season in a fortnight. This time o' year we keep movin' west, anyway. When the snow comes we'll be in the hills of Galloway. The *gaujes* won't never find us there. We'll git a bit o' peace at last.'

'*Gaujes*, Belle?'

'Folk wot live in houses. Farmers and such-like.'

Dumfries. Thirza tried to picture it on Katie Docherty's map on the wall of the Pittenweem Dame's school. It was about halfway along the north shore of the Solway. Galloway was a lot further to the left. Well, she thought with her heart lifting, she felt lucky today. In Dumfries she might find her destiny.

'You comin' along o' we, then?' Belle asked her.

'I might as well,' Thirza answered slowly, watching the women and children combing soapy water through their hair.

They were all using the same comb in increasingly brackish water. 'As far as Dumfries, anyway.'

Then the older children, excited at the prospect of moving, went so far as to help their elders bundle together cooking pots, baskets, canvas sheets, piles of rags, odd harnesses, old boots and all the hundreds of other bits and pieces which were part of their life. The hens had to be caught, the harness sorted out, the dogs tied on behind, the plug-chains wound up and the horses harnessed, all in a raggle-taggle muddle of noise and disorder.

Eventually everything was ready for the move. The horses were hitched-in to the various wagons and carts, the children were all stowed away inside, and some of the adults walked with the men leading the horses. Michael's van went first, heralding Belle's royal vardo, and behind that a procession of the rest of the Sharkey tribe, leaving behind a glory of rubbish and litter without so much as a backward glance. Sitting beside Belle on another glorious autumn day, Thirza could see that it was likely to be a very slow procession but, with the sun on her face and the open road in front of her, she felt more light-hearted than for many a long day.

22

T HAT night the Sharkeys brought their wagons to a halt, strung along a lane off the narrow, winding country road to Dumfries. Some slept inside the caravans and others outside, under the frosty, starry skies and all was silent.

Suddenly, the dogs under the wagons got to their feet, their hackles raised. They had heard a sound in the distance. The noise of horses coming from Dumfries got nearer and nearer. The sound became thunder and, as the dogs barked wildly, one or two of the Sharkey men sleeping outside opened an eye to see eight horsemen, each leading a second horse, galloping past the end of the lane,

The hoofbeats faded into the distance and the dogs gradually subsided. Belle Sharkey's soft snores continued uninterrupted – Thirza stirred a little in her sleep.

The horsemen galloped on eastwards, clattering through Annan, Dornoch, Eastriggs and Rigg. At the River Kirtle they hesitated briefly while one of the men spoke.

'Down here along the riverbank, boys,' he muttered. 'We should cut across country now, away from the road and as near to the sea as we can, until we come around the back of Sarkfoot Farm.'

'How can there be a cave hereabouts, Duke?' The leader of the band, Dick Marshall, dropped back to speak to him. They were all trotting cautiously now. 'The shore here looks very flat to me.'

'That's the beauty of it,' Duke Elliot grinned nervously. Only in utter desperation would he ever have holed up with the dreaded Marshalls in one of their Galloway hideouts and asked for their help. 'Nobody would expect such a thing. There are very few high banks here for the sea to tunnel into. But there are one or two outcrops of rock. My house over there,' he pointed across at Allison's Bank, 'is built on one of them. Sarkfoot Farm is built on another, and that's where the cave is, underneath the farm.'

'Somebody lives here,' Dick Marshall stopped and listened suspiciously. 'There's cattle here. I can hear them moving about.'

'The Bells live here, and a bloody Nosey Parker old man Bell is too,' Duke Elliot hissed, trying his best to placate the Marshalls and in an agony of suspense himself, now that the end was in sight. 'We'd better go on foot from here. Leave two of your men with the horses, Dick, and warn everyone not to make a sound. There's dogs here, and that old bugger has a gun.'

'I might have known,' Dick Marshall grumbled bitterly. 'Christ, I might have known!' He gestured to three more of his men to stay on top, one just above the cave, another a few yards back and the third within easy reach of the men by the horses.

Then, with Dick and Billy Marshall, Duke Elliot silently dropped down into the cave under what had once been Joe Dan Linton's cottage and, piece by piece, began to empty the shelves.

Billy Marshall, the youngest and the fittest, heaved the kegs, boxes and bales up to the man on the top who carried them one by one to the next man in the chain and, working at top speed, they quickly and expertly roped their cargo onto the pack-ponies.

After two hours, Duke Elliot was working more feverishly than ever in the cave. It was now well after three o'clock in the morning, and Farmer Bell would be up before five. Cursing and sweating, he quickened the pace. Then the cock crowed.

'Jesus Christ!' he panted. 'Listen to that bastard thing! We'll have to leave the rest.'

'Well, ye've got the most o' it,' Dick Marshall growled. 'Go on, Billy! Let's get out of here!'

They left as stealthily as they had come but, as Duke Elliot had anticipated, they could get up no speed now that the ponies were laden. 'Follow me,' he said. 'This may be strange ground to you, but I know every inch of it. We'll go up through Springfield and head north through the Solway Moss.'

'Ay,' Dick Marshall agreed. 'We canna be seen on the main road around here. The sooner we get up among the hills the better. Folk are used to seeing droves of cattle and strings of horses up there.'

But the sound of sixteen horses, eight of them heavy-laden – their hooves ringing out on the frosty road – couldn't pass so near to the dwelling-houses of Springfield without some people wakening from their sleep. A baby began to cry.

'God damn and blast his foxing eyes,' Duke Elliot cursed, and glared murderously at the light that sprang up in the cottage window.

'Hush, baby, it's only the gentlemen riding by,' the child's mother tried to soothe him, but the hairs rose up on the back of her neck.

It was still early, only eight in the morning, when Duke Elliot and the Marshalls, contriving to look like ordinary packmen, passed through Canonbie. The next town was Langholm and, after that, it was only another few hours to Moffat, beyond which lay the wilderness of the hills, criss-crossed by drovers' roads.

'I've done it, boys!' Duke Elliot slid off his horse when they had finally reached the safety of the hills, throwing up his hands in triumph. 'God, I never thought I could!'

Dick Marshall looked at him sourly. 'Ay, ye've done it,' he said, 'thanks to us. And a fine haul we got for ye, more than enough to double our pay.'

'Ay,' the other Marshalls chorused, agreeing with that.

'Dick, when have I ever reneged on you?' Duke Elliot's brilliantly white smile flashed around them. 'I *will* double your money as soon as we get to my father's house in Edinburgh. I promise you!' he vowed confidently. 'He's got the ready cash.'

'Ye'd better,' Dick Marshall's tones were deadly and, looking around the hardbitten, murderous faces of the Marshall tribe, Duke Elliot knew with a slight chill in his heart that he'd better or he'd lose not only his loot but his life, too.

191

'You know these hills better than I do, Dick,' he said, almost whining. 'You lead the way. You're the main man, now.'

'He always was,' Billy Marshall rode up alongside his brother, 'and dinna you forget it! Besides that, he knows Edinburgh a bloody sight better than you ever will, so ye'd better not try any o' yer tricks there, either. You're not the only one who's been inside India House, ye ken. So watch my brother, and watch yer back, Duke Elliot!'

The venom in Billy Marshall's voice shook him to his foundations. Their journey became the worst one of his life, instead of the most triumphant one. There was nothing to stop the Marshalls from murdering him then and there and making off with the goods. They were seven to his one. He wouldn't stand a chance.

Every mile was a nightmare and he kept his head down, terrified half out of his wits. Watching him, Dick Marshall's thin, grim line of a mouth relaxed into something resembling a smile when he glanced around at the others from time to time.

He had no intention whatever of making off with the loot. It was getting harder and harder to get rid of smuggled goods every day, as he knew to his cost. And he had no intention of getting rid of Duke Elliot, either, for the time being. Hard cash was what he was after nowadays, and there was no sense in killing the golden goose.

Duke Elliot got no sleep at all that night in the cold, freezing heather, while the Marshall men slumbered peacefully in a tight ring around him. The next day they continued their weary journey in changing weather, their view from the hills that of the storm clouds gathering and chasing across the sky. At last, on a cold, windy night with the first drops of rain slashing across their faces, Dick Marshall climbed down stiffly off his horse at the gates of India House, and named his grossly inflated price.

'We'll just wait here until you come out with the money,' he told Duke Elliot. 'No money, no goods. We'll dispose of them ourselves.'

With that, he leaned back against his horse's flanks, his legs crossed nonchalantly and his arms akimbo. To a man, the other Marshalls followed suit, their eyes like daggers in Duke Elliot's back as he ran up the driveway and hammered at the door.

'For God's sake, Father,' he shouted, falling inside as soon as it was opened, 'I need money, fast!'

'*Again?*'

'Oh, don't worry,' Duke Elliot was almost crying in his desperation, 'this time you'll have a return for it! Just give me your purse,' he said, grabbing the heavy bag from around his father's waist, 'and *then* you'll see!'

He ran back down the driveway, emptied the purse of all its golden sovereigns on the wet road and, retreating to the safety of his father's grounds, shouted at the Marshalls. 'There! Will that do, you greedy buggers?'

Dick Marshall didn't bother to reply. He knew a coward when he saw one, and this man was the worst one yet. He signalled to his brother Billy to pick up all the coins and the rest of his men untied the goods and piled them high in front of the door to India House. Then, contemptuously, they rode away.

The first clap of thunder echoed after them, and rain began to pour down. Left alone to carry all the goods inside, Duke Elliot was convinced that he had not seen the last of the Marshalls. Those bastards would be wanting both the money *and* the goods, he thought. By the time he had the last box inside, and had safely shut the front door, he was in a terrible state.

'You might have given me a hand,' he snarled at his father.

'I might have,' Marmaduke Elliot agreed, 'but why should I? I don't want all that stuff you've got lined up there.'

'What do you mean? It's worth thousands!'

'Not to me, it isn't. It wasn't to Dick Marshall, either. You're a fool, Duke Elliot! I used the Marshalls to get rid of the last illegal lot I collected in here a month ago, and how they avoided swinging for it, I'll never know. Somehow or another they wriggled out of it.'

Duke stared at his father. God, how he hated him! And how he hated this house! He had always hated it. Supposed to be a copy of an Indian Palace? It was a monstrosity, with all those silly towers above it. Minarets, his father called them. How had the stupid old man ever come to live here?

Just then, there was a brilliantly blue flash of lightning, followed by another clap of thunder. It rolled around the heavens until it merged with a tremendous roaring clatter from

193

somewhere at the top of the house. The noise seemed to rattle on and on.

'Jesus!' Duke jumped. 'What in the name of Christ was that?'

His father looked him up and down with disgust. 'Another of those minarets falling down, I expect. They're nearly all down now. There's hardly a room left habitable downstairs, let alone upstairs.'

'Why don't you get the roof fixed, then? This house is part of my inheritance, you know,' Duke Elliot complained.

'I might have, if you hadn't snatched every last penny I had in the world to throw at the Marshalls! And what makes you think you're coming in to an inheritance, anyway? How do you know you're my only son? Even if you were, I don't have to leave anything to you when I die – and I'm not ready to die yet!'

Duke stared at his father, resentfully. It was true that although now in his sixties he was still hale and hearty. He was still as upright as ever – and just as burly. The only difference the passing years seemed to have made was to change his hair from red to grey.

The old man had never looked at him with such open dislike and contempt, even hatred, before. Vainly attemping to hide his weakness, Duke decided to change his tune. It must be a lie, that there could be another son somewhere, and even if there were such a byblow, he could never be such a faithful reproduction of the old man as Duke himself. It was a lie, too, that there was no more money. There had always been money. Marmaduke Elliot had always been a money–shark, a crook and a thief. Thinking these thoughts, he smiled winningly at his father. It had always worked before.

But not this time.

'God help me, but you're like your mother,' Marmaduke jeered, 'and a useless, grinning, stupid bloody whore *she* was!'

Standing there – wet, tired, and tired of trying – something snapped inside Duke. It was a feeling he had had before. He walked straight past his father, into the sitting-room and over to the fire. 'Yes,' he said, picking up the heavy poker, 'and that was why you fucked everything in skirts that came your way, wasn't it? By the way, how did my mother die? With a broken heart, that I know. Was it with a broken neck, as well?'

Marmaduke was trying to escape up the stairs when his son got to him. A heap of rubble blocked his way, and he fell back, arm upraised to shield his head.

Screaming with rage, and swearing and spitting, Duke Elliot brought the poker crashing down. He flailed and hit out in a blind fury as blood spurted everywhere, over the stairs, and in splashes up the walls – until he had smashed the human being who had been his father into pulp. Then, horrified by what he had done, he threw down the poker, put his head in his hands and wept. He wept till he could weep no more.

Hours, and several brandies, later he lifted his father's heavy body and dragged it over to the French windows. He knew already where he would bury it. Oblivious to the blasting wind and rain, he opened the windows and stepped out to find the latest landslide from the roof, cursing all the way. He tore away at the rubble and stones in a frenzy, looking over his shoulder all the while. Was that something? Was something moving? Someone? The Marshalls? In a mad panic he dragged the body to the shallow hollow he'd dug out and covered it with as many stones as he could find again in the pitch dark and the rain. Then he rushed back inside and locked all the doors and windows on the ground floor. He spent what was left of the night drinking the rest of the brandy in fear and trembling.

When morning finally came he had a plan. He would have to leave his horse. He couldn't ride away, for fear of the Marshalls around every next corner. He looked at the clock. In an hour the baker's wagon would arrive, and in it he would leave. He still had a few coins to bribe the baker to take him to Leith, from there he could make his way to England. He must go somewhere until the heat cooled off – in Scotland he was a wanted man now, seven times over.

But he would be back.

Duke Elliot haunted the docks of Leith for three weeks before he heard of a ship carrying a cargo of hides that would call in at several ports down the east coast of England on her way to London. Drastically short of money, he signed on as a deckhand, carrying his few possessions in an old duffle-bag he'd found in India House, clearly marked with his initials, D.E.

The first port of call was Sunderland. There he jumped ship

and, making his way from east to west, and living from hand to mouth, he got to the Cumbrian port of Whitehaven. From there it was only a few miles to St Bees, his ultimate goal.

He hung around Whitehaven and the outlying district for months. Those people who took any notice of the tall, broad-shouldered, red-haired man got used to seeing him walking up to St Bees Head and back again three or four times a day. He went there even at night.

To them, he was just another stranger in the place, another eccentric who wandered into the taverns in the evenings, drank hard, sat morosely by himself, and slept God only knew where. Nobody really cared.

Duke smiled grimly to himself at their attitude. It conveyed to him that he had been successful in exactly what he had set out to achieve: to be a nonentity. It gave him time and space while he waited – and oh, how he waited. His patience was stretched to breaking point as each minute of every day and night slipped past, until at last – oh God, at last – came the sight he'd been praying for.

It was a sunny morning when he saw her first, the large barque painted jet black, hovering offshore. He whipped his spy-glass out of his pocket and read the name *Prince* on her bows. That was all he needed to see. He raced to the top of St Bees Head and positioned himself so that the sun would reflect on the mirror he'd been keeping in his other pocket, and began his frantic signals. Over and over he signalled his message, without response from the *Prince*.

'Did ye see someone flashing just now from the Head?' McKim asked Jordi.

'No,' said Jordi, who didn't admit to anything on this ship. He was in the business of keeping himself to himself, saying as little as possible, while he watched everything.

'Look! There it is again!' McKim exclaimed. 'What does it say?'

'You'll have to ask somebody else,' Jordi told him flatly. But already he had made out the message: it asked for a small boat to be sent out.

'I'll see Jack Hawkins, then,' McKim said, disgruntled.

Jordi smiled inwardly. McKim suspected that he could read the signals all right. He watched him going to the Captain and saw them both watch the flashes, ever more frantic, from St Bees Head.

Then he heard the *Prince* dropping anchor and saw one of the longboats being lowered and heading for Whitehaven. Immediately the man on the Head streaked towards Whitehaven's harbour to meet it. So, Jordi thought, there was to be another addition to the crew, was there? Well, he would be at hand when Hawkins received him.

When the longboat got back, Jordi just happened to be making sure of some of the rigging near the hastily lowered rope-ladder. He took the precaution of having his back half turned when the stranger set foot on the *Prince*, his duffle-bag thrown in ahead of him.

Hawkins was there to receive him. 'It's you, is it – '

'Quiet!' The stranger clapped a hand on his shoulder to stop him. 'Not so loud,' he muttered. 'Just trust me, Jack, for God's sake! From now on my name's Drew Ellis.'

Looking sideways, Jordi saw the man's duffle-bag had the initials D.E. – but that wasn't his real name. Whoever he was, the Captain knew him very well. Another smuggler, perhaps, Jordi wondered?

'What the hell have you been up to now, you fat red-headed bastard?' Captain Hawkins asked affectionately, laughing and clapping him on the back. 'Are you running away from the law?'

'Don't ask. Just let's take off. I don't care where to.'

'As bad as that?' Hawkins asked, leading the man off to his cabin.

That was the last that Jordi managed to overhear, but it was enough to cause turmoil inside him. He *knew* that man – somehow he knew him. But who was he? Rack his brains as he might, the answer wouldn't come.

The *Black Prince* sailed south that night into darkness, and for a long time after that, kept well clear of British waters. Jordi assumed that this was for Drew Ellis's sake. Nevertheless, she went about her business as usual, as she shadowed other ships from Gibraltar up the Spanish coast to France, moving in for the kill when any of them got into difficulties in the Bay of Biscay. In fair weather or foul, the Bay of Biscay was a happy hunting ground for Jack Hawkins and Drew Ellis. The two were as thick

197

as thieves. Drew Ellis revelled in every manoeuvre, especially when it came to killing. Jordi watched him, sickened by the man's brutality. But to Hawkins there wasn't a man on board who could match him.

To the extent that Ellis's presence took the Captain off his own back, Jordi was immensely relieved. But, as something about Ellis continued to haunt him, he grew more and more agitated. There was something in the way the man turned his head and in the way he spoke – even the very shape of him . . . Somehow Jordi was reminded of someone else, but all he knew for certain was that he hated him. He had hated him on sight.

And to make matters worse, the feeling was obviously mutual.

23

THE Sharkeys were well into the wilds of the countryside now and the order of the caravans had changed. A small yellow one, belonging to Snaky and Caroline, went first because it was the lightest. It was always sent on ahead, Belle explained, to test the hills for the bigger vans.

Snaky was small and slight, and sported a black walrus moustache, so luxuriant that it gave the appearance of supporting the man, rather than the reverse. The ends stuck out almost to his ears and, immensely proud of his fine moustache, he combed it every five minutes. He was also very proud that he was double-jointed all over, so that he could wriggle into spaces no other man could. What his real name was, Thirza never found out.

Snaky's wife, Caroline, was even smaller and thinner than he was, with a tiny triangular face and yellow teeth, due to her habit of chewing tobacco. She was very friendly and obliging, except to her husband – with whom she conducted a never-ending battle. Although, to judge from the number of their children, there must have been relatively frequent cease-fires.

The procession of wagons, covering about a hundred yards, rumbled on accompanied by the screaming and shouting of the children, the barking of the dogs, the squawking of the hens and the clanking of the tins and pans dangling from the wagons. All went well, if agonisingly slowly, until the pony pulling Snaky's van suddenly reared up.

'*Waaaaaaay*! Stand still, you bloody foxin' bastard!' he

shouted, clinging to the bit, and beating the pony vigorously about the face with a thick holly stick while he kicked it in the stomach for good measure until, eyes rolling, it quietened down.

'I don't like a lazy pony!' he laughed, pretending not to be upset by his pony's show of bad temper.

'Hm!' Belle said to Thirza. 'He'm furious, o' course. News of a wild wagon horse travels fast amongst we Romanies. He won't never sell it now.'

Caroline's little face appeared from behind her curtain. 'God cuss him wot 'witched me,' she yelled at everyone, pointing at her husband. 'He never takes a tellin'! He *would* buy that poxin' pony! There's no sense in the man, no sense at all!'

Round a bend and up a hill they went and then down again, applying the brake full on. Thirza and Belle trailed on behind, a few feet from the van belonging to Fangs and Lily. Fangs was singing a ballad at the top of his voice. That was bad enough, but when Lily joined in it was even worse. Fat, jolly Lily adored everything about her husband, his curly black hair, his pencil-line moustache above a wide mouth devoid of teeth – except for two lone fangs an inch or so apart in his upper jaw, hanging like those of a sabre-toothed tiger. He wore a wide-brimmed greasy felt hat pulled low over his eyes and a shabby overcoat.

Thirza thought that his wide-set expressionless eyes were very like Michael's, and in those eyes she detected more than a hint of insanity. Was that why, although she would die rather than show it, she was afraid of Michael? She made up her mind to keep well away from all the gypsy men, and just stick close to Belle.

They went up another hill and back down again, over a crossroads and still onwards.

'How far have we come now, Belle?' Thirza asked.

'Reckons 'bout three miles.'

'And how many more to Dumfries?'

'Fourteen, fifteen, maybe.'

'Will we get there today?'

'Not today,' Belle laughed. 'More like next week.'

Just then great consternation broke out around the next corner. There were roars and shouts of 'Stop! Stop!' from the men and, louder still, came the screams of a woman in distress.

'Oh, God! . . . Oh, the baby's killed! . . . The wagon's over! . . . Oh, me poor dead mother! . . . Oh, me blessed Jesus . . .'

'That be Caroline's voice,' Belle said. 'Wot's Snaky done now? Better get out and see.'

Thirza followed her around the corner of the lane just in time to see a shabby yellow-painted wheel rolling slowly and ponderously across the grass verge and toppling heavily into the ditch, where it vanished from sight.

'Oh, me blessed Jesus Christ A'mighty!' Snaky, distraught, swiftly pursued it. He, too, disappeared into the ditch, re-appearing within seconds with the wheel in his hand. It had come off while they were actually travelling along, leaving the yellow caravan leaning at a drunken tilt.

Little Caroline was jumping up and down in agitation, anger and shame. 'Oh, me poor wagon . . . It's all in pieces! . . . Oh, it's all broken! Oh, me poor dead father . . . I wish I'd never gone wi' that bugger Snaky . . . Wot's that wheel come off for?'

'Fangs! Michael! Samson!' shouted Snaky. 'Will you push the wagon up straight agin so I can put the wheel back on him? It ain't broken – 'tis only the pin wot's a-comed out of him. Look!'

All the other men had gathered around by that time, filling their pipes and offering suggestions. After a long discussion they eventually heaved the wagon upright, the wheel was slipped back on and a nail attached in place of the missing pin.

'Never knowed such a thing to happen in all me life,' Snaky muttered, jerking viciously at the pony's head, which was lowered as he cropped the roadside grass unconcernedly.

'You bin a-makin' that ole wagon shake too much at night, that's wot loosed that wheel,' Fangs grinned his toothless grin.

'Wot?' exclaimed little Caroline, her pointed face still work-ing with rage that such a thing should have happened to her wagon in front of the others. 'That man's an idiot! He ain't a-broke the banns wi' me fer these last six months – and he won't fer the next six months, my brothers, that's fer sure!'

They all laughed until Caroline, spitting brown saliva vehe-mently on the road, climbed back in again, cursing the wagon and her husband, and pulled the torn front curtain across behind her.

'Why don't we stop yere?' Belle asked her son. 'There's plenty o' hazels fer a few baskets. We might as well camp yere for the night.'

'I could do wi' some tea, anyway, after all that,' Michael said.

Thirza sighed. She could see it was going to be a *very* long, slow journey.

Soon the smoke was curling up from the fires and there was the smell of bacon, potatoes and onions frying. 'We'm be havin' a fresh egg wi' this,' Belle said, and afterwards showed Thirza how to clean her plate with bread. 'Water's too scarce,' she explained, 'and too heavy to carry. We save it to drink and fer washin' the clothes. We must drink to live, and Romanies can't live without puttin' out white washin's.'

'But how do you get a bath, then?' Thirza asked.

'Bless the gal!' Belle took her pipe out of her mouth long enough to enjoy a good laugh. 'We don't have baths! Nobody needs baths! Your skin scales off, dirt and all, my dear. Nature sees to that, so all you'm needin' is clean clothes to put on.'

Still laughing, she went inside the vardo and stretched herself out on her bunk. Thirza saw that everyone else was doing the same. There was no sense of urgency in these people. They would get to Dumfries when they got there, and that was that.

After their siesta the men climbed down again and went to cut the 'withies' from the hazel copse. Thirza watched while Fangs weaved his baskets, making a square for the base and then building the basket up in layers. Then he got out a tiny hammer, tacked the withies together with three-quarter inch nails, and finally added a hoop of hazel to make a decorative handle.

He made four or five of them and then shouted up at his van. 'Lily! There be plenty yere to fill,' and out she came with a selection of paper flowers and some moss to stick the flowers into.

'How much do you get for them?' Thirza asked curiously.

'Two shillings each, callin'. Half a crown at the Fair.'

Michael was intent on making pegs. He held a knife against his knee and pared off the bark of the hazel sticks in long slithers. To cut the lengths for the pegs he took another knife, razor sharp. Standing the lengths on a tiny block, he sliced them down the middle by hitting the knife with a small mallet, and then bound the two halves together back to back with a length of wire.

Within an hour his deft hands had produced about a gross of pegs, and Sasha came out to tie them into bundles of a dozen.

'Goin' to make any more today?' she asked her husband.

'No,' Michael said. 'Time to go and practise.'

'What are they going to practise?' Thirza asked Belle when they rose to go.

'Michael be the knife-thrower at the Fairs,' Belle told her. 'He throws twenty o' them around Sasha while she be standin' wi' her arms held out sideways. Come and watch them, iffen you like.'

Sasha was standing with her back to the side of their caravan. Michael got ready with a great flourish, showing the audience the knives before he laid them down in a ring on a table beside him. Thirza noticed that Sasha's unblinking eyes never left his face.

'Ready?' he asked.

She didn't nod. She just froze, absolutely still. Thirza thought she had never seen utter fear personified before.

Michael picked up the first knife. Thirza didn't even see it flying through the air. There was just a thud, and the handle was quivering within an inch of the crown of Sasha's head. With lightning speed nine others followed, finishing up all round her left side.

Then Michael changed hands. Using his left hand he threw the other ten knives around her right side. Belle and the others who were watching clapped, and Sasha walked away white-faced, but unharmed.

'But what happens if he misses?' Thirza whispered.

'He *never* misses,' Belle said proudly.

'I see his knives are all the same, and all the same length. They're beautiful. The way he throws them is beautiful.'

'He makes them that way. He takes the blades o' kitchen knives and makes the handles from wood he weighs hisself, very careful. He makes all the knives we use in the camp, too, but he's not so fussy wi' them.'

*   *   *

Every day, as the Sharkeys made their haphazard way over the miles to Dumfries, Thirza grew closer to Belle.

'I loved my children,' Belle told her. 'I had three o' them to that bastard Matt Sharkey wot up and died on me. Here's a picture of him,' she added proudly, dusting off a silver frame. It surrounded a portrait someone had tried to paint of a man in a yellow plaid suit, a red neckerchief, a green hat and large boots tied with string.

'He must have been very handsome,' Thirza said tactfully.

'Hm!' Belle snorted. '*He* thought he was, and so did a lot o' other women!'

Thirza thought she detected a note of pride in this statement, so she smiled and said nothing.

'Ay,' Belle went on after a reflective minute, 'he wuz good-looking, all right. The *chavies* took after him, Cathie and Isadora and Michael . . . So did half the children in a lot o' other camps,' she added bitterly. 'Matt was a great one to shake it about.'

'And where are Cathie and Isadora now, Belle?'

'Where they should be. On the road wi' their husbands, o' course. They both got hitched to Cumberland Romanies. Met them in Carlisle, Cathie one year and Isadora the next. So,' Belle sighed, 'I'm left with the runt o' the litter – Michael.'

'He seems to work hard,' Thirza strove to console her. 'He fairly took charge at the Fair in Annan.'

'Hm!' Belle snorted again. 'He wuz only runnin' up and down like that on the roundabout for *your* benefit, believe me. He saw you long before I did. He came and pointed you out to me. Yes . . . Michael thinks he's God's gift to women, so be warned, lady!'

But the warning only intrigued Thirza further. Of course, she didn't fancy Michael Sharkey, and him with a mouthful of black teeth . . . Ruth had been right about teeth, she sighed, remembering. No, she could never have anything to do with a man like Michael. There was something in his eyes she didn't trust. And in any case, what was she worrying about? He was married anyway, to the dark-haired pregnant woman.

But oh! He was a wizard with the knives! Those beautiful, flashing, deadly knives! She had fallen under their spell.

* * *

The villages grew bigger as the Sharkeys came nearer to Dumfries, and they all had to be milked dry of any spare coppers the *gaujes* might possess before the tribe would move on.

Thirza accompanied fat Lily when the women went out calling every morning with baskets full of pegs, wooden spoons, paper flowers and good luck charms, and she usually came back depressed at the insults and humiliations the Romanies had to suffer.

They were only trying to earn a living, after all ... On the other hand, Thirza could see the householders' point of view. They were frightened of the Romanies, of their rough appearance, their dark faces and their mystery.

As long as she lived she would never forget what she saw one day when Lily was knocking repeatedly on a door and getting no answer although there were movements inside. Thirza peeped in the window and saw a table inside, its long tasselled cloth twitching. Underneath it, she made out the figures of a terrified woman clutching her even more terrified children. It was no wonder that the Romanies were always being moved on. The *gaujes* hated them.

One village they came to had just been having a funeral, and Fangs stopped his wagon around the next bend from the graveyard and refused to move, backwards or forwards. 'I ain't a-movin' out o' this lane fer the next half an hour,' he said mysteriously. As the mourners left, the gravedigger filled in the grave and placed the wreaths on top of it before he, too, went home with his spade over his shoulder, locking the gates behind him.

The minute he was out of sight Fangs came to life. He took a running jump at the graveyard wall, scaled it and vanished. A minute later the wreaths came flying out. Lily picked them up, put them in their vardo and had the reins ready for him to make a fast getaway when he came panting back.

'What did he do that for?' Thirza asked, aghast.

'No luck'll come to that two, and that's as true as I'm yere,' Belle said darkly. 'I wouldn't take the flowers off a grave supposing I wuz dyin' o' hunger.'

'But what are they for?'

'We'll be in Dumfries tonight, won't we? Lily will be away hawkin' their baskets full o' fresh flowers tomorrow, wait and

see. I'll bet she's takin' those wreaths to bits this very minute.'
And, sure enough, Belle was proved right in the morning. While
the men were parking the wagons beside several caravans
belonging to other travelling people, Lily went out calling with
her head in the air. This time she went alone. Neither Thirza
nor anyone else would go with her.

As more and more wagons arrived, it became a Romany
reunion. The men walked up and down examining each other's
horses – the flashier the animal the better. With so much live-
stock to see and trade for, the bargaining went on till late
afternoon. There was a pause in the babble for a second when
Thirza heard a young boy bargaining with Fangs and Lily.

'Ain't that bird quiet, though?' he eyed one of their little
bantam pullets admiringly. Finally he and Lily struck a bargain
with the Romany slap of hands together, and he handed her
a young showy cock in exchange. 'His dee-little balls ain't
a-comed through yit – but he'll be all right when they does!'
he said.

Meanwhile the women were catching up with all the news of
births and deaths. Thirza realised that they would never send
each other letters, even if some of them could read or write. It
would only be at established meetings like this, held on a certain
calendar date, that one could ever be sure where the other might
be. It was a strange life, the travelling life.

The taverns of the Vennel were only a stone's throw away when
the lamps were lit. Most of the Romanys, welcome for their
songs, were there until closing time. Belle tried to persuade
Thirza to go, too.

'My mother always said strong drink was the drink of the
devil,' she refused, shaking her head.

'Ah, well, suit yourself,' Belle said, hobbling off.

Thirza was left alone in the semi-darkness, sitting on the
step of the vardo and listening to the river Nith tinkling by
the white sands. Well, here she was at her journey's end. This
was Dumfries. She could leave the Sharkeys now, if she liked.
She was wondering if she would, when she became aware that
she was not alone any more. The graceful, powerful figure of
Michael Sharkey was standing in front of her.

'Move over, then,' he said, 'and let me sit aside yer.'

'You haven't gone out drinking with the others?'

'Never do, the night afore I throw me knives. You need a clear eye an' a steady hand fer that job.'

Thirza shuddered at the thought of what might happen if he threw just slightly wrong. 'Not everyone would be so careful,' she said in genuine admiration, and he moved a little closer. Immediately regretting her display of civility she added, 'Your mother isn't here, if you were looking for her . . .'

But he only laughed. 'That's right,' he said. 'She likes a drink now and then. Left her tins locked up, did she?'

'Yes, and took the key.'

'Ain't a bad sort, me mother, iffen she'm gettin' on a bit now. But the head woman allus keeps the money, and anything might happen, so I keeps an eye on her. When she passes on, me wife will be the banker.'

'Sasha, you mean?'

'Sasha ain't my wife, gal.'

'But she's carrying your baby!'

'She'm carrying a baby, right enough,' Michael scowled, and when he turned his face to the side there was a meanness and a narrowness to it that reminded Thirza of a rodent of some kind. She said no more.

'Anyway, it was about Sasha I wanted to speak to yer. Tomorrow be the last day I throw the knives around her. She says it be not fair, and her a-feared for the baby.'

'Belle says you never miss.'

'I never have, so far,' Michael swelled with pride, 'and I don't never have a mind to.'

'What will you do without Sasha? Who will you get?'

'You, gal . . . I wuz hoping.'

'*Me?*'

'Don't get excited. There be no more Fairs until next April. That gives us six months to practise – and get used to each other,' he smiled at her obliquely, disappearing as quickly as he had come.

'Wot a grand night we had!' Belle told her when she came back. 'You woulda enjoyed it, Thirza! Did you git any visitors?'

'No,' she lied.

*   *   *

207

Next day the Sharkeys got up earlier than usual to change into their 'Fair Day' clothes. The children's faces and hands were washed, and the dirty, soapy water that was left was combed through their hair.

Then it was the women's turn, and by now the block of damp, greenish soap was softening up so that each woman was able to take a handful of it and rub it into her scalp before she tied her braids.

'We don't want to git them pesty dee-little beasties, do we?' Belle grinned, larding on the soap and then combing her hair flat and greasy to her head. 'Come here, gal, and I'll do the same for you.'

When Thirza saw herself in the mirror after this operation she didn't look like the Thirza Gourlay of the long, flyaway, auburn curls at all. With all that soap in it, her hair looked as black as treacle and, when she touched her braids, it felt just as sticky. Still, she thought, the wee 'pesty beasties' would have a struggle to tramp through that lot, so she didn't object.

Next, Belle donned several brightly-coloured dresses, one on top of the other, from the heap on the floor of the caravan, topping them with what she called a 'pinna' of shocking pink. With her purple handkerchief over her head and her best brown-button boots she was beginning to look the part of a gypsy queen.

'Choose somethin', then,' she said. And, after sifting through the pile, Thirza found a long brown skirt and a green tight-fitting velvet jacket. Belle surveyed her critically. 'Why, that won't do,' she said. 'Not that skirt. Try this one,' and she held up another, yellow with brighter yellow stripes. 'Yes, that's more like it! Now, plenty o' ribbons in yer hair, and a scarf – and better pin this in it,' she handed Thirza a huge silver brooch with her beringed, brown old hands.

It was just like dressing up. It was a wonderful game.

Transformed into a gypsy, Thirza sat on an upturned bucket and helped Lily to dress her little girls in white embroidered frilly dresses, given to her by some *gauji* who had been clearing out her cupboards. All this time the men were erecting the roundabout and putting up the stalls and, by eleven o'clock, Michael and Sasha were ready for their first show. But he had only given two shows before he closed down his tent and led an ashen-faced

Sasha back to their vardo. That night he went out with the other men and came back roaring drunk.

Belle said, 'I reckons Michael needs another gal to help him ... Oh well, we'm movin' on agin by twelve tomorrow. It'll be fine to git a bit o' rest at last, tucked up in the Galloway hills. And wot about you, my dear? Made up yer mind to stay, or to go?'

It was a question Thirza had been pondering for days. Life with the Sharkeys was rough, but they were so entertaining, without ever meaning to be, after the humdrum life she had lived so far. Besides, those beautiful, flashing knives of Michael's held her in a spell. She had no fear of them, nor of his expertise with them. No matter how much she disliked Michael, she would trust him with the knives. She wondered whether, if she offered to be his assistant, he would teach her all about them?

She remembered her father's bowie knife, the care he had taken of it, and how he used to sharpen it continually, testing it on a hair pulled from his head. 'It's got to be sharp, lassie, to gut fish,' he had said. 'A blunt knife's no use to anyone. In fact, it's dangerous. It's easier to cut your finger with a blunt knife than it is with a sharp one.' What would he have said if he could see her now, and know what she was contemplating?

Anyway, it had been a long time since she had learned anything of any value. This way, if she actually learned to throw a knife of her own she would be learning one of the arts of self-defence at the same time. It would be another phase of her education, she tried to tell herself virtuously.

And besides, where else could she go?

'I'll stay, Belle,' she said.

24

ONLY a month later, as the caravans lurched, sinking almost to their axles, along the way to Castle Douglas in the November downpours, Thirza came to regret her decision.

The horses had to heave and strain to shift the wagons from the clinging grasp of mud, hauling the Sharkeys, splashed and cold, out of the soft spongy ground on to the hard roads.

Mud was their enemy. Once it got on their boots it was caught by their trouser legs or their skirt hems and spread from there like a foul disease all over their bodies. It found its way into anything put down on the ground – into water-carriers, kettles, food-hampers, and all over the harnesses.

It clung to the coats of the dogs, matting and discolouring them, caked itself on the hens' feathers, seeped up into the vardo, even onto the bedding, until everyone else was in the same depressed state as Thirza. The further west they struggled the worse it became.

Occasionally, there was a fine day, and there would be an uplift in everyone's spirits and renewed activity. The whole tribe, young and old, concentrated on fetching clean water to wash the mud away.

'Wi' me bad leg I can't carry water nowadays,' Belle said. 'But iffen you fetch it I'll cook and clean up this vardo.'

'I'll wash all our clothes to begin with, then,' Thirza said, casting around for a suitable tree. She unwound the long rope hanging coiled from a hook under the roof of the caravan and,

once it was stretched out to the tree, she began the washing –
scarcely noticing that Michael had gone in to visit Belle. She was
too busy pounding the clothes in the soapy water, rubbing the
dirtiest parts up and down on the washboard, and then taking
it all to the stream tr be rinsed. Starting under the tree at the
furthest end of the rope, she began to peg it out. The nearer
she worked towards the vardo, the louder and clearer Belle's
conversation with her son became.

'Sasha won't like it,' Belle was saying.

'What the hell do I care what Sasha thinks? Listenin' to
you, Ma, anyone would think I jumped over the broomstick
wi' her.'

'It be your bairn wot she'm carrying, Michael Sharkey!' Belle's
voice rose in anger. 'An' iffen it be a boy this time it'll be the first
son any o' your women has ever given you. He'll be the king!
He'll be the king after you, some day!'

'Never you mind all that,' Michael's voice sounded savage.
'It could be a girl, like all the others . . . Anyway, first things
first. I got to git someone else to help me wi' the knives.'

'There be Anne-Marie. She would do it.'

'Anne-Marie looks like a dog, and you know it. The punters
wouldn't give a damn if I *did* stick a knife into the likes o' her.
Different if it wuz Thirza, now. She'm so beautiful.'

'So she'm beautiful next, is she? You bastard, you'm just like
your father!'

'All I want is a proper gal to help me wi' the knives. Will you
be askin' her, Ma? Try and find out if Thirza'll do it.'

'Hm! All right, but you needn't git any other ideas in that
direction. She'm a *gauji*. Don't you forget it!'

Thirza had her back to him when he stamped down the steps
of the vardo, but her heart was beating wildly.

'Oh yes,' she said breathlessly when Belle put it to her later.
'I'll try.'

'I not be too sure 'bout this, you know,' Belle eyed her
doubtfully, 'but iffen you be determined, go on down to that
old green wagon at the end. That be where he works wi' the
knives.'

When she got there Thirza stood and watched Michael for a
few minutes from the outside. The blades were not concerning

him, she saw. It was the balance of the handles, as he flung them from hand to hand. Then somehow she knew that he knew she was there. 'You'm come, then,' he said unsmiling, still testing the knives.

'What are you doing?'

'I be not happy wi' these two. I got to git them right,' he frowned. 'Go away! I'll let you know when I'm ready.'

'Not so fast, Michael Sharkey! I'm here, but I haven't said I'll do it yet. There's something I want, first.'

'Oh, yes? God, you women be all the same! Well, wot is it?'

'I want you to make me a knife of my own, and I want you to teach me to throw it.'

'Well, that's different, fer once,' he smiled blackly. 'All right then, Thirza. You couldn't throw these knives o' mine, anyway. They'm be too heavy. I'll make you a lighter one.'

The tribe moved onwards unsteadily for another two unhappy weeks, through Ringford and Twynholm until they got to Gatehouse of Fleet. All the men and most of the women escaped thankfully into the small bar at the side of the Murray Arms, and this time Thirza was in such a state of anxiety and suspense that she even accompanied Belle to the door. Little by little she progressed to the end of the bar and looked around for Michael Sharkey.

'We'm yere fer a few days,' said a voice in her ear. She felt a man's arm around her waist. Michael dropped it almost immediately under her icy blue stare. 'We can start practisin' tomorrow,' he said.

'But you're drinking.'

'Just this one,' he swore, 'and then I'm off.'

She watched him go. He seemed steady enough on his feet. The following day she peered into his eyes. They were as dark and as expressionless as ever, but the whites were absolutely clear. There wasn't a tell-tale red vein to be seen.

'All right,' she said, spreading her arms sideways along the side of the wagon as she had seen Sasha doing, 'let's try.'

She felt the wind whistling around her as the knives landed one by one. She strained every nerve to stand still, and the thought flashed through her brain that now she understood why Sasha's eyes had never left Michael's. One error of judgement

213

and she could be dead – or very severely wounded at the very least.

She saw by the sudden droop of his shoulders that the knives had all been thrown. The strain was over for the time being and, a minute later, she was walking away with her knees shaking a little, and laughing weakly.

'You'm a natural,' Michael told her. 'The best yet,' and after that they practised together at every possible opportunity.

Before the Sharkeys reached Newton Stewart and the weather got appreciably colder, Thirza realised that Michael was becoming more and more familiar with her. Furthermore, he was taking her acquiescence for granted. She remembered the rodent's expression she had seen on his face once before. Now when they were alone together he resembled a different, more predatory animal. With a sinking heart she became increasingly convinced that he wanted her for something more than just his assistant. And that was a complication she could well have done without.

They hadn't even left Gatehouse when she saw him coming out of Belle's vardo one afternoon. Thirza went in and immediately sensed that something was wrong.

'What's he been saying to you, Belle?' she demanded.

'I wishes I didn' have to tell you, Thirza.'

'Tell me,' she said, for now she scented danger.

'He'm be wantin' to jump over the broomstick at last . . . Wi' you.'

'I don't know what that means.'

'To be marryin' you.'

'I don't want to marry him or anyone else! I'm only sixteen.'

''Tis old enough.' Belle's head went down and she groaned. 'Oh, *dordi! Dordi!* There be no use goin' agin him. I wouldn't have had this happen fer a hundred pun! He could take one o' his knives an' stick me in the back, never mind iffen I be his mother. Then he'd be king all the sooner. Wot he sez would go. Thirza, we'm got to humour him.'

His own mother believed Michael might kill her if she went against him! His own mother was frightened of him! Now at last Thirza knew that she should have heeded all the warning signs. She realised she was indeed in danger and, through her, so was Belle.

'Sasha's not well, and he'm needin' a woman,' Belle said by

way of explanation. 'But I got him put off till Christmas Day. That's when you'm be jumping over the broomstick. T'wuz the best as I could do.'

'Christmas Day's a long way off, Belle. Three weeks at least.'

And between now and then I'll think of something, Thirza promised herself, smiling at the old Romany woman.

'Did you know Michael's made a bargain with me, Belle? He's going to make me a knife of my own.'

'Oh,' Belle's face brightened. 'He struck a bargain, did he? A Romany never goes back on a bargain. You'll git yer knife.'

'I want you to tell him to stay away from me until then, or else there won't be any jumping over the broomstick. Now, let's have some tea, Belle, and forget all about it in the meantime.'

Thirza intended to forget all about it for ever, herself. Soon she would be gone. She felt quite confident as the caravans headed west for Newton Stewart.

Before the Sharkeys left Newton Stewart they took on a small flock of sheep and several pigs, paid for out of the money in Belle's tins, counted out shilling by shilling while she kept her back to Snaky and Fangs who were doing the business.

'And meal! Don't forget the meal and the tea, fer God's sake. Asides that, a bag o' tatties fer each wagon, a box o' apples an' a sack o' oranges. And don't forget some onions,' she flounced around with more shillings. 'We'm be needin' it all afore this winter's out.'

Next she buttonholed Michael, pressed a golden coin into his hand and whispered in his ear. Thirza didn't like his grin when he accepted it. Later that day the sheep were tied onto the various wagons and the pigs were conveyed, squealing, into a flat-top of their own. They were off.

'Where are we going next?' Thirza asked as the caravans rumbled along.

'To the hills. Thank God,' Belle answered, but with none of her usual sparkle. She seemed sad, even worried and, not long after, Thirza caught her rising stiffly from her knees when she entered the vardo one day. She had been locking another cupboard, and Thirza could have sworn there were long, slim bottles of wine inside it. Why? Thirza understood the Sharkeys

215

drank only ale. They must have got the wine for a special occasion, such as a wedding. *Belle must be keeping up the pretence to Michael that the wedding was going ahead. She was actually making preparations for it.* No wonder she was looking worried. The little incident brought home forcibly to Thirza that somehow she must outwit the Sharkeys, and fast.

Every word Michael said to her now was suggestive, to her great annoyance. 'Just hurry up and make me my knife, Michael,' she said wearily. To her amazement, he began working on it. Day after day he honed the handle, watching her throw with a critical eye, until he was satisfied with the balance.

'Can I have it now?'

'Soon,' Michael promised, but the look of cunning and satisfaction she saw in his eyes alerted her. Clearly, he believed he had some ascendancy over her. Thank God neither he nor any of the other Sharkeys could read her mind.

At last the knife was finished. He presented it to her in a leather sheath ten days before Christmas. 'Put it up yer sleeve,' he said. 'A knife thrower's wife should have a knife up her sleeve. You can protect yerself for ever wi' that knife, wi' an aim like yours.'

She intended to, and she didn't need him to tell her that her aim was good. It was bound to be, at the rate she practised, even when he wasn't there, for Thirza had never done anything by halves.

The Sharkeys were now travelling northwards, and eventually they reached a huge forest. 'Where are we?' Thirza asked Belle.

'Glentrool. We have a place yere. We comes yere every winter. And we'm be just in time,' Belle added, glancing up at the yellow sky.

Each flake of snow scurrying across the road brought Thirza more and more pricks of panic. She strove to remain calm and optimistic, but every day now was one day nearer to Christmas and no opportune moment to escape was presenting itself.

She had been so perfectly sure they would meet a horse and cart going in the opposite direction on these country roads; a lone horseman at the very least. She had counted on people living here – in scattered cottages no doubt – but, if they did, they weren't using the same roads as the Sharkeys. She must make some other plan. After some thought, she made up her mind that once the Sharkeys settled down in their wintering place, and she got the lie of the land, she would slip away. It was her last resort.

The tribe skirted the Forest of Glentrool until, up ahead, the little yellow caravan belonging to Snaky and Caroline turned sharply to the right into the forest, and the other wagons following began to rock and sway ominously on a rough, narrow road. It wound upwards, on a gentle incline for a mile or two, until, going very slowly now, Snaky led them to the right again and finally came to a halt in a disused quarry shaped like a horseshoe. They had arrived. For a moment there was silence.

'I'd never come up yere agin – not fer all the money in the world,' Caroline's desolate voice floated back to the rest of them. 'It's near enough kilt me up yere. God cuss this place! Pass me the baccy, Snaky, pass me the baccy. Quick!' she shouted. However, ten minutes later she was outside unpacking her vardo quite happily, chewing her tobacco.

'The lilac caravan's not coming in the quarry,' Thirza said. 'Why is it staying out on the road?'

'It be the birthin' van when February comes,' Belle said, 'and the birthin' van has to be kept apart. No man, not even Michael, can go in there fer a month afore or a month after. Yes – look at him! He'm moving his stuff into his green wagon. Sasha's mother will move in wi' her instead.'

'When is her baby due, Belle?'

'End o' January, maybe.'

The next morning, when Thirza woke and opened her eyes, she saw frost crystals glistening on the wagon ceiling a few feet above her face. It was bitterly cold. Although it was the shortest day of the year, the light shining in the skylight was very bright, and there was a curious hush outside.

Muttering and groaning, Belle heaved herself, shivering, out of her bunk and limped over to open the top half of the door. 'Dordi, dordi!' she exclaimed, 'there be a foot o' snow out yere!'

Thirza put on her clothes quickly. She hadn't bargained for snow. It could ruin her plans completely. When she put an experimental foot on it she found that, worse still, it was frozen.

One by one the Romany men came out and cleared a spot for their fires. Thirza left the vardo when Michael came to light his mother's, and went for a walk.

Nobody paid any attention to her. She knew they would assume that she was going to the usual place, behind a hedge as a rule. This aspect of travelling life was the one that Thirza had hated most from the beginning. She loathed the dirt and squalor of it, and especially the lack of any sort of privacy. Now, she supposed, the open-air privy would have to be behind a snow drift and, when she found a suitable place, she took stock of the situation from there.

The sides of the quarry towered up above her. She doubted if she could have climbed them even in the height of summer. Iced up as they were at present, escape that way was out of the question.

Her gaze moved around to the mouth of the horseshoe quarry, with the lilac van slung across it. It might be possible to get around it and out on to the road. Slithering and sliding unsteadily on her feet she managed somehow to squeeze past it.

She heard the door of the van opening behind her and, glancing around, was just in time to see a body hurtling towards her out of the corner of her eye. Pregnant or not, Sasha jumped on her and threw her to the snowy ground.

'Brazen bloody bitch!' she screamed. 'Why you'm ever come yere? You'm taken my man!' In her upraised hand was a bar of iron, and in her eyes was murder. 'I'll kill you fer that! I'll kill you!'

In a flash Thirza pulled out her knife. Its blade glinted cold and blue against the snow. She pointed it at Sasha's throat and watched terror replace the red glow in her eyes, hearing the thud as the iron bar fell from Sasha's grasp.

'Get off me, Sasha,' she said calmly, still pointing the knife. 'Here, let me help you up.'

'Don't touch me!' Sasha screamed. 'You'm a bloody witch!'

'Come on now, Sasha. You're going to hurt your baby.'

'Wot do you care about my baby? Wot do I care, now?' Sasha sobbed passionately. 'You'm stole my man.'

Thirza put the knife away and dragged her to her feet. 'If you mean Michael Sharkey,' she said just as passionately, 'I wish your man was still in your vardo. God only knows I don't want him!'

To her amazement Sasha bared her decayed teeth in a horrible imitation of a smile. 'You'm stupid,' she said. 'You'm a silly cow. I knowed he would go to another woman when I got too far on. He allus does. He's been wi' four afore, one fer every time I gave birth – ay, and given two o' them girl babies. They'm here in this camp. But you! He'm going to jump over the broomstick wi' you, and he's never done that wi' any woman afore. You'll be his wife!'

'But I thought this was your first baby!'

'You'm stupid! I got four. Four girls. I can't get a son, but iffen he gives you a son, that son will be the king! I hate you. I hate you, Thirza Gourlay, and I hope the dear God a-years me axin' him to cuss you and make you suffer somethin' wicked!'

'Wot's goin' on yere?' A large woman came out of the lilac caravan, pushed Thirza backwards and hauled Sasha away. 'Wot you'm doin' to my gal? Go away! Go on, git back to Belle, or I'll shout fer Michael.'

Tears of rage and frustration blinded Thirza's eyes as she trudged back to Belle's vardo. Sasha was quite right: she was a stupid cow. If she'd had any sense she would have left the Sharkeys in Dumfries or Newton Stewart, instead of getting herself trapped like this in the back of beyond. If she'd played her cards right she wouldn't have presumed to take Sasha's place as Michael's assistant. She should have made friends with the woman instead of giving her not one, but two deadly reasons to hate her – usurping Sasha's place with Michael, and then, as his prospective bride, holding one of his knives to her throat . . .

If she'd played her cards better, Sasha might even have helped her to escape. As it was, she and her awful mother would see to it that she never got past their vardo. Sasha wasn't so much jealous of her jumping over the broomstick with Michael, as she was jealous of the result of the marriage. Sasha was convinced Michael would father a son, but that would be Thirza's and not her own. As for caring that Thirza was being forced into such a union – on the contrary, Sasha hoped she would really suffer as a result.

Sasha wanted revenge.

25

STILL shaken by this encounter, Thirza was lying miserably on her bunk in the afternoon dozing on and off when fat Lily came to visit. 'Does she know?' she asked. It dawned on Thirza that this visitation of Lily's was not a casual one. Lily had been invited.

'Not yet,' Belle said.

'Let's git on wi' it, then. There be only three days left atween.'

'Lily's speakin' about the weddin',' Belle explained. 'This be Monday. Christmas Day's on Friday, and there's somethin' should be done today so that you'm better in time. You'm got to be blooded.'

''S right,' Lily nodded sagely, and sighed. 'It be for yer own good.'

'Blooded?' Thirza didn't like the sound of that one little bit. 'What do you mean?'

'Well,' Belle took a deep breath, 'you'm be knowing wot a man does on his weddin' night?' she asked delicately.

Thirza gazed at the two gypsy women speechless with horror.

'His *pintle* gits hard, like a tube,' Lily told her. 'Them dee-little seeds o' his runs down through it and inside you.'

'Did any man ever touch yer privates afore?' Belle asked.

'*No!*' Thirza cried, shrinking away. Suddenly she was very frightened. Already she had made up her mind to use her knife on Michael if this farce was played out, but she had never reckoned on an attack from the women.

'Then you be still a maiden,' Lily informed her, 'and maidens has a maidenhead.'

'Just a dee-little skin inside you,' Belle took up the story, 'but men can be savage on their wedding nights, and then you suffers terrible pains and agonies, ain't that so, Lily?'

'Terrible pains,' Lily agreed. 'Wuss than water-pains. Wuss than month-pains. Romany women be more gentle wi' a bride. We do it gentle, a few nights afore she jumps over the broomstick.'

'Well, you're not doing it to me!' Thirza defied them, feeling for her knife in her sleeve.

'Now then,' Belle said soothingly. 'I'm took the knife away, my dear, when you were havin' a nap. You'm fetched the bloodin' stick, Lily?'

Thirza couldn't believe what she was hearing. She couldn't believe what she was seeing either, when Lily unfolded the white cloth in her lap to reveal a bleached, polished stick about seven inches long, with a handle on the end of it.

'It be clean,' she said. 'Been in boilin' water,' and suddenly Belle was standing over Thirza where she lay, holding her down and whipping up her skirts while Lily prised open her legs.

'No! No!' Thirza screamed, but the women held her down more firmly. She felt the stick entering her very cautiously and then a sharp pain. It was all over in a minute.

'Wot did I tell you, Lily?' Belle said above Thirza's sobs. 'She'm be a good gal! Now, it be done, my dear,' she said holding Thirza's hands. 'You won't feel any more pain, now. There be a little bit o' blood from where that skin was pierced, but it'll soon stop.'

Lily pulled her skirts back down. 'Not a drop went on that pretty petticoat, my dear. Wherever did you git such a pretty petticoat?'

'From my mother.'

Thirza turned her face to the wall and cried. She had never missed Ruth as much as she did now.

'Her pore mother be dead,' Belle explained to Lily over her head.

'Wot about a cup o' tea, then, Belle?'

'I'll git it.'

Tea, Thirza thought bitterly. Tea, the Romanies' cure for everything. But it was going to take a lot more than tea to cure *this*. She felt her temper rising to a pitch it had never risen before. She had been taken by surprise with the blooding stick, but she swore upon the memory of her mother a solemn oath that she would never be taken by surprise again. She wasn't going to take any more of this lying down, in any sense of the word.

Never. From now on, whatever happened, she would dictate the terms.

'Where's my knife?' she asked, sitting up and refusing the mug of tea Belle was holding out to her.

'In safe keepin', my dear. You'll be gittin' it back when Sasha gits her baby.'

'I want it *now*.'

'I can't give you it. I haven't got it.'

'Then,' Thirza said calmly, 'I'll think of some other way to kill myself. There are plenty of other ways to do it, besides by the knife.'

'Wot?' Lily cried in alarm. 'Oh, Jesus God A'mighty! Listen to that, Belle! Oh, my Jesus! Oh, my blessed Jesus!'

'But you promised me you'd jump over the broomstick on Christmas Day!' Belle wailed. 'You promised to git wed to Michael! Oh, my God! Wot you'm sayin', gal? You know wot he might do to me iffen he'm thwarted! Oh, me pore dead Matt . . . Oh, me pore dead Matt, me pore dead husband!'

'I know I said I would at the time, Belle. But I've been raped since then.'

'Raped? Raped?' Belle and Lily cried together, in alarm. 'Who did it?'

'You did it, the pair of you. You invaded my body against my will. That's rape, whether it's done by a man or a woman.' The two women clutched each other in fear and trembling, mumbling to each other and shaking. 'Oh yes,' Thirza went on, 'I could get the pair of you put in jail for that! You know it, don't you?'

She saw that they had never thought of such a thing. 'We do it to help all our women,' Lily sobbed.

'I suppose there's no way out of it,' Thirza said, trembling with fear. She felt sick at the thought of it. 'I know I'll have to go through with the jumping over the broomstick now. But,' she paused, and fixed them with her eyes, snapping, piercing and brilliantly blue in her rage, '*I refuse to become with child as a result. Do you hear me?*'

'Yes,' they replied.

'So what are you going to do about that, Belle? Or you, Lily? I promise you if such a thing should happen I'll not only kill myself, but the baby too, even if it's a boy. You've raped me. Now, you'd better help me.'

'Terrible, that look in her yoks! Tell her to stop *trashin'* us wi' her yoks!' Lily moaned.

'She means you be frightening her wi' yer eyes, Thirza,' Belle said, bowing her head and relapsing into silence.

'Romanies know cures for everything, don't they?' Thirza went on relentlessly. 'Belle, you've told me how to cure measles, croup, pneumonia and a lot of other things. You're bound to know about this,' she said desperately. 'You Romany women must know how to stop having a baby, as well.'

'Well, I don't,' Lily quavered. 'We'm got our two daughters, Fangs and me. I'm goin' to keep on tryin' till I gits me a son.'

Then Belle looked up. 'My Isadora once told me somethin',' she said. 'It was about a woman in her camp wi' eight *chavies* already, an' a-feared she would die iffen she had another.'

'Yes?' Thirza asked.

'So she got the orange skins.'

By now Thirza was used to the strange ways and remedies of the Romanies. The strangest thing of all was that they usually worked. Orange skins must also have some magical property. She was quite prepared to believe anything Belle told her in this predicament.

'Isadora said the woman cut an orange in half like we does and kept the skins. Then she put one of the half orange skin up inside her like an upside down cup to catch all them dee-little seeds. She tied little woollen strings to it so she could pull it back down again. Her man never knew any difference.'

'I never yeared o' that afore,' Lily said, open-mouthed.

Thirza could see now that the two women simply didn't understand how much they had offended her already. Now here they were, suggesting how they could offend her again. She looked at them and tried to imagine the simple, open lives they had lived. They had never known privacy. A woman's modesty didn't exist. They genuinely meant her no harm. They were only trying to help. 'I'll try anything,' she said desperately.

'We should collect orange skins, then, Lily,' Belle said. 'Wi' your hands you could tie on the strings. You'm be so neat.'

'And you'd better do it in such a way that they don't come off,' Thirza warned her emphatically. 'You've only got three days!'

'Come back in two,' Belle told her, 'Christmas Eve.'

On Christmas Eve Thirza and the two gypsy women prepared themselves for the second operation in Belle's vardo behind locked doors.

'Spread your legs and draw up your knees,' Lily instructed her, showing Thirza the inverted half orange skin with long woollen strings attached firmly to it. 'Now,' she said, pushing it up inside her as far as she could, 'it be in place.'

'Oh, God in Heaven,' Belle moaned. 'I hope it works and he doesn't notice. Wot iffen he notices, Lily?'

'It had better work,' Thirza scowled at them. 'Lily, you had better make a neat job of this, or else you two know what'll happen.'

There was a great commotion going on outside. The men had killed two sheep and set up spits over the fires which were much larger than usual. By Christmas Day itself the excitement had risen to a crescendo. The acrid smell of mutton fat hissing and spitting in the flames was overcome by the aroma of the roasting meat, and in other big pots the women were boiling a mixture of potatoes, carrots and onions.

'Time to get into yer Fair Day clothes,' Belle said.

There was no way out now. Terror invaded Thirza so that she began to shudder, but worse than her dread was the repugnance she felt for the man she was being forced to marry. 'Oh, God,' she screamed silently, 'why is this happening to me? You shouldn't let it happen to any woman!' She burst into tears. Neither Lily's, nor Belle's heart melted in the slightest as they went on calmly preparing the weeping girl.

'We'm seen all this before,' Lily assured her, placing the orange skin firmly in place. 'They be wedding nerves, that's wot. Now stand up and we'll put on that pretty petticoat o' yourn. Ain't it a pretty petticoat, Belle?'

The very sight of her petticoat, and all it meant to her, in the gypsy woman's hands infuriated Thirza. She snatched it away from Lily and stepped into it herself, dried her tears and squared her shoulders to meet whatever was in store for her. That was the trouble, she thought. She had no clear idea what would happen to her on her wedding night.

'That's right,' Belle nodded, slipping Thirza's dress over her head. 'Now give us a smile, gal, and remember – you'm to be Queen of the Sharkeys.'

Every fibre of her being was resisting the very idea of such a fate as she hesitated, a very unwilling bride, on the top step of the vardo while the Sharkeys all looked up at her.

It was a very important occasion. In a few minutes she would be married to their future king. In the world of the Romanies, their queen-to-be had much the same status as the Queen of England. Thirza supposed anyone would say she had arrived. As far as she was concerned she *had* arrived, but it was at her lowest ebb so far.

It all happened in a nightmare blur. A broomstick was laid down, black against the snow, right in the middle of the ring of fires. Fangs, looking important for the occasion, was clad in a very loud, ill-fitting plaid suit in which yellow predominated, a red neckerchief, a green hat and very large mudddy boots laced with string. Remembering the portrait Belle had shown her, Thirza supposed that this gorgeous apparel had once belonged to Matt Sharkey, Belle's dead husband.

With a demented look in his eyes, Fangs mumbled a mumbo-jumbo of words over the broomstick. They meant nothing to Thirza. Then Michael put his arm around her and carried her over the broomstick. The Sharkeys cheered and clapped. 'Now you'm my wife,' he grinned at her.

'Where's the wedding ring?' she glared at him.

For answer, Michael took the broad silver snake ring he always wore on his middle finger and held it out to her. Nobody else except a traveller would wear a heavy, wide ring like that. When Thirza put it on it slid around uselessly, many sizes too big. He was quite unconcerned. Belle had appeared at the door of her vardo with her arms around bottles of wine, and he was much more interested in them.

The feasting and drinking went on for hours until, at a prearranged signal, Lily and Fangs stood at either side of her and held her in a grip of iron. 'Time to go,' Fangs said, and they marched her down to the old green caravan and opened the door.

This time, an old straw mattress on the floor had been added to the furniture, which had never consisted of much more than Michael's bench where he worked with his knives.

'Just lie back,' Lily advised her before she left, leaving her in icy blackness. 'Think o' somethin' else. Wotever you do, don't struggle. Remember that orange skin and don't burst it.'

In the darkness Thirza felt all over the top of the bench. He might have been working on a knife and left it there. But there was no knife, nor on the floor, either. A strong sweet sickly scent led her to a heap of Michael's clothes, thrown in a heap in a corner but, though she searched his pockets thoroughly, she found nothing.

Minutes later, Michael lurched to the door. He was quite drunk, but not too drunk to throw her down on her back, and his smell when he pressed down on top of her was stronger and more sickening than ever.

Thirza thought she was going to vomit. Then she thought she was going to suffocate, he was pressing so hard. She tried to fend him off when, without a word, he punched hard at her jaw. While everything went black for a minute he thrust himself inside her. In spite of Lily's advice, in spite of her own awful predicament, she fought him to the bitter end through waves of sickness and, finally he won and she lost her viginity as well as the silver ring.

She didn't even look for the ring the following morning, after he had taken her again. That was twice now that Michael had invaded her, and neither Belle nor Lily had advised her about such an emergency. The skin was sure to have burst.

Thirza hurried behind the biggest snowdrift she could find, and found herself looking across at innumerable yellow and brown-stained patches in the snow. Now she added her own contribution, a bright orange skin, and thanked God it was intact. She buried it in more snow with tears pouring down her face. She couldn't put up with this. It was degrading. She had always believed when two people got married there was some sort of tenderness between them, even love. She felt none for her new husband and, quite clearly, he felt none for her. He had simply used her like any other convenience.

She felt like a whore.

She felt more and more like a whore over the next few weeks. She felt worse still every time she was forced to be the receptacle for Michael's 'dee-little seeds'. The brightness soon left her eyes. She felt destroyed and bitterly humiliated. Sasha had got her revenge, many times over.

Thirza often wondered if it was her own bitterness towards Sasha, or just her desire to know if the woman's baby was any nearer being born, that drew her every day to the lilac caravan. Every day she circled around it.

'There be more snow comin',' Belle warned her late one afternoon. 'You'm better not go far, Thirza. See, it be started already!'

'I won't be long,' Thirza said, and set off into the swirling snowflakes, Belle's scolding voice in her ears.

Within minutes Belle's voice seemed to be a hundred miles away. The snow hissed and seethed all round her, the wind whipping it up into her face. Thirza told herself not to be silly. Nobody could get lost in a quarry, even a big one, and anyway there was no way out.

Soon, she couldn't see a hand in front of her, and she began to wonder if she was only going round in circles, when she heard the faint screams of a woman, and ploughed on in their direction. By some miracle she had found the lilac van, and Sasha, to judge from the awful noise, was giving birth.

'Push that *chavi* out! Push it out!' she heard a woman grunt. It was Sasha's mother.

'Oh, me blessed Jesus!' Sasha was screaming. 'Oh, Ma! Oh, Ma!'

'*Push!*' the old woman shouted above her screams. 'Oh, yes! Oh, yes! That be the head! Now, once more, gal . . . That's right, one more push!'

There was a terrible scream. It went on and on. And then

came a shout. 'Oh, God be praised! Oh, me blessed Jesus! Sasha, it be a boy! A beautiful boy!'

Thirza waited no longer. If she ever got back to the vardo it would be a miracle, but one thing was sure, neither Sasha nor her mother would be able to venture out that night. Thirza battled on, gasping for air while the snow threatened to suffocate her, but her mind was thinking furiously all the while.

No one would know about the birth of the baby. She would be first with the news – and she had an idea. She stood quite still for a few minutes, and allowed the thick snowflakes to cover her. She arrived at Belle's vardo hoping to look like a ghost, an apparition all in white, and, when Lily screamed at the sight of her, she knew she had succeeded. Belle's vardo was full of people, Lily, Fangs, Snaky, Caroline and Michael, all staring at her with frightened superstitious eyes.

'We thought you'm be dead,' Belle said. 'Drowneded in the snow.'

'Well, there *was* something came over me,' Thirza admitted. 'I had a vision.'

'Wot did I tell yer?' Lily cried. 'There's somethin' wrong wi' that gal somewheres! She'm not natural!'

'Hush yer mouth! Silly cow!' Fangs said. 'Wot did yer see?'

'I saw you, Michael, holding a baby boy. You're going to have a son.'

'Oh, my!' Belle said, clutching her breast. 'Oh my!'

'I'll believe it when I see it,' Michael growled. 'But, better'n that! We'm got a fortune-teller in our midst, iffen it be true!'

'Oo-ah!' they all looked at Thirza in fear and admiration.

'Yes,' Michael said. 'And so now she's more valuable than ever!'

What had she done, Thirza wondered sickly? No matter how she twisted and turned there seemed no way out of it. Her nights were a hell from the moment that Michael arrived at Belle's vardo each evening and ushered her out of it down to the green wagon – and her days were almost as bad, dreading the next onslaught he would put her through.

Lily had been right, she thought gloomily. It was better and safer just to lie still and let him have his way, and no matter how he tried to rouse her she remained passive, with her head turned to the side in an effort to escape his horrendous breath. Her accurate 'prediction' had made no change in Michael's demands.

Thirza was miserable. She began to brood, seriously contemplating suicide. Angrily, she pushed these spectres away. She was Thirza Gourlay, and somehow she would survive. Then, one night in the middle of February, Michael came out with a statement that allowed her to glimpse a chink of light at the end of the long, dark tunnel.

'I be goin' back to Sasha now,' he said. 'A man should be with his son.' He demanded fewer and fewer favours from her the following week, while Thirza held her breath in the fervent hope that he was secretly visiting the lilac caravan already, whatever the Romany law. 'Sasha don't want to go back to the knives fer a while,' he added another night, confirming her suspicions. 'Will you be willin' to carry on helpin'?'

'We could make another bargain, then, Michael Sharkey,' she told him coldly. 'If you never make me sleep with you again, I'll carry on.'

'Go on, then!' said Michael, and his palm met hers in the smart clap which always clinched a Romany deal. 'You'm no good, anyway,' he told her flatly as he turned away, 'lyin' there like a dead fish. Sasha's got some spunk about her.'

It was as though he had thrown a bucket of cold water over her. She gasped at his effrontery. He had put her through . . . *all that*, for nothing. He had probably fancied her only as a convenience for a week or two until he could get back to Sasha. He had certainly never loved her. There had scarcely been a civil word between them. There had certainly not been one of love.

Well, Thirza thought, she'd known almost from the beginning that there was a streak of madness in him, and a dangerous streak at that — even his own mother was frightened of him and feared for her life. But at least now there was a glimpse of the sun behind all the black clouds of recent weeks hanging over both her and Belle. Thirza could scarcely contain her relief. He didn't want her any more . . . Oh, God, it was a miracle!

'Go to her with my blessing,'

Thirza smiled for the first time in two and a half months, for only that morning Belle had said, 'You'm got yer monthlies agin, then?' – a thing impossible to conceal in their close proximity in the vardo, and it meant that she was clear, unscathed in body at least.

This time she didn't care in the least that the Sharkeys were ankle-deep in mud again, with the melting of the snow. She helped them instead, happy and relieved.

The pigs had all been slaughtered for their bacon, and they were down to their last sheep. Supplies were running out, most urgently their supply of fresh water. Snaky examined the road at half-hourly intervals and the sky all day long, and the minute he pronounced that he and Caroline would try it in the yellow caravan, the tribe began to make ready to move again.

Thirza cried with excitement at the prospect of leaving this terrible quarry. She was not surprised that it all took the best part of a week. She wasn't surprised that it was a week of windy weather, either, for the gypsies knew every sign in the sky, and could usually foretell the weather accurately from hour to hour.

The road dried up quickly and the caravans set off as slowly and in as higgledy-piggledy a fashion as ever on the way back down towards Newton Stewart. After long stops for water, and to clean off all the mud again, they arrived at the outskirts of the town at the end of March, and Fangs and Snaky and Michael promptly smuggled their horses into a farmer's field to crop the grass overnight.

Belle shook her head and took her pipe out of her mouth long enough to cluck her tongue.

'They be fools,' she told Thirza, 'but men – they allus knows best! That ole farmer'll git them, wait an' see.'

Very early the next morning the men gave the farmer the slip when they went to retrieve their horses. Only Michael came back with two, instead of the one he'd put in the field the night before.

Smartly now, for the Sharkeys, the tribe made their way to the park where the first horse sale of the season was taking place. Nobody would have recognised Michael's extra horse. Originally a fine chestnut with a white blaze, he was now a black stallion. Only someone examining him closely would have seen that his coat didn't glisten and shine. It was dull and matt.

'Oh, *dordi, dordi*,' Belle muttered. 'Oh, me sainted Jesus. Oh, God help us iffen it rains.'

But rain it did, and all the black paint ran off the horse. The long white patch on his nose was coming into sight when the irate farmer found him and, in no time at all, Michael was being led away in handcuffs to the jail.

Belle and Sasha began weeping and wailing in a way that was pitiful to listen to. Thirza watched Michael's retreating, dejected back in thinly-disguised delight. She didn't think she would ever see Michael Sharkey again with any luck, but she fell to brooding over what he had done to her. Apart from the bitter memories of the terrible degradation she had had to bear, there was still the greatest worry of all. She was a woman married to a gypsy. Nothing could change that.

Eventually she saw that she could easily fall into a trough of despair and depression if she continued to brood like this. She must put these unpleasant facts to the back of her mind, wipe Michael clean out of it, and carry on with her own life as best as she could.

'Can I have my knife back now?' she asked Belle.

The old woman reached up inside her sleeve. 'Ay,' she sighed.

'You've had it all along,' Thirza accused her.

'I wuz meanin' to do right wi' yer,' Belle said mournfully, 'but Michael came first. In the end I did yer nothin' but harm, did I? An' now I've lost me son as well. Yere, take the knife! Stick it in me, iffen yer like!' She turned her woeful, wrinkled brown face up to Thirza. 'I'm not never felt so bad since me ole Matt passed away!'

'Oh, Belle,' Thirza put her arm around the gypsy's shaking shoulders, 'Michael will be back in a few months! You know that – and something else as well. Soon I'll be leaving you.'

'Don't go, Thirza,' Belle pleaded. 'I don't know iffen I could manage wi'out yer, now. An' there won't be any knife-throwin' till Michael comes back.'

'No.'

'We'm be needin' the money,' she whined. 'Wot about the fortune tellin'?'

'All right, then,' Thirza said. 'Get me a tent and I'll do the fortunes for a while, until one day I'll just disappear. It's got nothing to do with you, Belle. You tried your best to be good to me in your own way,' she squeezed the old woman's shoulders. 'I'll miss you when I go.'

'You'm the best dee-little gal I ever seed,' Belle dissolved into tears altogether.

26

ALMOST caught red-handed in an unsuccessful hijack attempt, the *Black Prince* scuttled out of the Bay of Biscay and into the safer waters of the English Channel. The whole crew, Jordi included, breathed a sigh of relief. Captain Jack Hawkins didn't hang about in the Channel, either. They were close to Whitehaven again before he slackened sail.

'Ay, lad,' Jordi heard him shouting at Drew Ellis, 'that was a close shave!'

'Too close for comfort, Jack. And where are we headed, next?'

'For the Solway.'

'The Solway?' Jordi watched Ellis's cheeks paling, 'Where, exactly?'

'Oh, come on, man! You should know! You masterminded the entire operation when we smuggled those goods into the cave at Sarkfoot Farm. I'm going back to get them, or the money Joe Dan Linton got for them. He's never coughed up, has he?'

'No . . . No, he never did.'

'And, of course, you'll be coming with me,' Captain Hawkins swept on. 'I've never actually landed there myself, but you know the place outside in.'

'You'll have to excuse me,' Ellis staggered off clutching his stomach, doubled-up as if in agony.

Hawkins stood for a minute and gazed after him with a

puzzled expression. Then he followed him. Barefoot, and at a discreet distance, Jordi shadowed them both and flattened himself against the wall outside Ellis's cabin so that he could hear every word that was said.

'What's wrong with you?'

'I don't rightly know. It's been coming on me for a while, but now the pain's settled itself in my gut,' Drew Ellis moaned. 'I'm sorry, Jack, but I'm no use to you like this.'

'Lie down on your bunk, then. Maybe that'll stop it. You'll feel better in the morning.'

'I wish I could think so! I've had these attacks before, you know. Oh, God . . .' Ellis moaned again. 'They usually last about a week. I'm useless for a week when this damned trouble hits me.'

'Well, well, then.' A note of irritation crept into the Captain's voice, as he prepared to leave. Jordi fled as soft-footed as a cat, and the last thing he heard Hawkins saying was, 'I'll just have to get someone else.'

'Jordi,' he said later when they were sailing cautiously under the cover of darkness into the Solway Firth, 'I had hoped to take Drew Ellis with me on a little matter of business tonight, but he's fallen ill.'

'Yes, sir?'

'Just a flying visit to a farm in Gretna which he's well acquainted with. There's a cave underneath it.'

'Yes, sir.'

But the Captain's attention had wandered from the subject. 'Look at those lights, lad!' he said. 'That's Dumfries over there, where my poor old parents live, God help me . . . If they're still living, that's to say.'

Ah! So Dumfries was the place, thought Jordi. That was the place where he would escape the *Black Prince* at last, somehow. If you sailed into the Solway estuary, the only way out was back the way you had come. Hawkins would have to sail past Dumfries again, in the opposite direction.

Perhaps tomorrow . . .

'Certainly, I'll go with you to the cave, sir,' Jordi smiled. 'How many of us do you want to go with you?'

'Just you, lad. We'll take one of the small dinghies . . . less noise . . . less chance of being seen . . . just the two of us,'

Hawkins said disjointedly, his mind obviously still on his father and mother.

Later that night, while the *Black Prince* lay off the coast in darkness, Jordi rowed the dinghy quietly ashore with a flowing tide to help him, past a little pier which seemed to be built at the side of the farmhouse just below a tumbledown cottage.

'It's dead ahead,' Hawkins whispered. 'I can see the opening. That's right, lad – row her straight in.'

The cave was as black as pitch. The sea lapped around them with an eerie echo, and Jordi thought the cave must run a fair way back. Hawkins scraped a light and lit the lantern. When he held it up for them to look around they saw natural shelves in the face of the rock sides, and every shelf was empty.

Jordi rowed the dinghy around a corner in the cave, as far in as he could, but it was the same story. The Captain's goods had gone.

'That cheating bugger, Joe Dan Linton,' he growled, and Jordi could sense the man's temper rising hysterically. Hawkins was having a run of bad luck. Twice in a row he had been cheated now, first of gold bullion in that last aborted attempt, and now this.

'Hush!' Jordi hissed vehemently, to stop the man's rage boiling over so near the farm. 'Let's get out of here, fast!'

Hawkins managed to contain himself until they were halfway back to the ship. Then, seething with rage and frustration, he burst forth with a string of oaths. He was positively ranting when Jordi shipped his oars and gripped his arms.

'Listen, sir,' he said quietly. 'The whole trip needn't be in vain. It needn't be wasted.'

'What does that mean?'

'We've to go back past Dumfries, haven't we? You could visit your parents, at least. How do you know when you might be back this way again?'

'You know I can't! You know I can't!' Hawkins shook him off angrily. 'I can't take the *Prince* in there of all places! Nobody must know that I am the son of the respectable Hawkins family in Dumfries. *They* don't even know themselves what my business is. They don't connect their son, Captain John Hawkins, sailing the seven seas and sending them home plenty of money, with the notorious Jack Hawkins of the *Black Prince*.'

'Of course, sir. I understand that you wouldn't wish to sail into Dumfries openly. But you could anchor around the back of that Head I saw further along – '

'Southerness.'

'Yes, sir. You could send McKim or someone ashore to hire a string of horses and take them to Southerness,' Jordi said calmly. 'Nobody's going to notice horsemen riding into the town, and it's been so long now since you were there that no one will recognise you. Not at night, anyway.'

Hawkins shuddered a great breath of release and delight. 'By God, Jordi, you've got it! You've hit on the plan! By God, that's what we'll do. I always knew it – you're clever. A bloody sight cleverer than that Drew Ellis, lying spewing in his bunk!'

'Sir?'

'He was in cahoots with Joe Dan Linton, wasn't he? How much does Ellis know about that cave, I'd like to know?'

'Forget about the cave and everything else, sir. Just think about seeing your family again.'

'You're right, lad. I should have listened to you all along. You'll come with me to see my parents? You should be at my side so that I can show them my adviser, by God! Yes, you'll be the first one I'll take ashore. If Ellis can get himself up out of that bunk, he'll be the second one. Then I'll abandon him, and let him look out for himself. He's running from something, you know, and I've sheltered him for long enough. You've been a great help, Jordi.'

'Thank you, sir,' Jordi said, helping him to mount the rope-ladder before he sprang up himself, and then raised the dinghy, shaking his head in wonder. For of course, there was nothing clever about his plan at all. Any fool could have thought of it long ago. But it had occurred to him at precisely the right moment, just when Captain Hawkins was too incensed to see how transparent it was.

Praying that he had set the framework for his escape, Jordi lay back on his bunk that night with his hands behind his head, staring for hours into the darkness, before he composed himself for sleep.

There was no use worrying any more. He had a whole day's work ahead of him tomorrow, and when night came round again and the game began, he would need a clear head. He would just have to worry about one move at a time.

It was just beginning to get dark that soft, balmy evening in May when the party from the *Black Prince* rode along the High Street in Dumfries. McKim went first with Ellis alongside him. Tucked in behind them were Jordi and Hawkins, and two other crewmen brought up the rear. Jordi noticed that Hawkins' hands were beginning to tremble with excitement.

'What about a drink, sir?' he suggested.

It was the answer to his prayer when the Captain nodded his head and grinned. 'Just what I was thinking myself,' he said, 'and I know the very place. McKim, keep going! We're not far from the Globe.'

The Globe Inn didn't look much from the High Street, but they all dismounted, tethered their horses and filed down a very narrow alley to the door. At first glance there didn't seem to be room to swing a cat in the tiny smoke-filled room, but the men there already shifted obligingly and eventually all six found seats. Their attention was drawn to the man at the end of the bar who was sitting on a high stool, reciting poetry.

'This was Robbie Burns's favourite Howff,' Hawkins told them, 'and that old man reciting his poems is sitting on his stool, silly old devil!'

'He's not so silly. I'll bet he never has to buy a drink for himself all night long,' Ellis laughed and downed his first whisky.

The barmaid brought another round of drinks. Hawkins paid again and ordered more, as the old man came to the end of his poem and someone else began to sing a Burns song. More and more men squeezed in, and now there was standing room only. Whisky flew fast and furious, the noise in the small, hot room was deafening, and everything was going far better than Jordi could ever have hoped for when Ellis suddenly jumped up.

'We could all do that, you know,' he yelled at the top of his voice, sneering at the old man who was in the middle of another poem. 'You're not the only one who can recite Burns backwards.'

'Let him be!' snapped the man behind the bar. 'He's a

regular in the Globe. You're not! We can do without trouble-
makers here.'

'For God's sake, shut up!' Hawkins hissed, his new-found
hatred of his erstwhile friend suddenly boiling over. 'And when
are *you* going to stand your hand, I'd like to know?'

'Me? I've got no money!'

'Oh?' Hawkins rose to his huge threatening height. 'What
about your share of the proceeds from that cave, then?'

'I don't know anything about that,' Ellis shrugged his shoulders, 'and you can't prove I do! Neither can that brown-skinned
bugger you've taken such a fancy to.'

Now all Jordi's bitter dislike of the man rose to the surface,
too. He took a leap towards Ellis and whirled him about. 'Here!'
he demanded, 'are you talking about me, you bastard?'

'Who else?' Ellis jostled him aside.

'Right,' said Jordi, 'you asked for it!' Somehow in that crowd
he managed to knee him smartly between the legs and, when
Ellis doubled up in his pain, he punched at the side of his jaw.

Ellis's head merely rocked a little on his shoulders. He came
back at Jordi with his fists flailing and, at that, the Globe
erupted. Every man's drinking companion became his bitterest
enemy in the space of seconds. There was uproar.

'Give him hell, lad,' Hawkins' voice roared above the commotion as he tried to battle his way through the brawling mob.

Out of the corner of his eye, Jordi saw that the Captain
wasn't going to manage it. In that split second – as he glanced
to the side – he felt a tug on his neck. Drew Ellis had jerked
his gold chain off. He couldn't believe it. He had worn it for
years without even thinking about it. But now that it had been
snatched away from him it suddenly became the single most
important thing in his life. It was all that was left to him of
his mother and, before that, of his father. He simply *had* to get
it back, there were no two ways about it. He tried to snatch it
back but his hand came away with only a small bundle – not
the necklace he wanted. Impatiently, he stuffed the bundle into
his breeches and, finding an almost superhuman strength from
somewhere, he summoned up a punch that knocked Drew Ellis
clean out of the open door. As he battled his way to follow
Ellis into the narrow alley outside, another part of his brain
thought of Hawkins and his men who were hemmed inside;

now here he was outside and, as soon as he had dealt with Ellis and retrieved his gold chain with the key on it, he would be on his way.

But the alley was empty. There was no sign of Ellis. He rushed out into the High Street and saw at once that there were only five horses instead of six, and from further up the street he heard the pounding of hooves fading into the distance.

For the second time that evening the townspeople of Dumfries scattered left and right off the middle of the High Street, as another horseman galloped along to the danger of everyone's life and limb. Jordi knew they were shaking their fists at him, but he galloped on grimly for at least two miles before he stopped to listen for the hoofbeats up ahead.

But they had gone. He had lost Drew Ellis, and he had lost his gold chain. It was gone for ever. The man was all bad, he thought in a fury of hatred. He brooded over it for another few miles until, gradually, the thumping of his heart steadied, the red mist of temper before his eyes cleared away and, with a shout of laughter, he realised that he was free.

Free, at last! And with a good horse beneath him!

To his left the River Nith glistened blackly in the dusk. A mist rose off the river, and with the chill of the night after all the excitement of the evening, he began to shiver. The best thing to do would be to find somewhere to sleep and carry on in the morning when he could see where he was going. He rode on until he came to a small farmhouse at the side of the road, in complete darkness, with a barn beside it. In the next field some horses were resting. Quietly, he slipped his horse in beside them, shut the gate behind him and crept up to the barn door. It opened easily and, finding the hay inside, Jordi clambered over it and hid himself over by the wall. Then he fell into a deep sleep.

In his dreams he heard the sound of voices, a woman's angry voice and the low rumble of mens' voices, followed by the beat of horses galloping away. But he only turned over contentedly in the warm hay. As he turned, he felt something digging into his side and, waking, remembered the bundle he had snatched from Ellis. Curious, he drew it out to see what it might be. A purse full of money! Counting it, he was astonished to find there were fifty pounds. But Ellis had definitely had nothing when he had boarded the *Black Prince* – he must have stolen it while aboard . . . Well, Ellis would get little satisfaction out of *these* ill-gotten gains! Smiling, he fell asleep again.

'Imphm!' A woman's voice woke him early in the morning, climbing over the hay towards him. 'And what are ye doin' here, may I ask?'

He thought she must be in her forties, broad, and with a sturdy pair of legs holding her up. She stood there regarding him with a pitchfork in a hand as large as a man's.

'I beg your pardon, madam,' Jordi said, getting up off the hay. 'I'll pay you for the use of your barn, and for the grass my horse has cropped through the night in your field.'

'Oh, ay?' she said, her expression still severe.

'Your house was in darkness last night when I got here. I didn't like to disturb you, or I would have asked your permission first,' he said, handing her some money.

Still she stood, barring his way. 'Four other men werena so particular about waking me up!' she scowled. 'They were looking for a young man. Dark-avised, they said he was. Did ye no' hear us?'

'I heard something – but I thought I was dreaming. Please take the money, and I'll be on my way. They might still suspect this house, and then you'll be in danger.'

'Och, no, laddie,' her expression softened. 'I knew fine there was someone in my barn. But I didn't like those men and so I never let on. They're long gone. Besides, there's enough money here to pay for yer breakfast as well. Leave yer horse and come inside!' She led the way and pointed him to a chair beside a scrubbed wooden table. 'Ye'll tak' some porridge?'

'I haven't had porridge for a long, long time, Mrs –?'

'Miss,' she corrected him. 'Miss Stewart. I've lived here alone since my father died. Why have ye no' had porridge for so long?'

'I've been at sea. I jumped ship last night,' he grinned at her. 'Those men must have been some of the crew looking for me.'

'But how did they know to come this way?'

'I was chasing another man who jumped ship. We both dashed through the streets of Dumfries, one after the other on horseback. I don't suppose that happens every night in

Dumfries! The people on the street would be angry enough to point out which way we'd gone.'

'Where are ye goin' now, then?'

'Edinburgh, if I can find the way.'

'Well, ye're on the right road. Keep straight on until ye come to a town called Thornhill. The road branches off there to the right. Ye go through the hills after that, through the Dalveen Pass. It's the drovers' road up to Crawford. From there ye'll easy find yer way.'

Waving goodbye to Miss Stewart, Jordi collected his horse and trotted along the empty road in the pleasant sunshine. There was plenty of time now to consider what he would do about Ellis. Where had he gone? Jordi had no idea where the man had come from originally. He only knew that he had joined the *Black Prince* at Whitehaven. Well, he would go to India House first, do his long-promised business there with Marmaduke Elliot and, after that, go across the Forth to St Fillan and the Gourlays' house, since he was in this direction. After that he would begin his search for Ellis, or whatever the man's real name was.

He was just breasting a hill overlooking a broad valley when he saw to his horror four men riding towards him, Hawkins, McKim and the two others. They must have decided to turn back. In five minutes they would be upon him.

And there was nowhere to hide.

27

THIRZA scowled at the men putting up the tent. Her bitter thoughts had been triggered off by Michael Sharkey's release from prison, when she had hoped never to see him again. But here he was, as large as life, and back with the tribe.

'It's not wide enough,' she snapped. 'How can a table, two chairs *and* a mattress go in that narrow space? Do I have to tell you *every* time?'

The Sharkeys got another canvas, lifted the pegs they had driven into the ground already and set them back another three feet. While two of them went to get the furniture, another pinned a sign above the entrance flap. It said 'FORTUNE TELLER' in longhand, and had been written by Thirza herself, since none of the others knew how to.

Inside, she supervised the placing of the straw mattress and then the curtain to draw across it, screening it from her place of business. She made the men lay down the card-table first this way and then that, and when they had placed the chairs to her satisfaction she waved them away imperiously before she walked over to Belle's vardo.

Belle greeted her with downcast eyes, still ashamed of herself.

'When I start telling the fortunes,' Thirza said, 'you know it goes on all day. Send down my meals and remember, Belle – I want Snaky and Fangs within calling distance.'

'Sure, I'll remember,' Belle sighed.

'I don't want any more trouble like I had in Dumfries, when that man tried to make off with the takings.'

'No.'

'And from now on I'll be sleeping in the tent all summer. I've got my mattress in it already.'

'So I see,' Belle replied, not daring to argue.

Thirza knew she wouldn't argue. None of the Sharkeys did any more, not now that her fortune telling tent was the best paying sideshow of them all – more popular even than Michael's, who was now back together with Sasha and the knives.

Thirza reckoned that already this season she had handed over more than enough money to Belle to pay for her keep since she had joined the tribe. She counted it all up in her head while she composed herself at the card-table to face her clients. Yes . . . It was more than enough . . .

An elderly woman came in first.

'Please sit down, madam,' Thirza pointed to the other chair and then adopted her best wheedling tone. 'You must cross my palm with silver. The more you pay, the better the luck.'

She studied the woman fumbling in her purse. She was in her late fifties, quite well dressed in black and carrying a large carpet-bag. Thirza diagnosed instantly that she was on her way to visit someone, but that huge swelling of her neck would soon obstruct her windpipe.

The woman put a whole crown into her hand. Five whole shillings, first thing in the morning! For that, Thirza knew she would have to be as kind as possible.

'Give me your right hand,' she said. 'Ah yes, my dear, I see you've been bereaved lately?'

'Yes.' The woman dabbed at her eyes. 'My husband died three months ago.'

'And you haven't been feeling too well yourself, lately?'

'Nothing great,' the woman admitted, 'but able enough to travel to see my son and his family.'

That was all the information Thirza needed. She ran the nail of her forefinger over the heart-line and the life-line in her client's palm in her most professional manner, noting that the life-line came to an abrupt halt.

'Well, my dear, I see your son welcoming you with open arms. This must be his wife standing beside him doing the same. I see your grandchildren at your knee. How many? Two, or is it three?'

'Two,' the woman said proudly, 'with a third one on the way.'

'No wonder they're so glad to see you, then! Your daughter-in-law will need you to help her. You'll stay with them until the birth.'

'But that's not for another three months!'

Long before that you'll be dead, Thirza thought darkly. 'What made you come to see me?' she asked aloud, curiously.

'I saw your tent from the road. I've been having a little trouble lately with my breathing. I just wanted to see a bit further into the future.'

Thirza managed to smile brightly at the woman. 'I'm afraid your ten minutes are up,' she said. 'Go and enjoy your family, my dear. Look after them, and they'll look after you.'

'Oh, thank you,' the woman said delightedly, picking up her carpet-bag.

For a minute after she left Thirza leaned her face on her hands. She couldn't tell anyone's fortune. All she did was look at the person for some possible clue. It was all a sham – the whole of the last eight months with the Sharkeys had been a sham, tricking people into parting with their money, and she was sick of it. Sick of the dirt, the squalor, the endless touting for money and just plain begging.

Thirza Gourlay had never been meant for this.

When she looked up, a young girl was hesitating at the entrance. Before the flap fell down Thirza caught a glimpse of a stout middle-aged man looking after the girl with a concerned expression on his red face. She went through her usual preliminaries, and realised that the half-crown the girl held in her hand had been given to her at the last minute by the man outside. Half a crown was a lot of money. The man waiting for her must be very anxious.

The girl gazed back at her with insipid eyes. The only thing Thirza could detect in them besides stupidity, was fear. It wasn't even fear. It was a sort of suppressed excitement.

'I see you're going to have a baby,' Thirza came to the point crisply, eyeing her client's swollen stomach.

The girl immediately burst into a torrent of noisy tears.

'And the father has left you?' Thirza saw it all.

The girl nodded.

'But an older man is willing to marry you, and take on the baby?'

The girl nodded again, but out from her silly, tear-filled eyes she shot Thirza a flirtatious, almost triumphant look. It took her by surprise. Without that, she would have advised her to accept the older man's proposal. Now, she saw nothing but treachery rewarding the generosity of the man outside the tent. He didn't deserve this.

'Where has your young man gone?' she asked.

'North, to a farm at Sanquhar.'

'Then go to Sanquhar,' Thirza said, putting what she considered was a well-earned half-crown into the tin under the table. At least she was sparing some fool of a man a lifetime of worry over a devious, lying wife. 'Follow your heart, my dear,' she smiled.

'Oh, I will!' the girl said and tossed her head. 'He's far better-looking, anyway.'

Thirza watched her go. 'But your young man won't be at Sanquhar,' she said silently. 'He'll be long gone, lady, and better off out of it. Wait and see.'

Desperately, Jordi looked around the fields up on the ridge of the hill. There wasn't a copse in sight, let alone a wood or a forest to hide in. There was only a hedge dividing two of the fields with a large old oak tree in the middle of it. He pinned all his hopes on the oak tree as he led his horse under its branches.

The four horsemen passed by. Jordi waited five minutes until he thought he was safe and then rode his horse back onto the road where the signpost pointed to Thornhill, down in the broad valley.

But from up above there was a cry from McKim, looking back. 'There he is!' he shouted.

Jordi heard him and saw Hawkins and his men wheeling around to follow him. Both he and his horse were in a lather of sweat when, off to the left of the town of Thornhill, on a broad green sward, he caught sight of a gypsy Fair.

He could hear the four horses thundering behind him as he

slithered off his mount, pushed the beast in amongst some piebalds and dived into the first tent he came to. He didn't even have time to read the sign.

Confronting him was a woman sitting at a small square table. For a fraction of a second his heart told him he knew her. But, of course, he couldn't. Not this woman with a red scarf pulled down over black braids, even if the set of her eyes reminded him of Thirza. But Thirza's eyes had always been brilliantly blue and flashing. This woman's were dull and dark and somehow very sad.

'Hide me if you can,' he panted. 'I'm trying to escape.'

'Trying to escape?' the woman smiled bitterly. 'Well,' she pushed him behind the curtain and pointed under the straw mattress, 'I know the feeling, Jordi.'

Belle presented a daunting figure when Hawkins and his men approached her vardo. In spite of the fine weather she wore a long checked overcoat on top of her Fair Day collection of dresses, a muffler around her neck to cover the rope suspending her tins of money and a brightly patterned silk scarf pulled as usual low over her forehead.

She didn't like the look of this quartet, and it showed in the flashing of her eyes in her brown wrinkled face, the agitated jingling of her silver earrings, and in the way she drew herself up, leaning heavily on her stick.

'Wot *you* want?' she asked them ungraciously, turning her fierce eyes next on the two half-naked children who had been following the men. 'Britty! Joey! Fetch Michael yere,' she commanded.

'We're looking for a sailor, run away from my ship,' Hawkins explained. 'He's here somewhere. We saw him coming in.'

'Ain't no sailor yere,' she declared. 'And stay where you are!' she raised her stick at McKim who was taking another step towards her vardo. 'Iffen you gits too close, young man, I'll lay me stick agin yer y'ears!'

'You can see for yourself we won't get into any of the caravans at this rate,' one of the other crewmen muttered, 'but then, neither will Jordi Wishart. He must be hiding in one of the stalls.'

'Ay,' McKim urged the Captain. 'There's a tent over there. That's where we should be looking.'

They moved off in that direction, followed by Michael who had arrived in answer to Belle's summons, and had gathered some more Sharkey men to accompany him. He saw them taking Snaky and Fangs completely by surprise, lolling half asleep as they were on the grass outside the entrance to Thirza's tent.

Inside, she was in the middle of an unusual thing, telling a young man his fortune, for her clients were almost always women, when Hawkins and his men pushed in. 'Fangs! Snaky!' she shouted. 'Come back later,' she told her client, who was scuttling away in any case.

At the commotion, Michael and the other Romany men ran in behind Fangs and Snaky. The little tent was overflowing with men when Hawkins boomed, 'Has a young sailor come in here?' 'Never,' Thirza said positively, standing with her back to the curtain, and hoping devoutly that Jordi had had the sense to roll out from under the mattress and also the tent.

'What's behind there, then?' Hawkins demanded, putting up his hand to draw the curtain away from the tent-pole. But his hand was caught in mid air. There was a whirr through the air and his sleeve was pinned to the tent-pole by a vicious looking knife, its handle still quivering. Immediately silence fell.

Thirza took out her own knife and pointed it at the Captain. 'Try anything else, and you're dead,' she said quietly. 'That man over there,' pointing to Michael, 'has another four knives in his hand, one for each of you. He only caught your sleeve that time, to warn you. He's the knife-thrower here and, believe me, he never misses his target.'

'No, he don't,' the Romanies agreed, pressing forward.

'However, if you want to see behind my curtain,' Thirza continued coldly, 'you had only to ask in a civilised manner. I have nothing to hide.' She raised it a little, enough to expose the straw mattress and also the fact that it filled what little space there was. To her relief, it lay flat and innocent. Jordi wasn't there. 'Now, sir, are you satisfied?'

'Hm,' Hawkins mumbled. 'Take this damned knife out of my sleeve and we'll be going.'

She pulled out Michael's knife and, a knife in each hand, jerked her head towards the tent-flap. 'Go!' she said. 'Get out!'

The Sharkey men escorted them to their horses. They mounted, and in a few minutes they were galloping away. The whole tribe stood and watched them until they were up on the ridge again, and then out of sight.

Gradually, they went back to their stalls. The people of Thornhill had scarcely noticed the disturbance. The music from the roundabout started up again, the Sharkeys shouted their wares and all afternoon the Fair carried on in its usual noisy way.

Thirza continued telling her fortunes throughout the afternoon. The silver coins mounted up in her tin but, for once in her life, she couldn't concentrate on money. She grew weary, puzzling and wondering, instead. It *was* Jordi. She knew it was him. Taller, older, leaner, and more than ever her dear Jordi . . . But he hadn't recognised *her*.

How could he, she fretted bitterly? Every day when she looked in the mirror she didn't even recognise herself. With her hair blackened and greasy under her gaudy scarf, her skin once so fair and so clear now dull and dyed brown from the smoke of the fires, she was no longer Thirza Gourlay as Jordi had known her.

She was Thirza Sharkey, wife of a gypsy man, and by this time Jordi would be miles away. He had been so near, she thought, closing up the fortune teller's tent in the twilight, and now he would be so far away, somewhere up in those dark hills all around.

One by one the Sharkeys' fires were lighting up. The appetising smell of bacon and onions floated on the night air. The last thing Thirza wanted was food. She couldn't eat. She couldn't even cry. She only wanted to die.

Miserably, she lifted the curtain inside her tent and lay down on her mattress. Then, from outside, almost in her ear, there was a whisper. 'Thirza! Is that you?' and Jordi crawled in beside her.

Then, at last, she cried.

With Jordi's arm around her she cried as though she would never stop, and all the while she patted his hair, his face,

251

his hands and his body as if to reassure herself that he was real.

'Yes, Thirza,' he said. 'It's me. I'm really here . . . What's that glorious smell?'

'Oh,' she laughed through her tears, 'that's just like a man! You're hungry, of course. Well, wait here, and I'll fetch you something to eat.' As she left him, she knew that she was making her way to Belle's vardo for the last time. She found her outside, cooking.

'I wuz a-goin' to send it down,' Belle said, slapping more rashers on the pan.

'I thought I'd fetch it myself this time, Belle.'

'Ah . . . I sees. You'm different tonight, gal. You'm leavin'.'

'Yes. I told you I would.'

'That sailor's still yere, ain't he? I just knowed it. I been waitin' fer this. You goin' wi' that sailor then, Thirza?'

'Yes, but not without saying goodbye to *you*.'

Belle got up stiffly and went into her vardo. She limped back down the steps again and held out something in her hand. 'Take this ring fer a keepsake, a good luck piece.'

'But it's gold,' Thirza protested, looking at the slim gold band.

'Yes, gold. But it be too small fer me or Cathy or Isadora. I wants you to have it, gal.'

'Oh, Belle! I don't need this to remember you,' Thirza said, slipping the ring on the third finger of her right hand. 'I'll never forget you.'

'Don't be taking it off, then. Let it be reminding you every day and every night that you can allus come back to ole Belle,' she said gloomily.

'Now, Belle, you know I'll never be back.'

'Wot about Michael, then? You'm be his wife.'

'Tell Michael I'm dead. Tell him any story you like. After a while make him jump over the broomstick again – with Sasha, now that she's given him a son. It's what he should have done in the first place, and the best ending for all the Sharkeys,' Thirza said, watching the smoke curling up from all the gypsy fires and listening to the cries of the children and the shouts and laughs of the tribe. She would never see them again.

'Yuss,' Belle sighed, piling bacon and onions and potatoes

high onto a tin plate, and pouring tea into her largest mug. 'Go wi' this then, while it be hot.'

Back in the tent she and Jordi demolished all the food and drank the tea.

'That's better,' he said. 'Now I'll go and fetch my horse. We've a long way to go.'

'Where to?' she asked when he came back.

'Edinburgh,' he said, pulling her up in front of him. For a minute he held her close, hardly daring to believe he had found her again – and in such an unlikely place too. 'Oh, I've missed you! I've thought so much about you.'

'I've missed you too, Jordi,' she said sadly.

'We'll get to Edinburgh through the Dalveen Pass. I hope you'll come out at the other end of it looking like Thirza Gourlay again, and not some gypsy woman. It was a miracle I recognised you.'

The mare trotted along obligingly with her double load for some time before Thirza replied. 'Yes,' she agreed. For, in amongst these dark hills in the dead of night, was neither the time nor the place to be telling him that she could never be Thirza Gourlay again.

28

JORDI and Thirza were less than a mile along the track of
the Dalveen Pass before their sporadic conversation petered
out altogether. The chilling, awesome atmosphere of the place
overpowered them. There was a fragile moon in the clear night
sky, but it did nothing to light Jordi's way ahead. Rather, it
pointed out the majesty of the mountains towering to left and
to right of them, dark, silent and haunted.

Thirza hoped that the eerie silence was disguising her terror.
Her vivid imagination conjured up strange people, strange
animals and strange things – ghosts, even – moving and alive
in the shadows all around them, and she shuddered, thankful
that Jordi was protecting her back.

'Cold?' he asked.

She shook her head and the silence continued. It went on
for miles, and all the while she tried to subdue her fear and
arrange her swirling thoughts. But they went round and round
and refused to be arranged, even with the first few streaks of
morning in the heavens.

As the light grew a little stronger and the moon became
just tissue paper, it served only to throw up the contours
of the mountains in sharper relief, brooding and frowning
down on them as she knew they had been frowning all
night.

A curlew rose up from a tuft of grass almost underneath
them, screeching and whauping mournfully, beating across the

heather, and the horse reared in shock. Thirza shook from head to foot.

'It was only a bird,' Jordi murmured in her ear while he reassured his horse, and they travelled on.

During those last few miles before the sun rose the early breeze seemed to clear Thirza's head. Some things fell into perspective. These last eighteen months since she had been separated from Jordi had been a terrible waiting period until she saw him again. Everything that had happened while she was in Springfield, and then with the Sharkeys, were all part of the experience, and this journey tonight was like a bridge between her old life with Jordi and the new life she was sure she would be living with him from now on. The most important thing was that he was here, by some miracle, and they were reunited. As long as they were together, surely nothing could go wrong.

Brought up in the strict Gourlay tradition that you never betrayed your emotions, no matter what, Thirza didn't betray hers now, either.

'I'm tired, Jordi,' she said instead, 'and I'm hungry. When can we stop?'

'Not yet. Soon,' he replied, and they rode on.

It seemed never-ending. Her bones were sore from being bounced around on the back of the horse. She was sore all over. And what was Jordi thinking all this time, she fretted? He had not given her a clue. He just seemed preoccupied, a thousand miles away.

Finally he broke the silence.

'That must be Crawford,' he said, looking down on it, when they were leaving the mountains behind. 'We'll find somewhere to rest here.'

'You don't mean in that inn?' Thirza pointed to a large white house picked out in black with a sign swinging in front of it.

'Why not?'

'Look at me, Jordi! They wouldn't let me in. They don't allow gypsies into places like that.'

'No, I suppose not,' he grinned tiredly when he looked at her. 'So I'll go myself and buy some food. In the meantime you can be looking around for somewhere to rest. Gypsies know about such things, do they not?'

She scowled after him, but all the same she scouted around until she found some flat ground behind some trees hidden from the road, and then sat waiting to direct him into it.

'I was lucky to get some bread and milk and cheese,' he told her when he came back, and tied up his horse behind the trees. 'It's too early in the morning for anything else.'

'What time is it?' she asked him when they had finished their meal.

'It must be about seven o'clock now. The landlord said it would take about three hours to get into Edinburgh from here. There's plenty of time for a snooze. Lie down, Thirza.'

'Oh, what a relief, just to stretch out!'

The last thing she saw before she closed her eyes was the horse, contentedly cropping grass. Jordi, lying down behind her, his arm around her, was the last thing she felt. Within ten minutes, if anyone had been looking, they were sleeping like children.

Nobody could have been looking, for they slept on for most of the day. When Jordi finally woke up, he woke Thirza . . . 'It must be three o'clock in the afternoon now,' he told her. 'How do you feel?'

'Stiff,' she stretched herself, 'but much better. 'How about you?'

'The same,' he said almost impatiently, 'but now we should be going.' Their weary journey continued along a road where there was much more traffic until, at one of the many crossroads they came to, Jordi stopped to get his bearings. 'It's that way,' he pointed.

'Where exactly are we going?' Thirza asked him, now that they were on a quiet road again and could talk.

'To India House.'

'I've never heard of it.'

'No,' he agreed. 'That's because you never listened. But your mother listened to everything I told her. Ruth knows it was the house I was brought up in. She knows that it was stolen from us, my mother and me, when I was too young to do anything about it.'

'My mother's dead, Jordi,' Thirza told him quietly, and after a long silence she told him how she had followed her mother

257

to Springfield. She began to tell him that her mother had gone to Allison's Bank to work for Duke Elliot –

'Duke Elliot?' he interrupted her. '*Duke Elliot* . . . That's strange. The man I've come here to see is called Marmaduke Elliot. He's the one who stole our house and ruined my mother. Don't you think that's a strange coincidence?'

Thirza regarded him thoughtfully. 'What age would this Marmaduke Elliot be?'

'In his sixties now, I suppose.'

'Well . . . Duke Elliot would be about forty. He had a father in Edinburgh. He often went to see him . . . Duke could be short for Marmaduke, couldn't it? They could be father and son. Oh Jordi, Duke Elliot beat my mother to death!' Thirza sobbed.

Jordi stopped the horse, jumped down and marched about agitatedly. 'Oh, God, oh God,' he said and seemed to gasp for air. 'It all runs on a parallel with that awful man in India House. It's a pattern repeating itself. Marmaduke Elliot raped my mother, and caused her to drown herself.'

'So that's what you've been brooding about all these years, Jordi?'

'I won't rest until I kill him for what he did to my mother,' he said passionately.

'I know how you feel, believe me,' Thirza said as Jordi got back up on the horse behind her, glad that her face was hidden when she said it. She wanted to hide the murder she knew was burning in her eyes. 'As well as my mother, Duke Elliot also murdered his wife and children,' she continued. 'The Bells of Sarkfoot Farm found their bodies.'

Jordi fell silent as he brooded over this new knowledge. Sarkfoot Farm, and the cave, and Drew Ellis who wouldn't go near them. *Drew Ellis*, again. His initials D.E. The pieces were beginning to fall into place. Drew Ellis was a false name. The real one must be Duke Elliot. Oh, God . . . he could be the son of Marmaduke Elliot. Had they stumbled on the vital connection? Was that why every time he looked at the man, he had reminded him of somebody else?

Blinking his eyes in the strong sunshine, Jordi came out of his trance and back to the present. 'That's India House,' he reined in his horse at the entrance to a neglected driveway up to a large house. It seemed to be in ruins.

'But it's falling to pieces!' Thirza said. 'Nobody could live there now.'

'It was falling to pieces before my mother and I left it, and I can see Marmaduke Elliot has done nothing to repair it. He's too tight with money. But I believe he's still here, all the same, hoping to sell it the way it is. That man wouldn't let a penny go past his nose, and the house could be restored if anyone rich wanted the site, I daresay. No, he'll still be around here somewhere, using the place for some evil reason of his own.'

'Oh, Jordi, I've seen enough evil connected with the name of Elliot already!' Thirza shuddered.

'What do you mean? Is there more?'

'You didn't give me a chance to finish. There was Joe Dan Linton.'

'Joe Dan Linton? What do you know about Joe Dan Linton, Thirza?'

'Duke Elliot murdered him, too. He strangled him with wire and pushed his boat out to sea. But the Bells found him later in the sands. The evidence was still all there . . . So now you know why I don't want to go into that house,' Thirza looked up at the ruin and shivered. 'Besides, you're only guessing that anyone lives in that ruin now. It looks deserted to me. Perhaps Marmaduke Elliot left and never came back.'

'Well, I'm going to find out! I've waited a long time for this! We'll soon see!'

Jordi spoke with such venom and suppressed rage that she scanned his face in surprise. Jordi was usually so cool and calm.

'But what if nobody's here now?' she asked. 'It could be days before they come back!'

He smiled down at her grimly. 'Well, we won't wait in India House, don't worry. There's a place I know, not far away. We can watch the house from there.'

He set the horse along a lane she had not noticed while they had been gazing at the house. Nobody would have seen it unless they had known about it before. It ran outside the wall of the grounds and was so overgrown with weeds and bushes that the horse had to be encouraged every step of the way.

Jordi urged it on, lifting long streamers of brambles out of Thirza's face at the same time, until they were past the worst of it. Now the path was clearly defined and she could hear the rushing of water somewhere near at hand.

'Here we are,' Jordi said. 'It's just around this next bend where the wall stops and the stream begins. It's still in our grounds, although quite a distance from the house. Anyone would have had to be brought up here to know about it.'

'It's a little wooden house!'

'A summer-house, built for my mother by an Indian man called Viaz. She loved the greenness all around, and the stream on hot days. She used to bring her embroidery here.'

'Is it locked?'

Jordi laughed and put his hand up to feel along the guttering. 'If the key's still here, nobody has used it for a long, long time,' he said. 'The gutter's full of rubbish, dead leaves and moss . . . Ah, here it is!' he held up a key triumphantly. 'So nobody has interfered here, after all. Let's try it.'

It was only one very dusty room, but it was dry and furnished with odds and ends obviously left here years ago. There was a sofa, two easy chairs which didn't match each other, nor the sofa, and a low table in the centre. To one side stood an old sideboard and, when Jordi opened the drawers, he found cutlery intact and, in the cupboards below, cups, saucers and plates were all still there.

'Yes,' he said. 'It's just the way my mother left it. But, of course, there's no food. I'm going to get some. You rest here, Thirza, and wait for me.'

As soon as he was out of sight, Thirza ran down to the stream. Its clear shallow waters reminded her of the river Kirtle after she had run away from Gretna Hall.

Then, it had been at the end of a summer. Now it was the beginning of another, almost a year later. The difference was that there was no clover to lie about in, and all the trees ran right down to the water here, but the feeling was the same. The sun was just as hot now as it had been then, and once again she longed to enter the dimpling stream. There was no sound except for the warm breeze rustling through the leaves overhead. There was nobody else here. She was alone and the temptation was too much.

Off came the silk scarf covering her head. Out came the gaudy ribbons tying up her braids. Thirza teased out her hair, stiff and greasy with soap and, undressing quickly, slid into the cool water with an indescribable feeling of relief and thankfulness.

She rubbed her hair in the soft water, and the bubbles swilled all around her. She realised that if she was quick she could wash herself all over and cleanse her skin at last.

A different girl came out of the stream and ran around delightedly in the sunshine to get dry. Finally she got dressed again, and sat mourning the fact that she had neither brush nor comb. She did her best with her fingers, remembering what Ruth used to say.

'God gave ye two hands and ten fingers, lassie. There's no' much any tool can do that they canna do better.'

She was still shaking her hair and running her fingers through the knots and tangles when Jordi came back and saw her sitting in the doorway of the summer-house with the sun full on her face and the red-gold tendrils framing it.

'Thank God you're Thirza Gourlay again,' he smiled, 'and prettier than ever.'

She didn't reply to that. She wasn't Thirza Gourlay now, no matter how much she resembled her, but too much had happened since then to begin to explain all that to him. 'What did you get, Jordi?' she asked instead.

'Two hot meat pies, for a start. Milk, apples, and some bread and butter for the morning.'

'It's just like playing "hoosies",' Thirza sighed contentedly as she ate a meat pie. 'Andra used to play "hoosies" with me on the washing green at St Fillan, but not often. Only when I caught him in a good mood. He was never the big brother I wanted him to be. Not like you, Jordi.'

'No? Well, while we're on that subject, Thirza, remember I'm not your brother, after all,' he frowned.

'No,' she heaved another great sigh and bit into an apple. 'I know that! What's the matter with you, Jordi? You never used to object.'

'Well, I'm objecting now,' he looked at her with eyes that were momentarily filled with an intensity she was unwilling to recognise, far less investigate. She knew he loved her. Merren Cheyne had alerted her to that in Shetland. But, still deeply hurt after Michael Sharkey's crude onslaught, she couldn't help drawing back, even from her beloved Jordi, to whom she could trust not only her heart, but also her life.

'What else did you see besides the shops?' she hastily changed the subject.

'I went for a scout around India House,' he said, looking aside and revealing his profile to her.

It was the first time she had ever seen anything 'furrin' as she used to say, in him. His nose seemed more acquiline. His thick black eyebrows drawn down as they were seemed very fierce. Suddenly Thirza realised that Jordi could be very fierce if he liked – just like her – and, from somewhere deep inside her, she felt a little thrill. He was a kindred spirit, after all, and there was no doubt that he had changed and matured in the space of eighteen months – just as she must have changed, almost out of recognition.

'And what did you find out?' she asked.

'There *is* somebody living there. And he's not alone. There's someone else, making an attempt to keep what's left of the place clean, and there were signs of cooking in the kitchen. I'm going back shortly to have another look.'

'Then I'm going with you,' Thirza said.

Several times that day they crept through the trees and the undergrowth, after Jordi had found the almost forgotten and overgrown path that led them to within sight and sound of the back door of India House. But it wasn't until six o'clock that evening, when the glorious summer day was fading, that he and Thirza were rewarded.

'He can either eat this tattie soup or leave it alane,' a woman's angry voice announced only a few yards above their heads. 'A few tatties, an onion and some withered carrots were all I could find to cook anything with.'

'Ye're a fool, Gladys Henderson. I aye said ye were,' a younger, lighter voice retorted. 'Ye made me come another week to work for nothing. Now here we are, on another Saturday night, and neither sight nor sound o' him to pay us any wages! He'll no' be coming now.'

'No,' Gladys agreed, 'he's no' coming now. Ach, things havena been the same at all since the old man disappeared.'

'I dinna ken why ye keep harking back to that old devil, Gladys.'

'He always used to pay me my wages.'

'Well, I'm gaun hame, and I'm never coming back!'

'You're right, Peggy. This is the finish.'

'So what are ye waiting for, Gladys?'

'Should we no' lock up first? Half the windows are still open.'

'No!' Peggy appeared indignantly at the back door. 'Why should we bother? There's nothing in here worth stealing, anyway. Are ye coming?'

'Ay, and good riddance to bad rubbish, I'd say,' an older woman came out to join Peggy, and they walked away grumbling to each other with the fine smell of the soup wafting out of the open window.

'I'm going in for that pan,' Jordi grinned, and ten minutes later he and Thirza were laughing together in the summer-house and enjoying the soup with the bread left over from the morning like two conspirators.

Although their real intentions had been put aside for the moment, they were, nevertheless just that – conspirators, in a deadly game of murder.

29

THIRZA was still smiling when she looked up at him afterwards. 'I feel better now,' she told him, 'thanks to that soup
– and especially thanks to you, Jordi. I always knew everything
would be all right when you came back again.'

'Oh, Thirza,' he took her hands in his impulsively, 'it won't
always be like this, I promise. All this running and hiding and
scraping for something to eat! Only bear with me until I see
this man. It's something that has to be done.'

As night came down the sky became inky, then studded with
stars, and the breeze changed to a light wind bending the trees
and rushing through the leaves. They sat and watched the moon
coming up, not thin and insubstantial as it had been last night
in the Dalveen Pass, but a solid silver disc in the sky, shining
and bright.

'Did you hear that?' Jordi whispered.

'No. What?'

'The sound of hoofbeats. I've been waiting for it. Those
women didn't make soup for nothing. They really were expecting the master of the house tonight.'

'Marmaduke Elliot?'

'I hope so.'

Thirza felt her heart pounding, and the blood rushing to her
head. 'Then what are we waiting for?' she asked. 'Come on!
Let's go!'

Well-used, by this time, to the path up to the back door, they crept along it silently with the fickle moon their friend for now, lighting up twigs whose snap under their feet would sound like the report of a gun. But that same moon could, only too easily, turn out to be their enemy if the wrong eyes saw them in its beams.

Cautiously they waited and watched, clutching each other's arms when someone with a lighted lamp began a tour of inspection inside the house. He made for the kitchen first, putting down the lamp on the table and poking about in the empty cupboards. But, Jordi saw to his disappointment, it wasn't Marmaduke Elliot, after all. It was a much younger man, one that he recognised instantly.

'That's him!' Thirza whispered when he took up the lamp again and moved to another room. 'That's Duke Elliot!'

'Duke Elliot? Drew Ellis, as I knew him,' Jordi muttered, 'but Drew Ellis or Duke Elliot, it doesn't matter. I've got a bone to pick with him, too. He stole my gold chain. Look, he's moving into the sitting room . . . He's sitting down with his back to the French windows . . . And Thirza, the French windows are open!'

But there was no answer from Thirza. She had melted away like a ghost. Jordi frowned into the darkness behind him, but there was no sign of her, and he didn't have time now to go looking. Mesmerised at the sight of his enemy under his very nose, Jordi continued to watch, shaking with concentrated hatred. The viper, Marmaduke Elliot, may have gone, but he had left his spawn behind him in his nest. Like father, like son, Jordi thought, regarding him with loathing. No wonder he had hated the man upon sight on the *Black Prince*.

Duke Elliot was almost hidden by the large chair he was sitting in. He bent down and his right hand went into the cupboard beside the fireplace. He took something out of it and stuffed it down the side of his chair. His left arm sprawled out over the arm of the chair except when he raised the bottle he was holding to his mouth. This he was doing often, and in an agitated manner. Duke Elliot would soon be drunk. Jordi smiled to himself, and silently made his move to the outside of the window.

The man was too agitated even to feel the draught which must be hitting the back of his neck – or too drunk already, Jordi thought. The night wind was blowing the window further open. The curtains, in tatters now, were fluttering and bellying in.

Agitated or drunk, Duke Elliot froze with the bottle half way to his mouth. Behind him, Jordi froze in horror as the door of the sitting room was flung back with a crash, and Thirza stood in the open doorway.

'Ah . . . The little daughter,' Duke Elliot came to his senses and sneered in a dreadful attempt to make light of it. 'Thirza Gourlay.'

'That's right,' she said. 'I've caught up with you at last, you bastard! How does it feel to be a minute away from death?'

Duke Elliot pulled a pistol out from the side of his chair, took aim at her and fired.

Then everything happened at once – within seconds – although, to Thirza, those seconds went by in such slow motion that they seemed like hours. She heard the bullet slamming into the doorpost beside her head, saw Jordi leaping in through the window and fastening his hands around Duke Elliot's neck in a stranglehold.

It could only have been seconds before her knife was out of her sleeve and flashing through the air. At exactly the same time as it landed in Duke Elliot's chest, there was a horrible crunching sound from his neck. Jordi's arms dropped to his sides, Duke Elliot's head lolled grotesquely to one side, and then everything went very silent. The room went around and around before it blanked out altogether in a grey fog.

'I killed him! I killed him! Oh, my God, I killed a man,' Thirza was mumbling when the fog swirled back a little as Jordi slapped her wrists.

'You did nothing of the sort, Thirza. I killed him. I broke his neck, remember?'

'That's my knife, sticking out of his chest. It's got a six-inch blade. Are you trying to tell me that at the speed I threw it, it didn't kill him? Of course I killed him! What's more,' she added weakly, gazing at the dead man, 'I meant to do it.'

'I'm not going to argue with you at a time like this,' Jordi said firmly. 'It's six of one and half-a-dozen of the other as to which one of us got to him first. Let's say we killed him together, if that will please you.'

'I feel sick, Jordi.'

'Sit still, then. I'll deal with this.'

She heard a squelch, and knew he'd pulled her knife out of Duke Elliot. Then there was no sound except the wind outside until, finally, Jordi was at her side again. 'Here's your knife,' he said. 'I've cleaned it. Put it away.'

'What now?' she asked, trying shakily to get up.

'Sit still, Thirza! I'm going to get rid of him. I won't be long.'

One by one, by the light of the moon, Jordi heaved out the stones that had once been a minaret. It took a long time, but he gradually dug deeper and deeper into the pile of rubble.

Then, to his horror, he came upon the remains of a hand, and then an arm. He worked faster until he uncovered the whole, badly decomposed, body of his bitterest enemy in the world, Marmaduke Elliot. Almost unrecognisable now, especially with half his head smashed in, nevertheless Jordi knew it was him.

He rushed into the bushes and vomited violently. Then, wiping his face and trying to compose himself, he went back into the house for Duke Elliot's body.

'What's the matter?' Thirza asked at once.

'I found what I think are the remains of Marmaduke Elliot,' he replied, dragging out the body.

'That disgusting creature killed his own father then, as well,' she said with complete conviction. She seemed to be much calmer now. 'By the way, you'd better remove your gold chain from around his neck before you bury him.'

Had Thirza changed so much, after all, Jordi wondered to himself?

He threw Duke Elliot's body into the stony grave beside his father, and decided that she hadn't. He was building up the stones around and on top of both Elliots when she appeared at his side.

'I'm glad that's where you've put them,' she said. 'It might be years before anyone takes over this house. Perhaps one day some workmen will uncover two skeletons.'

No, she hadn't changed. She was as practical as ever.

'In that case, there will be an official inquiry, Thirza.'

'It can only conclude that father and son were accidentally killed by falling masonry.'

'So long as nobody sees us. So long as we are never connected with it,' Jordi said grimly, finishing his task. 'We've got to get out of here, fast. But it's nearly morning now. We should stay inside all day and go when it's dark.'

'Where to?' Thirza asked as they made their way back down to the summer-house. 'We should have a plan. You can't be seen buying food again. Somebody will take notice. We've got to think.'

The next morning they regarded each other from heavy-lidded eyes. She had tossed and turned on the sofa, and he had tossed and turned on the floor beside her.

'I can't help it,' she burst out at him. 'For what that man did to my mother, I would kill him again ten times over. I just cannot feel any remorse.'

'Neither can I,' he agreed sadly, 'and now, Thirza, promise me that we will never speak of it again. We must leave it all behind us and move on. The most important thing to decide is what to do.'

She smiled at him in the same teasing way that she had done when she was just a child. 'So you *are* going to take me with you, Jordi? Is that because you think that now we're criminals, we'd better stick together?'

'It's because someone should look after you, Thirza. And anyway, we're both alone in the world, now.'

'Well,' she sighed 'that's what I always hoped for, anyway, whatever the reason. I just want to stay with you for ever, Jordi.'

Perhaps she meant it. Perhaps she didn't, but it was a step in the right direction as far as he was concerned.

'We'll have to get somewhere to live, to begin with,' he said.

'That costs money.'

'Oh, Thirza,' Jordi smiled, when he thought he would never smile again. She would never change.

'Well, don't worry.' She wriggled out of her petticoat and laid it across her lap. 'Mother gave me this last year on my sixteenth birthday. There's plenty of money here,' and the next minute her knife was in her hand again, this time to slit open the hem.

Out rolled the banknotes. Jordi picked them up. 'There's hundreds of pounds here!' he exclaimed.

'Almost three hundred,' she said calmly, 'from the sale of the cottage at St Fillan, your wages from the fishing and a small amount from my wages when I worked in the Jollys' bakeshop. Mother kept it for us and hid it from Duke Elliot. She gave it to me for my sixteenth birthday.'

'Oh, *Ruth* . . .' Jordi passed a hand over his eyes. 'She was a good woman, Thirza.'

'She made sure we could start a new life. Where shall it be?'

'Down by the sea, somewhere?'

'Yes,' she agreed.

'Then I must take a chance and go and find it.'

'You're not going anywhere without me.'

'I don't want to go without you, but I must. I could be away for as long as a week before I find anything. I'll probably have to sleep rough, and I'm not going to put you through any more of that, not when there's a perfectly good shelter for you here.'

She hung her head at that, but he could see she saw the sense of it.

'First I'll get you some food. Don't worry, Thirza. I'll go to different shops this time. I wouldn't do anything to put you in danger.'

Before long he was back, and making sure she was going to manage. 'You'll lock the door every time you leave the summer-house?' he asked her anxiously. 'And lock yourself in every night? Will you be all right, now?'

'I'll be all right,' she assured him, and watched as he rode away.

Later that day he began his quest in Leith. But two days later he was still looking without any success, and, dejected, he sat down on the sea wall, holding his horse's bridle.

Further along, an old seaman looked at him with interest. 'Ye're looking gey tired, laddie. I've been watching ye oot o' the corner o' my eye, walking up and doon. Are ye looking for someone?'

'Not someone,' Jordi smiled. 'Something. A house for sale.'

'Well, there's no' many o' *them* doon herabouts. Ye should be further up in among the streets.'

'That's the trouble. I want to buy a boatshed along with a house. You see, I want to repair boats. It's what I do best. To tell you the truth, I've been looking for the shed, more than the house.'

'Oh, ay?' the old man ran his hand around his chin thoughtfully. 'Well, as ye can see, Douglas Hunter is the big man here for boats.'

'Yes,' Jordi said, eyeing a massive roof with 'HUNTER' painted on it in large white letters. 'Nobody could avoid seeing it. But I suppose he builds ships as well?'

'Repairs boats and ships. Builds boats and ships,' the old man smacked his lips. 'Used to work for him mysel', so I did, after I gave up the sea.'

'And you think there's no room for anyone else around here?'

'Plenty o' room for someone cheaper – oh, ay! He's gey stiff wi' his charges, is Douglas Hunter. There's plenty would go to another Yard if only they could find one . . . But wait a minute! There's a man I know thinking o' selling off his old Yard and his house. They're not up to much. The shed's dilapidated. I've never been in the house to tell ye aboot it.'

'Where is he?'

'Come back here at eight o'clock tomorrow morning. I know he'll be in then, and I'll take ye to him mysel'.'

With that, Jordi had to be content. That night he decided to sleep in a proper bed for the first time in weeks, and found one in a seedy lodging house in Leith.

He examined the bedclothes suspiciously but, to his surprise, they seemed to be quite clean and free from bugs. He lay down, so tired he couldn't sleep, and his thoughts turned to Thirza and her sojourn with the gypsies.

She had explained all about Michael Sharkey and the knife-throwing, all about the fortune telling, and about old Belle and her vardo and their strange way of life on the roads. But there was something missing, he was sure of it. With a sigh, Jordi closed his eyes and fell asleep.

The days weren't so bad when Thirza was left alone in the summer-house. She spent most of them in and around the stream, bathing in it, carrying water from it to the summer-house and washing everything inside. She washed herself and her clothes again. She washed until there was nothing left to wash, and then she took to gathering wild flowers and putting them in cups all around the little room.

It was a shame they withered so quickly, she thought, but flowers, like humans, had their short time upon the earth and then they were gone. This gloomy thought haunted her when night fell, and the time came to lock herself in. Although she would never have admitted it, she was very frightened and was sleeping badly, constantly listening to the night sounds all around her in the trees. The sudden fluttering of wings when some stray bird brushed past the window in the middle of the night was enough to send her imagination wild. That could never have been a bird in the middle of the night . . . It must have been a human being, or a ghost – Duke Elliot risen from the dead . . .

But every morning the nightmares receded. The sun rose. The stream tinkled on. It was quiet and peaceful all around her, and yet her nerves were stretched to snapping point. It was some relief when, every now and then, she burst into tears. Thirza didn't know why she was crying. She just wept, thankful that no one else was here to witness her misery.

Sometimes she thought she was crying for her father and Andra, lost so cruelly at sea. Sometimes she thought she was crying because of the terrible drifting over the North Sea and what she and Jordi had endured before they were flung half dead upon the shores of Shetland. And always, she was mourning her mother.

Many of her tears were shed over the Sharkeys, and most of all over Michael Sharkey. Sooner or later when Jordi came back she would have to tell him about her gypsy wedding. He would take it for granted that there had been some sexual attraction between her and Michael. Could she make him understand that the gypsy had only used the ceremony to rape her?

It had made her feel used, abused and dirty. She would rather have been murdered than raped, given the choice. She felt it was such an awful stigma on her that she didn't want to talk about it to anyone. She dreaded telling Jordi. It would lower her in his estimation. Thirza wrapped her arms around her knees, put her head down and sobbed her heart out for both their sakes, especially Jordi's, because he thought he loved her. He was going to get a terrible shock . . . If he ever came back.

The fact that she had just murdered someone was a thought that Thirza put to the back of her mind, as she always did with her most pressing problem, believing as she had done as a child, that if you didn't look at it, it would go away.

Unhappily, it hadn't worked with the problem of her rape. That problem hadn't gone away. However, in the meantime the sun was shining again, and she decided to go down the lane that ran around India House to see if Jordi was coming back at last.

She never knew afterwards whether it was by some instinct or by some far-fetched coincidence, but she had hardly gone twenty yards along the lane when he was there, coming towards her with a smile on his face. He jumped down off his horse and took her in his arms.

'Oh, Jordi,' she said, kissing his face all over in her desperate relief, and then finally kissing him full on his lips, surprised at her emotions when he kissed her back, full and hard. Surprised by the feelings it raised, she stepped back from him.

'I know,' Jordi laughed. 'I must smell like a dog after some of the places I've been in! Before I do anything else I'll go down to the stream and bathe,' and he ran off, scattering his clothes as he went.

Thirza followed him slowly, picking up his clothes for him, her heart full of so many mixed emotions that she was quite confused. The only thing she did know for certain was that the moment of truth was at hand.

The moment of truth, when she arrived silently at the bank of the stream, was not as she expected. Jordi was standing with his back to her, knee-deep in the water, splashing it up and over himself. It was the first time she had ever seen a man without any clothes on. Everything with Michael Sharkey, she shuddered, had been conducted in icy darkness, but now here was Jordi with his skin gleaming golden and wet in the sunshine, and nothing was hidden.

For a few seconds she watched him, marvelling at the muscles rippling under that skin, admiring his tall lean frame and his broad shoulders narrowing to his waist, and amazed at the grace of his powerful legs. In that moment, before she retreated as silently as she had come, laying his clothes on the river-bank for him to reach, something pierced her to the very core of her being. Suddenly she felt tied to him, bound hand and foot in a bondage from which she never wanted to be freed.

Walking slowly back to the cottage, Thirza knew that she loved him. She had probably loved him since the first day she had seen him, but until now she had never known it. A few minutes later Jordi followed her into the cottage. He looked so happy that all the clouds of her doubts and fears rolled away, and she was happy too.

'Oh, I missed you so much! I love you, Jordi,' she said, and flew into his arms.

'I love you, too. I've always loved you, darling Thirza, and I've found a little boatyard in Leith,' he told her with his arms tight around her. 'There's a house up on the hill directly above it. It's not much, but it could be our first home.'

'How much does it cost?' she asked, true to form even at that moment.

'Two hundred and fifty, plus the horse when we get back.'

'Well, we won't need the horse,' she said.

'All I want is you,' he told her, kissing her passionately again. 'Will you marry me, Thirza? We could be so happy together from now on! I'll work night and day to make you happy.'

'I'll live with you, Jordi,' she said, delighting in his kisses, and wondering at the strange feelings they were arousing in her.

'What do you mean, you'll live with me?' Jordi raised his head.

'I want to live with you and be your wife. I will be, in every way,' she kissed him again, 'but I can't marry you. I'm married already. I'm not Thirza Gourlay any more. I'm Thirza Sharkey. The gypsies forced me into it.'

'What ... ?' Jordi couldn't believe the words that were coming out of her mouth.

'It's true.' Thirza burst into tears. 'Oh, Jordi, I can never tell you how awful it was! But I'm married to Michael Sharkey.'

'No, you're not,' he protested violently. 'Not unless you want to be. Not unless you want to go back to him. Will you ever go back to him?'

'*No!*' she swore.

'Then you're *not* Thirza Sharkey any more. You're Thirza Wishart, as you pretended to be once before. I mean, married or not, you'll be my wife.'

'I want to be. That's all I want,' she sobbed.

'Then we'll go to Leith a married couple. Nobody will ever know the difference. It will be just another little secret between us.' Thirza smiled tearfully and nodded her head. 'But you'll need a ring, if you're to be Mrs Wishart. I'll have to buy you one.'

'No, you won't, Jordi! For one thing we can't afford it. For another, I've got a plain gold ring already. Old Belle gave it me,' Thirza took it off her right hand and put it on the third finger of her left.

It was all coming true, she thought uncomfortably, the fortune the old Shetland woman had read for her. She would never wear a wedding ring, although she would be married three times.

First there had been Michael Sharkey. Now there was Jordi. But the old Shetland woman had been wrong about one thing, she reassured herself as they set off to Leith. There would never be a third man in her life. All she ever wanted was Jordi.

30

THEY arrived in the boatyard later that afternoon and gazed at the broken-down shed.

'The best bit about it is the tarred roof,' Jordi commented. As its new owner, seeing it for the second time, he felt quite downhearted. 'There are a lot of repairs to be done to this shed before I take on boats,' he added, but if Thirza was disillusioned, she certainly wasn't showing it. When he led her inside to view it, a man in his early thirties stepped forward to greet them.

'This is Bob Steele, Thirza,' Jordi introduced him. 'I've kept him on as my assistant. Bob, this is my wife.'

'Pleased to meet you, Mrs Wishart,' Bob said with a smile. 'What your husband means is, I come with the Yard. I've worked here all my life, so far.'

Thirza took to him at once. Nobody could help liking Bob Steele, with his round honest face covered with freckles and crowned by a thatch of sandy hair. It was parted in the middle, to give him an even more ingenuous appearance. Besides, he was the first person to call her by her new name. 'I'm pleased to meet you too, Bob,' she said.

'We're going up to have a look at the house,' Jordi told him. 'Your last job before you lock up for the day is to deliver this horse to your former employer. You and I will meet again at eight o'clock tomorrow morning.'

'Yes, sir,' Bob grinned, took the bridle with obvious relish and tied it to a post in the meantime. 'I haven't ridden a horse for a while.'

'Well, she's a gentle enough beast,' Jordi advised him. 'You won't have any trouble, providing you give her none. Now, Thirza, we have to cross that road,' he pointed it out to her. 'It's a cul-de-sac, and that's Constitution Street at the end of it where all the shops are. Here's our house.'

A large iron number eight was nailed to the squeaking gate. They could see as they climbed the wide, shallow steps winding up to the house that there had once been terraced gardens on either side of them, now sadly overgrown and neglected.

'Oh, it looks important!' Thirza became more enthusiastic the nearer they drew to the granite-faced frontage. 'Look, Jordi, it's even got pillars at each side of the door, and the number in gold on the glass! Oh, I like it – and what's more, it's *number eight*!'

'What's number eight got to do with it?'

'It's lucky. It's bound to be lucky, after St Fillan.'

'Why?'

'Our cottage was number eight, The Braehead.'

'I never knew that. Are you just making it up as you go along?'

'No, I am not, Jordi Wishart! There were eight cottages and ours was the last one, number eight. Oh, I just *know* this house is going to be lucky!'

'I hope so, too. But you should never judge a book by its cover. The front looks quite respectable. Wait till you see the rest of it.'

Thirz's spirits refused to be dampened as they wandered from one dirty, decaying room to the next. Upstairs, it was in an even more dilapidated state. 'I love it,' she said. 'All it needs is a lot of hard work . . . and money.'

'We've got nearly fifty pounds left of the money Ruth saved for us,' Jordi told her, 'and that, plus another fifty I managed to take with me off the *Black Prince* makes a hundred. It won't go too far.'

'But we don't have to worry about that tonight, do we, Jordi? Not the first night in our new home?' Thirza lay down on the floor with all her clothes on.

She didn't seem to have any intention of taking any of them

off, either, Jordi thought when she snuggled in to him and composed herself for sleep. 'No, I suppose not,' he sighed, unwilling to push her into something she didn't seem to be ready for.

The next morning, he and Bob Steele set to work to clear out all the wood piled up around the inside of the shed. Only then did they see the full extent of the repairs that would have to be done.

'A lot of this wood is rubbish,' Jordi said as they surveyed the view out of one of the larger holes in the walls. 'Still, it'll do in the meantime to mend these walls and to keep out wind and water. We'll keep the best for boat repairs.'

'Och, old man Forbes let everything slide these last few years,' Bob confided, 'ever since his wife died. He just lost interest. But now I hear he's taken up wi' a widow in Newhaven. That'll be what he wants the horse for, randy old bugger,' he laughed. 'But never mind, I've managed to get us a wee job already. If ye come outside I'll show ye. It's only a couple of hours' work on a rowing boat belonging to a friend o' mine.'

'You work on the boat then, Bob. I'll start fixing up the shed . . . So there hasn't been much business here for a few years?'

'None to speak of, sir.'

'The sooner we change all that the better. But how to set about it? The problem, Bob, is how to get some trade back again.'

'There's only one way: by word of mouth. Folk soon get to know, and one job leads to another. Of course,' Bob added darkly, 'there's Douglas Hunter along the way. It's like farting against thunder – begging your pardon, sir – competing wi' the likes o' *him*. The only thing in our favour is, he's awfy dear.'

'So I understand. That's not the first time I've heard it. Well, Bob, we'll just have to undercut him. It'll mean low profits and low wages for you and for me to begin with.'

'I'm game if you are, sir. I'd like to see someone stealing some o' Douglas Hunter's thunder for a change,' Bob said, lining up a plank of wood to patch up his friend's boat, and then attacking it viciously with his plane. 'Old man Forbes just handed him work we should have had, on a plate. He'll have left the house in a fine mess, too, has he?'

'Don't ask. My wife's got her work cut out for her, I can tell you. Now that you mention it, I'd better take her up a pint of milk and some rolls. We haven't had our breakfast, yet.'

Up in number eight, Thirza was battling with her priorities – everything seemed to need doing at once – and gazing in horror in the early morning light at all the dirt.

There was no running water in the house and consequently no sink, but she was used to that. All the water would have to be fetched and carried from the outside well and heated if she could get the fire to take. She got to work, and, when Jordi came in with the milk and the rolls, he found the air quite blue, between Thirza's language as she cursed the fire up hill and down dale and the smoke that kept blowing back.

'It's the chimney,' he told her. 'It needs a cowl to divert the wind. I'll get one and go up on the roof as soon as I have time. This afternoon, perhaps.'

Back in the boat shed Bob Steele handed over the money for the work on his friend's rowing boat. 'He's been, while you were out, and taken his boat away. He had a bit o' news, as well. There's a Pittenweem vessel over here in trouble just now, needing some planking done to her deck in a hurry, but the skipper can't get a Yard to take him on at such short notice.'

'I would, Bob.'

'That's what I told him, sir. He's away to find the skipper now.'

'What if he doesn't know the place? He could miss this Yard if he blinked his eyes.'

They both ran out to see a rowing boat leading a much larger vessel in. In a few minutes, looking very familiar to Jordi from his fishing days at St Fillan, the burly figure of the skipper, Fred Joss, came ashore.

'By God, it's you, Jordi!' he said. 'I didn't dare to hope, when I heard the name Jordi Wishart!'

'Yes, it's me, Fred. What are you doing in a boat this size? Have you given up the fishing?'

'Long ago, lad. I'm carrying cargo, now.'

'Oh?' Jordi said, as they stepped on board and he examined the damage. 'What cargo?'

'Cooking ranges, from an ironfounder in Devon. We canna

get them up here fast enough. But they're heavy buggers o' things. One slipped and went right through the deck.'

'So I see. You've got a lot of rotten wood there, Fred,' Jordi frowned. 'You should really come in as soon as you can and let me have a look at the hull. If one part's weak, the rest is suspicious. But you're in a hurry today, Bob says?'

'If I could get the deck done, I'd chance another trip and go today, yes. But I suppose that's out o' the question?'

'Not for the Wishart Yard, it isn't! There's such a thing as running repairs. We'll get the wood and the tools I need on board, and I'll come with you. How long will the trip take, do you reckon?'

'Good lad, Jordi! A week at the outside.'

'I'll be back in half an hour, then,' Jordi smiled and took the steps up to the house two at a time while Bob piled wood onto the boat.

'A *week*!' Thirza exclaimed, taking a deep breath. 'Well, never mind, Jordi. I'll have a surprise waiting for you when you get back.'

'And I'll bring you home a present, sweetheart,' he promised. 'I'll leave Bob in charge. See him if you have any trouble.'

She stood at the front door and watched the boat going out, wondering as she waved what it all reminded her of. It was Ruth, of course, waving goodbye to her father when he went off to the fishing at St Fillan, and then pacing the house like a tigress until she saw him coming back. Well, she was going to be too busy for any of that!

In a few minutes she was heading for Constitution Street, and only minutes after that she was wandering around the first saleroom she came to.

'Found anything?' a salesman with a limp approached her.

'I'm afraid it's all too dear for me in here. Where else should I try?'

'What sort of things do you need?'

'Everything.' Thirza enchanted him with her frank, beaming smile. It worked as usual – especially, as she had discovered, with men.

'Don't say I told you,' he muttered behind his hand, 'but who you want to go and see is Secondhand Rose. She's up the street a bit, on the left-hand side.'

'Thank you, sir,' Thirza flashed him another brilliant smile and, sure enough, as the man had said, she came upon a tiny slit of a shop, so tiny that some of its goods were spilling out onto the pavement. She read the sign: 'ALADDIN'S CAVE – Prop. MRS ROSE', and ventured in.

A tiny woman with dark eyes, a hooked nose and a smiling mouth seemed familiar, somehow. She was lifting things and looking at them half way up the shop. She reminded Thirza so much of little Caroline Sharkey that she felt quite at home with her. She squeezed past junk of every kind, piled high from top to bottom of the long narrow shop and smiled radiantly again. 'Oh, I love this,' she whispered in the woman's ear. 'I'm sure to find exactly what I want in here . . . What are you looking for?' she asked with interest.

'I'm just trying to tidy up, lassie,' the woman said. 'I'm the owner, Mrs Rose – or as they call me around here, Secondhand Rose.'

'Oh dear, Mrs Rose, I'm sorry! We're new here. I didn't know who you were. I thought you were just another customer.'

'So ye like my shop? What exactly are ye looking for?'

Thirza had found out long ago that straight talking usually worked best with women, not charm. They could always see right through charm.

'We've moved in to a dirty filthy house,' she said, deciding to tell the truth, 'without a pot, a pan, a dish or a stick of furniture.'

'Dear, dear, lassie! Ye're in a bad way.'

'Desperate, I would say, Mrs Rose. Besides that, we're very short of money. The fire won't burn. My husband says the chimney needs a cowl. I don't even know what a cowl looks like. I need a kettle, if we ever do get the fire to burn. Then I can heat up some water to clean the dirt.'

'Harry!' Mrs Rose shouted. 'Go out the back and fetch a cowl.'

A boy of about sixteen rose up from the heart of the bric-a-brac and disappeared at the back of the shop.

'I've got a kettle,' Secondhand Rose said, digging under an old table. 'It's black with soot, but it's whole. Where are you sleeping?'

'On the bare floorboards.'

'Well, there's a brand new mattress ticking here, never been used. All you need is a bag of straw to fill it with, and some clean paper to lay down underneath it in the meantime.'

'How much for the lot?'

'Let me see. A cowl, a kettle and the ticking. That'll be two shillings.'

'*Two shillings?*' Thirza looked scandalised, and a quick look of amusement flashed in and out of the other woman's eyes. 'Oh, I can't afford that! The man in the saleroom said to come here, but I can't afford that!'

'Oh, ay . . . A man wi' a limp?'

Thirza nodded.

'Jimmy Rose, my brother-in-law. We're all in the secondhand trade in this family. All right, one and six for the lot.'

Thirza shook her head again.

'What about sixpence, then? Now, I can't say fairer than that, lassie!'

'Even sixpence is a lot of money to us, Mrs Rose. But thank you.'

'Ay, all right, then. Sixpence it is, and I'll throw in a bag o' straw and a bucket as well. Harry, you go wi' this lady, and carry her things.'

'My name is Mrs Wishart,' Thirza said, holding out her hand. 'Thirza Wishart. Thank you, Mrs Rose. I'll be back.'

Bob Steele shut the boatshed in the afternoon, and went up on to the roof of the house to fix the cowl onto the chimney. Then he came into the kitchen and helped Thirza to light a fire. To her great relief, it burned well, and no more smoke came down the chimney.

'It might need adjusting later,' he said. 'I think I'd better have a look at the well while I'm here. I daresay it needs cleaning out, too.'

While he was doing that, Thirza filled her mattress with straw and threw it over the washing line out of her way. When Bob came back with a bucket of water, she was ready for serious action. 'Thank you, Bob,' she smiled. 'I'll manage now,' and he turned to go, shaking his head at the state of the kitchen.

'You've got plenty to do, Mrs Wishart,' he said sympathetically.

She spent the rest of that day attending to the fire and heating water to scrub the floor. She scrubbed and scrubbed until she got the floorboards back to the colour they had started out in life, pale brown and yellow. When they dried up she put down the mattress, fell into her improvised bed, and plotted her next move. Tomorrow, by hook or by crook, she was going to get a bed before Jordi came back.

She arrived quite breathless at the door of Aladdin's Cave the following morning at nine o'clock.

'Lassie, lassie,' Secondhand Rose clucked her tongue, 'sit doon and catch yer breath! What is it the day?'

'A bed,' Thirza gasped. 'Please, Mrs Rose, do you have a bed?'

'I dinna ken aboot *that*,' Secondhand Rose shook her head doubtfully.

'Ay, ye have, Ma,' Harry Rose shouted from the back. 'This old one, here.'

'Och, that's nae use to man nor beast! It's only got three legs.'

'Would you let me see it, anyway?' Thirza pleaded.

The little woman nodded at her son and a gigantic upheaval began in the small cluttered shop. Chairs, tin baths, wheelbarrows, tables and bric-a-brac of every description landed out on the pavement, where Harry guarded it all from passers-by. Meanwhile, Secondhand Rose demonstrated by climbing over the top of what was left that she was not only nimble, but athletic too.

'Here's it!' she cried triumphantly, and indeed, there it was in all its glory, lop-sided, covered in cobwebs, but with a fine oak railing top and bottom and a decent spring. 'Ay, that's been a bed and a half in its day! Double, too.'

'Three quarters, Mrs Rose,' Thirza said briskly.

A gleam of amusement lit Secondhand Rose's eyes for a second. It was enough to tell Thirza that they were about to embark on the bargaining. Well, little did the owner of Aladdin's Cave know that she was up against the best haggler in the business — or used to be, with the Sharkeys.

'I'd need a couple of pounds for that bed,' Secondhand Rose started at the top, as Thirza expected.

'It's not much use with only three legs,' she sighed. 'I don't know what I'd do with it.'

'All ye need is a joiner to make another leg, lassie.'

'Joiners charge money, though.'

'One pound, then! And that's a bargain!'

'Let's see . . .' Thirza said, half turning away, enjoying this exchange. 'A joiner will charge for the wood and charge for his time . . .'

'My God! Ye're fairly out for a bargain the day! Ten shillings, then. Noo, I canna say fairer than that, can I?'

'It's very fair, Mrs Rose, until I count up all the hidden charges attached to it – ten shillings for the bed, ten shillings for the wood to mend it, and ten shillings for the joiner's time. I just can't afford it.'

'Ach, awa' ye go, lassie! Half a crown, and that's my last word.'

'Thank you, Mrs Rose. You're very kind.'

'I need my head looked at, ye mean!'

'Ye might as well let her have the wardrobe to match while ye're at it, Ma,' Harry's face appeared above the pile of goods at the doorway. 'It would gi'e us a lot more space.'

'Ay, all right,' his mother sighed.

'But I've got no more money!' Thirza said, gazing at the wardrobe behind the bed with a calculating eye.

'Ye're a fly wee torment,' Secondhand Rose observed. 'Tak' it for nothing. It's like Harry says. We need the space. I ken the mirror on that wardrobe needs replacing, but ye shouldna look a gifthorse in the mouth.'

'Two and sixpence, then?' Thirza said and, in the heat of the moment, raised her right hand. 'It's a deal?'

'Deal,' Secondhand Rose slapped it, laughing. 'I might ha'e known it! Nobody ever beat me down like you did, lassie, and nobody strikes a bargain like that except another Romany! Which tribe did ye come from?'

'None. I joined the Sharkeys for a few months, that's all, before I married my husband.'

'Ay, Jordi Wishart. Harry made it his business to find out when he helped ye home yesterday. Ye've bought Davie Forbes's Yard and his auld hoose?'

'We have indeed,' Thirza sighed, 'and now there's very little money left over for anything. We're penniless, more or less.'

'Ach, cheer up, dearie, and call me Meggie. I was Meggie Lee once, of the Lee tribe, born a traveller mysel'. Ye're no' in that much o' a hurry, are ye? We'll ha'e a dish o' tea.'

Afterwards Thirza raced back to the boatshed. 'I've got a job for you, Bob,' she announced. 'Can you get another three men to help you? I've bought a bed and a wardrobe from Secondhand Rose.'

'I daresay I can,' he smiled and took another bite out of his bun.

'Oh, dear! I've interrupted your lunch.'

'That's all right, Mrs Wishart. Up to the house, is it?'

'Well, no, Bob. You see, they need a few repairs. Would you have a look at them . . . Before my husband gets back?'

Two days later, during their lunch break, Bob and his three friends toiled up to number eight with the bed and the wardrobe. Nobody would ever have known that the bed had been damaged, and as for the wardrobe, the mirror had been taken out, the speckled edges cut off, and the space around it filled with marquetry.

Thirza washed them and polished them lovingly, with tears in her eyes. They were the first two articles of furniture in their new home. After that she sat on one of the orange boxes she had acquired in place of chairs to admire her handiwork, before she lay down to sleep on the mattress on the floor. She would not get into that bed without Jordi, she vowed. It wouldn't feel right without him. It might even be bad luck.

Now that she had got together the basic essentials for their new life there was no time to waste. Everything must be got ready to perfection, for Jordi's homecoming. She went out early in the morning and bought some pieces of rabbit and, after she'd washed them and floured them, put them in her heaviest pan – one of a set she had bought at a bargain price – with plenty of onions and carrots, adding a little cold water. Belle had taught her how to cook this stew, very slowly on the fire, so that by nightfall it would be tender enough to look and taste like chicken, Jordi's favourite.

Jordi arrived back, as promised, exactly a week from the day he'd left and, after a lot of commotion at the Yard, came running up the steps to the house, carrying a bottle.

'What's that?' Thirza asked.

'Cider, from Devon.'

'Do people get drunk if they drink cider?'

'Not very. Especially if they drink it with a meal – and I smell something cooking.'

'It's rabbit stew, Jordi. What else do you see, besides the fire Bob got to draw at last?'

'You've been missing me. I can tell,' Jordi grinned as he looked at the bed.

'What about the wardrobe to match?' Thiza flushed and ladled out some stew onto his plate, while he poured the cider into two cups and set them down on their orange-box table.

'Never mind the wardrobe, Thirza. I'll admire that later. First of all I want to admire my wife.'

'I feel quite strange,' she said in the middle of her second cup of cider, 'but this is lovely, isn't it? It goes so well with the rabbit.'

'Just like me, sweetheart. I go so well with you,' Jordi said. 'I promise you, soon you'll find that out. As I recall, we never did have a honeymoon, did we?'

They looked at each other for a long exquisite moment in the candlelight and then there was no need for words. Thirza moved into his arms and they kissed, over and over again. Jordi drew her hard against him, both to gratify himself and to prove to her how unmistakable his need was. She laughed softly. 'Let me undress you, Jordi.'

'And I'll undress you,' he said breathlessly.

They fell eagerly into the bed, warm and deep. Silence fell upon them like some delayed blessing, and in that silence and warmth they came to know each other's bodies with ever-growing intimacy. Their responses to each other seemed insatiable and of endless variety. Thirza felt almost drugged with love, though her senses grew keener as the night and their passion went on. The pleasure far exceeded the wildest dreams she had ever had of what love between a man and woman really could be.

So this was what it was supposed to be, she thought in ecstasy. Orange skins were the furthest thing from her mind.

31

NEXT morning Jordi asked her to go down to the boatshed with him. 'I want to show you the present I brought back for you,' he said.

'I thought the bottle of cider was the present.'

'That was only a little celebration, Thirza. The real thing is a bit bigger than that,' he said, opening the Yard gates. 'It caused quite a stir last night, taking it off the boat.'

She could see why. It was about six feet long, three feet tall and made of iron. In fact, she had never seen anything like it. The middle section of it had perpendicular bars and seemed to sit on a box. The left section looked like a cupboard door with a handle on it. The section on the right had a little tap instead of a handle, and all three were housed beneath a flat, cast-iron top. 'What is it?' she asked.

Jordi roared and laughed. 'I wish you could see your face! It's for your birthday, darling. It's the twentieth of August. Had you forgotten? You're seventeen today! I was so worried in case I wouldn't get it here in time.'

Whatever it was, it didn't matter to Thirza, not when there was someone still living in the world who loved her enough to remember her birthday. He was the only one who knew, now. He was her entire family.

She wanted to cry. She wanted to laugh. Above all, she wanted him to know how much he had touched her heart. She felt all these things passionately inside. Last night in bed she had managed to express them, in one way. But this morning she couldn't for the life of her put them into words. 'What is it, Jordi?' she asked again, instead.

'A cooking range. The fire goes in the middle to heat the oven on the left and the water tank on the right. Now you'll get all your kettles and pans on the hot plate on the top, you can bake or roast in the oven and you'll have hot water always ready. What do you think? You'll be the first lady in Leith to have one.'

'Oh, Jordi, I don't know what to think, except I'm the luckiest lady in Leith, that's for sure, to be Mrs Wishart! But we'll never get it through any of the doors of the house. It's so big!'

'We won't even try, sweetheart. We'll tear down the kitchen wall and get it in, that way. It's got to be built in, anyway, along with the flue to take the fumes and smoke up the chimney. As soon as Bob comes, we'll shut the Yard for the day and make a start.'

Thirza felt very doubtful when she saw Jordi and Bob, together with four other men, heaving the range up to the side of the house, and apprehensive when the bed, the wardrobe, the orange boxes and her little bits and pieces were moved into the next room. Then the hammering began. Dust from the kitchen wall crumbling under the sledge-hammers flew from one end of the house to the other like smoke until, at eleven o'clock, she could stand the din and the dirt no longer. 'I'll go and get something to eat,' she said, and made straight for Secondhand Rose. 'Oh, Meggie,' she almost wept, 'can I sit here with you for half an hour?'

'What's happened?'

'Jordi's come back with a cooking range instead of wages. The men are tearing down the kitchen wall right now for it. The noise is terrible.'

'I've heard o' cooking ranges. Some call them "kitcheners". I'd like fine to see one.'

'Come home with me, then. Will Harry manage the shop?'

'For a wee while. But wait, Thirza, how many men are working?'

'Six.'

'Have ye got enough dishes?'

'I never thought of that! I took only enough money for rolls.'

'You get the rolls and I'll look out some dishes. I'll leave a wee pan o' soup for Harry. If we walk awfy slow, we could carry up this big pot o' tattie soup between us, and the rolls and the dishes.'

When they arrived at number eight, the men downed tools and they all went out into the sunshine of the back garden.

'Never mind the weeds,' Thirza said, ladling out the soup.

'Pretend it's a picnic,' Secondhand Rose sped around the small circle of men, handing out the rolls.

'Don't go near the kitchen for another half an hour,' Jordi advised them. 'We're going to sweep the chimney next.'

'Oh, no . . .' Thirza wailed. 'What about my nice clean floor?'

'Better get all the dirt over and done wi' now,' Bob Steele smiled.

'Come on, then, Meggie,' Thirza sighed. 'You might as well see the rest of the house while you're here.'

'Oh, dearie me!' Secondhand Rose clucked her tongue when Thirza flung open the first door. 'Na, na! It gets worse!' she exclaimed as the tour went on. 'My God, Thirza,' she said when they got upstairs, 'I see what ye mean now. By the way, those dishes were a wee present. Ye're going to ha'e a struggle, lassie. What a mess! It's a good job ye're young!'

Back downstairs again they took one look inside the kitchen and retired, coughing. Dust and soot lay thick everywhere.

'But oh!' Secondhand Rose went into raptures, 'ye've got a right fine stove there! Think o' it, all black and shining in the light o' a roaring fire in the winter – which reminds me. I'll gi'e ye a tin o' black lead to polish it the next time ye're in the shop.'

The range was installed and working before dark, and the brickwork and plastering finished off the following day. But it was a whole week before Thirza got the walls white-washed twice and the floor back to normal. In the meantime, the honeymoon continued in the new bed, and that made it all worthwhile.

In September, Thirza made a determined assault on the garden while the weather held fair, tearing out weeds that were threatening to choke the Canterbury Bells, the peonies and all the other perennial flowers she recognised. She chopped down the flowering currant hedge mercilessly, in the belief that it would bloom all the better in the spring, and tied back the honeysuckle that roamed over all the walls. Not knowing what to do with the rose rambling over an arch at the front door she simply tied it up and hoped for the best next year.

Next, she turned her attention to something that had been worrying her for some time. 'We've got to join a church here,' she told Jordi. 'Today I'm going out to find the nearest one and, if possible, have a word with the minister.'

'No, you're not, Thirza. Today you're going out to the shops, to buy a new dress. You can't go to the Kirk, let alone visit the manse, dressed the way you are. Neither can I. It's Saturday, anyway, so I'll close the Yard this afternoon and come with you.'

In Constitution Street he steered her past Aladdin's Cave very firmly. 'Oh, no you don't,' he said when her footsteps wavered outside the door. 'It's something new I meant. You deserve it.'

'But the money, Jordi!'

'To hell with the money. Here's a shop with a pretty outfit in the window. Do you like it?'

'Yes, it's very nice.'

'And they've got mens' suits in their other window. We'll go in here.'

Half an hour later they emerged, Jordi in a dark blue suit, and Thirza in what the assistant called a "costume", in a paler shade of blue, with their old clothes respectfully wrapped up, as though they had been made of gold threads, in a brown paper parcel.

'Now, we'll find a church,' Jordi said, 'and you're not going to speak to any minister alone. We'll go together.'

'Mr and Mrs Wishart,' he announced firmly when the maid opened the door of the manse to them, and showed them into the parlour.

'I'll fetch Mr MacPherson, sir,' she said.

'We've come to introduce ourselves, Mr MacPherson,' Jordi told the short, stubby minister when the maid fetched him. 'We're new here. Tomorrow we hope to attend your service.'

'Fetch some tea and biscuits, Ruby,' Mr MacPherson told

the maid. For the next half an hour he chatted to them about the virtues of being churchgoers at all, considering the way the world was going in wickedness, and questioned Jordi delicately about his Yard.

'Did you like him?' Thirza asked on the way home.

'He was as I expected.'

'What does that mean?'

'To go to church, or even to be a respectable person, costs money. He was trying to find out how much we are likely to put into his collection plate on Sundays.'

'I never thought you were so cynical, Jordi Wishart! Well, we are likely to need the services of a minister all our lives, whatever it costs, so we will have to discuss our donation,' Thirza said, practical as ever, and just as cynical.

Before she knew where she was, it was the third of October and Jordi's twenty-second birthday. That day, she managed to afford a fine fat chicken and stuffed it with oatmeal and onions. It was roasting nicely in the oven when she set two cheap candles on one of their latest acquisitions, a kitchen table with the wood scubbed white.

'You're wonderful,' Jordi smiled at her lovingly over the flickering candle flames.

'I know it,' Thirza tossed her head playfully, 'and not only that, but this chicken is done to a turn. So why aren't you eating it?'

Jordi shook his head, smiled and took up his knife and fork again in a great show of appetite, but then he paused again.

'I'm not very hungry, Thirza, not today. It's not the chicken. It's a few business worries, that's all.'

'What business worries?'

'None for you to bother your pretty little head about, anyway.'

'What business worries, Jordi?' Thirza insisted.

'It's just that we've finally run out of decent wood. It costs too much to buy any more, just when the small boats are flocking to our doors.'

'That's because of the money spent on the range and new clothes.'

'It was money well spent, Thirza. The way we are dressed

is an advertisement for the business. We don't want anyone to think we're not doing well. And as for the range, I want you to be warm and clean and happy, as we all were at St Fillan. It's how you were brought up. You'll never go backwards as long as we're together.'

'Oh, Jordi!' she rushed around the table to hug him. But she was thinking desperately, nevertheless, until at last she had an idea. It might be difficult to carry out, but she wanted Jordi to be happy at all costs. 'Don't worry any more,' she kissed him. 'I'll think of something. Forget about it tonight. It's your birthday.'

Forget about it they did for a few blissful hours, but Thirza lay awake long after their lovemaking, making her plans. Early the next morning, she escaped from Jordi's loving arms and stood in her nightgown on the floor.

'I'm going to wash all over,' she announced, too shy and modest even now to allow him to see her naked in the cold light of day. 'Go on down to the shed, Jordi. You can brew up some tea in there. I'll see you tonight.'

'Why? Where are you going?'

'Never you mind. It's a secret,' she said and shut the door on him.

So they needed wood, did they? She continued brooding over her plans and swilled cold water all over her, flinching when it cascaded over her nipples. They were unusually sore. She thought that Jordi must have been too enthusiastic in his foreplay last night. He had certainly aroused her to new, unexplored delights before they sank back together, utterly satisfied.

A little smile etched her determined lips in the glorious memory of their lovemaking when she presented herself at the Pittenweem Ferry at nine o'clock. She was very startled to find Jimmie Gilmour, son of Bertha Gilmour – the midwife who had brought her into the world – at the helm.

'Oh yes, Thirza,' he said as he cast off. 'I took up this job when we had our first bairn, Marie and me. She never liked me going to the fishing, you see. You remember Marie?'

'Of course I do. How is she?'

'Expecting again.'

'And your mother?'

'She's fine.'

'Well, I'm glad for you, Jimmie,' Thirza smiled wanly.

She wasn't feeling too well as she stepped back into Pittenweem and into her past. It took her a minute or two on dry land to recover and ask her way to Fraser's Sawmill. Clem, that was her uncle's name. It had come to her when she dredged her memory last night. She had never met him. When Ruth had gone to visit her brother, she had gone alone – as she had done that time they had needed wood for the loft room at St Fillan. Ruth had rarely mentioned his name. Thirza understood there had been an estrangement.

When she got to the sawmill she marched into the whining, screaming, whirring of huge saws ripping through the tree trunks which were moving inexorably up the channels to meet their fate.

'Mr Fraser?' she asked the first man she came to.

He looked at her blankly for a minute before he took out his earplugs. 'What did ye say, lassie?'

'Is Mr Fraser about?' she raised her voice.

'He's in his office,' he pointed to a small, glassed-off partition.

She knocked at the door. A middle-aged man writing something down on a paper rose up from his seat to open it. 'Ay?' he asked. 'Can I help you?'

'I hope so, Uncle Clem,' she shouted above the noise. 'I'm Ruth's daughter, Thirza.'

'Come in,' he said, and all at once they were in a cocoon of comparative silence. 'You're Ruth's daughter?'

'Yes, sir. I'm Thirza,' she said looking at him curiously. Andra had been his very double.

Clem Fraser stared back at her suspiciously. 'So what might you be wanting? Neither of my two sisters have been to see me in years, and now you turn up, Thirza Gourlay!'

Thirza didn't have all day for recriminations or to argue about family feuds, whatever they had been. She decided on shock tactics. 'Both your sisters are dead, Uncle Clem,' she said quietly.

At that his face went grey. His knuckles, gripping the desk, went white. 'I shouldn't have been so stubborn,' he said, 'but I could never accept the men my sisters married.'

'Well, my father and brother are dead too. Thirza rammed it home. 'The men you didn't like are all dead now. I'm the only one of the family left. Mother told me that you had never married, so I must be your only living relative.'

'Oh, God,' he said. 'Oh, my God . . .'

'And my name isn't Thirza Gourlay any more, either,' she added. 'It's Thirza Wishart. I'm married now.'

'But I thought you were only a wee lassie,' he protested.

'Wee lassies grow up, Uncle Clem.'

'Well, you'd better come awa', into the house,' he said. 'You and I have a lot to talk about.'

She was just in time to catch the three o'clock ferry back to Leith. She couldn't believe it when, five minutes out across the Firth of Forth she was suddenly and disgracefully sick, vomiting violently over the side of the ferry-boat. Jimmy Gilmour guided her sympathetically up the slipway at Leith, handing her a fry of haddock.

'Will ye be all right, Thirza?' he asked in concern.

'I don't know what came over me,' she said, wiping her eyes and her mouth. 'I've never done that before. But yes, Jimmy, I'll be all right now.'

She felt better as she got nearer to their house, and she was smiling and bright and pink again when Jordi came home to a fry of fresh haddock and tatties.

'I've been to Pittenweem,' she told him. 'That was the secret. I went over to ask Uncle Clem for wood. You'll get it tomorrow morning, and from now on you'll get all the wood you need at cost price.'

'Oh?'

'Don't look so doubtful. There's no catch.'

'No?'

'No. All he made me promise him is to go across and see him every now and then. He's lonely. Besides, he's a nice man.'

But the rocking, sickening sensation returned to Thirza that night. It still hadn't settled when she got up early, and she was violently sick again. She recovered again through the day, and this went on for the whole of the following week.

'I don't understand it, Jordi,' she said. 'To be seasick is

one thing, but for it to continue for days after on dry land is another.'

'I think you'd better go and see Dr Browne,' he said, smiling.

Thirza glared back at him. For once he was so unfeeling – he didn't seem concerned at all.

'I would say you're three to four months pregnant,' Dr Browne told her after he had examined her. 'The womb is now about the size of an orange. Come back again in three months. I'll look at you again and appoint a midwife for you.'

Jordi laughed, almost delirious with happiness. 'Our own little son, or or own little daughter, Thirza! It's a miracle!'

32

T HIRZA'S pregnancy dragged on through the spring. Most days she was well, but at least once a week she became depressed, asking herself if she really wanted this coming child. She kept these dark doubts hidden from Jordi.

She remembered the high hopes of her childhood and despaired of ever being a fine lady now – rich, elegant and, therefore, happy. Her life wasn't going the way she had planned it, not at all. Here she was, grindingly poor, and about to become poorer with another mouth to feed and another back to clothe. They were too poor . . . That was the bottom line when she added it all up.

One windy, sunny afternoon in April, restless and unable to settle, she walked into the room next to the kitchen. She had managed to clean and furnish it, courtesy of Secondhand Rose, and had grandly named it the drawing-room, for she was still determined to elevate their status one way or another. She inspected it for any stray speck of dust that might have dared to settle on the furniture and then walked over to the window and looked down over the terraced gardens, aware of a nagging pain in her back.

Someone must have planted daffodils in the past. They were dancing in the breeze, nodding their heads to her and all the trees and bushes were covered in a green haze of buds. Wherever she looked there was fresh life. She had never seen the cycle of the

299

year unfolding as she saw it so vividly today, not even when she was travelling on the roads. Another pain struck, low down in her back. She put her hand on it, but it took longer to go away this time.

'What's wrong?' Jordi took one look at her face when he came home.

'Oh, it's nothing. I've got some pains in my back, that's all.'

But by eight o'clock that night she was feeling dreadful. At ten, water gushed out of her, and wouldn't stop. She had no idea what to expect. She was frightened when the pains began. They were so bad that she was sure the baby would be born any minute.

Jordi helped her to bed and sat with her. At the end of half an hour, when she had had three severe pains, they both thought he'd better go for the midwife. He came back alone.

'She says to go back for her when the contractions are coming every five minutes,' he told her. By the time they were, Thirza was becoming very distressed.

'Don't worry,' he told her before he set off again. 'If the worst comes to the worst I'll be here. I'll deliver our child myself, if I have to. After working with the animals in Shetland, I know exactly what to do. It's the same principle.'

She couldn't speak to him when he came back. She just kept gripping his hands.

At midnight, the midwife arrived in a leisurely fashion, took a look at Thirza and then all around. 'I see ye've got a good fire on,' she said. 'Keep it up. I'll need plenty of hot water and sheets and towels.'

She kept him busy for another half an hour before she dismissed him. 'Awa' ye go, Mr Wishart,' she said. 'Ye needn't stay here. Go and lie doon yersel'. I'll let ye ken when the bairn comes, but that'll not be for a while yet.'

Thirza heard her and couldn't believe her ears. The baby *must* be coming any minute, to judge from the hell of *unceasing* pain she was in at that moment.

'I'm not leaving her whatever happens,' Jordi said firmly. Just knowing that he was there, somewhere outside this red ring of pain, gave Thirza the courage to endure it all night long.

It got worse, early in the morning. Someone kept wiping the

tears and the sweat out of her eyes. She was aware that a sheet was ripped up and tied round and round the bedhead, and that her hands were being directed to it.

'Hold on to that, lassie,' she heard the midwife saying. 'There's no sense getting splinters in yer hands. Ye're going to need yer hands soon now, to hold the bairn.'

Thirza could hardly hear her. She was going to die. She knew it when the worst pain so far ripped through her. The very bones of her hips were grinding apart, and the midwife was at the foot of the bed.

'Push, lass!' she said. 'Here's the head . . . Now, once more – push!'

If anything, that second searing pain was worse than the first. Somewhere in Thirza's brain common sense told her that here were the baby's shoulders, coming now. There was a slithering, the midwife's grunt of satisfaction and, after what seemed a long time, Jordi's radiant face above hers, kissing her. 'He's here, Thirza! Our beautiful little boy! We have a son, darling.'

Thirza felt she was swimming in deep waters. Sounds were coming and going. She thought she heard a slap. She knew she heard a baby cry and instinctively she opened her arms. She found that she was looking down at her very own child.

He was beautiful. He had the most perfect, beautiful face she had ever seen. But the midwife had wrapped him up so tightly in a towel that she couldn't see the rest of him and, too weary to speak, tears fell from her eyes.

Now the baby's face was red and angry, and he was bawling louder every minute, until Jordi took charge. 'My wife wants to see him all over,' he told the midwife, who was more concerned with attending to Thirza's afterbirth than her tears. Suddenly all Thirza's terrors evaporated. Everything was all right again. Jordi would make them all right. And it was more than all right; it was wonderful when, with a great shout of laughter, he whipped the towel off their son and showed the baby to his mother.

'He's all there! Ten fingers and ten toes, and everything else in between. He's a proper little man,' he said wrapping him up again and putting him back in Thirza's arms. 'What shall we call him?'

'It's usual to call a first son after his father,' the midwife put in, clearing everything up.

'Yes, Jordi,' Thirza agreed. 'That's what I want. Jordi.'

'Sweetheart, my real name is George,' he smiled and bent down to kiss her again. 'My French mother gave me my by-name, and it stuck. So, shall it be George Wishart, after his father and his grandfather?'

'George it is,' Thirza smiled tiredly.

'And he's needing to be fed,' the midwife said. 'I'll stay with you to make sure you can manage.' The liquid was oozing from Thirza's breasts, so that it was a relief when George took to them straight away. 'Ay, ye did well, Mrs Wishart, considering yer red hair,' she smiled at Thirza, 'and he seems to be feeding all right. Ye'll remember he must be winded after each feed?'

'Yes. But what do you mean, considering my red hair?'

'Och, nurses like me think red-haired women have the hardest births, lose more blood, and are more of a problem than anyone else.'

'Why should that be?' Jordi asked.

'Nobody seems to know, but some folk say that red hair is a mixture of the dark and the fair, and its a dangerous combination.'

'Now you know, Jordi,' Thirza laughed weakly when she left. 'I'm a dangerous combination.'

'I always knew you were different, anyway,' he smiled at her fondly.

George was two years old, a plump adorable baby, before she realised one day that she didn't like his name. In fact she resented it. George was such a solemn name for such a tiny boy. Worse than that, the child was living up to it, for try as she might by smiling and laughing, even by tickling him for a response, George remained a dark, solid, solemn child who hardly ever laughed.

Thirza simply couldn't understand how any child of hers could be so serious, but he was. In the end, one day when she was taking him across to Pittenweem to see Uncle Clem, now a monthly occurrence when the weather allowed, she decided he must be like his father, or his father's family.

She discussed it with Uncle Clem, who would have none of

it. 'He's a proper little man, Thirza,' he kept saying. 'Wait and see. He'll go far,' and there was nothing George seemed to like better than to be in the sawmill anyway, knee-deep in sawdust and wood shavings, playing with the latest toy his besotted grand-uncle had made for him.

On the fifteenth of April, George's fourth birthday, Uncle Clem sent across a rocking horse, beautifully painted, and with a blond mane and tail.

By the time he was six, the Wishart Yard was breaking even, at last, and there was a little more money to spend. Jordi took him down to the Yard to play about some afternoons, while Thirza managed to clean out more and more rooms downstairs, furnishing them with the help of her friend, Secondhand Rose.

All seemed to be going well until one day, when Jordi brought George back home, she could hardly look at the child in a sudden anxiety. The force of it took her completely by surprise. She tried to avoid her son's dark eyes, but whatever she did, wherever she went, she was drawn to them. There was no doubt that they were crossed.

It couldn't be. It simply couldn't be that any child of hers and Jordi's could be less than perfect in every way. Jordi had assured her of it when George was born, yet here he was himself remarking on it.

'Rubbish!' she said. 'It's a trick of the light. You're imagining it, Jordi. His eyes are perfect.'

'Perfect, but squint. The left one is turning in,' Jordi said, confirming her worst, most terrible fear. 'It'll have to be seen to. He must see Dr Browne.'

'No!' Thirza protested. 'How would *you* like it if someone interfered with your eyes? Think of the pain and the agony! I won't have it! Leave him alone,' and she clutched her child to her breast.

'He's going,' was all that Jordi said. He took George's hand then and there, and led him out of the house.

Then Thirza knew a different, agonising pain, the pain of worry. She bitterly resented the reason for it, and Jordi for putting her through it. She waited and watched until the tall, handsome figure of her so-called husband came back, leading their small son by the hand, their son who was utterly desecrated in her opinion. He was wearing a patch over his little right eye.

'How could you *do* this to him?' she screamed, and tore the patch off.

'He has to wear it, Thirza,' Jordi explained patiently, putting the patch gently back over George's eye, and comforting him. 'His left eye is lazy, that's all. It's very common, Dr Browne says. By wearing this patch over the right eye, his left one is forced to work.'

Thirza couldn't take him out, not to see Secondhand Rose, not even to see Uncle Clem. For weeks she was black affronted. Afterwards, however, she was forced to agree that, on close inspection, George's eyes were responding to the treatment.

'There's nothing wrong with his eyesight, you know,' Jordi assured her, 'and, in time, he can do without the patch.'

A few weeks later Thirza took him to see Dr Browne herself. She wanted to consult him on a little matter of her own, as well.

'Oh, I think we can throw this patch away now, George,' Dr Browne smiled. 'Your eyes are as good as new. You've been a very good boy, and good boys who come to see me get a sweetie.'

'That's wonderful, Dr Browne!' Thirza said overjoyed to see the last of the eyepatch.

'It wouldn't have worked without good parents who cared enough about him to see it through, Mrs Wishart.'

Thirza had the grace to feel ashamed of herself for a minute.

'And now, if you'll lie down on the couch for me? Oh yes,' he said a few minutes later, 'you're pregnant again, my dear, but I suppose you suspected it yourself.'

'I did,' she said. 'When?'

'October, I should think. But come back again in three months, and we'll work out a date for you then.'

George had been admitted to the local school when their second son was born.

'The choice of a name is yours this time, sweetheart,' Jordi said. 'Perhaps you want to call him David or Andrew, after your father or Andra?'

'Oh no,' she shuddered. 'Not after anyone dead. That's

bad luck. I think he should have a name of his own, a plain name like John. Yes, John. John Wishart sounds lucky, doesn't it?'

33

JOHN reminded Thirza of Andra in so many ways. When the black hair he was born with fell out, reddish-brown hair grew in, and his blue eyes were merry, if not downright mischievous. She never had any trouble getting John to smile and laugh, and by nine months he was on his feet and ready for action.

'Ay, just like Davy Gourlay,' Uncle Clem said when he saw the new baby and, from the way that he said it, Thirza knew he had never liked her father. She wondered why, and in the end came right out and asked.

'Your mother married beneath her, Thirza. She had to get married. It was a terrible scandal at the time.'

She was stunned at this discovery. She thought about it for weeks afterwards. To think that Ruth, always so strict and so prim, had committed one of the most heinous crimes of all, the unlawful, unlicensed crime of passion and the flesh . . .!

Yet it explained a lot; why her mother had kept herself to herself ever since, to the point of being misunderstood and considered 'that stuck-up Ruth Gourlay'; why the family always had to be cleaner and smarter than everyone else on the Braehead, and why she had been so determined to educate her daughter so that she could better herself. To Thirza, it all pointed to her mother's efforts to cleanse herself and atone for her own fall from grace. Thirza was only just beginning to understand how great her mother's frustration must have

307

been, with that history behind her, when she fell into Duke Elliot's arms.

The truth of the matter was, she was feeling very frustrated herself, tied down now with two small children to look after when she could have been going out to work. Her life was going past too quickly. She was twenty-three already, with none of her ambitions realised. Very soon she would be considered too old to employ.

'George is a very clever child, his teachers say,' Jordi reported one day, after he had been to the school to fetch his son. 'He's the most intelligent in the school. Already they say we should be aiming at a university education for him.'

'But he's not even seven years old yet!'

'It doesn't matter. A child has to be prepared for university, years ahead.'

'Besides, they'll want to see records, I suppose.'

Thirza brooded about it all to such an extent that it wiped her usual shine clean off her. Her eyes became dull, her quick smile disappeared, and Jordi was the first to notice it.

'What's the matter, Thirza?'

'I've been thinking.'

'Yes, I can see that. What about?'

'There are new laws and new regulations every time I open a newspaper. I never knew about the Six Acts until I read an article about them the other day – the dispersal of seditious meetings, any publication that might be used for propaganda against the government to be further taxed, justice to be administered promptly – '

'Well, we did that,' Jordi said. 'Where might we be today if we had waited for justice from the authorities? We might both be dead ourselves. What else?'

'Oh, other laws concerning guns and pistols. What I've been thinking is that soon our whole lives will depend on little bits of paper . . . Like marriage records, for example.'

'Now, Thirza, we would have been married long ago, if you hadn't been married already to Michael Sharkey. Why are you bringing it up now?'

'Because I want both boys to be christened, at least.'

'How can we? We still can't produce any marriage lines. We've been living in sin for years, sweetheart,' Jordi grinned.

'Shh, Jordi! There's got to be a way around it. In fact I've already thought of one. Listen . . .'

The following Thursday morning they set off to see Mr MacPherson at the manse, by appointment. George was at school and John was romping about under Bob Steele's watchful eye in a wooden slatted cage he had erected in the boatshed. 'Don't worry. I'll do all the talking,' Thirza said, as they approached the manse.

'I know you will,' Jordi smiled. 'And I'll do all the paying. The usual dangerous combination.'

This time she refused Mr MacPherson's polite offer of tea and biscuits. Her hands were shaking so much inside her gloves that she could not have held a cup and saucer, anyway, without them rattling about and so betraying them.

'We should like to have both our sons christened, Mr MacPherson,' she began.

'I see . . . I have wondered for a long time why you haven't spoken about this before.'

Thirza smiled, and hoped that Jordi would remain silent, too. She intended to approach this in a roundabout way.

'Well,' Mr MacPherson said, when he saw that no explanation was forthcoming, 'it's a simple little ceremony, although so very important, as you both know.'

'Indeed, sir,' Jordi agreed. 'We understand that we shall be asking God's blessing for our sons.'

'In the name of the Father, the Son, and the Holy Ghost,' Mr MacPherson assured them so austerely that Thirza's very soul shuddered at the magnitude of the deception that she was about to undertake.

'Afterwards,' she heard the minister saying next, 'I shall write out certificates to say that I have done so. You have your marriage lines, of course?'

'No,' Thirza said with tears in her eyes. Jordi reached across and took her hand in his. 'You see, Mr MacPherson, ours was a runaway marriage, conducted in a hurry over the anvil in Gretna Green. We were warned that we should see the Sheriff in Dumfries about it . . .' her voice trailed off.

'But we were being pursued at the time,' Jordi took up the tale. 'Very hotly, too,' he smiled steadily and fondly at Thirza while he pushed one of the last five pound notes from Thirza's petticoat across the desk in a casual way.

'Yes,' she smiled back at him lovingly, noticing that Mr MacPherson was picking it up very smartly, 'by both sets of parents, too!'

'Dear me! An extraordinary story,' the minister commented. The five pound note had vanished. 'Romantic, too.'

'One we would like kept as quiet as possible, sir, and our mistake rectified,' Jordi exhibited a note of steel in his voice for the first time.

'Of course. Well, well! Now, you good people mustn't worry about this. Not at all. I know the Sheriff here very well. In fact, he's my brother-in-law,' the minister paused delicately.

'This interview is all about keeping things in the family, isn't it?' There was a distinctly cynical note in Jordi's voice when he handed over the last five pound note.

'Yes. So if you give me a few details, we'll get a copy certificate of your marriage drawn up.'

'Oh, Mr MacPherson! Thank you,' Thirza gasped, and Jordi smiled his quiet smile.

'Now, it was at Gretna Green, you say? In the blacksmith's shop? And the date?'

'June the eighth, 1829,' she answered, having carefully worked it out to well over a year before George was born.

'Your parents' names, my dear?'

'David and Ruth Gourlay.'

'His occupation?'

'Fisherman.'

'And your parents, Mr Wishart?'

'George and Madeleine Wishart.

'Your father's occupation?'

'Captain, in the army of the East India Company.'

'All very interesting – in fact, unique,' Mr MacPherson was still murmuring as he showed them out. 'A week on Sunday, before the service, shall we say? That should give me time to make the necessary arrangements.'

'Well, we got away with it again,' Jordi said on the way home. 'Ten pounds poorer, but for that you'll have your three pieces of paper, one of them bogus.'

'Don't say it like that, Jordi,' Thirza shuddered. 'You make it sound as though one day our luck will run out.'

Any luck they had had began to run out when John was eighteen months old. He caught a very bad cold. His nose and eyes ran, and he wheezed terribly. When he began to cough alarmingly, Thirza sent for Dr Browne.

'Let me see . . .' he frowned, looking at the spots inside John's elbows, behind his knees and all over his little hands. 'I see he has a rash?'

'A rash that never goes away, Dr Browne. I wash docken leaves and wrap them around the spots to try and soothe the itching, and I've made him little cotton gloves to stop him scratching.'

'You're doing your best, Thirza. Keep him warm, give him plenty to drink and I'll come back tomorrow. By the way, have an old kettle handy and get some friar's balsam. Try steaming the room with it if he ever has another attack like this.'

That bout passed, as did the next and the one after that, and Thirza managed to contain them with Dr Browne's help. But, by the time John was four years old and stretching out tall and thin, with a concave chest, she could see that the doctor was very worried.

'These are not ordinary colds, are they?' she asked him.

'I'm afraid not, my dear. John has asthma.'

'I've heard of it. What exactly is it?'

'We don't know very much about it, I'm sorry to say, but it's a disease that seems to change every seven years. Just look after him as you have always done, and perhaps when he's seven years old he'll grow out of it, with God's help.'

During the next few years Thirza had more than enough to cope with. Not a single breeze that blew was allowed to come near her John. She draped the sides of his little bed with blankets in case of draughts. She allowed him to go outdoors only in clement weather, and school was out of the question.

Throughout all this, George clung almost exclusively to his father. Thirza shed tears over it, remembering the first time she had tried to put him in a bath, when she was so unused to babies that she was too frightened to put him in the water.

It was Jordi who had calmly taken over, supporting the infant's wobbling head and back with one of his large, capable hands. It was Jordi who helped her until she felt confident enough to do it herself. She remembered how Jordi had been a tower of strength to her then, and to George as well, ever since. It was only natural that her beloved firstborn should turn to his father, and never more so than now when she was so preoccupied with little, ailing John. But all the same, it was breaking her heart.

She had another nagging worry, the greatest of all, that she and Jordi would drift apart over the years. She berated herself for not paying enough attention to him, and sometimes she voiced these fears at the end of another long day when she was very tired and depressed. But Jordi always comforted her, and he never stopped loving her.

Then she would pull herself together again and try harder than ever to inject some fun into their lives. She insisted that Jordi took time off his business to take George out to sail his model yachts, and she saw to it that, when they returned from their favourite pastime, there was always something special for tea.

When John was well enough, she held little parties for the boys and the friends George introduced. And, every now and then, like oases in a desert, she and Jordi went out to see a play or listen to a concert, leaving their sons in the hands of Secondhand Rose. But still, no matter how she tried to relax, she had not conceived the third child that she and Jordi wanted so desperately.

And life went on until the June of 1845 when John caught his most severe cold yet – where from, and in the middle of June, Thirza was too tired, too anxious and too despairing to care. In such an emergency, when John wheezed and coughed, Dr Browne could do very little to help him. Then Thirza resorted to the old Romany ways in a frantic effort to ease John's breathing any way she could. She tied old socks around his neck. She strung onions around his waist. She forced warm water laced with cinnamon down his throat, but all to no avail.

In spite of everything, his convulsions of wheezing and coughing took a new and terrifying direction. This time Thirza heard him whoop.

'He's got the whooping cough, Thirza,' Dr Browne confirmed. 'Now he'll have even more difficulty in breathing. Don't let him lie down to sleep. Keep him in a sitting position all the time. I'm afraid you're in for a few sleepless nights.'

She and Jordi took it in turns to sit up all night with John, watching over him. A few nights later, when it was Thirza's turn, John's face went blue all over and his lips went purple. The sounds of his awful struggles for breath filled the whole house. Thirza shouted for Jordi to come.

He raced for the doctor. Thirza held her child, willing him to get a breath in the steam-filled room, gently rubbing his back until Dr Browne took him out of her arms twenty minutes later and laid his now silent little body back on his bed.

'He's gone, Thirza,' he said. 'No more struggling for John, now.'

'No! No! No!' Her terrible screams came from the very depths of her being, while Jordi held her tight. '*Oh no, not our little John . . .*'

So great was her grief that she forgot about George for the next twenty-four hours. He emerged pale-faced, clinging to his father's hand, when Jordi faced her with the brutality of their loss.

'The undertakers have been, Thirza. The funeral will be on Saturday. John looks very peaceful now. He's in the drawing-room.'

The last thing she wanted to see was her child lying in his coffin, but she dragged herself through, and sat beside it dry-eyed wondering why this should have happened to an innocent child. Was there anything else she could have done – should have done – for their beloved John? She tortured herself still further until, on the third day, from the silent, darkened house, she and Jordi and George set off to the church for the funeral service.

But they had to wait while the mourners from another funeral came out, chief amongst them Jordi's arch-rival, Douglas Hunter. His face was grey, his eyes dark-ringed, and Thirza immediately felt tremendous sympathy for the man. Her eyes met his in a silent bond.

Then another minister, one they had never seen before, came out behind the flower-bedecked coffin, and all the people bowed their heads as it was taken away.

Mr MacPherson came out last of all and murmured to Jordi. 'That was the service for Mrs Helen Hunter. Her brother wanted to conduct the service himself in our church. I'm sorry for this slight delay, Mr Wishart, but if you and Mrs Wishart and young George would allow me to seat you first? There seems to be quite a crowd come to pay their last respects.'

They sat down in the front pew. The undertakers brought in the small coffin and laid the family flowers on it, and then the other mourners came in and almost filled the church.

What could the minister possibly find to say about a little seven-year-old boy, Thirza wondered, while they sang the first hymn? But Mr MacPherson rose to the sad occasion superbly, dwelling on John's christening, not so many years ago in this very church, and the fact that his little life had only been preserved as long as this because of the loving care and attention lavished on him by his parents. Now, he was happy and at peace in a better world.

Thirza lived through it somehow without fainting, but she only did so by concentrating her mind on the tortured face of Douglas Hunter. He had endured all this public display of grief for his wife only half an hour ago. She was so far away in her thoughts that she neither saw nor heard Jordi leaving the pew, and the first thing she was aware of was the congregation rising respectfully when Jordi and Bob Steele carried out John's coffin between them.

She began to cry. She would never see her son again in this life. Thirza could never have explained to anyone how surging and tremendous a comfort it was when she felt another small hand creeping into hers, and she looked down at George's solemn face, betraying emotion for once, with huge tears in his dark eyes.

Thank God, they still had George.

34

AFTER so many years of anxiety and stress, Thirza found it very hard to relax and take up the threads of normal living again. She and Jordi drew closer together than ever in a grief that wouldn't go away, comforting each other in every way they could.

Before long the comfort they gave to each other flared into a passion more fiery than it had ever been, and as a result Thirza bloomed again.

Jordi leaned one elbow on the pillow and smiled down at her in the early morning of the twentieth of August. 'You're so beautiful, Thirza,' he marvelled, 'far more beautiful now on your thirty-second birthday than when you were a young girl. All our experiences are etched on your face, to make it so interesting and attractive . . . And as for your body . . .' He made passionate love to her again.

Their happiness was reflected in George, who was now fulfilling all the promise of his early years. He was interested in everything that was going on in the world, and was very clever. Thirza understood at last that this was the reason why he seemed to live in a world apart from her, a world she couldn't reach, which was full of the dreams and aspirations of far-sighted men.

He read about the railways, about William Hedley's *Puffing Billy*, about George Stephenson's *Rocket*, and spoke about them to his parents with tremendous excitement.

'It's Railway Fever, all right,' Jordi smiled at him. 'Britain is full of Irish navvies. Armies of them are advancing across the country building cuttings and tunnels and embankments, and laying down mile upon mile of track.'

'And there's a man called Isambard Kingdom Brunel, Father.'

'Yes. He built the Great Western Railway to Bristol and then thought there was no reason why the route shouldn't be extended to New York by ship. Brilliant! Do you know the name of his ship, George?'

'I know he designed the *Great Western*. Oh, Father, that's what I would like to do, to design a ship!'

Jordi smiled at George's enthusiasm. Thirza saw only his shining dark eyes, so like his father's, as she listened to their conversation with one ear. She had more important things to think about. She was pregnant again.

The Wisharts' third child came in a hurry before Annie Begbie, the midwife, could get there. Jordi delivered their daughter himself.

'A gorgeous little girl, Thirza,' he said, with the tears raining down his face. 'She's an angel, just an angel!'

Thirza smiled and cradled her in her arms. She had known from the beginning that it was going to be a girl. The easy pregnancy and her whole well-being told her that it was going to be a change of birth. A golden aura had been all around this child from her very conception.

'Well, you've named her yourself, darling Jordi,' she said. 'Her name is Angela Wishart.'

Her parents and her brother doted on her. There never was a child born into this world like Angela. Later, she smiled through the pain of her teething, tottered to her feet with George's help and, with her hair a mass of curling blonde fronds in contrast to her huge black eyes, she enchanted everyone.

'I don't know where she got this hair from,' Thirza said, tackling it with a hairbrush and unconsciously echoing her mother, years ago. 'It wasn't from any of the Gourlays, I'm sure.'

'My mother was very fair,' Jordi smiled.

'But she's got your glorious eyes,' Thirza kissed him, uneasily wondering if she should cross her fingers at the same time. In this state of bliss, something was bound to go wrong.

It did two years later, when George dug in his heels and refused to go on with his education, at least at university. Thirza was sympathetic, Jordi was furious and Bob Steele who, despite the thirty years' difference in age, had been George's best friend all his life, did his best to sit on the fence and pass no comment while the battle raged.

'I want to build ships that can sail the seven seas, Father.'

'There's no college or university for that,' Jordi protested.

'No, there isn't. But there's a very good man employed by Douglas Hunter called Edward Gibson who's always coming out with new ideas for ships. Why do you think Hunter's Yard is bigger and better than anyone else's? It's all because of Edward Gibson.'

'And what makes you think that a man from a rival Yard would get leave from its owner to train any son of mine?' Jordi demanded.

Thirza said nothing. Unconsciously copying Ruth again, she waited until they had both left the house – Jordi to go to the Yard and George to go to school – before she took off her pinafore and led Angela by the hand to Hunter's Yard. The men working there chose to be ribald when a strange woman appeared in the Yard with a baby.

'Och, ay,' one big slovenly man sniggered, 'Douglas Hunter wisna long finding company after his wife died.'

'How d'ye ken he waited till then, anyway?' his straggle-whiskered companion asked. 'That bairn must be twa years old, at least.'

Thirza's flashing, brilliant blue eyes glared at them, and at all the others who were laughing. She was at her best when she rounded on them. 'I'll remember *your* faces in the future, don't worry!' Her voice produced a silence. She didn't talk like a Leith wifie, even if she had obviously just come out of her kitchen. 'And I'll thank you to point me in the direction of Mr Hunter's office. I have some business with him and now, after this introduction to his Yard, a few complaints, believe me.'

'The office is over there, lassie,' one of the men pointed.

Thirza made as dignified an exit as she could, and the jeering laughter persisted behind her back. She was so angry by the time she was shown the door of Douglas Hunter's inner sanctum, that she just marched in, her fury transmitted to Angela who, for once, was howling at the top of her voice. 'Those men of yours!' she said. 'They're animals! And to think I came here today to ask you to take my son into this Yard!'

Angela yelled louder than ever.

'Please sit down, Mrs Wishart.'

'How do you know my name?'

'Have you forgotten? We met at a funeral, as I recall. You and I know all about the trials and tribulations of this world, far more important than worrying about those men out there. Now, please calm yourself.'

'But they insulted me! They thought I was your whore, and my little daughter your by-blow!'

'You're delightfully out-spoken, Mrs Wishart,' Douglas Hunter laughed, while Thirza was regretting the words she had used. They were not the words of a lady, she thought, struck dumb by the sheer charm of the man sitting opposite her. In the eyes of a man like this, any woman would want to be considered a lady. 'How can I help you?'

'It's our son,' she explained, outlining the problem. 'He has the idea that only Edward Gibson can help him.' She finally faltered to a halt.

Douglas Hunter's hair, almost as black as Jordi's only three years ago, was iron-grey now, and the lines on his pleasant face were etched deeper, but when he got up from his chair and went over to the window overlooking his Yard she saw that his figure was still trim and attractive, in spite of his fifty or so years.

'So you would like your George to be trained by Edward Gibson?' he asked. 'He would need to have very good references for that.'

'You'll get them, Mr Hunter,' Thirza tossed her head, 'and within a week. I'll see to it.'

His admiring gaze followed her, stalking out past the gauntlet of his men in the Yard. She had plenty of courage, that lady. But she was asking a lot, and she had to justify it. He sighed, and went back to his work.

Angela continued to be a delight to every person who saw her, but most especially to her family. Sticking her little legs out at grotesquely funny angles, she insisted on showing them her dancing steps. Her tuneless voice regaled them with her childish songs. When, if ever, she was naughty she remained enchanting, and her family adored her more with each passing day.

'She'll be ruined and spoilt at this rate,' Thirza frowned.

'I don't think so,' Jordi disagreed. 'She's got too much sense, herself.'

'And she's got so much energy that it should be channelled. I want her to learn to dance and sing properly. She should start now that she's three, before she goes to school.'

'I daresay we might manage to afford it.'

'I don't want you to worry about the money, Jordi. I've been thinking a lot about this and watching the newspapers. There's an advertisement in the paper tonight by J.J. Millar for a Book-keeper and Accountant.' She passed him the paper to read where she had marked it, and had underlined the salary. 'I'll probably be too late for that position, but there will always be others coming up. If I got a nursemaid for Angela, I could pay her wages, pay for Angela's lessons and we'd still be in pocket.'

'Oh, Thirza . . .' Jordi frowned.

'You want your daughter brought up a lady, don't you? I do,' Thirza insisted. 'In fact, I'm going to put an advertisement in Secondhand Rose's window tomorrow for a nursemaid. I'll get plenty of replies. Work is so scarce, and Secondhand Rose won't allow anyone unsuitable to be sent here.'

A fortnight later, having secured the position with J.J. Millar after all, Thirza engaged wholesome, honest Florence who, on sight, loved Angela as much as Angela loved her. It was a very satisfactory arrangement, made even more auspicious when a letter arrived inviting George to be apprenticed to Edward Gibson, and to come and talk to them, signed by Douglas Hunter.

'How did this happen?' Jordi demanded angrily. 'I was never told about this!'

Thirza was forced to confess what she had done, but no matter how she tried to get around him, he remained cold and angry with both her and George. For the first time the thin edge of a wedge was driven into the Wishart family, and they all relied on Angela more than ever to ease the situation.

George immediately took to Mr Gibson, a tall rangy man in his late forties who always had an unlit pipe in his mouth while he was working. Mr Gibson looked at him kindly over the top of the spectacles perched on the end of his long nose, shook his hand and put him at his ease while he showed George around the pattern shop.

'Well, well, George . . .' he smiled at the end of their tour. 'So you want to find out how ships are built?'

'I think I'm very lucky to be here to learn from the best in the business, sir.'

'Ho! We'll see what you think in six months' time! You might change your mind before that.'

'No, I won't,' George said seriously. 'I'd better not. I had a falling-out with my father to get here. He wanted me to go to the university.'

'Not many boys get such an opportunity, George.'

'No, sir. Did you go?'

'I never had the chance, lad,' Edward Gibson was laughing, when a young girl came in and danced up to him. 'But then, I was a lot like you. Ships were all that were in my head.'

'Your morning rolls, Father,' she said, laying down a brown paper bag in front of him.

There must have been room in his head at some time for other things besides ships, George thought, admiring Miss Gibson. She reminded him of a sunbeam. Everything about her gleamed, from her shiny brown hair down to her little button boots.

'Tessa,' her father said, 'we have a new apprentice just started today. Allow me to introduce Mr George Wishart to you.'

'How do you do?' Miss Gibson shook his hand politely.

'I hope you've put butter on them?' her father enquired.

'Oh, Father! You know I always do!'

'Yes, so you do . . . When you remember.'

She laughed and went away. George thought she didn't walk, so much as dance, but then, that was what sunbeams did. She must have been all of fifteen years old. George deliberated about her and about his future for at least ten seconds before his mind was as usual, implacably made up.

Some day he would have his own ship. He would name her *Tessa*, after his wife.

*   *   *

The only sunbeam in his father's life at that time was his dearly beloved Angela. Jordi was still angry with George for defying his wishes. He simmered about it for a long time before he calmed down sufficiently to realise that the boy might not have done well at the university anyway, if his heart was set on something else.

He remained outraged by Thirza.

First, she shouldn't have gone behind his back and wangled George into the employment of Douglas Hunter of all people. He was pleased that his son seemed to be climbing up the ranks of the apprentices at such record speed, but that made no difference to her offence. He sighed, Thirza had always been clever herself . . . And very devious, even for a woman.

Secondly, he was far from pleased that she had gone ahead and taken up the post with the grocer, J.J. Millar, against his better judgement, no matter how well she was getting on there, either. She should have been at home looking after Angela, although he could find no fault whatsoever with the nursemaid, Florence. It was a conviction he couldn't shake, and so he couldn't forgive.

Sometimes he wished that the house had never been finished, but Thirza had taken it by the scruff of its neck in her usual way and – by hook and by crook – had painted it, papered it and furnished it from top to bottom long ago. Even the gardens were immaculate, he thought gloomily.

In fact, he had dreaded the day when it would all be ship-shape and Bristol fashion as it was now. He had always known that Thirza would have to find something else to occupy her, especially her mind. She had more energy than three women put together, and she was still as thorny, still as spiky as the first time he had ever clapped eyes on her.

Jordi built a wall of quiet disapproval around himself, except when he was with Angela.

Thirza had been working for about a year, indisputably swelling the family coffers, when he watched Angela and her nursemaid coming out of the front door one Saturday morning to go to her dancing class. He had forgotten about it, until he saw her shiny black patent dancing shoes.

His little four-year-old daughter skipped down the steps happily, holding Florence's hand. Jordi watched her, smiling, unable to take his eyes off her in her blue dress and coat and her pretty blue bonnet over her dancing blonde ringlets. Her little legs were encased in white stockings above her shiny shoes.

Those shoes were twinkling down the steps now. Angela saw her father on the other side of the road, waving and smiling at her. Somehow she slipped out of Florence's hand and ran over the road towards him.

It was like something out of a nightmare when she tripped and fell. The coalman had just looked over his shoulder a minute ago to see a clear street. He was encouraging his horses to go backwards to get out of the cul-de-sac.

The wheels of the dray rolled nearer and nearer to the fallen child on the road. Jordi screamed at the pitch of his voice, and as at all such crucial moments in life, everything happened in front of his eyes in slow motion, to be indelibly imprinted on his heart for ever.

Yelling and screaming at the coalman who was still shouting at his horse and pulling the reins in his hands, Jordi raced to stop him with legs suddenly made of lead. He couldn't get there in time. Desperately, he held on to the side of the wagon, trying to stop it himself when, right there in front of him, one of the huge wheels rolled straight over Angela, squeezing the life out of her.

The coalman felt the bump and stopped, leaping down off his seat. When he saw what had happened he collapsed in the middle of the street. Florence was still screaming on the pavement, and it was Bob Steele, hearing the commotion, who rushed out of the Wishart Yard and took charge.

A small crowd had gathered around the prone, sobbing figure of Jordi, stretched out over his daughter. Somehow, Bob prised him off her, got someone to go for Thirza, got someone else to go for George, got others to support Jordi into the house and, with his coat over her small dead body, carried Angela up to the house himself.

Overnight, the wings of Jordi's hair above his ears turned white with shock. He was speechless, inconsolable. In the distance somewhere he saw Thirza's face turn to white marble. He saw George retreating into himself. He was powerless to do anything about either of the two of them. He was in some kind of a limbo where Angela's happy smiling face was forever coming towards him, over and over again, and the only sounds he heard were coming out of her mouth.

There was no comfort for any of the Wishart family in the months that followed, no passionate coming together in grief this time, for Thirza and Jordi.

Every night they lay rigid, Jordi at his side and Thirza at hers, side by side on the mockery of their marriage bed.

But life had to go on, however bitterly. Thirza resigned from J.J. Millar's. George went back and forth to Hunter's Yard every day, and Jordi threw himself into his small business. Nothing mattered much, any more.

He awoke one winter morning to find Thirza already dressed in a black costume. It suited her, one part of his mind told him, especially teamed with that frothy white blouse. She was pinning a black feathered hat over her auburn hair, which she was wearing now in a coil at the back of her head, and her expression was as stony as usual.

'I can't stand this any longer,' she told him when she saw he was awake. 'I've lost two children too, you know. It seems I've lost a husband as well. I've got to get out of this house before I go mad altogether.'

'Where are you going?' he asked wearily.

'To try for another job. Douglas Hunter is advertising for a book-keeper.'

Jordi's mouth set in a bitter line as he watched her go.

35

D OWN in Hunter's Yard, Douglas Hunter was a worried man and a lonely one. His wife, Helen, had helped him to run the business until the time of her death. Not strong since the birth of their only child, a stillborn son, she had never visited the Yard. Because he could well afford to engage servants for her, she had been glad to keep the books for him at home, saying that it made her feel of some use in the world again.

She had always been there to talk things over with in the evenings. He missed her company, and he missed her. He felt that, without her, he was drying up like a wrinkled old prune, dusted with white.

Since her death he had been forced to engage a succession of book-keepers and accountants. Two or three had tried to tamper with the truth so that they could steal money from him. Others had been plain incompetent, and so here he was again today setting out pessimistically on another round of tedious interviews. His young clerk, Mattie Howie, was receiving the hopefuls at that very moment, ten o'clock.

'There's eight o' them arrived, sir. Seven men and one woman.'

'Better get started then, Mattie. Send in the first one,' he sighed.

An hour and a quarter later he reflected that he had been right to begin with. He didn't like the look of any of the seven men. He wouldn't have trusted one of them.

'Well, well, Mattie,' he said despondently, 'I suppose, for the look of the thing, I'd better see the last applicant even if she is a woman. What's her name?'

'Mrs Wishart, sir.'

'Good God, boy! Why didn't you tell me this sooner? She's been kept waiting out there for well over an hour, all for nothing! Show her in immediately, and then fetch us coffee.'

Thirza saw at once that the years between had not been kind to Douglas Hunter. At his wife's funeral he had been a handsome dark-haired man, tall and well-built. The last time she'd seen him, when she had asked for a job for George, he had still been as handsome as ever, with greying hair giving him an added air of distinction. Now he was looking tired and sad, and his hair was snow white.

'Come in, Mrs Wishart,' he said. 'I'm sorry to have kept you waiting for so long.'

'Perhaps I deserved it,' she smiled, 'after the way I burst in on you the last time I was here, so angry with those two men.'

'They were dismissed that same day.'

'Oh,' she said, disconcerted. So he had taken notice of her distress that day.

'Yes, I remember it all clearly . . . You brought your little daughter . . . I was very sorry to hear about her death, my dear. You've had more than your fair share of trouble, much more than most people of your age.'

'I'm thirty-seven, Mr Hunter,' Thirza said bluntly, without taking her eyes off his face. After all, this *was* an interview.

'Well,' he smiled charmingly, 'I have always believed that ladies are at their best at that age. Still young, but with an intriguing wealth of experience behind them. It seems to refine their faces, somehow . . .' He coughed, as if aware that he was embarrassing her, when they heard a knock on the door. 'Ah, here's Mattie with a pot of coffee. Set it down here, lad. Will you join me, Mrs Wishart, before we get down to business? Young George is doing exceptionally well in the pattern shop, Edward Gibson tells me. He has risen to the top.'

'He's extremely clever,' Thirza acknowledged gravely. 'Mr Gibson regards him as his protégé.'

'He also says that George and his daughter Tessa are close friends.'

'More than that, I think, Mr Hunter. They intend to marry.'

Douglas Hunter smiled and paused delicately, obviously trying to choose the right words to say next without causing offence. 'Then he'll be a lucky young man, as well as a very able one,' he said in the end. 'Mrs Gibson is a wealthy lady in her own right, and Tessa is their only child.'

Once again Thirza looked him straight in the eye. 'We know that, sir. But strange to say, money has nothing to do with it. They love each other, that's all. They always have done, ever since they first met.'

'Yes,' he said. 'Sometimes it's like that. One look says it all.'

Thirza's thoughts winged back to the day of the double funerals when she and this man across the desk first exchanged glances. He set down his empty coffee cup. 'It's only a formality, of course,' he said, 'but perhaps I should see your credentials?'

'They are very few on paper, I'm afraid,' Thirza said, and quickly outlined her meagre work experience.

'It doesn't matter in any case. The position is yours, if you care to take it on.

'I should be delighted, sir.'

'When can you start?'

'Tomorrow morning, Mr Hunter, if you want me to. There are just a few little arrangements to be made today for my husband and George, so that no one will miss me when I start work.'

'No one?'

'Not now,' Thirza said sadly.

In her expressive eyes during that interview Douglas Hunter read a depth of inconsolable grief such as he had never encountered before. He sat back afterwards and wondered what losing two young children would have done to him and his dear wife Helen. Shuddering, he could not imagine it. It was kinder by far that they themselves had lost their own child at birth.

Somehow, after that tragedy, and during Helen's subsequent ill-health, they had grown closer together. That had been a tremendous blessing and a great consolation. He suspected that such was not the case in the Wishart marriage, although Thirza Wishart had not betrayed it by look or by word. It was just a feeling he had when he looked into her bleak eyes.

Yet there had been no tremor in her voice, no quivering of those firm lips of hers and she had presented herself to him cool and immaculate. She had been an arresting woman before, vivid and beautiful, one that he had admired. But now, after speaking to her again, he admired her even more for what he could only describe as an element of steel in her, an indomitable spirit. Yes, that was it. She had a backbone of steel, that little lady, and God knew he needed such a prop nowadays.

And what about her husband, Douglas Hunter wondered? He knew that the Wishart Yard was managing to survive, that Jordi Wishart worked hard at his small business and, in fact, had done more than could have been expected of a man with very little capital.

Douglas knew within himself that he would not have succeeded half so well as Jordi Wishart. He had never been put to such a test, but merely walked into his father's business when he died. There had been plenty of money at his disposal to expand the business. Money made money, indeed.

But now his thoughts were moving into dangerous channels. Little pains thrilled uncomfortably across his chest. There it was again, the spectre that haunted his lonely old age. Sometimes he wished that the money would simply evaporate, but of course it never did. It just kept rolling in instead . . . and what was to be done with it when he died?

One thing was certain. It would never go to that bastard Jake Hunter — that viper nephew of his — he thought savagely. By now the pains were ripping across his chest, wave after wave of them. He felt very sick.

He sat still, and gradually the pains and the sickness subsided, but they had left him feeling quite weak. The money should go back into the business, of course. The days of sail were coming to an end. It was only a question of time before those wonderful new steam engines would be fitted into ships and the Hunter Yard would need all its capital then.

If only his son had lived! If only there was someone he could trust to carry out his dreams! But there was no one.

'Going out, sir?' Mattie Howie looked up from his desk in the outer office in some surprise.

Mr Hunter never left the Yard during the day. He liked soup and a sandwich from Mrs Mutch's bakeshop to be sent in to him in the middle of the day. In fact, Mrs Mutch's message boy would be coming at any moment now.

'I'm feeling a little under the weather, Mattie. I'm going home. But I'll be back first thing in the morning to deal with anything that crops up during the rest of today.'

'Yes, sir,' Mattie opened the door for him.

Mr Hunter's face was grey, right enough. In fact, it was ashen.

George had just turned twenty when he was accepted into the Gibson family as Tessa's future husband and the son they had never had. Jordi and Thirza were invited to the Gibsons' house, the Wisharts invited them back, and the two sets of parents became socially well acquainted. Upon these occasions Thirza and Jordi did their best, for George's sake, to appear a happily married couple.

It helped that they were genuinely fond of Tessa. It was a pleasure to them both to see how happy George was with her and, after each of these encounters with the Gibsons, the tension between Thirza and Jordi eased for a few days.

They spoke to each other, but then they had always spoken to each other, through thick and thin. They had been friends first and they remained friends, but almost imperceptibly the wall went up between them day by day, barring the way back to their love. Jordi went to work as usual, and Thirza went to the Hunter Yard, and life went on as drearily as before.

Soon, Thirza was finishing her work with time to spare. Mr Hunter couldn't help noticing it sometimes, when he had occasion to open his door and speak to her or to Mattie Howie in the outer office, where they had their desks.

One afternoon he called her into the inner sanctum for one of his little chats about the business. 'Would you care for a cup of tea, my dear?' he asked her in the middle of it.

'I would indeed, Mr Hunter. That would be most acceptable.'

'And don't you think you could call me Douglas now, after all this time?' he smiled kindly. 'No one does, nowadays, and often that feels so lonely.'

Thirza's kind heart was pierced to its core. Lonely? She knew what that felt like, now. 'Of course I will, Douglas, if you will call me Thirza.'

'It will be a pleasure,' he was assuring her when Mattie came in with the tea-tray. 'Mrs Wishart, will you pour out?'

'Of course, sir.' She lifted the teapot with – at last – a twinkle in her eye.

'Now, see you have a cup yourself, lad,' Mr Hunter said, as Mattie closed the door behind him, and he and Thirza laughed out loud.

'Oh, Thirza! I'm so glad you came for my "situation vacant"! Let me see . . . How long ago was that?'

'Seven months.'

'As long ago as that? Well, well!' he beamed. 'It must be one of the best appointments I ever made. But there's not enough work in it for you, is there, my dear?'

'Well . . . I'd rather have more to do. It would give me less time to brood.'

'Is it no better yet?'

'Not really.'

'To tell you the truth, I've been seeing that for myself, and I know from experience that although it cannot cure grief, hard work certainly helps. So I was thinking of moving you in here with me, to be my assistant. That way, you will be able to do your own work, and help me with the running of the Yard as well. *That* should keep you occupied! And there will be a raise in salary, of course.'

When Thirza told Jordi about her promotion, he was, as she expected, less than enthusiastic. 'You should be taking on less, instead of more,' he told her. 'It isn't for the money, is it, Thirza?'

'George's wedding isn't far away,' she reminded him.

'Well, I won't argue with you. You know best how you feel.'

So Thirza's desk was moved into a corner of Douglas Hunter's office, and gradually she met all his business associates, although she remained quietly in the background. Afterwards, he discussed each interview with her and she began to understand their implications; not only that, but how far-reaching the Hunter business really was.

She gave it all her attention. She studied every man who came in and it wasn't long before Douglas began to rely heavily on her feminine intuition. If his glance met hers during a business deal which was somehow not quite right, in her opinion, she gave a little shake of her head, and the interview was soon terminated.

But she never shook her head during a visit from Douglas Hunter's lawyer and friend, the tall and gentlemanly Andrew Phillipson. If Douglas now seemed to her almost like a second father, soon Mr Phillipson seemed like a kindly uncle, two elderly gentlemen she not only respected, but came to dote upon.

One day, when she had just run out of the Yard on an errand, she came back to see a man slowly pacing the pavement outside the gates, stopping occasionally to kick at the pavement aimlessly, with his head bent in thought. He must be waiting for someone, she thought, studying him from the back as he sauntered away for a few steps.

Tall and well dressed in dark clothes, he walked with a cat-like grace. She was wondering what his face looked like when he turned on his heel and they were face to face.

His eyes stopped her dead in her tracks.

She had never seen eyes like his before, royal blue and far-seeing, eyes that seemd to be scanning the horizon behind her. She knew at once that he was a sailor, and she knew at once that she wanted him to to see *her*, never mind the horizon.

A long minute passed, during which neither of them said anything. Thirza just looked at him helplessly. He was exactly the same as Douglas must have been when he was younger. He could have been his son.

'Are you going in?' he asked.

His smile was the same, too, with those strong, gleaming square teeth. Only the expression in his eyes was different from Douglas's. It was not only admiring, it was knowing and somehow very exciting.

'Yes, I am.'

'I've been waiting for someone to escort me inside. That fellow on the gates wants some sort of authorisation before he'll let me in to see Douglas Hunter.'

'Come with me,' Thirza said. 'I'll take you to Mr Hunter myself.'

Up in his office Douglas Hunter's face paled at the sight of the visitor Thirza was ushering in. Then it contorted and went scarlet with rage. He came around from the back of his desk shouting and swearing at the man, bundling him out into the corridor and slamming the office door behind him. Inside, Thirza was petrified, listening to the terrible row going on.

'I told you never to show your face here again!' Douglas was shouting.

Then it became a confusion of Mattie's voice joining in, and then the voices of other men rushing up from downstairs. The hub-bub moved away from the office door and down the stairs, and when Thirza looked out of the window she saw the stranger being frog-marched off the premises.

'Douglas, I'm so sorry,' she said when he returned alone, shaking with temper. 'I would never have done that to you, knowingly.' She went across to one of the mahogany cupboards and poured him out a little brandy. 'Here, drink this.'

'You weren't to know, my dear. That's what he was banking on,' he said, with some colour coming back to his cheeks. 'That was my nephew, Jake Hunter.'

'What did he want?'

'What do you think? What he is always wanting! What he expects one day to inherit . . . My money.'

Thirza smoothed back a lock of silver hair disarranged in the brawl. 'Well,' she comforted him, 'he'll have a long wait.'

'I don't think I'll come in to work tomorrow, Thirza,' he said, rubbing his hand over his chest, 'and I had meant to go over the books with you as soon as possible. I feel a bit sick. It's a perfect nuisance.'

'You'll go right home and lie down, Douglas. I'll ask Mattie to get a cab. I don't think you need to worry about the books, but if it will set your mind at ease I could call round this evening and let you see them – just for half an hour, mind!'

'Thank you, my dear. I'll leave the front door on the latch.'

But the incident of Jake Hunter had shaken Thirza more than she cared to admit as she smiled at Douglas, soothing him and agreeing with him until the cab arrived. She hadn't liked the effect on her of its sudden violence, like a thunderclap, and she certainly hadn't liked the mauve-grey of Douglas's face in the aftermath of the shock.

That evening she got the family meal ready, eaten and cleared away in record time. As soon as she did, Jordi and George spread maps and drawings out on the table and pored over them. She was glad that they were friends again. It seemed that there had been a meeting of minds over steam, and the new steam engines. Their discussion was all about pressures and gauges – too technical for her. She went upstairs to change her clothes and comb her hair.

'I've got to go back to work tonight,' she told them on the way out, 'up at Mr Hunter's house. He's worried about the books. The auditors are coming at the end of the month.'

Jordi and George nodded abstractedly, deep in discussion.

'Goodbye then,' Thirza said, setting off, dressed in a very correct dress of lilac trimmed with white lace that summer evening. 'I won't be long.'

Neither of them noticed her going, not even Jordi. For that she cried a little as she walked along to Douglas's house. It really was all over between her and Jordi, then . . . If only he had been making more money all along, she would never have gone out to work in the first place. Then their beloved little Angela might still be living.

She chose to forget that it was Jordi who had been supporting them all for years, it was boredom that had driven her out of the house the first time, and grief the second time – not necessity. She ignored the fact that he may have become bored, too, and was still grieving. She forgot that she didn't even need this job with Douglas Hunter now, that it was only a pastime, keeping some other much needier person out of work – some man, it may be, who had a wife and children.

The real truth of the matter was that she needed to be loved, and in her eyes Jordi had deserted her in her time of need. When had he last looked at her with love or even admiration in his eyes? She had almost forgotten how that felt, until she had seen something like it in Jake Hunter's eyes this afternoon.

At last she arrived at Douglas's door, knocked and stepped inside. Douglas was standing beside the mantelpiece in what she took, through the open door, to be his sitting room. He looked like a burned-out shell of himself, gripping the mantelpiece with one hand and pressing his other to his chest. 'Oh, God, Thirza,' he gasped. 'These pains across my chest . . .'

She supported him to the nearest couch. 'You need a doctor, Douglas,' she told him. 'I'll send for him. Which one?'

He struggled to tell her, but no words came out before he collapsed in her arms.

36

THIRZA laid Douglas back on the couch and felt for a pulse at his wrist and his neck. She thought there was a faint one. In such a dire emergency she hardly knew what to do first. Surely there was a housekeeper somewhere? She flew through the house calling and asking if anyone was there, but only silence answered her.

Then she would have to run for Dr Browne herself, and as fast as she could.

'Douglas Hunter?' Dr Browne said when he came to his door in his shirt sleeves. 'No, he's not a patient of mine, Thirza, but I'll come at once.' Pausing only to collect his coat and his bag, he bundled her into his carriage, taking the reins himself.

'It's not good,' he said, after he'd examined Douglas. 'Who *is* his doctor, do you know?'

Thirza shook her head. 'I can't find out until tomorrow.'

'He shouldn't be left here all night alone. He needs nursing.'

'I'll stay here with him all night. What should I do?'

'Just keep an eye on his pulse.'

'And if he wakes up?'

'He won't wake up in a hurry. He's very ill. Are you sure you don't mind staying, Thirza? You're not afraid?'

Afraid? Of poor Douglas Hunter? Of death?

'No,' she said, 'only worried for Jordi's sake and for George's when I don't come back home.'

'I'll call in and tell them on my way to see Dr Ingram.

Mr Hunter might be one of his patients. If so, you can expect him to visit later this evening. I expect he will make his own arrangements, but I'll tell him you are here. You work at the Hunter Yard now, don't you, Thirza?'

'I was in his office when he started to feel ill.'

'I'll tell Dr Ingram that, too. He'll want to know what brought this attack on.'

Two hours later, Thirza was relieved when Dr Ingram made plans for Douglas to be properly nursed.

'I'll go and fetch one of the night nurses I use immediately,' he said. 'Tomorrow morning she will be relieved by a day nurse and, of course, the housekeeper, Mrs Wright, will come in as well. He'll be well looked after, don't worry. In the meantime, I'd like to examine him a little more thoroughly, without disturbing him too much.'

'Thank you, Dr Ingram,' Thirza said, and withdrew to the hall.

Fifteen minutes later the doctor came out to speak to her again.

'It's a while since I saw him,' he said. 'To tell you the truth he's not very fond of doctors. He would have to be pretty bad before he called me in of his own free will.'

'How is he, Doctor?'

'His heart condition has deteriorated badly, I'm afraid. I understand you work with him at the Yard?'

'Yes, sir.'

'Has anything happened there recently to upset him?'

'His nephew, Jake Hunter, tried to see him this morning.'

'Hm!' Dr Ingram peered at her over his spectacles. 'Well, that would be enough to do the damage, I should think!'

'I didn't even know he had a nephew.'

'He had a brother too, once, a rake. He died. Jake is Jacob Hunter's son, Douglas's only living relative, as far as I know. They are estranged.'

'It seems a pity, especially now,' Thirza said.

'Well, Mr Hunter must have no excitement whatsoever and I must forbid all visitors in the meantime except yourself, Mrs Wishart. I suppose you'll want to see him every day?'

'Yes, sir.'

'When you come to see him, don't bring him any bad news, then.'

'Indeed, I won't.'

To Thirza's great relief, Douglas slowly recovered. After a month he was able to sit up in bed and talk to her for an hour or two in the evenings when she came back from the Yard. Anything that she thought would worry him she kept quiet, and tried – usually successfully – to deal with it herself.

It was after suppertime when she got back home one night. Jordi was in bed already. Exhausted, she lay down beside him. Although she knew he wasn't sleeping, he didn't say a word. Eventually he just sighed, then turned over and went to sleep.

It was a stupid little hair to break a camel's back, but it broke Thirza's at last. The next morning she was still tired and very irritable. 'If I have to be late again I'll sleep on the settee in the drawing-room,' she told Jordi coldly.

'Look, Thirza,' he said. 'I'm as sorry for the man as you are. But must you spend so much time with him?'

'He has nobody else.'

'There's a nurse there all the time, isn't there?'

'Yes, but how would you like it yourself, if you had only a strange nurse to speak to? I'm sorry, Jordi. I haven't got the heart to leave him.'

'No. But you've got the heart to leave us,' he said bitterly.

After another two months of Douglas Hunter's illness, Thirza spent every night on the settee in the drawing-room rather than disturb Jordi again and provoke another scene.

At last Dr Ingram was allowing Douglas to receive another visitor, his lawyer and his friend Mr Phillipson, but only for an hour on Wednesday afternoons. To her surprise, Thirza also received a visit from him after one of the Wednesday afternoon visits.

'How is he today?' she asked him anxiously.

'He seemed a lot better this afternoon, my dear, so much so that I fear I stayed longer than my allotted time. We had some business to attend to, and then we had a long talk.'

Thirza longed to ask him what about.

'He wanted to talk about his past and his family, Jake Hunter in particular.'

337

'Oh, no! Didn't that upset him?'

'He was remarkably calm. You see, he had made up his mind on a certain course of action to take as regards Jake Hunter. I think it must have been worrying him for a long time. Anyway, he got it all off his chest today.'

'I know nothing of Jake Hunter, Mr Phillipson. Is there anything you can tell me about him?'

'Very little, my dear, except that he is a sea-captain, plying mainly between Glasgow and America. When he is ashore he comes to Leith a lot, I believe. Douglas doesn't like him, and has forbidden him to come to the Yard. Why, I do not know. There is some secret there, some mystery concerning the Hunter family – but what it is, Douglas has never confided in me during all the years I've known him.'

'A family feud?' Thirza sighed. 'They happen.'

'Perhaps,' Mr Phillipson said.

Only a week or two after that conversation Thirza was sitting with Douglas Hunter. His bed had been brought down to the sitting room, she was pleased to see. It was so much brighter there, and much warmer. She fussed around him, plumping up his pillows and smoothing his top sheet, although the nurse had just been attending to him and was now in the kitchen preparing his next dose of medicine. He was smiling and talking when he suddenly stopped in mid-sentence.

'Oh, it's so cold!' he shuddered. 'Oh, Thirza,' he held out his arms to her, 'I'm so cold . . .'

'*Douglas*, my dear!' She held him gently in her arms until the chill should pass over, but his head lolled to one side. A great dread filled Thirza's heart. 'Nurse! Nurse!' she cried, and the nurse came running.

'Ah . . .' she said, after just one glance, 'he's gone this time, dearie.' She took him out of Thirza's arms and laid him back in the bed. 'Mr Hunter is dead.'

Everyone else in Hunter's Yard looked as shocked as Thirza felt when she told them the news. In a fog of sadness and disbelief she wrote out the notice closing the Yard until after the funeral. She stayed late to see that everything was closed and locked up properly. George waited with her and took her home.

'What will you do now?' he asked.

'Go to the funeral, I suppose. After that Mr Phillipson will let us know the conditions of the Will.'

'You look terrible, Mother. You should go and lie down on your bed.'

She knew she couldn't do that. She couldn't share a loveless bed with Jordi tonight of all nights.

'It's fresh air I need, George,' she said. 'I'm going for a long walk.'

Nobody else was there when she walked past the gates of the deserted Yard and on down to the sea. At last she could give vent to her feelings. She sat down on the grass and, with her arms wrapped around her legs and her head bowed, Thirza thought her heart would break.

Many more people attended Douglas Hunter's funeral than there were seats in the Kirk. The Wishart family, along with the Gibson family, were there early and people crowded into the church till there was little room even to stand. Douglas Hunter had been regarded as a philanthropist in Leith. He had gone out of his way to help everyone he could.

Jordi glanced at Thirza's face from time to time. It was hard to know what she was thinking under that veil falling from her black feathered hat . . . *That hat*, he thought, and yet another funeral. The last one had been for Angela . . . Bitterness flooded his heart. He felt stifled with it. It had been going on for so long.

He and Thirza should have talked after their little one was so cruelly killed, he knew that. But they had never talked properly again. Jordi considered that he was as much to blame for everything as Thirza, but the longer the silence continued between them, the harder it became to try and break it, and now they were drifting apart.

The house at number eight, the Wishart Yard – everything had been for Thirza. She didn't seem to want any of it any more, and she certainly didn't want him. She was so unhappy. And he was miserable himself, and tired of it all. The only thing to keep him going was the new ship that George was involved with. When that was finished, and his obligation to his son over . . . Jordi bent his head to pray, but what he prayed for most was some way out of this misery, somewhere far away out of it, like India.

He startled himself with this stray, but powerful longing. It was pulling him across the seas, when he had not thought of India for years, nor of his real father, Viaz, either.

Up in the cool foothills north-east of Calcutta, Viaz Mohammed was becoming very agitated. In his hand he clutched a golden key. His wife tried in vain to calm him. He was dying, and he knew it, but it wasn't his approaching death that was worrying him. It was something else.

'I want Jorjeela,' he said. 'Fetch her *now*, Ameera. There is something I must say to her. There is still a lot to be done, before it's too late.'

He sank into another of the blacknesses that were becoming ever more blessedly frequent now. He didn't want to return to this tortured world, full of pain, even for a few brief moments. But he must. He opened his eyes again to see both his wife, still beautiful and desirable, and their even more beautiful daughter, Jorjeela, at his bedside.

Jorjeela . . . Lady Jorjeela Justin. She had married Paul Justin after all, and he had risen to the top of his profession before he died and left her a young widow. If only she would marry again! She should marry another Englishman, he thought. Instead, she seemed to be turning native, consorting every day with tall young Indians, heavily bearded and turbanned, and pursuing her latest charity work amongst the poor.

The scent of attar of roses lay heavy about both Jorjeela and Ameera, induced as he knew by the mysterious ritual of the Seven Orifices which every Indian woman of any lineage at all scrupulously observed morning and night. His ladies were there beside him dressed in silken saris heavily encrusted in gold and silver, and Viaz smiled at them both proudly.

'Father,' Jorjeela put her hands together, bowed her head over them and sank to her knees at his bedside, waiting for his instructions.

'Take this key,' he said, 'and go to Edinburgh in Scotland with it. As Lady Justin you will be well received there. Go to a lawyer named Alistair Fisher. Tell him that this key is for George Wishart's son, to open the trunk Wishart left with him.'

All Wishart-Sahib's treasure would still be lying there. They had to be, for there had been no key on his dead body when he had searched it. The worry of what had happened to Jordi, his child and Madeleine's, had gnawed at him all these years, but he had never been well enough to attend to the matter himself as he had intended.

'Do not delay, Jorjeela,' he frowned. 'There has been delay enough.'

'It shall be done, my father.' Her head sank to his bed alongside Ameera's.

The wails of their mourning rose in the early morning, and within two months Jorjeela, Lady Justin, was in England and staying with her late husband's relatives.

The congregation rose to their feet when Douglas Hunter's casket was carried out of the church by Edward Gibson and five other senior members of Hunter's Yard. Then they trooped out behind it, followed by the Wishart family, amongst others. That was when Thirza saw Jake Hunter again, standing just inside the door.

He was immaculately dressed in black, and his expression was quiet and respectful when he came forward to shake Thirza's hand.

'His death must have been very sudden,' he said.

'He had been ill for a while, before. I'm sorry for your loss, Mr Hunter. Your uncle was a very popular man here, as you can see today.'

'I am only sorry that he did not see eye to eye with me when he was living, for I was fond of him, you know. Well, it's too late now to patch up an old misunderstanding. I shall attend at the graveside,' he said, moving off with the people going to the cemetery, 'and then go back to my ship in Glasgow.'

He bowed, and put his hat back on his head. She could not have said it was at a rakish angle, but it was at an interesting one. Thirza stared behind him feeling as full of regrets as he had genuinely sounded. It was a pity that Douglas could not have been close to the last of his relations. She sighed, but then she knew, none better, that such things blew up in families and when they did no quarrel, no feud and no misunderstanding was more bitter.

She was glad when the Yard opened again and she could throw herself into her work. Work was the only cure she knew for so many ills, and she was seated at Douglas Hunter's desk, trying to sort out his papers, when Mattie Howie knocked at the door and came in.

'Mr Phillipson's here to see you,' he said.

'Show him in, Mattie,' she said.

Mr Phillipson took the chair opposite. It was the first time she had seen him since the funeral and he looked weighed down with problems. Thirza didn't know quite what to do or to say. 'Mr Hunter kept a nice Madeira,' she got up and went over to the mahogany cupboard to hide her concern. 'May I pour you a glass, sir?'

'Yes, my dear, you may – and I think you should pour one for yourself too. You may need it when you hear what I've got to say.' She wondered what was coming. Her hands were trembling suddenly. 'Do you remember that afternoon when I stayed too long with Douglas Hunter?'

'I remember, Mr Phillipson.'

'He wanted to make a new Will, that was why. I'll read it to you when you come to my office,' he smiled. 'In the meantime I've come to tell you that instead of leaving everything to charity as he did at first, he has left it all to you, Thirza.'

'To me?' she said, and almost fainted. 'What do you mean?'

'Take a sip of wine, my dear . . . Yes, to you. Everything – Yard, house, money, lock, stock and barrel.'

'But what could *I* do with it?' she asked, confused beyond measure. 'I'm not a man. I can't run a business.'

'He certainly thought you could, and I agree with him. Why shouldn't you run the business? You know more about that side of it than anyone else here.'

'I suppose so,' Thirza said numbly, 'but I certainly don't want to.'

'I came here today, first to tell you in advance, and secondly to get the papers I imagine are here, if you would be so kind as to find them for me,' he said, giving her a list. 'It's quicker this way. The work of the Yard must go on while I transfer it into your name.'

'Of course, Mr Phillipson,' Thirza said in a daze.

'Now, Thirza, I need a few details from you, too. When you come to see me I shall need all your papers, as well.'

Thirza looked at him in a sort of agony. A terrible crisis

was looming up in front of her. 'Oh, my God,' she said. 'Oh, my God,' and put her head down on the desk and burst into tears.

'My dear Thirza! Whatever is the matter? Are you ill?' Mr Phillipson got up and came around the desk to pat her back in his concern. 'The shock has been too much for you. Can I fetch you anything?'

'No, thank you. I'm all right,' she struggled to control herself. She sat up straight and wiped her eyes, and Mr Phillipson went back to his chair, still looking at her anxiously. 'I'm all right, except that I'm a fraud. My whole life has been a fraud,' she told him, while the tears threatened again. 'I've wondered for years when I would be found out. A person like me should not be put into a position of trust.'

'What are you saying, Thirza?'

'I'm not only a fraud, Mr Phillipson, but also a trickster. I tricked Mr MacPherson, the minister, into believing that Jordi and I were married. It was easy. I said we were in Gretna at the time, and so many marriages there were irregular anyway. Jordi had nothing to do with it. It was all my idea.'

'And *are* you married?'

'Yes, but not to Jordi. My name is Thirza Sharkey,' she said, and went on to tell him about her gypsy wedding, and how she had posed as Thirza Wishart ever since.

'Well,' he said at the end of it, 'from what you say, the gypsy wedding was not a proper marriage at all. You were never Thirza Sharkey. I don't even want to know how to spell it. It is quite inadmissable.'

'Do you mean to tell me I needn't have worried all these years about being bigamously married to Jordi? If we *had* gone through a proper ceremony, that is?'

'No, and you should have confided in me sooner, my dear. In any case, your marital status has nothing to do with this issue. Douglas named you specifically – Thirza Wishart – as his benificiary.

So she and Jordi could have been married after all? Only now, he wouldn't have her, anyway.

'What is your maiden name, Thirza?'

'Thirza Gourlay. Oh, Mr Phillipson, what am I going to do?'

343

'I'll tell you exactly what you are going to do, my dear. You'll let sleeping dogs lie – for George's sake, if for no other reason. Your name will go down in the records as Thirza Wishart or Gourlay. That is how married ladies are recorded in Scotland, anyway, so there is no difficulty there. Now, to give me a rough idea so that I can get things moving, what do you intend to do with Douglas's house?'

'I don't know. This morning I didn't own another house to worry about. I don't want it this afternoon either, or his money, or the Yard.'

'You're upset, my dear. Think about it for a few days. You can let me know on Thursday.'

She got up and paced around the room while he prepared to depart. 'I've thought about it already,' she said. 'I can tell you now.'

'But Thirza . . .' he said, sitting down again to listen to what she had to say.

'You may as well hear it, Mr Phillipson. I won't change my mind.'

On Thursday afternoon she went to his rooms to sign her name.

'That's it. *Thirza Wishart*,' he instructed her firmly. 'Now you do understand it will take several months to clear up the estate?'

'The order books are quite healthy in the meantime,' she told him, 'but there's no business so flourishing nowadays that it can refuse a cash injection. Before the house is sold, the contents have to be auctioned?'

'If that is what you want, Thirza.'

'I have only one stipulation about that.'

'Yes?'

'That Mrs Rose of Aladdin's Cave, Constitution Street, is to be given first option.'

'Secondhand Rose, you mean?'

'I've had a lot of fun with Secondhand Rose, Mr Phillipson. But I can foresee a slight difficulty with her. She will offer only a nominal sum for anything she chooses to buy, in the expectation that someone will bargain with her.'

'Ah . . . Someone?'

'That someone had better be me, or she will quite happily walk off with the lot for next to nothing. She comes of gypsy stock, you know, and bargaining is the stuff of life to her. But I was once a gypsy, too, so I'm fit for her.'

Mr Phillipson laughed.

'After all, they are Douglas's possessions we are talking about, aren't they? The revenue from them should go back into the Yard.'

He nodded in agreement.

'However, if I can help her to upgrade her own business with one or two good deals in her favour, I shall. She has been very good to me over the years.'

'And Douglas Hunter knew what he was doing when he changed his Will,' he smiled at her.

'Of course, when the house itself is sold, all the money for that will be ploughed back into the Yard. The same goes for Douglas's money when it is all rounded up.'

'You *must* take some of the money, Thirza. It is considerable, you know. I must insist that you keep at least five thousand pounds. It's not fair to Douglas if you don't.'

'I will accept one thousand pounds, if you insist. No more.'

'And you still intend to hand over the Yard?'

'I told you I wouldn't change my mind, Mr Phillipson. Hunter's Yard will be held in trust for George until I consider that he is mature enough to handle it himself. In the meantime, only you and I are to know this.'

'Thirza! Whatever is said by a client to her lawyer is absolutely sacred.'

'I didn't mean to offend you, Mr Phillipson. I will continue to run the business to the best of my ability in the meantime, but I intend with your help and advice to reorganise it. It is too much for one person the way it is now.'

'Well, it killed Douglas, that's certain.'

Thirza threw herself into the business of the Yard with all her energy for the next month. By the end of it, though, she knew that no one person could be expected to carry on with it on their own. If she continued, it would kill her.

Wearily, she went to see Edward Gibson. Crossing the Yard to his shed she was glad to be out in the fresh air for a few minutes, and she took her time. There were several things she wanted to discuss with him. Top priority, of course, would be the forthcoming wedding between Tessa and George.

For months now Mrs Gibson had been relaying the latest details of the arrangements through her husband, who saw Thirza every day. She and everyone else had understood that Thirza had been rushed off her feet at the Yard all the way through Mr Hunter's illness, and then, when the poor man died . . .

Thirza liked Mrs Gibson. She wasn't quite down to earth, perhaps a little airy-fairy, but then she could afford to be, with her servants at her back to be practical for her. The wedding had thrown her into an excited flurry of preparations. She was in her element, and Thirza was only too happy to leave her to it.

'Jordi and I insist we pay our share, Edward,' she began.

'Oh, I shouldn't worry about that!' He took his pipe out of his mouth long enough to laugh. 'My wife is revelling in every penny she's spending. She's been waiting for this since the day Tessa was born. Today they've gone to Edinburgh to search out just the right gloves, regardless of price. I only hope Tessa hasn't inherited her mother's extravagance. She'll have poor George a bankrupt within six months if she has.'

'Edward, believe me. Money is no problem,' Thirza assured him. But that was all she said. Nobody had to know what fate Douglas Hunter had decreed for Hunter's yard. Jordi didn't even know. Of course, she would have to tell him, but she wanted to wait for the right moment. 'Whatever Tessa is or is not, we love her more than words can say. You will be getting George for a son and we will have darling Tessa. She will go a long way to make up for the loss of our own daughter.'

Edward Gibson put his hand over hers in a little gesture that brought sudden tears to Thirza's eyes. She dashed them away impatiently. 'As for the business, Edward, Mr Hunter's lawyer says affairs won't be cleared up for at least a year. I've been thinking of a few changes in the meantime.'

That was the official line she intended to take with everyone.

'Dearie me! Is that what Andrew Phillipson said? That's a long time.'

'I don't know about you, but I have been finding things rather difficult. I'm managing to keep things ticking over but, really, it's a man's job.'

She saw by his face that her suspicions of being resented weren't far wrong. 'So do you think it would be a good idea to call a meeting of the heads of all the sheds, such as you, to see what can be done?'

'A capital idea, Thirza!'

'Shall we make it for three o'clock next Monday afternoon, then? Will you spread the word? I'll ask Mr Phillipson to be present also. He can keep order.'

Edward laughed, and Thirza went back to the office.

'Mattie, what's that room at the end of the passage used for?' she asked. 'The one with the big table?'

'It's never been used in my time here, Mrs Wishart.'

Perhaps Douglas had been intending it for a meeting-room, she thought.

'Well, it's going to be used on Monday afternoon at three o'clock. By that time I would like it to be cleaned out, the table polished with twelve glasses and carafes of water set around it, and a dozen chairs in place. Now then, Mattie,' Thirza smiled, 'there's a puzzle for you! How can it be done?'

Mattie smiled back at her and wrinkled his young brows. He wasn't much older than George, bless him. 'My mother is a good cleaner, Mrs Wishart. She would see to it.'

'Tell her she'll be well paid, then.'

On Monday afternoon, with Mr Phillipson at her side, Thirza brought the meeting to order. 'Good afternoon, gentlemen,' she smiled calmly. 'Of course, you all know Mr Phillipson. He is dealing with Mr Hunter's personal affairs, and the affairs of the Yard.'

There were a few nods, and a deathly hush.

'And, as you also know, I have been trying to carry on where Mr Hunter left off. It hasn't been easy. I've asked you here today to appeal for your help.'

Again there was a stony silence. Even Edward Gibson's eyes flickered away. There was no doubt about it. In their united opinion a woman's place was in the home.

'What Mrs Wishart is saying, gentlemen,' Mr Phillipson came to her rescue in smooth, cultured tones, 'is that she believes that the supervision of the workings of this Yard should be delegated to you. You are all heads of your own departments as it is, and know best how they should be run. She wants you to have a full, free and democratic say in the overall management, too. In other words, to set her free – '

'Please, gentlemen,' Thirza smiled,

'– You are to take over the running of Hunter's Yard yourselves.'

A ripple of satisfaction and relief ran around the table.

'Gentlemen, you will be the Committee. From now on I shall only be the Chairwoman,' Thirza told them.

'With a casting vote at your regular meetings,' the lawyer added.

'Once a month?' she suggested. 'Or every three months?'

In the end it was decided that every three months would do. During that time they could collect the suggestions and grievances of everyone, to be thrashed out around the table.

'Take a vote on it,' Mr Phillipson said, and every hand went up. 'And now, would you please vote on this next proposal? Mrs Wishart is prepared to carry on with the financial side of the business in the meantime, if that is favourable to you all?'

Again, every hand went up, this time enthusiastically.

'You did a good job there, Thirza,' Mr Phillipson assured her over a glass of wine afterwards.

'Only with your help,' she sighed wearily. 'Thank you. I don't know what I would have done without you.'

'You look tired, Thirza. You can afford to take a day off now. Why not tomorrow?'

'Why not, indeed? I've been struggling for the chance to go across to Pittenweem to invite my Uncle Clem to George's wedding. It's ages since I've been there, or he's been over here, and he does like to keep in touch with our family. He's suffered through our tragedies with us, and shared our good times too, but George has been his favourite ever since he was born. I'd like to go across and invite him specially.'

Sailing across the Firth of Forth that Tuesday was as good as a week's holiday to Thirza. She trailed her fingers in the water and turned her pale, tired face up to the sun, feeling all her cares and woes slipping off her. Uncle Clem, still spry, was delighted to accept her invitation.

'Oh, God, Thirza,' he said, 'how can I believe our wee boy is old enough already to marry? I know he was over here not long ago with his Tessa – but marriage? It's such a big step!'

'Well, you'll see him taking it on the first of June.' She hugged him. 'It's not far away.'

Afterwards she wandered back down to the ferry alone, with plenty of time to spare, and reluctant to leave her native heath. She passed her old schoolhouse on the way and all at once old memories came flooding back.

She saw Jordi again, just a boy, sitting in the corner and filing down the coins. She saw the path she had trotted along at his heels back to St Fillan. In every house, every stone and every blade of grass she saw his face, his smiling eyes and his helping hand. A terrible sense of desolation and loss came over her. It was all so long ago . . .

'This is your life now, Jimmie?' she asked when Jimmie Gilmour helped her onto the ferry boat. 'Shuttling back and forth over the Forth?'

'It beats fishing,' he laughed, 'and it's fair enough money.'

'Ah yes,' Thirza agreed, sinking down on her seat, 'it all comes back down to money, doesn't it?'

She was tired again, and dispirited as they approached Leith Harbour. Her eyes were roving over the small crowd waiting to go back across to Pittenweem when her heart lurched sickeningly and she felt the blood draining from her face. She closed her eyes to shut out the sight, for behind everyone else *there stood the image of Douglas Hunter.*

She couldn't move off her seat. Everyone else was walking away up the slipway and the new passengers coming down.

'We're here, Thirza.' Jimmie Gilmour was bending over her. 'Are you all right?'

She was aware of a man's strong arms around her and a voice in her ear. 'I'll look after her. She'll be all right with me,' and she looked up into the royal blue eyes of Jake Hunter.

37

'I GOT an awful shock,' Thirza said. 'I thought for a minute I was looking at your uncle. You're so very like him.'

'What you need is a stiff glass of brandy. Your face is white.'

'No, thank you.'

'Well then, a good strong cup of tea with plenty of sugar in it,' Jake Hunter insisted, propelling her across to the nearest inn on the harbour front. 'We'll sit down in here until you recover.'

'I was being silly. I'm just tired, that's all,' she said shakily, but even as she said it she despised herself. Thirza Gourlay was never tired or weak. Gourlay women didn't get tired or weak. What, she asked herself while he was ordering the tea, had happened to her backbone?

'So you're still slaving away in Hunter's Yard?' he asked lightly. 'Why?'

'Why?' she repeated the short, sharp, dangerous little question. The combination of that, those startling eyes of his so near her own, and a sip of almost gypsy tea brought her back to herself with a vengeance. Here she was, actually speaking to the man Douglas had disinherited. 'Because I need the money.'

Jake Hunter laughed teasingly. 'No, you don't.'

Thirza rose to the challenge immediately. 'How do you know?'

'Oh, I know quite a lot about you, Mrs Wishart, Thirza Wishart, beautiful Thirza . . . You can call me Jake, if you like.'

351

'You've got the cheek of the devil.' She couldn't help smiling. 'Anyway, what are you doing here? I thought you had gone to Glasgow to sail your ship.'

'There you are, you see! You have been thinking about me! And your cheeks are suddenly very pink. In fact, you're blushing!'

'Enough! Enough!' she was laughing when, almost as if a shutter had been pulled down over them, his eyes became bleak.

'To answer your question, I'm here to visit my sister. I come here often. You see, she is very ill in hospital.'

'I'm sorry.' The laughter faded from Thirza's face to be replaced by sympathy. 'Mr Hunter never told me you had a sister.'

'No?'

'No. In fact, he said very little about you.'

'And all of it bad, I suppose,' he said bitterly. 'But yes, I have a very dear sister. Her name is Caroline. When I'm here I go to see her every day, although she doesn't know me.'

'She doesn't know you?' she repeated, aghast.

'She doesn't know anyone, Thirza.' The royal blue of his eyes was even more startling now that it was washed with a suspicious glistening. 'You cannot imagine the ordeal of it, but of course there's nobody else to be interested, and so I always go alone.'

'I'm so sorry. How much longer do you have here?'

'This is my last day on this trip. I shall leave for Glasgow after the evening visiting hour, and hope to be back again in less than a fortnight. I've been keeping my trips short and local recently. Caroline's condition is steadily deteriorating, they tell me.'

'I do hope she will improve,' Thirza said, getting to her feet, 'but now I must go, I'm afraid. Thank you for the tea.'

'No, it is I who should thank you for some company at last in this wretched town. May I come to the Yard the next time I'm here, to talk to you? It means so much to me that somebody else in the world actually cares whether my sister lives or dies.'

'I'll give the gateman instructions that you are to be allowed in.'

'Then, will you allow me to walk you home after the shock I gave you earlier?'

'No,' Thirza smiled and held out her hand. 'My house is only a stone's throw away.'

'Oh,' he said, grasping it and sending shivers down her spine at the contact with him, 'I know where you live, Thirza.' On a sudden impulse he bent down and kissed her cheek. The contrast between his bristly face and the velvety hotness of his lips was enough to startle her even more. 'I've got your number,' he said as she walked away. 'Number eight, isn't it?'

How did he know, she wondered, climbing slowly up the steps to the Wishart house? When she thought over the whole incident she was left in two minds. There had been little prickles in that chance meeting and conversation almost like tiny barbs, which left her feeling quite uncomfortable.

Was it a chance meeting in the first place, she pondered? It had to be. Only Jordi, George and Mr Phillipson knew she was going to Pittenweem today.

Jake Hunter hadn't harrassed her about Hunter's Yard . . . Not really . . .

In any case, she had learned enough about him to find out that he was a kind, caring man to be so very concerned and upset about his sister. There must have been something far back in the Hunter family, perhaps connected with Jacob Hunter, to make Douglas disinherit his nephew.

'Your day out has done you good,' Jordi commented when she entered the house. 'The roses are back in your cheeks.'

'It was the sun. Yes, I do feel better, but I think I'll go straight to bed.'

Secondhand Rose had managed to find two single beds some time ago, and the three-quarter bed had been relegated to what Thirza called the 'guest-room'. She undressed and fell into her own narrow bed, tired out with the sun and the sea air, and exhausted with her life.

The guest-room was used soon afterwards. On the night of the first of June, when all the wedding celebrations were over, Uncle Clem had to be put to bed, rather the worse for wear.

'Lassie, that was a grand wedding!' He tucked in to a hearty, if belated, breakfast the following morning. 'Not that I saw much of it towards the end, I must say.'

'Did you sleep well?'

'After all that whisky? God, I *must* have been drunk.'

'You were well on,' Thirza agreed, laughing. 'Why don't you stay with us for a few days now you're here, Uncle Clem?'

'Well, I could. I'd like to see Jordi's Yard again. He and Bob were fairly branching out the last time I was here. What's he doing now?'

'I'm not sure, Uncle Clem. He doesn't speak much about it.'

'He doesn't speak much about it?'

'That is, I haven't been at home much recently, for him to speak to.'

'Thirza, ye're not still at Hunter's Yard?' Uncle Clem asked sternly. 'Jordi was complaining about it when I saw him last. When are ye going to give it up?'

'Soon, I hope. There's been a committee appointed since Douglas Hunter died. Hunter's Yard should more or less run itself from now on. But, to go back to Jordi. What was he saying to you?'

'Not much, but I got the impression that he wasn't too happy with you working for a rival Yard.' Thirza looked uncomfortable, and Uncle Clem patted her hand. 'Ay, lassie, a marriage is a very private thing, and I wouldna like to intrude – but is everything all right between you and Jordi? You've not looked happy for a long time.'

'I'm just tired, that's all,' Thirza lied.

'Ye should take a wee holiday, then. What about the happy couple? Are they away today for a honeymoon?'

'No,' Thirza smiled when her uncle changed the subject. 'You should go and visit them in their new home. It's only the loft over the boat shed, you know. They wouldn't accept a penny from anyone, and that's all they could afford. They paid Bob Steele to convert it into a tiny flat, and I think they'll be quite happy there for the time being.'

'They're happy, all right,' Uncle Clem assured her a few days later. 'That Bob Steele did an excellent job.'

'With your wood! Dearest Uncle Clem,' Thirza flung her arms around him, 'all the wood you've let us have for years and years has been put to good use. Do you have to go back to Pittenweem this afternoon? I love you. George loves you, and you haven't even seen this ship he's so intent on yet, have you?'

By the middle of June, with the wedding well past, the new

ship was all that was talked about in number eight and at Hunter's Yard. The excitement was mounting every day. Such a huge ship had never been built before at the Yard, not with sail and steam.

In the meantime, Thirza had been thinking about what Uncle Clem had said, and she decided the time had come to act. Something would have to be improved, she announced, at the Extraordinary Committee Meeting she had called. She proposed that an accountant, with an assistant, should be appointed to look after the finances, knowing full well that there was still a small element who would prefer Hunter's Yard to be an all-male establishment, anyway.

As she expected, it was accepted unanimously, and she began the business of advertising, drawing up the list of candidates, collecting their *curricula vitae* and their references, and arranging another committee meeting for their interviews.

Finally it was done, and Thirza found herself at the end of June almost a free woman again, merely supervising the two accountants from time to time.

On one of the afternoons she went back to the Yard, she decided to visit her daughter-in-law on the way – and not before time, it seemed.

'Oh, Thirza,' Tessa implored her, 'how can I ask my mother? I don't think she ever cooked mince and tatties in her life!' Her voice rose to a wail. 'I don't know where to start.'

Thirza took off her jacket, donned Tessa's pinafore and walked over to their new little stove. 'Come in about, dearie,' she said calmly, 'and watch me. You just brown the meat very hard to begin with like this,' she swizzled the pan over a high heat while separating the particles of meat with a wooden spoon. 'Now move your pan to the side, add your carrots and onions with some water, put the lid on and simmer gently.'

'What about the tatties? I always boil them to mush.'

'A panful of tatties only takes twenty minutes to be ready, Tessa. Don't put them on until half an hour before George is due home. Then try them with a fork, and when they're soft pour off the water and dry them until they're fluffy, shaking them all the time.'

She hadn't told Tessa about the herby doughboys, she reflected as she continued on to the Yard. That would have to be lesson number two, for now it was time to go to work, and start to clear up her desk and all the books before she could leave for home. She worked hard all afternoon and it was at five o'clock when she was nearly done, that Mattie announced a visitor.

'Mr Hunter, Mrs Wishart. You said to let him in.'

Once again Thirza's heart leapt up at the sight of him and her pulses began to race, but Jake Hunter's visit could not have been more blameless. He flung himself into the chair on the other side of the desk.

'You're here to see your sister again?'

'This evening. Oh, God, Thirza, I hate going. It's very depressing.' He looked at her with an expression in his eyes she could not define. It was meant to be agonised, she knew, but it was mixed with a challenge as if he was trying her out. Never one to resist a challenge, she responded.

'What if I came with you?'

'You would? Oh Thirza, you would?'

'If it will make any difference.'

'You know it will. I'll be waiting with a cab at six o'clock. What will you tell your husband?'

'The truth of course. I always do.'

'He won't mind?'

'Why should he? I'm only going to the hospital to visit a sick lady. I'll leave him a note.'

Jordi came out of Wishart's Yard early that night at five past six, and saw a cab just moving off from in front of number eight. When it passed him he saw a man and a woman inside it, sitting very close together. The man was looking down at the woman and she seemed to be gazing up into his eyes. He was sure it was Thirza.

He ran down to the harbour and jumped into the first cab waiting there for sea-passengers. 'There's a cab just gone up Constitution Street,' he told the driver. 'See if you can catch it and follow it. I want to know where it's going.'

'The wife's gone off and left ye, has she?' the young man grinned and picked up the reins.

'Something like that,' Jordi slammed the door.

It would be something quite innocent, he told himself. Thirza
was as honest as the day. Besides, she could never hide anything
from him. Her face said it all.

The cab hadn't got half way up Leith Walk before Jordi was
cursing himself for a fool. If she ever had to go away somewhere
she always left a note, and he hadn't even gone into the house
to look. The driver opened the slat in the roof to shout down.
'We're right behind them, now.'

'Keep back a little. Don't let them know we're following
them.'

The cab bowled along smartly again. The whole journey took
three quarters of an hour before the driver slowed down, guiding
the horse to a halt alongside the pavement.

'They've stopped,' he spoke down to Jordi. 'A man and a
woman are getting out.'

Out of the window he saw that it *was* Thirza, and that fellow
Hunter was taking her arm and leading her into a building that
looked like a hospital.

'What place is that?' he asked the driver.

'A place ye want to keep well clear o'. That's Bedlam.'

'*Bedlam?*'

'Ay. They'll be away in to see some poor mad soul.'

'Just take me back,' Jordi said, and closed the slat.

What on earth was Thirza doing in Bedlam, for Christ's sake?
He hoped she knew what she was in for. The stories he had heard
were horrific. No one they knew was in any kind of hospital, let
alone that one.

No. Jake Hunter must have inveigled her in there. Why? Jordi
couldn't imagine the reason. Jake Hunter was a man to whom
he had taken an instant dislike. His instincts about men had
never been wrong in the past. They wouldn't be wrong now.

At home he found Thirza's note.

'Douglas Hunter's niece in hospital. Gone to visit with her
brother.'

Douglas Hunter's niece? When everyone in Leith knew
Douglas Hunter had had no other relative in the world besides
his nephew Jake whom he'd detested? There was something very
fishy here.

'What hospital is this?' Thirza asked Jake Hunter when they

357

stepped inside. The place gave her an eerie feeling. It was all white-tiled, and the tiles were running with water. Why did they have to keep sluicing them down?

She found out as they walked further up the corridor. The stench of urine and faeces was overpowering and, even worse, were the noises – queer noises – sobbing and screaming. She clutched his arm in fear.

'Caroline isn't like *that*,' he said, urging her on. 'She's different.'

At last they arrived at the ward where she was. Inside, it was complete chaos. One woman was hunched up on the floor, continuously rocking. Another was running around screaming and jabbering with two nurses vainly trying to restrain her. While Thirza stood there in dismay a man in a white coat came to help them. She didn't want to believe what she saw him doing to the poor creature, but it stopped her effectively. When she looked around she saw on every face the look of madness. She was in the mad-house.

Horrified, and almost in tears, she felt Jake pulling her over to a lone figure sitting on a chair and staring at the wall. The girl wasn't just silent and unmoving. There was a sort of ferocity in her rigid figure.

'This is Caroline,' he said. 'Caroline! Caroline! Can you hear me?'

A tall, middle-aged nurse wearing a floating white hat came over as soon as she heard his voice. 'Oh, it's *you*, Mr Hunter?' she said, glaring at him.

Why should she sound so angry and surprised when he came here so often, Thirza wondered?

'Of course it's me!' he said with a look of suppressed rage on his face. 'Who else?'

The nurse didn't answer that. 'She's much the same,' she said before she walked away with tightened lips. 'Her outbursts are coming oftener. It's not a good sign.'

Caroline didn't move a muscle. Thirza thought she didn't even blink. She just stared and stared at the wall, holding on to a doll, holding it so tightly that her fingers had gone right through the doll's dress and into the rag body.

Jake Hunter looked at his sister with a strange, hard expression on his face. Thirza couldn't diagnose it. For a second she thought she saw his eyes turn almost black with hatred. Of course she must have been mistaken. She knew how much he thought of her.

'Oh, God,' he said. 'How long must this go on? Come on, Thirza, let's get out of here!' He dragged her out of the ward, almost running down the corridor, until they were out in the fresh air again. 'I hate that place!' he said violently.

'How did she get like that?' Thirza asked. 'What happened to her?'

'Some man attacked her and raped her, they said,' he averted his face, grinding out the words. 'She was very young at the time, only thirteen. After that, she became violent like some of those other women in there. When they gave her that doll she became as you see her now. She thinks it's her baby.'

Thirza had never heard anything so tragic. 'What age is she now?'

'Seventeen.'

'She's been in that hell-hole for four years? Who was the man?'

'Nobody knows. Do we have to speak about it any more?'

'Of course not. I can see you're very upset . . . And I'm very tired, Jake. Call me a cab now.'

'If you're so tired,' he said as they went back to Leith, 'why don't you take a holiday? A long holiday?'

'I've never had a holiday in my life. They cost a lot of money. Besides, where would I go?'

'Surely my uncle left you some money, after all the work you did for him?'

It was the first time anyone had asked her that question, either directly or indirectly. She hadn't even told Jordi about Hunter's Yard or the money, yet. She didn't like being questioned but, when he bent down and covered her lips with his, she forgot about it instantly. She kissed him back, and found she was enjoying it. She liked it very much, indeed.

'Come away with me,' he urged her in between kisses. 'I'm sailing to New York on the tenth of August. That would be a wonderful holiday – for us both, Thirza – and it wouldn't cost you a penny.'

'To New York? How long does that take, there and back?'

'I have a lot of business over there. A trip to America usually takes six months, before I see to it all.'

'*Six months!*'

'Come with me, Thirza,' he said, undoing the buttons of her blouse.

'Jake . . . Jake . . .' she moaned.

'Christ, you're a hot one, all right,' he panted. 'Think of it, all night long, every night on a long sea voyage. Come with me . . .'

'Stop it, Jake. I'm home,' she said, rubbing the steam off the window. Jordi must be home. There was a light in the window. 'I'll have to think about it,' she kissed him quickly, rearranging her skirts.

'I'll ask you one last time when I come to see Caroline on the fourth of August,' he told her when she got out.

The cab moved off and Thirza ran up the steps. Oh, God, did she have the strength to throw caution to the winds? She thought she might already know what her answer would be.

38

J ORDI saw that Thirza was very flushed when she came in, and her eyes were shining a brilliant blue. 'How did you find Miss Hunter?' he asked.

'Oh,' she answered with a shudder, 'she's very ill.'

'Which hospital is she in?'

'The Royal Infirmary.'

It was the first lie she had ever told him. He wouldn't have believed such a thing could happen, not out of Thirza's mouth. Then she definitely did have something to hide. Fear clutched at his heart, and he felt his face going as cold as stone.

'No, you didn't go to the Royal Infirmary, Thirza,' he said quietly. 'You went to Bedlam. I know because I followed you there.'

'You followed me? Why? Didn't you get my note?'

'I was on my way home when I saw you in a cab with Jake Hunter. So I jumped in another and followed you. I wanted to know what that man was doing with my wife. I couldn't believe it when I saw him taking you into Bedlam.'

'I knew you wouldn't like me going in there, if you got to know about it.'

'You're quite right. I didn't. Especially to see someone who doesn't exist.'

'What do you mean by that?' Thirza glared at him angrily, her face scarlet now.

'Miss Hunter doesn't exist. There isn't such a person.'

'Of course there is! I saw her myself, less than an hour ago!'

'You saw someone, I don't doubt that. But she was no sister of Jake Hunter's.'

'What are you saying? What do you mean?'

'I took the cab back to Edward Gibson's. He knew Douglas Hunter very well. He said that he's known the family for years. Jake Hunter never had a sister.'

'You went and asked Edward Gibson? How could you? You've been spying on me!'

'To try and protect you from that bastard. He's been telling you lies, and now you're telling them to me.'

'I'm telling you, I saw Caroline Hunter this evening. I'm not surprised the Hunter family kept her hidden away. She was very young when she was raped and then went mad.'

'Oh, Thirza . . . What has that man been saying to you? What is he to you, anyway?'

'A friend,' Thirza blazed, 'and God knows I need one!'

'I'm the best friend you ever had, or ever will have.'

'*You*!' she rounded on him. 'You haven't even spoken to me properly for the best part of two years! You needn't start now, by giving me your advice. It's too late. It's too late for everything!' she sobbed, 'And from now on I'll sleep in the drawing-room all the time. I'm not even going to go upstairs!' she flung over her shoulder, slamming the kitchen door so hard on the way out that the whole house shook.

He couldn't remember her ever being in such a flying temper before, not even during some of her childish tantrums with her mother.

In the drawing-room Thirza knew better than anyone that she had never been so angry before in her life. There had been the Umphrays in Reawick, and their cruelty. She had been angry enough with them. She could have killed any one of them quite cheerfully for what they did to Merren Cheyne.

Then there had been Duke Elliot in Gretna, and the horrendous thing he had done to her mother. She was still, and always would be, totally enraged over that. It didn't matter if she and Jordi had murdered Duke Elliot between them in revenge. That had nothing to do with the deep resentment she still felt burning inside her. Her mother's life had been cut short. Ruth had never deserved that . . .

As for the Sharkeys, she could hardly bring herself to look back at them. They, perhaps more than anyone else, were responsible for what was happening now, and all because of that stupid jump over the broomstick. Why had she never realised that it wasn't legal?

Her fury gathered force. Why hadn't *Jordi* thought about it? That was more like it. He was a man, wasn't he? He was supposed to see about these things. She had been a single woman all along and, thanks to him, had brought three little bastards into the world. Her beautiful little Angela . . . just a bastard . . .

When she faced Jordi next morning he could see that she was more than ready to carry on the quarrel where she had left off when she went to bed.

'You *had* to stand on the other side of the road and wave to her, didn't you?' she asked bitterly.

'Well, well! You always *did* have a way with knives, as I recall,' he blazed back, 'and that one was certainly aimed straight at my heart.'

'Angela might still be here, but for that!'

'Angela might still be here, if you had been at home to look after her yourself.'

The terrible battle raged on and off over the next three days, while all his resentment flashed out at her, and all her frustration became very clear to him, until it became dangerously close to the date for the launching of George's ship. Jordi spent as much time away from the house as he could, with Thirza in the mood that she was.

It finally came to a head on the evening of the sixth of August, when he heard her running up and down to her wardrobe in their bedroom and banging about in the drawing-room next door. He went in and found her packing her bags.

'What next?' he asked. 'You're not planning to spoil the launch tomorrow, are you? Jesus Christ, you're not going to ruin George's life, as well?'

'The launch will go ahead tomorrow, never fear,' she spat at him.

'Why were *you* ever chosen to do it, anyway?' he asked suspiciously.

'There's a very good reason for that, but I don't have to

tell you what it is. You don't believe a word I say, anyway.'

'See if you can answer this, then? You are packing your bags to go away somewhere? Unless you are determined to shame George and me both, don't you think you should tell us where you are going, at least?'

'Oh, George knows! Everyone in Hunter's Yard knows. I didn't think you would be interested but, since you ask, I'm going away for a long holiday.'

'Well,' his tone softened a little. 'I'm very glad to hear it, Thirza. You've been looking so tired, lately. Perhaps that's the reason why you've been so touchy.'

'I'm going to New York.'

It was as though she'd punched him in the face. 'New York? How do you propose to get to New York?'

'On Jake Hunter's ship. This holiday is his idea.'

'Oh . . . I bet it is,' Jordi said savagely.

Up to that moment he had never really understood when people said there was a very thin line between love and hate. Now he knew. He could have wrung her neck.

'I'm leaving directly after the launching. I've got nothing to hide, believe me,' Thirza rolled up her best starched blouse with angry abandon and crammed it into one of her bags. 'I never have,' she added with a toss of her head.

'You've got a hell of a lot to hide, Thirza. Murder, for one thing. Bigamy, for another, if you can call ours a marriage.'

'You swore to me that we acted in self defence. If we hadn't killed Duke Elliot he would have shot us for certain. He very nearly did.'

'As long as we were together we could defend ourselves from everyone and everything. United we stood. Divided we shall fall, mark my words, Thirza. You've been recognised here for a very long time as my wife.'

'Oh, didn't I tell you?' she asked with an infuriating mock innocence, 'Mr Phillipson confirmed that the gypsy wedding was just a load of rubbish. I was never married to Michael Sharkey, after all. And, you said yourself that the bogus record of our marriage was only a worthless bit of paper. I'm a free woman. I can do what I like.'

Jordi couldn't stand any more of it. He simply walked out and went up to his bed. The next day dawned as hot and as clammy as ever. Thirza looked jaded, even ill, thought Jordi, when she climbed onto the platform erected at the bow of the ship. The name the ship was about to receive remained a mystery to the very end. Thirza must have sworn the men in the paint shop to secrecy long ago. The curtains covering the name were tied down, ready to be cut adrift at the last minute.

'Give it a good hard throw,' Jordi heard Edward Gibson saying at Thirza's left side when he handed her the bottle of champagne.

She took the glove off her left hand to give her a better grip. It was only then that Jordi saw that she wasn't wearing what she had always called her wedding ring, and his heart plummeted.

'I name this ship *Tessa Wishart*,' Thirza crashed the bottle up against her bows where it smashed into smithereens, 'and may God bless all who sail in her.'

Well, she had got *that* right, Jordi thought sadly, watching the dribbles of wine foaming over the newly painted name. *Tessa Wishart*. One day, and not too long from now, Tessa would be the mother of his grandchildren. But where would their grandmother be? God alone knew.

The vessel glided slowly down the slip inch by inch until, at the end, she gathered momentum and plunged into the Firth of Forth before she righted herself proudly.

'Thank God,' Edward Gibson sighed audibly. 'She's going to be lucky. And now, Thirza and Jordi, I can let you in on another secret. George has asked me to go with him on her maiden voyage.'

'Where?' Thirza asked.

'Wherever he decides when the finishing touches are made to her.'

'Oh, Thirza!' Tessa took her arm, smiling. 'The name was your idea, wasn't it?'

Thirza hugged her. 'You're the wife of the man who designed her, aren't you? You'll always bring luck with you, dearie.'

Everyone waved when Thirza climbed into the waiting cab. Everyone, that is, except Jordi. The last thing he wanted to do was to say gooodbye to Thirza, however hard and scratchy his life had been with her these last two years.

He would do nothing to speed her on her way. He couldn't

imagine trying to live without her, deadly barbs and all. It was after the cab disappeared into the distance that Jordi suddenly knew the harsh truth.

She had no intention of ever coming back.

Home alone that night, the silence hit him like a sledge hammer. It was the silence that only a deserted house produces, rather than that of a quiet, peaceful household when everyone was out, but due back soon. This was a horrible blankness, like a fog.

Nobody would be coming back at all, he realised, sinking down on a chair in the kitchen. It was as if a death had occurred. He put his head down on the kitchen table and wept for the first time in years. His little Angela . . . His beloved Thirza . . . Oh, God, he had lost them both.

Much later he raised his head again. In the deafening silence a tiny clink directed his eyes downwards to where the cobra key, on its gold chain, was hitting the table.

He took it up in his hand. He had worn it day and night for so many years that now it was a part of him he scarcely ever noticed. His mother's words were ringing in his ears. 'Alistair Fisher, Jordi.'

Some day, he thought drearily, he might try to find him.

The days after Thirza left stretched out unhappily, ever more emptily, and all the time George was giving him excited reports of the finishing of the *Tessa Wishart.*

Jordi listened to him with one ear and to the persistent voice of his mother with the other, until at last he told himself irritably that he would *have* to go and find this Alistair Fisher, wherever he was. After a few enquiries he discovered that the lawyer had his rooms in Edinburgh. That same day he downed tools and left Bob Steele in charge.

Jordi was sitting in Alistair Fisher's stuffy little waiting room. He seemed to have been sitting there for hours when a lady came in and sat down on the only vacant chair, the one beside his.

She came in on a glorious wave of scents, and lifted the veil of her dainty hat. Jordi stole a glance at her and saw that, although she was exquisitely dressed in the western fashion, somewhere in her lineage must be traces of the east.

Her skin was the colour of a ripe apricot. Her black eyebrows were delicately arched over huge and beautiful eyes, not black like his own but the colour of the peat-water he had seen in Shetland, with little gold flecks in them.

'Have you been waiting long?' she asked in faultless English, so that he was almost persuaded to change his assessment of her.

'For hours,' he assured her, when Alistair Fisher's clerk stood in the doorway.

'Lady Justin,' he announced. 'Mr Fisher will see you now.'

Jordi's beautiful companion rose and went through, wafting the scent of attar of roses around that small, stale room. Within minutes, Alistair Fisher himself appeared at the door she had entered. 'I'm very sorry,' he said flatly, 'but the work in front of me prevents me from seeing anyone else today. Please make another appointment, if you wish, on your way out.'

Jordi made his for the following week and, as he sat once again in the waiting room the memory of that gorgeous lady and her perfume wafted back to him.

'Mr Wishart,' the clerk interrupted his dream, 'please come this way.'

'How can I help you, sir?' Alistair Fisher looked up from his desk and slowly gestured to him to sit down. He seemed to be bemused. 'Excuse me for staring at you, Mr Wishart. I remember another George Wishart who came to me many years ago, when we were both young men. And now here you are, the only Wishart I have seen since that day.'

'I was called after him,' Jordi smiled. 'He was my father.'

'That's why I'm staring. Of course, I do not disbelieve you, but you do not resemble him at all. You are the very image of his Indian companion.'

'It's a long story, Mr Fisher,' Jordi said, laying his necklace with the gold key dangling from it on the desk between them. 'I can see I should tell it to you from beginning to end, but I warn you it will take some time.'

For a second Alistair Fisher only stared at the key. Then he opened a drawer in his desk and pulled out another, identical, cobra key. 'This is the greatest coincidence of my entire working life,' he told Jordi. 'A lady, Jorjeela, Lady Justin, was here only last week and left this. She said that her father, Viaz Mohammed, had asked her, before he died, to bring it to Edinburgh and that it was for George Wishart's son, if I could find him. I was just about to advertise. Now, I will have to go and dismiss the rest of my waiting clients once again. You understand that I need proof?'

'I think I shall have given you all the proof you need in a couple of hours' time,' Jordi said, saddened by the news of his real father's death.

'In that case, what about a pot of tea? Or would you prefer something stronger?'

'Tea would be most acceptable,' replied Jordi.

Two hours later Mr Fisher stood up. 'The trunk is down in the basement in the strong room, where it has been all these years. The final proof will be when both these keys can open it.'

When they had made their way down to it, he tried one of the keys in the lock and it turned. Then he locked it again and tried the other. It turned the lock, too.

'That's it, then, Mr Wishart,' he smiled and handed Jordi both keys. 'The trunk is yours, without any doubt.'

'Let's see what's in it, then, shall we?' Jordi said, flinging back the lid.

Diamonds, sapphires, pearls and huge red rubies glittered and glistened in amongst the gold.

'Good God, there's a fortune here,' the lawyer said in shocked tones and took out his handkerchief to mop his brow.

Jordi was silent for a minute, equally dazed. The next minute he was even more angry than he had ever been with Thirza. 'This is the fortune my mother should have had,' he said. 'If she had only come to you as I tried to persuade her when I was a young boy, she might still have been living.'

'Yes,' Alistair Fisher said sadly, having heard the whole story.

With all that money might Thirza still be with him, Jordi wondered? And Angela? He snapped the lid shut and locked it again before he put his own key back around his neck and handed Mr Fisher the other.

'You'll need this, Mr Fisher,' he said, 'if you will take on the job of converting it into hard currency and placing it in the Royal Bank of Scotland. As you can see, you will be able to name your own fee. In the meantime, where is Lady Justin?'

'Gone, sir. Lady Jorjeela sailed for Calcutta last week, after she had seen me.'

'But, of course, you have her address?'

'I do. It's back upstairs.'

'That's good enough for me,' Jordi said, and within an hour was sitting in George's little flat above his own boatshed.

'Have you decided on your destination for the maiden voyage?' he asked his son.

'Not yet, but somewhere far away to give the *Tessa Wishart* a good run.'

'How far?'

'To the other side of the world, if need be,' George grinned.

'Calcutta?' Jordi asked.

'Very well, then,' George accepted the challenge. 'To Calcutta it shall be. We should be there and back by Christmas. Early spring, at the latest.'

'I do hope so,' Tessa put her hand anxiously on her stomach, but said no more.

39

As she was driven away in the cab after the launch of the *Tessa Wishart* Thirza gazed straight ahead. Tessa had taken her arm and helped her into the cab.

'Have a wonderful holiday, dearest Thirza,' she had smiled, and then whispered in her ear, 'Who knows? When you come back home again I think you may be expecting your first grandchild!'

Everyone waving . . . Everyone smiling . . . All except Jordi . . . To Thirza it was all a blur.

A grandmother.

How could she possibly become a grandmother, when her own life hadn't even started yet? At least, not properly.

The longer the journey lasted, the more her stomach knotted up. Jordi hadn't even waved goodbye. If they had clung together as they did after John's death, this would never have happened. Why had they not? The loss of a second child had been too much to bear, so that she had become dried up and shrivelled inside and hard on the outside, just like a walnut. And just as difficult to crack. As for Jordi, he had simply retreated with his pain, like some wounded animal, into a corner impossible for her to reach, even if she had found the strength to try.

If they had held out a hand to each other earlier, if they had never had that blazing row stretching out interminably over the three stormiest days of her life, if the words they had hurled at each other had never been uttered . . . If only, if only, if only.

If only she had listened to his point of view! But no. She had just exploded, and dashed off. Jordi had been quite right to accuse her of acting first and thinking about it later. If she hadn't rushed off on this holiday Jordi would have married her properly. He had said so. He had said he would marry her a hundred times over, if that would please her. He had even begged her.

But there was no way back, after all that. How could there be a way back? She knew why he hadn't waved goodbye, why he had just stood there with his face as hard as granite. It was because, as he said, too many of her knives had cut him to his heart.

Besides, he had reached the stage now when he didn't even trust her any more. He had been very, very suspicious of this 'holiday'. He was quite right, too. Thirza began to feel physically sick. It wasn't to be a mere holiday, she thought defiantly. It was going to be her honeymoon, a legitimate one this time.

Jake Hunter had murmured it whilst murmuring other sweet nothings in her ear, while fondling her and arousing her, as well as himself, almost to the point of full-blown intimacy. He had cast a spell over her with his lips, his whisperings, his utter charm and his uncanny resemblance to Douglas Hunter – dear, kind Douglas, whom she would have trusted to the very gates of Hell. She was sure she could trust his nephew in the same way – wasn't she . . .?

The sick feeling wouldn't go away, and it changed to outright panic when, in an awful moment, a trickle of doubt entered her mind. Jake Hunter *was* going to marry her, wasn't he? Of course he was.

Of course he was.

In Glasgow, she leaned upon the rail and watched the foam-streaked water widen between Jake Hunter's ship and the shore, and with some of her irrepressible optimism returning, saw the new life she was entering opening before her like a vast sunlit plain stretching away towards unimaginable horizons. A plain across which she could travel at will, choosing her own path across America and taking her own time. She was as free as a bird.

The *Columbine*, which only a few minutes before had shown nothing but bare spars, was now covered with her loose canvas from the royals to the decks. All hands were summoned to the falls and the anchor brought to the cat-head. The light sails were set one after the other with the precision of clockwork, and soon the clipper was under full sail and heading for the open sea.

Thirza stood aft on the weather side of the poop, gazing across the widening stretch of water at the receding shores of Scotland, with none of the thoughts appropriate to the occasion. She did not recognise any of the landmarks. She had never been familiar with the west coast of Scotland before. Now she could only vaguely discern them, but she was fully aware that she was leaving her homeland, never to return.

She became aware that Jake Hunter had joined her.

'And now?' she asked.

'Now for the open sea, and America.'

She shivered at his lack of reassurance. He knew perfectly well what a tremendous effort it had been to leave Leith behind. If he didn't know that it was only to marry him that she had done it, then it was time he did. They stood in silence for several minutes until the lights of Glasgow were mere pin-pricks of orange in the blackness astern, and the town had lost all shape. She shivered again, this time in agitation.

'You're shivering, Thirza. Take this coat.'

She allowed him to slip a coat over her shoulders.

'You should go below. You have your own cabin to go to.'

So they were not to get married right away, then. And he was the one who had spoken to her about nights of passion on his ship. He must have decided they would have the ceremony when they reached America. But she wished he had discussed the arrangements with her before this evening.

The tiny pin-prick of doubt that had been stabbing her grew in size and intensity. She wondered, feeling sick again, if he intended to marry her at all. She had visualised that they would have been in each other's arms straight away, especially when she caught her first glimpse of the romantic *Columbine*.

'Not yet,' she said. It was her duty to stand here, to accept the cold spray in her face, to strain her eyes for glimpses of land, to pay at least this small physical tribute to her country . . . And, in some strange way, to Jordi.

'Once we round this point there'll be nothing more to see, so you might as well go below,' Jake Hunter repeated.

She stole a sidelong glance at him. It felt very much as if he was trying to get rid of her. Well, she had something to say to him, and the sooner she said it the better. She would brook no arguments, either. It was now, or never.

'I was never married to Jordi Wishart,' she said, 'and that is one reason I left him. Another was that you gave me to understand that you would marry me, and that we would be happy together. You do understand, Jake, that it will be necessary for you to marry me?'

He did not reply.

'Jake, did you hear me?'

'I heard you.'

'And you said?'

'I didn't say anything. But if you think it necessary . . .'

'I certainly do.'

He shook his head in amusement and she felt, rather than saw, his smile.

'You'll marry me, then?' she pressed.

'If that's the way you want it.'

'That is the way I want it,' she said, and the words echoed and went on echoing in her head. They had a bitter ring.

She stood there on the poop, cold, damp, desperately tired and very close to tears. Was she going to have to fight for *this* now when he had led her to believe it was all he wanted?

'Very well,' Jake Hunter drawled. 'We can get married the day after tomorrow, if you like.'

'*The day after tomorrow*? How?'

'I'm the Captain, and the captain of a ship is the Law. I can marry people if I choose, or bury them at sea. I have all the power. Don't forget that, Thirza. So now you *shall* go below. I insist.'

'But how can you marry yourself?' she persisted when they reached the door of her cabin.

'I've told you,' he said shortly, and opened the door. 'On the *Columbine* my word is law.'

As if to emphasise his words the ship lurched, Thirza was thrown across the cabin floor and the door slammed behind him.

Of course he hadn't deliberately thrown her into this tiny cabin without even the space to fall flat. On the way down to the floor something hit her left side and something else cracked up against her head. She shook her head, but it wouldn't clear, and she felt ill. Somehow she hauled herself up onto the bunk and passed out completely.

She had no idea how long she had lain there when she opened her eyes. All she knew was pain as the *Columbine* rolled from side to side. She was feeling giddy, even lying down, when the door opened. Her first thought was that she wished she had been looking better for her future husband.

But it wasn't Jake who came in. It was a small, wiry seaman with a wizened-up face like a monkey's, bearing a tray. Even before she looked at it she was suddenly and violently sick.

'Christ,' the man muttered. 'Has he started already?'

She felt his strong hands holding her head while she vomited again. Then he wiped her face with a cold, wet cloth.

'I'm just seasick,' Thirza whispered. 'I'm sorry.'

'That's not seasickness,' he said. 'That's the result of that knock you've taken to your head. Let me see it. How did it happen?'

'I fell in the door, that's all.'

'I see you've hurt your side as well. The bruises are beginning to show. Did you fall, or were you pushed?'

That was the question Thirza couldn't face up to. She asked another instead. 'How long will it be before I'm better?'

'If I were you I'd be in no hurry to get better, Caroline.'

'My name isn't Caroline,' she stared at him. 'It's Thirza. Caroline is Captain Hunter's sister. Why did you call me Caroline?'

'He calls them all Caroline, the ones he brings on this ship.'

'You mean, there have been others?'

'Yes.'

'Well, there won't be any more,' Thirza said with dignity. 'Captain Hunter and I are getting married tomorrow.'

'Oh, yes?' he sighed.

'Has he been asking for me?'

'He's been busy,' he replied heavily while he busied himself about the small cabin.

So he must have had his sister with him on board at some stage or other, Thirza supposed as the ship ploughed on. But there was no visit from Jake so that she could ask him. Only the little seaman came in morning, noon and night and nursed her. That was the only word for it, she thought gratefully. He was an expert at the job.

'I still don't even know your name,' she tried to smile a few days later.

'Monkey.'

'*Monkey?*'

'That's what they call me, Thirza. It all started when I went to sea with a name like Monty Rench. From there it was a small step for my ship-mates to 'monkey-wrench' and I've been called Monkey ever since. My face didn't help, either,' he laughed.

'Well, I can only thank you for all you've done for me, Monkey. Do you think I could try getting up, now?'

'We're rolling a lot,' he said doubtfully. 'I don't think you should.'

Thirza sensed that Monkey was trying to prolong her captivity in her cabin. 'Tell Captain Hunter that I wish to speak to him,' she said.

Jake didn't come that day, or the next, or even the next.

A week later she thought that either the weather was coming from a different direction or she was getting used to the prevailing wind and the roll of the vessel. She was up on her feet again, but as weak as a kitten.

Three weeks out to sea, she found Jake's cabin, and she found out something else. She was almost frightened to knock on the door, after such a long time. While she stood there she thought she heard laughter. So Jake was inside, all right. She was just putting up her hand to knock when she heard someone else in there with him, someone with a little feminine giggle.

After a long pause, he opened the door.

'I'm ready now,' she said.

'Ready for what?'

'Ready to be married, of course.'

'Oh, yes! The marriage service!' He smiled at her. As ever, his smile was as attractive as his fascinating eyes. But he didn't ask how she was feeling, she noticed. 'It's a while since I performed it, but I'll read it up again. I shall have to, won't I?'

His tone was mocking. He was a changed man from the Jake Hunter who had suggested this trip.

'Yes,' she said. 'When?'

376

'I've been thinking about that. This has turned out to be a very busy trip for me.'

'Doing what?' Thirza asked, trying to see who else was in his cabin.

'Minding my own business, for one thing. I suggest you do the same until we're a few days from shore. Then I shall be able to give you my full attention. We shall be Captain and Mrs Hunter and live happily ever after,' he sniggered.

She stared at him suspiciously. 'Where? Not on this ship, I hope?'

'Oh, no. You'll be happy in the States, in one of the little towns just like Leith along the Maine coast. You can choose when we get there, but just now I'm busy.' Jake closed the door in her face. She didn't know what she felt. Insulted? Defeated? But then, she had a vivid imagination. She could be wrong, because at the same time she was filled with a huge relief. He *was* going to marry her, after all. He wasn't going to make a fool of her.

Hugging that knowledge to herself, Thirza tried to be satisfied with what he had said. 'How long before we get into port?' she asked Monkey.

'A week or two yet.'

'Let me know, Monkey. We're getting married a few days before that.'

'Not on board ship?' he said, looking very disapproving. 'Why don't you wait just another few days, since you've waited so long now, and get married in a proper church?'

'It's his wish, Monkey. He doesn't want to wait any longer than that,' she said almost happily. But still she worried. Jake hadn't been very romantic when he spoke to her. In fact, he had been quite rude. And who was the someone in his cabin?

All hands were on deck to witness the marriage when Jake announced it. Monkey had attended to Thirza's hair, fetching and carrying warm water to her for her toilet, although he seemed to be in a very bad mood.

'You're sure this is what you want, Thirza?' he asked anxiously as he was leading her up top.

'Of course,' she answered serenely. 'This is why I'm here.'

Monkey didn't look happy. The sailors didn't look happy either, when Jake pronounced a version of the wedding service with the Bible dangling nonchalantly from one hand, and they took their vows.

'I've forgotten the ring,' he laughed and turned to one of his sailors. 'Freddie, lend me your ring again for a minute.'

Again?

Immediately afterwards, Jake removed Freddie's ring from Thirza's hand and gave it back to him. 'Never mind, my love,' he whispered in her ear. 'I'll buy you a proper one in New York.'

Thirza felt her smile was watery. She didn't know why the tears were in her eyes, but she did know that she should not have left Belle's old ring in the dressing-table drawer at home. She felt naked and vulnerable when she went with Jake into his cabin.

'Now you're Mrs Hunter,' he said, 'and we must have a feast to celebrate that, and your return to health – although I must say, my dear, you are still looking a bit pale. A few years older, as well . . .'

Thirza felt cut to the quick. 'Oh, no. I couldn't eat,' she said.

'A feast we shall have, my darling, whether you eat it or not,' he said when the cook, accompanied by Monkey, appeared from the galley to spread great platters of food in front of them. 'And now, the wine,' Jake commanded his men.

They came back with the wine and the glasses, Monkey with an angry scowl on his face. He glared at Thirza, almost as if in warning, when he placed a glass in front of her with a thump, before he and the cook retired.

Jake threw himself into the feast, the first meal they had ever shared. His table manners were quite disgusting, Thirza found to her amazement, averting her eyes from his greasy lips. She was used to the appetites of men, but not even one of the Sharkeys had behaved like this, like an animal.

'So now you're Mrs Hunter,' he repeated through a mouthful of food. 'My wife . . .'

'Yes,' she smiled tremulously.

'And everything I possess is yours, Thirza. All my worldly goods. Even the *Columbine*.' As he paused to tear the flesh of a chicken from its bones she knew there was more to come from those food-encrusted lips. 'By the same token, everything *you* possess belongs to me,' he levelled a deadly look at her out of his dark blue eyes, eyes that were suddenly ice-cold, reminding her of how she had caught him looking at his sister in Bedlam.

'Of course. I'm only sorry there isn't more to offer you, Jake. All I have is what you see.'

He took another swig of wine and smiled a slow and crafty smile. 'Oh, no, Thirza. I know better than that ... After all you *were* Douglas Hunter's whore, and since he didn't leave his money to me, he had to leave it to you.'

She felt her blood run cold. 'Or to Caroline,' she reminded him.

'Not to Caroline in the mad-house! Don't be a bloody fool. No, you've got it, and now that you're my wife, it belongs to me as much as to you.'

'I haven't got it,' she protested, 'and I wasn't Douglas Hunter's whore, either.'

'Oh, no? Do you think I didn't follow you everywhere you went, for weeks – months. I *saw* you going into his house night after night, you bitch! Where's the money?'

'I haven't got it,' she repeated, terrified half out of her wits now. 'It's true Douglas left the Yard to me, but before I left Leith I handed it over to my son, along with all the money.'

He laughed and shook his head. 'No, you didn't, Thirza. You wouldn't do that. Only a bloody fool would do that.' Then he drained his glass, got up from his chair, came around the table and put his arms around her. Even in the lamplight his eyes were just as vividly blue and, she thought, passionate.

'God, Jake, I love you!' she said, weakly. 'You didn't have to say those terrible things to me. You know I'd give you anything I possess.'

But it was a passion of a different kind that was inflaming him. 'Oh, you will,' he sneered, and slapped her face.

Thirza stepped back. None of this could possibly be happening.

'And I did need to say those things,' he shouted at her. 'We're coming in to land shortly and then I'll have some fresh young meat, not some bloody old cow like you. I'm sick of white, greedy women. They say that black ones are better, anyway.'

'In God's name, why did you go through that charade this afternoon, then? Why did you marry me?'

'I told you. For the money.'

God, the money . . . there it was again. Greed for it domi-nated life.

And now she had been through another wedding ceremony, another one that had meant nothing, except as a way for Jake Hunter to gain the inheritance he had coveted so much.

But there was only one way for him to lay hands on the fortune. And that was if she died.

He confirmed it.

'Today I'm your husband, but watch out! Tomorrow I could be your widower,' he screamed, and punched her in the eye with his right hand, and then in the mouth with his left.

When she fell to the ground he kicked her in the stomach, and then again in the region of her kidneys, before he lurched out. In a haze of pain she heard him reeling along the passageway past the galley.

Within seconds Monkey and the cook were lifting her up and carrying her to her cabin. They both looked shocked beyond measure.

'He's nearly killed you!' Monkey said as they laid her on her bunk. 'One of us will have to stay with you at all times from now on to keep this door locked from the inside. He'll be back!'

'He's never been as bad as this before,' the burly cook agreed. 'My God, he threatened to kill you, lassie! We heard every word in the galley.'

'Look in the groove above my head, Monkey,' Thirza said sadly.

'A knife? Where did this come from?'

'It belongs to me. I don't know why I did it, but I hid it there a long time ago, when I came on board.' She gasped as the pain, especially in her back, got worse. 'Ahhh . . .' she groaned. 'Oh, God, I believe you, Monkey! He'll be back all right, and when he comes I want you to open the door and let him in.'

'You don't mean that, Thirza! You don't know what you're saying.'

'I do mean it! He's hurt me once. He'll never do it again,' she said, dredging up from somewhere an authority and a certainty neither man could argue with.

But Jake Hunter didn't come back that night. All the next day, while Thirza only felt worse, the two men took it in turns to sit with her at the side of her bunk, and the door was locked again.

It wasn't until almost midnight that Thirza and Monkey heard his footsteps stumbling back along the passageway.

'He's drunk again, Thirza. He'll be more dangerous than ever!'

'Let me sit up,' she commanded, with a face gone so white that he tried to reason with her.

'No! Help me, Monkey,' she said, 'and open the door.'

Then the yelling and the banging began.

'Open this door, Rench, or I'll bloody kick it in! I know you're in there with that cow! Open it, I tell you!'

Monkey looked at Thirza sitting propped up with a face like death and with her knife in her left hand.

'Now,' she said.

For less than a minute Jake Hunter swayed in the doorway, one foot inside the cabin and an expression on his face of dawning horror. The next minute the knife had plunged into his chest right up to its wooden handle, and the last thing he did in this life was to look down at it in total disbelief. Then he slumped to the floor.

'Jesus Christ . . .' Monkey whispered, looking at Thirza. But she, too, was slumped across her pillows.

They were both dead, he thought, in complete panic.

40

THE *Tessa Wishart* carried good luck and good weather with her all the way to Calcutta, and on the way Jordi, George and Edward Gibson found no difficulty in sailing her. Nor, when there was a flat calm, in turning on the steam.

As the voyage went on, and the temperatures soared, Jordi felt all his muscles relaxing. It felt strange not to have to labour physically every day as he had been doing for over twenty years now. And gradually, in the heat of the sun, the strain in his back that he had been feeling for the last five years, began to wear off.

He knew it wasn't only physical strain he had been suffering, but he hadn't realised he'd been so tense. He must have been wound up like a corkscrew. Looking back over his life so far, he could see that's exactly how he had been since Angela's death.

Above all, he had not understood Thirza over the two years since the accident had happened. During that last terrible quarrel with her she had even accused him of loving Angela more than he had loved her, or else he would have spared a thought for her grieving, too.

How could she possibly have thought that? In vain he had tried to tell her that what he had loved in Angela was the child she reminded him of. She was Thirza Gourlay all over again – with different colouring, of course – but with all the little ways of her mother's earlier years. The very way Angela had danced, so delightedly, so grotesquely, with her diminutive legs

383

flung out just anywhere, was exactly the way he remembered Thirza, long ago. Even Ruth could never help laughing at Thirza affectionately, just as they had laughed at Angela . . . and loved her. Oh, how they had loved her!

Deliberately, he buried these memories. Perhaps later – if they became less painful – he might be able to take them out again and look at them lovingly, but not now. If only, when he did, he could share those memories with Thirza! She was the only human being with whom he could ever share them, the only one to understand completely, and laugh and cry about it all.

Perhaps he and Thirza had loved each other so deeply that they simply couldn't cope with the loss of a second child – or they wouldn't be half a world apart today.

He had thought before he came on this voyage that there was no way back to her. He must somehow live another life without her. God alone knew how but, perhaps because India was part of him, that new life was meant to be in India. Leaning on the deckrail he gazed at the sea rushing past and wondered, until George's voice interrupted his reverie.

'I think you were right, Edward, when you said this would be a happy ship.'

'She's a happy ship, all right,' Jordi turned around and smiled at his son.

'Yes, a splendid trial run, Father. We put her through her paces, didn't we?'

'There was never any fear of the *Tessa Wishart*', Edward Gibson said firmly. 'We'll be putting in tomorrow, I should think. That'll be one leg of her maiden voyage over.'

'We'll stay only as long as we need to, before we turn around and go straight back home on the other leg, then,' George said

'You're not going to see something of India first?' Jordi asked.

'Not this time. I'm thinking of Tessa. I want to get back.'

'I think I'll stay for a while, George. You and Edward can easily manage the ship and the men without me.'

Jordi waved farewell a few days later as the *Tessa Wishart* set sail on her return journey. He hadn't said that he was never going back home. He couldn't hurt his son like that, and George and Edward sailed away quite happily, convinced that he was merely taking a holiday, the same as Thirza.

'But it's strange,' Edward Gibson observed. 'Your mother's gone west and your father's stayed east. There's half the world between them.'

'They're Scottish, aren't they, Edward? They're only dancing.'

'*Dancing?*'

'Dancing away from each other just now, as couples do in an Eightsome Reel. They'll make the figure of eight and dance back together again. Wait and see.'

The White House was far bigger, far more splendid than Jordi had ever visualised. He saw it first from the dusty road, almost a palace, set in jewelled gardens.

Servants bowed before him when he stated his business, and conducted him into a room which reminded him of India House in its hey-day with its ornate furnishings, silken draperies and priceless ornaments.

There he waited until a very different Lady Justin presented herself. Gone were the tight, high-heeled buttoned boots she had worn in Edinburgh, and the even tighter corsets she must have been wearing to lace in her waist so cruelly. Gone were the innumerable petticoats, and the pads of wire and wool over which her hair had been rolled and skewered under that veiled flower-bedecked hat.

Instead, an alluring, golden-skinned, dark-eyed beauty stood before him in floating, shimmering silks and gauzes. She seemed to sway to the music of the sitars somewhere in the distance when she walked towards him, a living, breathing replica of one of the voluptuous goddesses smiling at them from the frescoes. Jordi saw and felt immediately that indefinable quality that a generation as yet unborn was to call 'sex-appeal', and this she possessed in abundance.

'Of course I remember you,' Jorjeela said. 'You're the man I spoke to in Mr Fisher's waiting room in Edinburgh. If only I had known then that I was speaking to George Wishart's son! You would have been saved this long journey, which I'm afraid can only end in sadness.'

'Sadness?' Jordi smiled at her. 'Seeing your face again doesn't make me sad. You were beautiful before, but in your own dress you are like a flower . . . Exquisite.'

Jorjeela flushed a little at his words. Over her dress of paler blues her sari was dark blue, edged with gold, and the gold was reflected in the flecks in her magnificent eyes. Now, he saw, they were filling with tears.

'I mean my mother, Ameera, is very ill. She is only lingering in this world now. It means I cannot spend much time with you. But already a room has been made ready for you, and a meal is waiting. I shall come back when I can.'

She floated away in a cloud of perfume and he was conducted to another room, just as luxurious. Two female servants bowed and brought in water which they poured into a marble sunken bath at one end of the room. He watched while they poured in scented oils and scattered the surface with rose petals. Then to his horror, they took off his top clothes.

He pushed them away, but their dark expressionless eyes remained aloof. Their dark, businesslike hands removed the rest of his clothes. They urged him into the water, and when he lay back they stepped in beside him and washed him from head to toe.

He got the impression that he was no more than an object to them, just something it was part of their duties to attend to, and the fact that he was a man was of absolutely no interest nor account whatsoever.

Next, they dressed him in a suit of snow-white cotton, the trousers narrow and the tunic straight and buttoned up to his neck. When he looked in the mirror it was the Viaz of many years ago looking back at him. It was uncanny.

Then they took his own clothes and departed. Another servant brought fragrant rice and chicken and waited on him at the table. Soon afterwards Jorjeela returned. She, too, was freshly bathed and her blue dress changed for another, more diaphanous and even more revealing, of white.

'It's cooler now,' she said. 'We could walk in the gardens.'

Jordi fell hopelessly under her spell over the next week, hypnotised by her beauty, with the Indian blood in his veins at boiling point. He longed to possess her. He thought of nothing else. Jorjeela smiled and played with him, torturing him.

Ameera was always there in her bed by the windows which were thrown open for the evening air, staring at him. At last, one evening, she summoned him and Jorjeela to her sickbed.

'I have seen it,' she told Jordi. 'You desire my daughter, but you think it cannot be, because Viaz was your father, too.'

Jordi nodded miserably. He would have to go away. To desire his own sister was against every law of nature. Just when he had found the woman of his dreams her mother was pointing out what he already dreaded in his heart. Such an illicit love was not allowed in any culture.

Ameera smiled painfully. 'But you are wrong.' Her smile was more like a grimace when she took her daughter's hand. 'Jorjeela, you have never known this before. Viaz was not your father, although he loved you so much. Wishart-Sahib was your father. George Wishart. You were called after him. Jorjeela was the nearest Viaz and I could come to it in our language. It should explain to you why you are so light-skinned.'

'You mean, we are not related?' Jordi asked joyfully.

'Not at all. You both had different parents. You are free to marry.'

Two days later Ameera slipped away. They lit her funeral pyre under a blazing sun and, within a week, Jordi and Jorjeela were lovers.

Thirza woke up in a small, whitewashed room. Her first impression was that it was very noisy. The second one was that her injuries must have driven her mad, too, for she couldn't understand a single word of the jabbering voices of the people around her.

She was all alone in a nightmare of white walls and white sheets, except for the times when a plump woman came into the room to attend to her. For days she believed she was back in Bedlam. But the white walls here were dry. She couldn't understand any of it. She only knew that she was very ill.

Then one day the door opened and the plump woman showed in a visitor. 'Signor Rench,' she said.

'Monkey!' Thirza cried, trying to sit up.

'Lie back,' he said – the first English words she had heard for a long time – and sat down on the chair beside her bed.

'Where am I? What happened? Oh, for God's sake tell me, Monkey! I thought I was dead or in a nightmare.'

'Cook and I thought you were dead, too, at first. But there was still a thread of life there. We got you to this house on the waterfront before the agents for the shipping company searched the *Columbine*. This family agreed to look after you. They're Italians.'

'Oh,' Thirza almost sobbed in her relief. She wasn't mad, after all. She didn't understand Italian, that was all. 'What about Jake Hunter?'

'We threw his body overboard. It was good riddance to bad rubbish as far as all the crew were concerned. Nobody will talk.'

'What will happen to his ship?'

'The *Columbine*? He didn't own it, Thirza. He was only sailing as skipper. The company accepted that he was a man overboard, lost at sea, and paid us our wages.'

'So it's your wages that have been keeping me here, Monkey! It must be costing you a small fortune.'

He shook his head and smiled, but Thirza insisted. 'Fetch me my travelling bags, Monkey. Thank you for bringing them as well.'

'They were very light. We looked inside. They contained only womens' things, but we hoped that one day you would live to need them again.'

'What are you going to do now?' she asked him. 'How long are you staying here?'

'I was going to stay until you were better, lassie. Then I was going to work my passage back home in the first ship going to Glasgow.'

'Where's my knife?'

'At the bottom of the sea. Why?'

'I need a knife or a pair of scissors.'

He left the room and came back with a kitchen knife. 'I'm not too sure I should be giving you this, Thirza,' he said, handing it over.

Thirza laughed for the first time in many a long, painful day. She reached inside the smaller of the two bags and drew out a petticoat. Monkey looked the other way.

'Don't be silly,' Thirza hugged him. 'After all we've been through together? It's only an old petticoat! Now, watch this,' she said, slashing open the hem. 'It's an old trick I learned from my mother.'

'Jesus . . .' Monkey said as banknotes rustled onto the floor. 'There's hundreds there!'

'Ten hundred, Monkey. One thousand. More than enough to pay you back and buy us both a passage home.'

'So this is what that bugger almost killed you for?'

Thirza laughed again. 'Only a very small slice of it. But I never go anywhere unprepared.'

'I believe you. I've seen you in action,' Monkey laughed with her.

The following day, and for days after that, Thirza rested, waiting for Monkey to come back, able to concentrate again and in a much happier frame of mind. She may not have seen much of America, but her enquiring mind was gradually soaking in the Italian language from her loquacious hosts. It may be a *dolce vita* after all, she thought hopefully.

At least she was still alive.

Jordi opened his eyes and saw that there were only a few stars left in the sky. The moon had gone and the other wing of the White House showed up a dark grey oblong. The dawn was near.

Jorjeela was still sleeping, breathing deeply and softly at his side, and stark naked. He remembered last night and all the other nights with her, soft and supple in his arms, feeling the ripple of her hair all about him, long silky strands that smelt of roses and slid over his skin like a cloak of feathers.

They were nights of passion and of wonder and he wished they would last for ever, but even now there was a smell of morning in the air. That indefinable smell that tells of coming day as clearly as the growing light. He could do nothing to hold it back. The last star faded in a wash of pale light that was creeping up from the horizon. The sky was already turning yellow in the east.

The truth was, Jordi didn't like daytimes in the White House. He was lonely, and even when he travelled down to Calcutta he was still lonely, with no one to talk to. Jorjeela had what she called her 'work' to do.

What that was exactly, he was not too sure, but he knew when she dressed up in narrow cotton trousers and a high-necked tunic with her hair bundled up in a turban, she was pretending to be a man. Every morning the same tall, thin, bespectacled Indian man, dressed exactly as she was, came to collect her.

'Where did you go today?' Jordi asked her the first time it happened.

'Calcutta.'

'But why do you have to dress like a man?'

'Zarin says it is safer. We are working in the worst slums of the city, Jordi, too dangerous for women.'

'Zarin is the tall man I saw this morning?'

'He is our organiser. We are trying to help the poor children. Many of them are offered for sale, and if they are not sold, they're quietly disposed of. It is wholesale slaughter,' her voice rose fanatically.

'Yes,' Jordi put his arms around her and calmed her. After that, he looked for her and Zarin whenever he visited the steaming, crowded streets of Calcutta but, of course, he never saw them in those teeming millions.

In the evenings she was his beautiful Jorjeela, feminine and desirable again, but all day long he had missed her, and was in no mood to hear her talk of nothing else but the plight of the children.

'There is always the possibility that you could have our child, Jorjeela,' he said, 'and then you would have to stop your charity work.'

She looked at him in sheer astonishment. 'I can never have a child, Jordi. That was found out long ago, when I was married to Paul. These poor infants are my babies. Making love is only for pleasure.'

It was true. She did get enormous pleasure out of love-making. She was totally abandoned, hot-blooded, a very alluring woman – even in what must be the last flush of her youth. It was possible that, like a rose, she was now at the height of her beauty, full-blown. Jordi even seriouusly wondered if he was the only man she made love with.

She may not be 'working' with the poor children all day long. He didn't believe she was. For one thing, it would be impossible at noon when the sun was at its height. That was the time that everyone sought shelter and rested. Where did she go to rest? Wherever it was, he didn't believe she would be alone. Jorjeela's appetites included daytime love-making, as he knew.

He watched her with narrowed eyes as the days went past and she would give him no promise of commitment; he was amazed to find that the longer this delay continued the lighter his heart became, when the opposite should have been the case.

Did he really want to marry Jorjeela? Would such a marriage work? For the rest of his life? He might live for another twenty years and, looking back over the last twenty years with Thirza he knew without doubt that it took a very special sort of love between a man and a woman for a marriage to endure as long as that, through all the inevitable ups and downs.

What would he do with himself in Calcutta anyway? What was there here for him, except Jorjeela? And when all passion was spent, and they had nothing else in common, all Jordi could see was a wilderness of empty years stretching in front of him.

Then one night, she didn't come home at all.

Four miserable days later, during which the servants looked at him sideways, she was back. She went directly to her room and didn't come out for hours. When she did she was bathed, oiled, perfumed and attired in her gorgeous silks as usual.

'Where have you been?' he asked her.

'I'm so sorry, Jordi. The situation became a crisis. We had to get money in a hurry. I managed to get it,' she flushed a little and swept the silken curtain of her hair across her face so that her eyes were hidden from him.

'How much did you manage to raise?' he asked her.

'A very great deal,' she smiled, but still wouldn't meet his eyes.

Her lips were swollen, he noticed. Some mornings, if his kisses had been too savage during the night, they looked as if they had been stung by a bee. He thought wryly that Thirza had been right in one of the accusations she had flung at him. He must have a suspicious mind.

'In four days, Jorjeela?'

'It was hard work,' she admitted.

'But didn't Viaz and Ameera leave you their fortune?'

'They did, but even that was only a drop in the ocean of what is needed here! We are speaking about millions of children and millions upon millions of rupees!'

'How did you manage to raise so much in only four days, Jorjeela?'

'I was brought up so strictly and kept so secluded by my parents, Jordi, that it is only recently that I have been able to meet some very wealthy men of whom they disapproved. I have been applying to them.'

'And they have been generous?'

'Very generous.'

It was true that some rich men would give openhandedly for such a good cause, and expect no reward. Douglas Hunter in Leith had been one example. But the longer Jordi lived, the more he was becoming aware of political motivation for many such gestures. They were cloaks for corruption and greed.

'I see,' he said quietly, wondering if Jorjeela had offered her body as the inducement for all this generosity. 'Well, no one gets something for nothing in this world, Jorjeela,' he added. Immediately her black lashes swept down to veil her beautiful eyes from him. She retreated behind them in a feminine and mysterious Eastern fashion.

'We have set up a trust, Zarin and I, and from now on I must spend every minute I have raising funds in whatever way I can.'

There was a note of defiance in her voice. And he had thought she was a lady . . . That night the attar of roses had a slight whiff of decay.

He thought back over all the other nights when he had looked into her eyes in the middle of their love-making and found they contained nothing but lust. Her artfulness in bed was too artful, too mechanical and all too empty.

It meant nothing to her except the gratification of her desires, and to his surprise it suddenly meant nothing more than that to him, either. Jorjeela had been like Turkish Delight, and now he had lost the taste for it. He was tired of her, and he was tired of India, as well.

He longed for the cool mists and rains of Scotland, and the tang of the sea breezes to blow all these smells of scents and spices away. They were only there to cover up something unpleasant. He longed for the clean, fresh scent of heather, and even the spikes and thorns of the stinging Scottish thistles.

He wanted Thirza.

Uncompromising, tough, barbed and spiked with vinegar as he knew all too well she could be – yet, when she liked, she was softer and sweeter than all the roses and *jellabies* in India.

'I have been reading your face,' Jorjeela said. 'You are no longer happy here.'

'Jorjeela . . .' He took her hand, sadly.

'I have more Indian blood in my veins than you. We would not have been suited, Jordi. That's why I never arranged our wedding.'

'And Zarin has had nothing to do with it?'

'He has asked me to marry him. Perhaps I shall.'

Well, that would be very convenient for Zarin, Jordi thought. The title 'husband' would cover a multitude of sins, including pimping. No matter how good the cause, that was all it boiled down to.

'I wish you both every happiness, and every success,' he smiled.

He was ready to go back home to Scotland.

41

'THERE is a ship, the *Lorna Doone*, sailing to Glasgow next Saturday, Thirza,' Monkey said. 'But you don't look ready to travel.'

'Oh, I'll be ready! Make the reservations today!'

'But you can hardly walk, lassie.'

'I've been right round this room twice now without stopping.'

'It's a lot further than that to the pier. How will you manage?'

'I'll practise. Between now and Saturday I'll practise until I can do it *six* times without stopping! Besides, Monkey, I can always lean on you.'

'Ay,' Monkey smiled. 'You can always lean on me.'

The voyage to Glasgow was fair and comfortable. During it, they kept themselves to themselves as much as they could. But they knew there was speculation about them amongst the other passengers.

'You are so lucky,' one particularly inquisitive lady said when she managed to speak to Thirza alone. 'Your manservant is devoted to you.'

She was rewarded with one of Thirza's icy blue stares. 'Mr Rench is not my servant, madam. He is a friend. I have been very ill and he is only helping me back to Scotland.'

'Oh, I see,' said the lady, and retreated.

Suffering no more interference after that, they docked in

Glasgow in the early hours of the morning. Early or not, there were plenty of cabs waiting on the pier for anyone who had the money to hire them. Thirza watched Monkey, the first to disembark, carrying their bags. He darted over to one of the cabs and in minutes he was back to help her down the gangway.

'Take us to join the Edinburgh Fly,' he ordered the driver.

'Thirza! Home so soon?' Tessa led her inside their tiny flat. 'Does George know you're back?'

Thirza looked at her daughter-in-law's swollen belly, smiled and shook her head. 'No, I took a cab here directly.'

'You don't look very well. Are you ill?'

'I became very ill before I even arrived in America. You see me now very much improved, Tessa, and all I want is to go back home.'

'Well, I've kept number eight aired for you. All the beds are washed and clean – and, by the way, George had the three-quarter bed shifted back into your bedroom. He thought the single beds were more suitable for visitors,' Tessa chattered as they climbed the steps.

'Oh, it's good to be home,' Thirza said when they both paused for breath.

'The dry goods in the pantry have been replaced, and I'll send George up with fresh milk and eggs and butter. Oh yes, and bread . . . Perhaps a few slices of cold beef?'

'I can see Jordi isn't home, Tessa. Where is he? Down at the boatshed?'

'Oh dear! Oh dear!' Tessa looked at her in consternation. 'Of course, you don't know! How could you know? Jordi is still in India.'

'In India?' Thirza sank into a chair. 'What do you mean, in India?'

'Oh, Thirza . . . After you went on your holiday Jordi and my father accompanied George on the *Tessa Wishart's* maiden voyage. They went to Calcutta. Father and George brought the ship back. They were delighted with her. But Jordi stayed behind. He is having a holiday, too.'

So he had gone back to his roots, Thirza thought dismally after Tessa left. And she couldn't blame him after all she had put him through. It was a long time before she rose from the chair and walked through the gentle old house with its shabby secondhand furniture. Nothing had changed. Every single object in it was familiar to her, yet she felt disoriented.

Everywhere she turned, from the stove in the kitchen to the three-quarter bed she had shared with Jordi upstairs, she felt that something was missing. It didn't feel right. The heart had gone out of the house, and it would never come back, now that Jordi was gone.

The snowdrops were showing in the garden, and the scent of the winter-flowering jasmine she had planted under the kitchen window wafted all through the house during the weeks that Thirza rested. She knew that if ever she were to regain her health and strength it could only be here ... She squared her shoulders. There was a lot to do.

The crocuses hadn't begun to wilt before she attended to the first item on her agenda. She took a cab to Bedlam to coincide with the visiting hour one early evening. The same tall nurse with the floating cap met her at the door of the ward. She looked surprised.

'I've come to see Miss Caroline Hunter,' Thirza said. 'How is she?'

'There's no Miss Caroline Hunter here,' the nurse said. 'There never was. There was a *Mrs* Caroline Hunter, wife of the man you came with last time, but she died.'

Thirza stared at her dumbly.

'She died a very rich young lady in her own right. But of course, you knew that?'

Thirza shook her head.

'Oh, yes. It was her own money that was used to keep her here. After her death it all went to the Crown, I'm happy to say.'

'I didn't know any of this,' Thirza said. 'Mr Hunter said she was his sister.'

'No. He was the man who raped her. Then, when she fell pregnant, her father forced her to marry him. For propriety's sake, he said.'

'What happened to the baby?'

'When her father admitted her here she had just miscarried the baby, due to mysterious injuries she had received. To begin with she was very violent. She was raving.'

'Thank you for telling me this,' Thirza said, preparing to leave.

'It was when she was raving that she used to curse a man called Jake. Well,' the nurse said with triumph and contempt in her voice, '*Captain* Jake Hunter can't touch her money now!'

'No, not now. He died,' Thirza told her and stumbled out.

On the voyage home Jordi rarely spoke to the other passengers. He had too much to think about. He had learned a lot. Irrespective of the Indian blood in him, he understood now that – born and bred in Scotland – he was a Scotsman through and through. Scotland was his real homeland.

He had many people to think about, as well. Jorjeela, for one. He thought about her for the first few days of the voyage, mostly with pity, and he remembered all the old stories George Wishart and Viaz had told him about their adventures in the Marigold Palace.

Yes, his fortune had come from India, and there was far too much for his lifetime – too much even for George's lifetime. A large share of it should go back to India. He would send it to Jorjeela's Trust Fund. He admitted to himself that it might be conscience money, but he wanted the question of Jorjeela disposed of, paid off, and forgotten once and for all.

Next, he turned his attention to his own Yard. He would invest a large sum in it and then hand the business over to faithful Bob Steele. George wouldn't need it. George would one day inherit the fortune himself to do with as he thought fit.

Jordi wrestled for a week or two on the voyage with the vexed question of what to do with so much money, and finally asked himself what was the point of the young couple having to wait until he died? No, George would get some of the money right away to buy a proper house, and enough to plough into his next project.

That left only Thirza to consider, and she was somewhere in America. Well, he would touch along Leith, long enough to reassure George and Tessa, and then he would set off to find her – even if he had to search the four corners of the earth. Jordi was sure that he would find her, and knew what he would say to her when he did.

He should have remembered her background. How could he

have forgotten her narrow Presbyterian upbringing? He had even lived with it, and Ruth who enforced it. He should have been quicker that time they went to see Mr MacPherson, the minister. Instead of allowing Thirza to invent her elaborate story of why they had never been properly married, he should have looked into the legality of the Romany charade she had told him about.

Jumping over the broomstick indeed! Yet Thirza had sworn she was married, and he had been easy to convince. He had believed everything she said. He had believed in her in every way, and he still did, now that he had had time to think about her from a distance.

He had been in the middle of an adventure when he was shipwrecked at the Gourlays' door. He had been about to go right around the world. Well, he had no doubt now of what his next adventure would be.

When he caught up with her he would ask Thirza to marry him. She could choose for a wedding ring any of the rings she liked from his father's trunk. There were thick, solid bands of gold, intricately carved bands, and even jewelled bands. If she said yes, and he wouldn't stop asking her – begging her – until she did, he would continue on his travels right round the world, but with Thirza by his side.

Throughout all his deliberations Jordi never considered stopping off at their old house. He had been home alone in it after Thirza left for America. It was a very unhappy experience he would never wish to repeat.

When the daffodils danced in the breeze of a glorious spring day, Thirza imagined they were nodding their heads to her to tell her that her first grandchild would be born soon. It could be today.

But at eleven o'clock in the morning she saw Tessa down at the gate, still out and about. Thirza's brows knitted in a frown. She should not be climbing those steps in her condition.

Tessa didn't come any further, she saw to her relief. She only bent down to lay something inside the gate before she waved and turned back. It was a fine, plump chicken, she discovered, when she went down to pick it up. She watched her daughter-in-law walking slowly and heavily back to her

own house, and suddenly Thirza was shot through with longings.

She would be holding a soft little bundle again, running her
hand lovingly over the baby's downy head, smelling the soft
sweet smell of her grandchild.

No! That wasn't it!

Through all her contortions Thirza had always tried to be
honest with herself – *and that wasn't it at all.*

The truth was she wished with all her heart that she was
the one walking slowly and heavily. She wished she was just
about to give birth to another of Jordi's children. And, she told
herself, she would not have been too old yet. But all that was
an impossible dream now, and it was all her own fault.

She took the chicken up to the house with the never-ending
tears blinding her again. It took some time for them to dry, and
it was only the thought of what her mother would have said that
they dried at all.

'Och, away ye go! Ye're like a broody old hen!'

Thirza smiled and dried her eyes. Later, she promised herself
wearily, she would go down and see that the young ones were
all right.

Jordi arrived in Leith about seven in the evening and went
straight to George's flat. It took half an hour before they all
finished greeting each other, and he found out that George had
not gone back to the Yard in the afternoon because he had a
feeling that the baby would be coming any minute now.

'What would you like, Father?' George asked. 'There's brandy
in the house in case Tessa feels faint. And someone brought us a
bottle of sherry. It's not long been opened.'

'I'll have a glass of sherry, then,' Jordi smiled, 'on condition
that you sit still, Tessa. I don't want you to cook anything
for me.'

George got up and poured out the wine. As usual, his father
admired the set of him, tall and broad across the shoulders,
like his grandfather Davy Gourlay had been before him. The
only difference lay in his colouring. Instead of Davy Gourlay's
ruddy hair and complexion, George's hair was dark and his skin
was olive.

It was strange, Jordi thought in that fraction of a second, that a man could father a son, love him, protect him, and proudly watch him growing up. Then, before he knew where he was, his son was another man, self-contained, whom he really didn't know at all.

On the trip out to Calcutta George had shown no fear of anything. Around him there existed a circle of confidence and calm. It was just as well, Jordi thought, at this particular moment. Mrs Gibson wouldn't be much use to Tessa.

'Oh, if only your mother were here now, George,' Jordi sighed.

George was quite confident and calm now as well, in spite of the impending crisis in his life. He went over to the window and looked up at number eight. 'Well,' he said, 'I see the smoke's coming out of your chimney, Father.'

'She'll be cooking that chicken,' Tessa said.

'*What*? Are you saying that Thirza's home? Why didn't you tell me sooner?' Jordi jumped up and rushed out.

Thirza had cleaned the chicken, stuffed it with her own dried sage and onions and put it to roast with the tears running from her eyes. It was only the onions, she told herself, dashing them angrily off her cheeks.

But she knew perfectly well that it wasn't the onions. As well as all the other things she regretted, there was the thought of a new baby coming. It was strange that she had only ever become pregnant herself every six years or so, by some whim of nature. No wonder she was broody. If she had still been with Jordi she might have been pregnant herself at this very moment.

She flung her apron over her head and sobbed as if her heart would break, facing at last what she had been shying away from for far too long. Once, she had had Jordi, the best man in the world, and she had simply thrown him away.

Thrown him away! She couldn't believe it. And then there had been her stupid childhood ambition to be a rich lady one day. Now, that *had* been really stupid. She had found out how stupid when she actually did become a rich lady, and all she wanted to do then was to give the money away. Money, when she had actually got it, meant nothing.

Only Jordi Wishart did. He was her life.

She remembered when he had been washed up almost underneath their cottage in St Fillan. Then she had been only a child, still going to Katie Docherty's school. Oh, that Dame School! The maps on the wall, of places she thought she would never see!

Well, she wasn't much further forward, was she? To have actually gone all the way to America and seen nothing of the country . . . When what she would like most would be to see the wonders of the world . . . With Jordi. Nobody else would do.

As soon as this grandchild of theirs was born she would hand over Hunter's Yard to George. Of course, there would be a condition: 'HUNTER' must be removed from the roof, and 'WISHART' must be painted over it, for all to see.

By now, the chicken was glazed a golden brown, and there was a bottle of wine cooling. Not that she could eat or drink anything without Jordi, she thought sadly. On a sudden impulse to feel closer to him she went upstairs to her dressing table drawer and looked at Belle's old ring.

It might not have been a proper wedding ring, but she would wear it now, and never take it off again. It was the only wedding ring she ever wanted, no matter what the old Shetland fortune-teller had said.

Thirza wiped her eyes finally, gasped a sobbing sigh and went to the door for a breath of fresh air . . .

And there he was, galloping up the steps. One minute she was staring at him – she couldn't believe her eyes, nor her luck – and the next, her lips were compressed into a tight line. Look at him! He would have a heart attack next!

George and Tessa watched as his father threw his arms around his mother and swung her round and round. They could hear them laughing.

'What have I always said?' George demanded. 'Well, now you've seen it with your own eyes! That's the end of the dance.'